WILD SCOTTISH BEAUTY
THE ENCHANTED HIGHLANDS
BOOK FIVE

TRICIA O'MALLEY

LOVEWRITE PUBLISHING

WILD SCOTTISH BEAUTY
THE ENCHANTED HIGHLANDS SERIES
Book 5

Copyright © 2024 by Lovewrite Publishing
All Rights Reserved

Editors: Marion Archer, David Burness, Trish Long

Cover Design: Damonza Designs

All rights reserved. No part of this book may be reproduced in any form by any means without express permission of the author. This includes reprints, excerpts, photocopying, recording, or any future means of reproducing text.

If you would like to do any of the above, please seek permission first by contacting the author at: info@triciaomalley.com

To my sweet soul puppy, Blue. Forever in my heart, always in my soul. Safe home will you go.

"In order to be irreplaceable one must always be different." —Coco Chanel

GLOSSARY OF SCOTTISH WORDS/SLANG

- Away and shite – go away, you are talking nonsense
- Bit o' banter – Scots love to tease each other; banter is highly cherished
- Bladdered – drunk
- Bloody – a word used to add emphasis; expletive
- Bonnie – pretty
- Brekkie – breakfast
- Burn – river, small stream
- Clarty – dirty
- Crabbit – cranky, moody
- Dodgy – shady, questionable
- Drookit – extremely wet; drenched
- Eejit – idiot
- Get the messages – running errands, going to the shops/market
- Give it laldy/laldie – do something with vigor or enthusiasm

- Goes down a treat – tastes good; successful
- Hen – woman, female
- "It's a dreich day" – cold; damp; miserable
- Mad wi' it – drunk
- Och – used to express many emotions, typically surprise, regret, or disbelief
- On you go then – be on your way; get on with it
- Scunner – nuisance, pain in the neck
- Shoogly – unsteady; wobbly
- Spitting chips – angry, furious
- Tatties – potatoes
- Tetchy – crabby, cranky, moody
- Tea – in Scotland, having tea is often used to refer to the dinnertime meal
- Wee – small, little
- Wheesht (haud your wheesht) – be quiet, hush, shut up

CHAPTER ONE

WILLOW

I wasn't doing it *just* for the wine.

Okay, so maybe that played a small part in my decision to accept an internship at a Milan fashion house, but only, like, ten percent. Fifteen, tops. The rest was rooted firmly in my need to get away from a failed business venture that doubled as a bad breakup.

If you're going to fail, you might as well do it catastrophically. At least you'll be the best at something.

I laughed, amazed that my innate optimism could somehow turn even my most recent dumpster fire of a life into a positive thing. But maybe it was. If my boyfriend hadn't stolen all the money I'd invested in our fashion line —along with the heart of the very first employee we'd hired —well, I wouldn't be able to take this internship in Milan, would I? Instead, I'd still be stuck in a closet of a studio, desperately working on designs, sucking down instant ramen from the bodega next to the artist warehouse in Brooklyn, and dreaming of being able to afford a one-bedroom apartment someday.

Moving to Brooklyn from the Midwest had been like jumping into an icy lake in the dead of winter where at first, you're so shocked it hurts, and then you're so busy frantically kicking your legs to survive that you just grow numb to it all. I was in the numb stage—perhaps *too* numb—after my boyfriend had charmingly talked me out of all my savings and taken off with our new seamstress.

Now, as I stared at the snow gusting across the frozen tundra of my father's backyard in Minnesota, I dreamed of warm Italian nights, good food, and learning at the helm of a larger fashion house. Maybe I just needed to set aside the dream of starting my own line for a while, get more experience, and see where it took me. It was standard operating procedure for me, really, to dive in headfirst, which was also what had landed me in my most recent pickle. Ah, well. Live and learn.

Some would say I needed to learn faster.

"Hey, Threads. You doing okay?"

I turned to see my father hovering in the living room doorway, two glasses of red wine in his hands, a concerned look on his face. He'd started calling me Threads when I became obsessed with fashion after we'd gone on a trip to Chicago and a woman dressed in high, high heels, a leopard-print dress, and screaming red lipstick had enraptured seven-year-old me. Upon return, I'd thrown myself into playing dress up with a vengeance, demanding trips to the store for more material, and had become the clothing designer for my dolls.

My father says my mother would have been proud.

It's hard to know, really, as she died four years after I was born. It had been just my dad, and my older brother, Miles, and me for years now, a small team unit. Miles fancied himself the captain of our team, and if I didn't love him so much, his overbearing nature would be enough for me to hem all his pants too short.

"Actually, I am." I beamed at him and accepted the glass he offered me, leaning up to kiss his cheek. He smelled like Old Spice and cedar, likely having come in from his workshop where he built custom cabinetry, and the scent was as familiar to me as the feel of a sewing machine under my hands. "I just got a new opportunity, and I think I'm going to take it."

"New opportunity?" I glanced up to see my brother, my complete opposite, standing in the doorway. Tall, wickedly handsome, and dressed in what I referred to as Minnesota chic—Carhartt chinos, a flannel, and a Twins baseball cap—Miles was confident in a way that I aspired to be some day. He'd always been so certain of his path in life, and doors had just opened for him. Whereas for me, even though I *knew* what I wanted to do, it seemed like I had to lose my life savings, slam into a few walls, fall into the bushes, climb a hedge, trip on a boobytrap, and tumble down a hill before I made any headway in life.

Which was fine. It was totally fine.

"Yes." I beamed. We settled into the living room, Miles stretching out in a lounge chair, feet crossed, fingers steepled at his chest as he regarded me. My dad sat with me on the couch, curiosity in his warm brown eyes.

"Tell us, Threads. You look excited."

"I just got accepted for an internship at Dolce and Gabbana in Milan!" I squealed, doing a little happy dance in my seat.

"Italy?"

"Internship?"

They both spoke at once, and I sipped my wine, anticipating their reactions. Dad would be upset that I was leaving again. Miles was going to lose his mind when he heard it was an unpaid internship. There *was* a meager stipend for living expenses, but based on apartment prices in Milan, I knew it would be much like trying to find a place to live in New York.

"Is this paid?" Miles asked, his eyes narrowing, confirming my suspicions.

"There's a living stipend," I assured him quickly, taking a gulp of my wine.

"A stipend? What about an actual wage?" Miles shifted, leaning forward into his interrogation position.

"Yes, well, that's the goal, isn't it? You have to work up to that."

"Willow, what are you even doing? You just lost everything that you've worked for. Now you're going to run off to Italy with no money and no promise of an actual job? This is idiotic, even for you."

I flinched, stung by his words.

"That's enough, Miles. Let's just talk this through, and we'll figure something out. Your sister has every right to chase her dream," my father said, always the voice of reason, and I calmed down.

"For how long though? The fashion industry is notoriously difficult, and she's too nice. New York already chewed her up and spat her out, so what do you think Milan's going to do? There's a language barrier, she has no money, and we don't know anyone there who can help her."

"Come with me then," I purred at him, and Miles rolled his eyes in response.

"Unlike you, I have gainful employment. Here. Where you should stay as well and start looking into other career options. Maybe you can go into something fashion adjacent, I don't know ... merchandising or marketing and branding. Something like that. This is getting ridiculous, Willow. How often do we have to bail you out?"

"Excuse me? There's only been like—"

"Three times now," Miles said.

"Oh, come on, you can hardly call the first two instances bailing me out. This was the worst of them, wasn't it?" I rolled my eyes. Annoyance bloomed. Miles dearly loved holding up my failures for me as reminders that I should be heading in the direction he wanted, which appeared to be firmly settled into Minnesota forever, where he could ensure my safety.

A few years older than me, losing Mom made Miles overly controlling of those he loved, as though if he could keep a constant eye on them then he could ensure their safety. I tried to remember that when he was annoying the shit out of me, like now, but it wasn't always easy. My temper heated.

"Miles, back off. Her Scottish is heating up."

It was rare for me to get well and truly angry, but when I did, look out. My mother was Scottish, and my father always said she and I shared the same temperament. Calm, even keeled, until pushed too far. It was true, too. I could feel the anger boiling.

"Let me read this offer."

Standing up, I grabbed my laptop and opened the email with the offer and handed it to Miles before returning to the couch. I was far too angry to engage verbally right now.

"Are you sure you want to do this, Threads? What opportunities will come from something like this?" My dad reached out and squeezed my arm, concern in his eyes. *How can he not know how interning for Dolce and Gabbana could influence my future so positively?*

"It's a foot in the door. If I'm lucky, I might be able to work my way up to in-house designer, maybe contributing ideas that get used in collections, that kind of thing. If anything, it will look great on my résumé. It's an internationally successful, upmarket brand, somewhat exclusive, and I might get a recommendation out of it too. It's a step forward, albeit a small one, since I won't be designing my own label, but I guess that's just how the industry works. I think I'll always be fighting for opportunities."

"And is that what you want?"

"I mean …" I tapped my fingernail, painted in Chanel Ballerina, against my wine glass. "I don't think I'm in a position to say no to opportunities."

"One hundred euro a month is hardly a living stipend." Miles handed my closed laptop back to me, and I glared at him.

"I'll get a second job. Like everyone else in the world who has to make ends meet."

"I can help—"

"No, Dad. *No*. I can do this. Trust me, it's going to be great." I drained my wine, picked up my laptop, and stood. "Now, I need to research flights and look at housing options. I love you both. Thank you for caring, but this is what I want to do."

With that, I left the living room and climbed the stairs to my childhood bedroom, which my father had left exactly as I loved—colorful, chock-full of art, and stacked with books on fashion. Flopping onto the bed, I stared at the ceiling, my heart hammering in my chest. It wasn't like their concerns were unfounded. It was just that they were people who wanted every *T* crossed and every *I* dotted before they took a risk. I was a touch more haphazard with my approach to life.

Opening my laptop, my emails flashed on the screen at the same time my phone rang.

An international number?

"Hello?"

"Hi, I am looking for Willow Barlowe?"

"Yup, that's me." The woman had an American accent, but her number certainly wasn't local. "And who is this?"

"My name is Sophie, and I run MacAlpine Castle in Scotland."

Scotland. A ripple of recognition went through me, as it always did when speaking of my mother's homeland. We'd spent many a summer there, my father leaving us with our mother's family, and it was a country I loved dearly.

"MacAlpine ... is that in Loren Brae?"

"It is! That's awesome you know it."

"My mother grew up nearby, so I've visited a few times over the years."

"Did she? Even better."

My email pinged on my open laptop, and I automatically went to silence the sound, but my eyes caught on the subject line. It was a reply to my internship offer.

Except I hadn't replied yet.

Sophie's words faded into the background as I clicked the email open, my stomach plummeting as I read the words.

Thank you for your reply. We've offered the position to the next intern on the list.

Tears flooded my eyes as I saw the reply that my brother must have written, declining the offer on my behalf. *What the hell?*

"Willow?"

"Oh, shoot. Sorry. The line must have broken up for a moment. Can you repeat that?" Dashing the back of my hand against my cheeks, I slammed the laptop shut, trying to tamp down my fury. I wanted to run downstairs and kick my brother in the crotch for interfering in my life. Again.

"Of course. I'm calling because we have a unique opportunity to offer you at MacAlpine Castle. Our castle is rich in history, and we're working on increasing the tourism to the area. We have a gift shop that really could use some help. Apparel is our largest seller, but frankly, our designs aren't that great. We'd like to offer you an opportunity to come work with our kiltmaker to design an exclusive line of merchandise for our visitors."

"Wait, you're offering me a job?" My brain was sluggish to catch up to her words.

"Absolutely. Full-time, with accommodation at the castle."

"I could live in a castle?" I sucked in a breath, shock propelling me to standing. "In Scotland?"

"Aye, lassie." Sophie's laugh rang through the phone. "Sorry, I tried, but my Scottish accent still isn't great."

"Why me? How did you even find me?"

"Your website! You had some great tartan pieces in your last line, and your background says you have ties to Scotland. If you're interested, I can email you the offer."

"Oh, I'm interested. *Very* interested."

"Great, I'll ping it over now. Do you want me to stay on the phone while you review it?"

"Please." If this was as good an opportunity as I hoped it might be, I wanted this signed, sealed, and delivered before Miles could get his grubby mitts on it. I scanned the exceedingly generous offer, my mouth dropping open at the salary, and the list of perks that came with it. "How did you end up in Scotland? You sound American."

"Oh, I am." Sophie laughed again. "It's a long story. I'm from California, and while I dearly miss the sunshine, Scotland has my heart now. Basically, I inherited the castle, and now I'm determined to bring tourists back to Loren Brae."

"Sophie, you know what?" Nerves hummed, causing me to pace my room. There was a shiver of recognition—a knowing of sorts—that had come to me at key points in my life. I listened to that instinct now. "I'd love to come work for you. This sounds fantastic."

"It is. Trust me, you won't be disappointed. If you send me the dates you can come, I'll arrange your flights."

"You don't need me to book them?" I asked, incredulousness filling my voice. Sophie laughed again.

"No, Willow. We'll handle that. You're part of the team now."

At that, my heart sighed, happy that I had a place to go. *I don't have to give up my dream.* I needed to pack. And then, only when I was at the airport, would I tell my brother where I was really going.

Nobody was going to take my chance away from me again.

CHAPTER TWO

Ramsay

"Three. Solid. Corner pocket." I leaned over the pool table and neatly pocketed the ball, while Munroe groaned, and Lachlan chuckled.

"I told you to watch out for him, Munroe." Lachlan, manager of MacAlpine Castle and childhood friend of mine, beamed at Munroe's annoyed expression.

"The lad's lost his touch now that he's on the way down the aisle," I said, poking Munroe's buttons.

"You're not wrong. Who knew planning a wedding would be so involved? I just want to throw money at it and tell Lia to do whatever she wants so long as she shows up at the aisle on the appointed day. Her mother …" Munroe shook his head, real fear entering his eyes, and he swallowed. "I thought the Scots were bad, but an Italian mother-in-law? Man, when she's not mothering me to death, she's ordering me around like a drill sergeant."

"Och, lad, you love every moment of it," Lachlan said, topping up our glasses with a fine Islay single malt.

"Coming from the Ice Queen, can you blame me?" Munroe lifted his glass in thanks.

"The Ice Queen?" I asked, rounding the table and lining up another shot.

We were in the games room at MacAlpine Castle, a fire crackling to ward off the mid-winter chill, the promise of a home-cooked meal luring me from my shop. Hilda, the castle caretaker, and substitute mum for those who needed some extra nurturing, had badgered me into coming up for the night on the pretext that Lachlan needed more time with his friends. I suspected it was more that Hilda needed to make sure I was well fed, and frankly, why would I turn down the offer of a free meal? One less task for me to take care of, as more often than not, I'd defer to eating cold beans out of a can along with a loaf of sourdough or a meat pie in my workshop. Nutritious, filling, and requiring little effort on my part, the latter being the most important. If I could cut out one less decision in my day-to-day, I was happy to do so.

"Munroe's mum might as well be an ice queen for all the emotion she shows," Lachlan explained. "Could cut coal into diamonds on her frigid face."

"Family can be tough," I said. I would know, better than most. I pocketed another ball, to Munroe's deep annoyance.

"Ramsay can commiserate with you on that part,"

Lachlan said, crossing his arms and leaning against the wall. He looked at ease here, man of the manor so to speak, and it fit. Even so, I'd never known him to treat anyone differently based on their bank balance or where they'd come from. Not that that ever stopped me from poking him when I thought his upper-class upbringing was showing.

"Aye, can you then? It's a bitch, isn't it?" Munroe slid me a glance.

"I don't dwell on it." I shrugged one shoulder and pointed my cue at another pocket. Bending, I lined up the shot. "Nothing can be changed, so why fuss over it?"

"Is it your parents? Or other family?" Munroe asked as I was about to take my shot and I glared at him. Raising his hands in apology, he stepped out of my sight line, and I took my turn, missing by a small miscalculation. Annoyed, I looked at Lachlan who grinned.

"This is how people make friends, Ramsay. We share about our lives with each other."

Whereas Lachlan and I had known each other since childhood, Munroe was a newer acquaintance, having only passed through Loren Brae during the summers when I was working every hour of the day to help my family make ends meet.

"Should we paint each other's nails and talk about boys too?" I asked, not remotely interested in discussing my messed-up family dynamics.

"Oh, Matthew would be pissed if you do that without him." Sophie, Lachlan's partner, trailed into the room with a tray full of snacks in her arms. A stunning woman, with ample curves, an American cheerfulness that I often found daunting, and whip-smart mind, I liked her for Lachlan. And they clearly liked each other, as their eyes heated when they met across the room. "You know how much fun he had the last time you helped him on Tinder when he was here over Christmas."

"He has poor taste in men." Lachlan sniffed.

Sophie threw her head back and laughed.

"As I've been telling him for a while now. At least you managed to snag him a good date for his holiday."

"Of course I did. I have great taste." Lachlan winked at Sophie as she put the tray down on a side table. Turning, she clapped her hands together and zeroed in on me. *Oh shite.* I knew that look in her eye.

"No," I said, turning away from her to watch Munroe take his shot.

"But you don't even know what I'm going to ask yet." It came out as a whine, and I couldn't be sure, as I wasn't looking at her, but there may have been a foot stomp as well.

"Still, no."

"What if I was going to ask you if you wanted a million pounds?"

"Don't need it."

"Everybody needs a million pounds."

"Nope. My needs are met." I rounded the table, thinking about my next move.

"You could donate the money to a charity of your choice. Think how much they'd love you."

"I already donate to charities."

"A million pounds though?"

At that, I lifted my head and sighed.

"Are you actually offering me a million pounds, Sophie?"

Sophie screwed up her face and sighed, her shoulders slumping.

"No. But ..."

"Then, no, my charity of choice is not going to be upset about a fictional amount of money that they've lost out on."

"I suggest you just get to the point, darling, before Munroe wins this game. You're distracting Ramsay."

"Please, distract away, Sophie. I haven't won a game yet today and money is on the table." Munroe, owner of Common Gin and likely able to buy all of us several times over, grinned at Sophie.

"If I must." Sophie sidled closer, her eyes huge as she planted herself in front of me. Sighing, I straightened, holding my pool cue, and looked down at her. She fluttered her eyelashes. Despite my annoyance, my lips quirked.

"What do you want?" I asked, knowing she wouldn't leave until she said her piece.

"Have I told you how much I love your shop? The kilts you make are ..." Sophie leaned in, widening her eyes, and stage whispered, "better than cheese."

I looked to Lachlan in disbelief. "Is that meant to be a compliment?"

"The highest form of flattery, no doubt."

"Is it a kilt you're wanting for Lachlan then, lass? I've no trouble making one for a friend," I said, the tension easing from my shoulders. That was an easy enough wish to fulfill.

"Oh, well, now that you mention it, I wouldn't mind getting him a new one."

"I have plenty of kilts, Sophie," Lachlan said.

"But we ripped that one when we were out by the stables the other day …"

I snorted and Munroe coughed, covering a laugh.

"Must not have been a Ramsay kilt then. Ours are made of the highest quality. Meant to last through battle, lass."

"Oh …" Sophie's lips rounded as her eyes went to Lachlan. "Through battle, you say?"

"Darling, I don't want Ramsay to skewer you with a pool cue." Sophie shook her head, returning to her attempt to charm me into whatever it was that she wanted.

Which she would likely get because from what I'd learned so far, Sophie was an incredibly determined woman. She'd inherited MacAlpine Castle a little under a year ago, and in that time, she'd managed to not only neatly step into the role of owner, but she'd done innumerable good deeds for Loren Brae and a cracking marketing campaign to draw new tourists to the castle. She also managed to put up with Lachlan, and he'd never been happier, so that was extra points in my book for the lovely American who now danced around whatever she was trying to wheedle out of me.

"I do love a good skewering," I said.

"Oh right, okay, soooooo, I couldn't help but notice how busy your shop is, yet you don't have any help."

"No." The last thing I needed was someone in my shop chattering at me all day long.

"You can't keep doing business the way you are. I heard

you turned the sign to closed for a parking lot full of customers."

"And?"

"Ramsay! That's a horrible business decision."

"Those same customers came back the next day, didn't they?"

"What are you? Playing hard to get with your kilts?"

"It's a VIP experience." I bent and took the shot, since it seemed Sophie wasn't leaving anytime soon. Munroe swore under his breath as I pocketed the ball and straightened.

"It's bad for business. If you had an intern, you'd be able to work on the kilts and they could handle the customer service. Just think … you wouldn't have to talk to people anymore."

That had me pausing. I tilted my head as I considered it.

"See? Wouldn't that be nice? They could handle the phone calls, do intake forms, chat people up about what they want, and you'd only have to come out for measurements or whatever step of the process that you need to be there for."

"It sounds like you're implying that I'm not good at customer service, hen."

"Um." Sophie's eyes darted to Lachlan's, and she grit her teeth through a pained smile. "I wouldn't say it's your strong suit."

"You just haven't been around when I turn it on." Pausing, I leaned over Sophie, putting one arm on the pool table behind her, and gave her a heavy-lidded look. Lowering my voice to a rasp, I moved a wee bit closer. "Is it a kilt you're interested in, darling? I've got some of the best fabrics in the world. Soft as silk against your naked skin."

"Oh." Sophie's eyes widened and she fanned her face. "Matthew would faint."

"That's enough of that." Lachlan hooked an arm through Sophie's, pulling her away from me and shooting me a death glare. I bit back a smile, amused at Sophie's response, hoping I'd thrown her off track.

"I think you need a new kilt," Sophie said to Lachlan, dazed, and I chuckled, turning back to the pool table. Taking my shot, I won the game, causing Munroe to curse again as he handed me the winnings.

"I'm up next." Lachlan stepped forward and put twenty quid on the table.

"Fine by me. I enjoy taking your money, you posh bastard," I said, dropping twenty over his.

"Posh? Like Posh Spice?" Sophie asked, twirling a lock of her strawberry-blond hair around her finger, derailed from her mission. Munroe laughed, sidling over to the table to examine the snacks Sophie had brought in.

"Exactly like Posh Spice. High-maintenance yet oddly loveable." Munroe gestured with a small mince pie in his hand.

"I am not high-maintenance," Lachlan protested, furrowing his brows.

We all went silent, Sophie included, and Lachlan's mouth dropped open. Whirling on Sophie, he put a hand on his hip, the very picture of an angry diva. "You think I'm high-maintenance?"

"Of course not, baby. You're just temperamental." Sophie patted his chest.

"Temperamental? Was I the one stomping my foot a moment ago when she didn't get what she came in here for?"

"Yes, but I'm American. We're very loud with our emotions."

At that, I outright laughed, loving Sophie for Lachlan. They were entirely too well matched, and their banter was top shelf.

"Whereas us Scots like to have small explosions of our emotions through the day. Very understated we are," Munroe agreed.

"Except for Ramsay, I hear." Sophie turned, narrowing in on me again, and I sighed. She wouldn't leave us in peace until she got her way. "Didn't you make a customer storm out the other day?"

"He wanted polyester and for the kilt to be made by the end of the week. I don't do fast fashion."

"So you made him cry?"

"I did not. That's just Loren Brae overexaggerating the gossip." Okay, there had been one tear, but I wasn't about to admit that to Sophie.

"Again, if you had an intern, you wouldn't have to deal with people."

I sighed, putting my pool cue against the table, and turned, crossing my arms over my chest.

"Out with it. Tell me what you want so I can kick lover boy's arse at pool."

"Not likely," Lachlan grumbled.

"It's a two-part request. First, I want to bring someone in to intern at your shop, a person with a fashion background, who will then also partner with you to create an exclusive line of kilts and other tartan accessories for MacAlpine Castle's shop."

The last part piqued my interest. I obviously wasn't going to let her shove an intern in my shop, but I would be interested in designing for the castle. I'd grown up playing in its gardens, running through the halls with Lachlan, and watching as tourists fell in love with our history. It would be an honor to design for the gift shop, knowing tourists could take a small part of its history home with them. *Even better, knowing that I'd created it.*

"Now you have my attention." I tapped a finger against my lips as I thought about it. "What kinds of gifts for the shop? Nothing tacky, I hope?"

"I'd leave that to you. Not only do we have historical apparel on display that you can take inspiration from, but we also have boxes of old clothes preserved in storage. I'm sure you could find some ideas there."

Now I was definitely intrigued. I loved the history of kilts and kiltmaking, which was a significant part of Scottish history. Telling me that she had a treasure trove of historical apparel was like offering a wee child the keys to a sweetie store.

"And this intern? Why?"

"We need help at the castle, and you need help at your store, no matter how much you try to deny it. It would be a win-win for everyone." Something flashed behind Sophie's eyes, and while I sensed she was telling me the truth, it felt like there was something else she was holding back.

"What's the catch? You've got a look in your eyes."

"No catch," Sophie lied, radiating truth and honesty.

"Sophie, darling, you're a shite liar."

Sophie sighed and looked to Lachlan. He nodded.

"We need help with the Kelpies. This person can help."

I froze. The Kelpies had increasingly become a problem in Loren Brae over the past few years, running people out of town and closing businesses. It was one of the reasons I'd decided to bring one of my shops back to Loren Brae. That and I wanted some peace and quiet from running my other locations. I'd grown up knowing, in the same way you know the sky is blue, that the Kelpies were as much a part of Loren Brae as MacAlpine Castle was. They'd been dormant for years, but now that they threatened the town again, everyone was trying to figure out a way to subdue them so the town could thrive once more. If Sophie said this intern could help in some way, then I had to believe her.

"Fine. Bring them through. But no talking before I've had coffee, and they don't get to touch the music."

"Understood." Sophie leaned up to plant a kiss on my cheek before I could stop her and sailed from the room, happy now that she'd gotten what she'd wanted.

"How do you ever get your way living with that?" I grumbled to Lachlan.

"Och, lad. I don't even try anymore. It's much easier to give in."

"You're a wet lettuce." I pointed at the table. "Play."

"Maybe so, but I'm a deeply satisfied wet lettuce."

"That's an odd image." Munroe cocked his head as he thought about it. "What does a satisfied lettuce look like?"

"I'd say your mother after I had a night with her, but it sounds like nothing warms the Ice Queen up." I grinned at Munroe's shocked look, before he threw his head back and laughed.

"I knew I'd like you," Munroe said.

"I swear if this games night ends in us hugging and crying ..." I shook my head.

"Only if we're lucky," Lachlan singsonged.

I sighed and bent to the table. "Prepare to get your arse handed to you, lad."

CHAPTER THREE

WILLOW

"Dublin? As in Ireland?"
"Correct," I said, cheerful despite missing my connection to Scotland and having to wait five hours for the next flight. The flight on Aer Lingus from Minneapolis had been, well, honestly, amazing. Sophie had upgraded me to business class, and I hadn't been able to sleep a wink in case I missed out on something fabulous. I'd been rewarded when the flight attendant came around with ice cream while everyone else was napping. I had boldly asked for seconds because I didn't want it to go to waste. The flight attendants were happy to indulge me, and I was just keen to keep them talking because their gorgeous Irish accents made me smile. Now, I could barely keep the grin off my face as I shamelessly eavesdropped on everyone around me in the

airport just to hear the rhythm of different accents being spoken.

"Knock it off, Willow. I've had a shit day at work. What do you need?" My brother's annoyed tone cheered me up even more.

A woman walked by in a gorgeous wool cape that had my head turning. Pinned at the neck and draped neatly so the material didn't overwhelm, the cape was so flattering. It made me instantly want to wear it with leggings and my Vince Camuto equestrian boots or perhaps even with my ripped straight-leg jeans and a chunky loafer …

"Willow!"

"Ope, sorry." I drew my mind back to the conversation at hand instead of mentally building outfits around that fabulous cape. "I don't need anything. I'm calling to tell you that I left, and that I'm in Dublin on my way to my new job."

"Italy … but how—"

"How did I still get the job even though you sabotaged it for me?" I asked, injecting my voice with sweetness.

"Listen … Willow. I'm *not* going to apologize for that. It was a crappy job offer. It was the right decision."

Not a hint of chagrin entered his voice. I rolled my eyes.

"The right decision for *you*, Miles. Not for me."

"I did it for your own good. It's time for you to stop messing around and get serious about your life."

Not even an apology.

My breath left my body as a deep-rooted anger threatened to surface.

I hated being angry.

In fact, ever since the shift in the household after my

mother died, I'd actively sought out happiness. I always tried to look at the sunny side of things and did my best to act as peacemaker between my father and Miles when things got tough. Maybe that was the real reason Miles never wanted me to follow my dream—he liked when I was home to temper his sharp edges and bring some joy into his miserable existence.

Okay, that wasn't fair. He wasn't miserable. Just a very dedicated, focused, and determined older brother who insisted on trying to run my life on some misguided notion that he knew more about what I needed than I did.

I think, beyond anything, that was the most infuriating part. The simple fact that Miles refused to recognize or understand that I could be trusted to know what was best for *my* future. Every time he shot down my dream, it was as though he was calling me stupid or infantile because I hadn't yet had success. Life came easily for Miles, well, easily enough, and he'd been running his own in-demand construction firm for years. There was no room for error in Miles's exacting world of measurements and project budgets, and apparently, he applied that same principle to my life, wherein mistakes were failures instead of lessons.

"I've always been serious about my life, Miles. It's just not the life *you* want for me."

"I want you to be safe, Willow. I want to not have to worry about you, wonder if you're eating, if you're living in a dump, if you're getting taken advantage of by a shitty boyfriend. I want you home, in a stable job, living a normal life. Find a husband, settle down. Why is that so hard for you to do?"

The anger bubbled.

"So let me get this straight." I eyed a woman's quilted purse and wondered if it was Chanel. "If I come home, find a nine-to-five, marry, and settle into a house with a picket fence down the road from you, you'll be happy?"

"Yes, I will be. What's wrong with that life, Willow? It's safe, it's normal, it's respected. You've never even given it a chance. You might love it."

I considered his point for a moment, giving him the benefit of the doubt because that's who I was as a person, even though my simmering anger wanted me to fly home and nut-punch my older brother until he backed off and realized that I had every right to live my life my way. I pictured myself waking up in a little box of a house—or in reality, a studio apartment, which is all I'd likely be able to afford—making coffee in the morning, talking to my faux plant because I absolutely couldn't be trusted to keep a real plant alive, shivering through an icy morning commute on my way to work. Smiling at my co-workers from the confines of my cubicle, meeting for after-work happy hours, spending endless hours on online dating apps trying to make a real connection with someone who would see me for me, and then counting the years until he'd propose, before I'd dive into wedding planning, and then settle into making babies.

There was nothing inherently wrong with that image. Certainly, I'd probably painted it more negatively than I should have because I hadn't added an exciting career or a sexy boyfriend, all of which could be possibilities if I stayed in Minneapolis. But it wasn't what I wanted *right now*. I was only twenty-six years old. Maybe in the future, that could be my life—*and Miles will feel very self-satisfied. I'll be "safe."*

I couldn't help wondering if he was comparing me to my best friend, Melissa, though. She loved that life. She craved stability in a way I never had, and she was thriving, embracing the suburban mom life with a gusto that I admired. And I couldn't be happier for her. The one difference between her and Miles? Melissa knew that I needed something different and accepted that for me.

"I don't think I would, Miles. I wish you could see that. I'm allowed to do what I want with my life. This is my dream, and even if I don't achieve success at the rate you deem to be appropriate, that doesn't mean that I should give up. Ever heard of failing forward? Every mistake I make is just a data point. It's something for me to learn and grow from."

"Like not sleeping with your business partner?"

I winced.

"It's not like I planned that, Miles. We just fell in love."

"Was it love when he stole all your money? Left with the seamstress?"

"Yes, please, let's revisit that. Great fun for us all," I muttered. My brother seemed to think that relentlessly pointing out my past failures would somehow stop me from making any mistakes in the future. Shifting in my seat, I turned my head to look at the line of shops. One of them showcased purses and those woolen capes that I'd seen on more than one person now, and I knew where I'd be heading once I ended the call with my brother.

"Well? I'm just saying … you can't be trusted to know what's best for you."

"Actually, I can. I have all of my mental faculties, which means I do get to be in charge of the decisions that I make. For *me*. So I took a chance on love and it failed. Spectacularly. But now I've learned—no mixing business with pleasure. It's a tough lesson that millions of other people have likely learned. It's not like I'm some anomaly that is the first ever to go into business with her boyfriend and fail. Everything is so black and white with you, life or death, and it's just not that serious."

"Not that serious? We had to come bail you out, Willow. When does this stop?"

"It stops right now." My anger finally surfaced, and I stood and grabbed my carry-on, unable to sit still. "Right now, Miles. I didn't ask you to come to New York to bail me out. And I'm not asking your opinion on this, either. I get to make my own choices."

"Then you live with the consequences. I'm not flying to Italy this time to fix everything for you."

"Good. Because I won't be in Italy anyway. I'm going to Scotland."

"Scotland? *What*?"

"You know, our mother's home? Maybe I just need some time to take a pilgrimage to find my roots." I knew that would set him off, because there was nothing Miles hated more than an unplanned and unstructured vacation. He was the type to research everything in advance and have an itinerary for the whole week. "I'm just going to wander, I think. See where the wind takes me."

"You've got to be kidding. At least tell me you're staying with Gran."

"I'm not."

"What about Ramsay?"

"What about him? He's *your* best friend, not mine. I haven't seen Ramsay since I was a freshman in high school." Ramsay, my brother's gorgeous best friend, had been over on a break from university. All of my friends instantly fell in love with the tall, strapping Scotsman with the delicious accent. Had I harbored a crush on him? Just a bit. Was I ever going to tell my brother that? Nope. Not a chance.

"Call him. He'll take care of you."

"Miles! For the last time, I don't need taking care of. I'm an adult. Stop it."

"From the way I see it—"

"I don't care how you see it. My gut says this is the right choice for me. I have to listen to that."

"Do you though? Your little flashes of 'knowing' haven't exactly landed you in great situations in the past."

"Every situation is a learning opportunity. You know what? I'm done with this conversation. Especially because all you've done is point out my faults. And that's not okay or fair. Tell Dad I'll call him when I get in. And for the last time, back off, or you'll lose me forever."

"Lose you? God, Threads, you're always so dramatic—"

I ended the call on his words, rolling out the tension that had knotted my shoulders, and wheeled my bag toward the little airport store where I'd spied the capes. Perhaps some shopping would be just the therapy I needed, even though I didn't have the budget for anything other than looking. While my salary with MacAlpine Castle was a generous one, my first paycheck was still a ways out, and all

I had was the emergency ration that my father had pressed into my hands when I'd told him I was leaving.

If this all worked out, I was going to bring my dad over to Scotland, his first real vacation in years, and show him my fabulous new life.

Miles could stay home.

Sticking my nose in the air, I sailed into the shop and beamed at the woman behind the counter who welcomed me in a lovely Irish accent. I swear, it was like listening to wind chimes singing in the wind, the way the *R*s rolled over her words. It was one of the things that I'd loved about New York City, aside from the fashion and the hustle and bustle. Being surrounded by so many different accents and cultures had reminded me just how big the world was and how there were still so many places for me to explore.

Other shoppers came in the store, needing assistance, and I turned to the rack holding the wool capes. Lifting a corner, I ran my hand over the fabric, enjoying the weight of it, and flipping it over to see the craftsmanship. Well-made, and with a price that reflected it, I realized after a discreet glance at the tag. I'd have to draw up a design once I was in Scotland. The cape appealed to me, as someone who fluctuated between sizes, because it would be forgiving of weight gain or loss and still look stylish.

Being a plus-sized woman and wanting to look fashionable was sometimes a challenge. Not as much as it had once been, but it was partly what had driven me into the fashion industry. I wanted to design clothes that looked good on my tall, strong, Midwestern body. Built for plowing fields and surviving a famine, I'd always joked to people, even though I probably was not likely wrong. I fluctuated between size sixteen and twenty, depending on the label, and took great care to track down brands that supported that sizing. It made shopping a touch more difficult at times, but I loved the direction that the fashion industry was going where inclusivity was becoming more common. It just made sense, in my mind, to offer a larger range of sizes. Why cut off an entire market of people who had the money and were willing to spend it on quality made clothing?

Already, the anger from Miles's phone call had dissipated, now that I was in my happy place surrounded by clothes, and I breathed out a sigh of relief as I returned to my baseline of cheerful and breezy. Reminding myself that Miles being overbearing was nothing unusual and came from a place of love, I checked the time on my phone and left the shop, looking for a spot to grab a coffee where I could jot down some sketches. Though I really had no idea what, specifically, I'd be designing with the kiltmaker, I loved tartan prints and had already compiled a folder of ideas that ranged from a basic kilt to a fun tartan bralette, which I likely knew would be instantly vetoed.

But that was what sketchbooks were for—dreams.

And unlike Miles, I was full of them.

I wasn't going to listen to his doubts though. *I* had been approached for this gig. *Found.* Contrary to what Miles believed about me, I had talent, and this window to explore and grow was a once-in-a-lifetime opportunity.

"We'd like to offer you an opportunity to come work with our kiltmaker to design an exclusive line of merchandise for our visitors. You had some great tartan pieces in your last

line, and your background says you have ties to Scotland." Sophie's words rang in my head.

And if I was honest, I already felt somehow tied to Loren Brae and Sophie's MacAlpine Castle. Even if I had no idea why.

CHAPTER FOUR

Ramsay

"That should do it, lads."

Munroe grinned at Lachlan and me. We'd been recruited to help move a heavy stack of timber for the new distillery into an old outbuilding near the castle that Munroe was in the process of converting. Even though he'd hired a crew of joiners to help, with the rain lashing down, it was quicker to get the timber inside when more of us were there to help.

"We'll collect on that pint later." Lachlan wiped his brow with the back of his arm.

"Or you can name a gin after me," I suggested.

Common Gin had quickly become a household name in Scotland, and Munroe's determination to keep it local, accessible, and a favorite of the people was what made it so beloved. His decision to build a distillery in Loren Brae would not only bring a significant volume of tourism back to the town but was also part of what had made me consider coming home and opening a shop here.

That, and my father needing more of my help.

It had been an easy enough solution, returning to Loren Brae and establishing a new shop, and one that had allowed my father little in the way of protest. If I had told him that I was coming home to help him, he would have discouraged that decision.

Even though some days he had trouble remembering which of his sons were speaking to him.

A recent stroke had impaired my robust father, causing him both neurological and physical damage, and his recovery had been slower than he hoped. The day we received the call to say he'd collapsed had been an enormous shock, but to see him struggle with basic, daily tasks had been grim. *How can someone so strong seem so feeble?* My mother, the calm saint that she was, carried on easily, never asking for help and weathering my father's frustrated outbursts with an equanimity that I could only envy. It was only through her that I knew how annoyed my brother was that I had returned to Loren Brae, putting me near our parents, and thus earning the "favorite one" title that he apparently so desired.

I gave zero shits what Andrew thought. As far as I was concerned, I had no brother.

"You have to do a lot more than lift a bit of wood to get a gin named after you," Munroe said.

"Isn't that what Lia did to get a gin named after her?"

I threw my hands up to block Munroe's punch, laughing as I ducked out of the way.

"Och, never talk about a man's bride-to-be, Ramsay," Lachlan chided as I held up my hands in defeat.

"Apologies, mate. It was too good of an opening to leave hanging."

"Fair play," Munroe said, lifting his chin at the castle behind me. Turning, we saw a car come up the drive.

"Sophie's back." Lachlan, as though he was a dog answering his master's whistle, took off toward the castle, the rain having abated the minute we finished unloading the lorry.

"Does he do this every time she comes back from the shops?" I asked Munroe, following at a more sedate pace.

"Any time she enters a room, really."

"I'm surprised he hasn't dragged her to the altar yet."

"Oh, he's planning to. But she's insisting on running MacAlpine Castle for a full year before she considers any relationship advancement. Something about proving herself and there was a spreadsheet with a timeline involved, I think."

"Ah yes, the spreadsheet approach to love. Very logical."

"And your favored way is …?" Munroe slid a glance at me, and I grinned.

"To love 'em and leave 'em, naturally. I'm not really into relationships. I like my space."

"I get that. More time to play board games."

"There's that." Munroe was a bit of a board game freak, so that must have made sense to him. Being a touch competitive, I was typically down for any game, so long as it didn't require hours of my time to learn. Which, I'm told, separated me from the true board game lovers.

Like I had an entire day to waste learning the rules of Sir Toadfrog the Fairy King or whatever.

Sophie wasn't wrong, I really did need to hire an assistant. Not particularly to run the shop, but I needed more help to run my business as a whole. My business manager, a steely-eyed lass by the name of Elaine, who had whipped my entire company into shape, had recently moved to the States, and I was left with more paperwork than I knew what to do with. That, coupled with my father's health issues, and the recent opening of my Loren Brae shop, had left me gasping for a moment to myself.

The sound of barking had me turning, a smile at my lips. Sir Buster, a snarly little chihuahua who vacillated between charm and hate, rounded the corner of the castle with a stately dame of Corgi mix following on his heels at a more leisurely pace. Lady Lola, the only one who could tolerate Sir Buster regularly, had been a welcome addition to the castle.

Sir Buster skidded to a stop at my feet, shivering in the cold, and growled.

"Aye, wee man. It's a blustery one today," I agreed.

Lady Lola, as charming as could be, bumped her head against my leg, and I bent down to give her a proper hello.

I loved animals. All kinds. I wasn't a dog person any more than I was a cat person or held strong viewpoints on their veracity as pets. I didn't care. If a cute fuzzball wanted to make my acquaintance, I was happy to do so, frankly far more so than with any people that wanted to chum up to me. Pets, I liked. People, I could do without. Sir Buster, seeing Lola getting all the attention, dropped the tough guy act and sidled closer, shivering as a gust of wind pushed him backwards on his teeny feet. Risking a lost finger, I scooped him up and tucked him in the crook of my arm, where he instantly settled into the warmth of my jumper. He growled at me once, as though to let me know he was still in charge, and then his eyes slid to half-mast as I carried him toward the castle car park.

MacAlpine Castle, as stately as she was understated, loomed over manicured gardens put to bed for the winter. With half the castle kept historically accurate and offering tours, MacAlpine Castle typically did a brisk business in the summer. Winter and early spring were the slower months, but even so, there should have been a few visitor cars scattered in the car park. Instead, it was just Sophie's car next to mine.

A statuesque woman got out of the passenger side of Sophie's car, the wind blowing her auburn hair across her face. She tossed her hair back with a laugh, and I was too far away to make out her features, but her laugh punched me in the gut. It had a raucous vibe to it, as though inviting me to join in on the joke, and my interest piqued.

If I were to date, she was the type I liked, at least from a physical standpoint. Ripped jeans covered thick thighs, and the wind molded a heather grey jumper against sizeable breasts. Black and white Adidas trainers, big hoop earrings, and a cheerful grin on her face made her seem casual, cool, and approachable. Being a big man myself, I liked a woman who didn't feel like she would snap under my hands. This woman's body looked like a virtual playground to me, and I had to dart my attention away before I was caught staring too long.

I wondered if her jumper was real wool.

Nerd. I snorted lightly to myself. I was such a fabric nerd when it came to the products I used for making my kilts. It was one of the reasons I'd gone into the business, to preserve the history of Scotland, and I only used locally sourced textiles for my kilts.

Sophie popped the boot of the car, and I almost dropped Sir Buster in my rush to step in front of Lachlan and offer a hand with the luggage I saw there. Whoever this woman was, she was staying for a while, and even though I'd just told Munroe that I was off relationships, I certainly wasn't off sex. There was nothing wrong with a casual holiday fling, as far as I was concerned. Handing Sir Buster off to Lachlan, I offered a hand.

"Here, lass, let me get that for you."

The woman turned, a smile on her lips, and her face froze. A myriad of emotions flashed through her eyes, the most damning being anger, before the smile returned.

"Ramsay?"

I squinted, my brain scrambling to place where I'd met this beautiful woman before. Had it been that one-night stand in Glasgow last year?

"Ramsay, it's Willow." Willow looked at me, her eyebrows raised in expectation, and then it all clicked.

Oh shit.

Shit. Shit. Shit.

I'd just been ogling my good mate's little sister. I hadn't seen her since she was in high school, and her hair had been bleached blond with odd green streaks at the time. Now, the auburn color brought out the turquoise tones of Willow's eyes, and I blinked at her as my brain struggled to move from picturing her straddling my body to friendly acquaintance.

"Willow. Wow, what are *you* doing here? Is Miles here, too?" I looked around, as though he would pop out from behind a bush or something. It also gave me an excuse to force my eyes away from Willow's sparkling eyes and rid myself of indecent thoughts.

"You two know each other?" Sophie asked, tilting her head at me.

"Kind of. I mean, we do, but we're not like ..." I stumbled over my words, immediately annoying myself.

"Ramsay is one of my brother's good friends." Willow's eyes narrowed at that, and there was that flash of anger again. I wondered if I had done something when I visited, and she'd harbored some secret grudge against me all those years.

Then immediately chastised myself. Inflated ego much? She probably hadn't thought a thing about me since.

"You look great," I said. So much for keeping my mind off her luscious body.

"That's great you two already know—"

"I haven't seen Ramsay in years. Odd you show up now, isn't it?" Willow said, interrupting Sophie, tilting her head at me. I definitely hadn't imagined that flash of anger.

"Odd, how? I live in Loren Brae, lass."

"Do you? Miles hadn't mentioned that. I thought you were running some fancy business somewhere."

"Ramsay is—"

"Fancy business? Miles must be talking me up." I smiled, wondering why Willow seemed so on edge.

"No, he rarely mentions you except for when you go on your yearly trip together. In fact ... I hadn't heard about you in ages until a few hours ago when I told my brother I was coming here. *Then* he brought you up. Weird, right?" Willow tapped a shell-pink painted nail against her pillowy lips, and I had to swallow against the surge of lust that ran through me.

Down, boy. Friend's sister. Not yours to touch.

"Not that weird, no. I do live in Scotland, so it seems pretty natural for him to bring me up."

"Willow, Ramsay is—"

"I don't need you reporting back to my brother," Willow said, once again interrupting Sophie. She put a hand on her hip and pushed her lower lip out in a pout.

I wanted to bite it.

"Is there something you plan to be doing here that requires me to report to your brother?" I raised an eyebrow at her. Turns out, Willow must have grown up into one of those prickly women annoyed by anything and everyone. Which was the last thing I needed in my life.

"Would it matter? It's my business. Not my brother's."

"Why don't we get you settled?" Sophie said as I tried to figure out what Willow was hiding from me.

"You're staying here then? In one of the flats? Are you renting them out now? Holiday rentals?" I asked Sophie as I heaved Willow's two bags easily from the boot and started toward the castle, forcing Willow to keep up with me.

"No, it's just that—"

"Oh my God!" Willow shouted and I almost dropped her bags at her shout. Turning, I caught her staring in awe at the castle. "This place is incredible. And do the dogs live here? Please tell me they live here."

"They live here." Lachlan stepped forward, his hand outstretched. "I'm Lachlan, and welcome to MacAlpine Castle."

"Hi, Lachlan. It's so great to meet you. This place is just ... words fail me. Wow."

Lachlan smiled. He loved when people delighted in his castle.

Not wanting to provoke Willow, because she was certainly a lot sweeter in her greeting of Lachlan, I kept my mouth shut while she cooed over the dogs, exclaimed over the castle, and chattered with Sophie like they were best friends. I'd missed a step somewhere, that was for certain. Once I'd dropped her bags at the flat she must be renting, I stepped back into the hallway while Sophie walked farther into the apartment with Willow.

"I'll just ... catch you later?" I interrupted, feeling awkward and uncertain of my role here. I mean, technically, Willow was a friend, right? And if that was the case, would it be out of reason to invite her to the pub for a drink later? Just to catch up. I hadn't spoken to Miles in a few months, so to see his sister out of the blue was surprising, to say the least. But her words ... *"I don't need you reporting back to my brother. It's my business. Not my brother's."* What was with that? I opened my mouth to speak, but Willow just fluttered her fingers at me in a little wave.

"Bye, Ramsay. Tell Miles I'm fine."

At that, I arched a brow, opening my mouth to retort, but then thought better of it. It wouldn't do for me to be hulking over this woman as she settled into her bedroom. Best for me to head back downstairs and gather information from Lachlan.

And I would definitely be on the phone to Miles later.

CHAPTER FIVE

Willow

I excused myself from speaking with Sophie by professing a need for the bathroom, promising to meet her downstairs shortly. It might have been a touch rude, since she'd been in the middle of showing me this gorgeous castle apartment that was apparently my new home, but I needed a moment to collect myself.

I was fuming.

How. Dare. He.

How had my brother managed to weasel his way into my plans? Now I couldn't help wondering if this incredible job opportunity had somehow been manufactured. *Just so Miles could keep an eye on me.* Far-fetched? Maybe. Had he faked his surprise at my destination of Scotland? This was just wild enough that my brother could pull it off.

Which sucks. Truly sucks.

This would be a real kick to my pride if Miles had arranged this for me. *Would Sophie lie about how she found me?* She'd sounded so genuine. It would be one thing if I'd gone to Miles and asked him for help, but I hadn't. And all I felt was anger. Disbelief in myself. Again. I paced the pretty living area of the substantial apartment that had been part of the package deal that had been my admittedly generous job offer.

I'm so stupid.

Of course MacAlpine Castle wouldn't just call me, a relatively unknown designer, out of the blue and offer me a sweet job. That was the stuff of fairy tales and or movies like *Pretty Woman*. Yup, I was a dumbass.

This was too good to be true.

Pausing, I took a few deep breaths, trying to settle myself. This wasn't the first time that I'd found myself in an unwanted situation, and it was far better than the time I'd been ordered to "service" the lead designer with my mouth or lose out on showing my collection.

For what it's worth, I'd ignored the offer and left with my collection, and my pride, intact. While that moment had stung, because I'd been so close to seeing my designs on a runway, this felt even worse. Was I really just that naïve?

My gut said no.

My head said yes.

And there it was, the war that I always had with myself. Drying my hands and looking in the ornate mirror hung over the bathroom sink, I studied my reflection as I schooled my breathing. Thus far, I'd had one hundred percent success rate in surviving bad days, so I would be fine.

Leaving the bathroom, Sophie had indeed left the apartment, which gave me a moment to look around. Grey stone walls showcased watercolors of the loch, colorful rugs were thrown across the floors, and two arched windows allowed the wintry light through. Crossing, I stood at the window and took stock of my situation.

Sophie hadn't pinged on my radar as being a bullshit artist. Everything she'd told me so far she'd delivered on in a timely manner, and she'd been bubbly and excited on the drive down, regaling me with tales of her own mishaps in moving to Scotland the year before. We hadn't spoken about the job, as though we both understood there was a time to jump into work talk, and instead had begun to forge the beginnings of a friendship. I'd only met Lachlan for basically a millisecond, but the way his eyes had heated when he'd seen Sophie made me instantly approve of him. There was just something about seeing a man deeply in love with his woman that made my heart flutter.

The clouds shifted outside, and a single ray of pale sunlight broke through, spearing a little island smack dab in the middle of the lake. Loch, I corrected myself. Loch Mirren. Even though I came from the land of ten thousand lakes, I'd never seen one like this—discounting Lake Michigan, of course—and being near water instantly soothed me. Rolling hills dusted in snow hugged her shores, and the buildings of Loren Brae stood out against the wintry landscape like colorful confetti left on the ground after a party.

Stay.

It was the same voice that had guided me in the past, even when the outcome had been considered a failure by others. This voice was the one that had led me to take chances, to learn from my mistakes, and to build on every new opportunity. It was the voice I trusted above all else, the same one that occasionally gave me flashes of insight about other things that I couldn't quite explain, and I knew I needed to trust it now.

Seeing Ramsay had unsettled me. But at the end of the day, if this opportunity resulted in a huge win and great step for my career, then maybe, just maybe, I would be able to bring myself to thank my brother for meddling in my life once again. Even though the loss of the Dolce and Gabbana internship still felt bitter, I reminded myself that I could always apply for another. Nothing in life was set in stone, it was all a matter of choices.

And I chose to see the good side of things, even when it was a struggle at times.

The skies opened, icy rain drifting down in sheets, and my eyes were drawn once more to the small island in the loch.

There was *something* there.

I didn't know what, or why I thought that, but once the idea came to me, it stuck like a burr to my skirt.

Maybe I'd get a chance to go there one day, when the weather wasn't so moody.

Pulling myself away from the window, I glanced once more around the apartment, excitement finally breaking through my anxious thoughts. This place was seriously cool, and I got to live in it, like a real freaking princess. I mean, I would pay to stay in a rental like this, so the fact that it came as part of my job was a huge bonus. Already imagining the many cool photos I could take when I posted my outfit of the day on Instagram, I opened the door and stepped into the hallway, a smile on my lips.

A flicker of light, a shimmer in the dim light of the stone hallway with high ceilings, was the only warning I had that something was off before a massive cow jumped out at me from the wall.

I lost it.

Screaming, I turned and ran straight into the door that I had just closed, my hands only just catching me before I broke my nose, and I wrestled with the doorknob in panic. When it wouldn't budge, I whimpered, too scared to look over my shoulder, and when I couldn't get the door to open in time I turned to run.

And slammed into another wall.

This one being a decidedly warm and more forgiving wall. Ramsay's arms came around me and he lifted me into them, cradling me against his chest like I weighed nothing more than the chihuahua he'd been carrying earlier, and I gaped up at him.

"What happened?" Ramsay's eyes scanned the hallway, on alert, his jaw set. In profile, he looked ready to go to battle, and when he glanced down at me again, I shivered at the barely restrained violence I saw in his eyes.

This man could do some damage.

"Um ... it's just ..." *Shit*. How was I supposed to tell him that I saw a cow jump out of the wall and not sound like I'd well and truly lost the ability for coherent thought?

My hands were pressed against his chest, the hard curves of his muscles making me itch to explore more, and my eyes widened. No. No. Absolutely not. Sure, Ramsay was smoking hot, and seriously built, but that was not a tree I would be climbing. No, ma'am. He was my brother's friend and likely involved in this scenario of finding a "safe" place for Willow to land.

But I could still appreciate a muscular chest when pressed against one.

Angling my head, I glanced over my shoulder to the empty hallway, where sconces in the shape of lanterns warmed the stone walls and shed light across stately ancestral portraits. Surely I'd just imagined the cow. It seemed I should have slept on the plane over here. That was it. Just a bit of jet lag making me see things.

"Moooo?"

I stiffened in Ramsay's arms. The moo had been a whisper in the air, barely discernable, and my face froze, waiting to see if Ramsay had also heard it or my sleep deprivation was now leading to me hearing voices.

"Moooo?" Again, just a whisper. Bracing myself, I glanced up at Ramsay.

His head was tilted, as though listening for something, and a perplexed expression hung on his face. Relief filled me.

"Do you—"

"Don't move." Ramsay's arms tightened around me, and honestly, I wouldn't have been able to move if I had wanted to. And, frankly, I really didn't want to. Do you know how incredible it was to be hugged tightly and cradled against a delicious man who wanted nothing more than to protect you from harm? I mean, I wasn't one for the whole damsel in distress thing, but I was beginning to see the perks. And, *God* did he smell good.

Following his gaze, I froze.

In the once-empty hallway one of those cows with the big horns now stood, tilting its head at us, whispering its "moo" at us.

Yes, whispering.

Not to mention, he was semi-transparent.

Oh my God. He was a ghost. A ghost cow. A freaking ghost cow.

Torn between excitement and fear, I blinked as the cow executed what seemed to be a little dance, a jig maybe? His hooves tippy-tapped on the floor, and his eyes were wide with excitement. He ended on a flourish and nodded his head at us.

"Moo?"

"You must be Clyde," Ramsay said.

"Moo!" The ghost cow bellowed so loud, racing up and down the hall like a dog with the zoomies, that we both jumped and held on to each other tighter.

"He has a name?" I gasped.

"Clyde is the Highland ghost coo that haunts MacAlpine Castle. I've never had the pleasure of meeting him."

Clyde dove through a wall at the end of the hallway, and then popped through the door to my apartment, executing another round of zoomies as though he couldn't contain his excitement.

"A coo?"

"We call our cows 'coos' here, lass." Scotland drifted through Ramsay's words, the soft roll of the *R*s making me shiver, and I wanted to keep him talking just to listen to his beautiful accent.

"Right. A ghost coo. And this is normal?" I was torn

between what I wanted to look at more—Ramsay's handsome profile or the ghost executing a series of acrobatics behind me—but the ghost won. I mean, who was to say when I'd ever see this ghost again? It didn't sound like it made an appearance much if Ramsay hadn't yet seen him.

"Great job, Clyde!" Ramsay called and I glanced up at him in question. I didn't know Ramsay well, but the enthusiasm in his voice struck me as out of place for him.

"Great job doing what? Scaring the shit out of people?"

"I'm told you're supposed to compliment him, or you'll hurt his feelings."

"Hurt his … the cow, I mean, coo, has feelings?" Sure enough, Clyde pattered closer at Ramsay's words, bobbing his head as though he was happy, and I smiled.

"He's right, Clyde. You did the best job ghosting of any ghost I've seen."

Clyde perked up, doing his little jig again, and then disappeared. I blinked at the empty hallway, my heart still hammering even though I'd managed to bring myself down from sheer panic to simple anxiety, and blew out a breath.

"Are you okay?"

The hallway shifted, and I realized that we were moving. Ramsay was carrying, yes *carrying* me, downstairs. I wanted to stop him, but the experience was so unexpected and novel, that I decided to relish this moment.

My ex-boyfriend had stood on a chair while I'd cornered a rat in our studio.

I suspected Ramsay would set me on the counter, tell me to put my feet up, and catch the rat one-handed all while cooking me breakfast. He just had that vibe, you know? It was a quiet confidence that made me think that not much rattled this man. Which also immediately made me think about how fun it would be to see him come undone.

Bad Willow.

Ramsay carried me all the way downstairs and into a living room area where a fire roared in the fireplace. Sophie and Lachlan were cuddled on a love seat, and an older couple sat in matching tartan chairs by the fire. The dogs jumped up at our arrival, the chihuahua racing over to growl at Ramsay's feet, and Sophie popped up as well when she saw Ramsay carrying me.

"What's wrong?"

"Clyde," Ramsay said, putting me gently down and making sure I was steady on my feet before stepping away.

It was like losing a warm blanket on a cold winter's night.

I instantly missed his nearness, my body wanting to be snuggled up to his, and I had to force myself to take a step away from him to steady my nerves and pull my thoughts away from just how right it had felt to be cradled in his arms.

Let's just say my ex-boyfriend hadn't exactly been a knight in shining armor type, okay? He'd been hot, in his own art school vibe way, but not like this tall muscle-bound man who oozed strength and confidence. Really, could anyone blame me if my mind went to certain places around Ramsay? I imagined he cut a wide swath through the supermarket, women tailing him like lost puppies, pretending to reach for something on the highest shelf just to ask for his help.

Ramsay also had an impeccable sense of style. All of

which ticked some of the boxes of what I found attractive in a man. His jeans were the perfect fit of not too tight, not too loose, cuffed casually over thick-soled boots. A heather-green wool sweater worn over a faded tartan shirt, both sleeves rolled to reveal intricate tattoos snaking up his arms, and a chunky watch at his wrist.

I'd forgotten just how green his eyes were.

It was one of those weird memories, which itched at my brain and took me back to being seventeen, dreaming over boys and clothes and makeup, and Ramsay had been the most exotic man I'd ever seen before. His soft accent, striking eyes, and taciturn attitude had sent my friends and me into a tizzy. None of which I'm sure he remembered, since he'd spent most of the trip fishing and camping with my brother on Rainy Lake.

"Oh, no. Willow, I'm sorry. I should have prepared you for that. Clyde is ... well, he's an experience, let's just say?"

A plaintive moo echoed through the castle and Sophie grinned. A curvy girl like me, with rose-gold hair and a casual style, she had that fresh-faced American look that California girls seemed to effortlessly exude.

"And we love you for it, Clyde," Sophie called, directing her voice toward the corridor.

"So ... that's a normal thing, eh?" I asked, making a mental note to never sneak downstairs for snacks in the middle of the night. Nope, I would be stocking the mini fridge in my apartment with any needed midnight munchies, thank you very much.

"Normal would be a stretch, I suppose, but Clyde is part of MacAlpine Castle's charm." The woman sitting by the fire rose and walked forward, hand outstretched. With short hair, an efficient and motherly air, her presence instantly soothed me. She wore fitted navy corduroy pants, buttery-soft Chelsea boots, and a cream-colored cable-knit sweater. Country cottage chic. "I'm Hilda, one of the castle caretakers, and this is my husband, Archie. I largely run the interior and Archie handles the maintenance and gardens, but if there is anything you need, we're both available to help."

"Thank you, Hilda. Nice to meet you."

"Welcome, lass." Archie lifted shaggy brows and nodded at me from where he tied flies by the fire.

"You fish?" I asked, angling my head at him.

"It's a passion, I'll admit. Do you?"

"I do," I said, because, well, it was hard to grow up in Minnesota and not try your hand at fishing on occasion. Particularly when you had an older brother who would drag you along on his days to watch you. So I'd learned, reluctantly, and had quietly come to enjoy the peaceful times at the lake. It had given me time to sketch designs and dream over my future.

"That's a good lass."

The way Archie said it made me want to preen, as though I'd just received the highest badge of honor, and my lips quirked in a smile.

"Well, honestly, this is going far better than I expected. Since I have you both here, do you want to just quickly talk about your schedules this week? Ramsay, I'd like to get Willow down to your shop at some point so she can scope the place out and make some notes on what she'll be doing for you."

I blinked at Sophie, my brain scrambling to catch up to

her words. My mouth went dry. I turned slowly, my eyebrows at my hairline, and met Ramsay's eyes.

"Notes?" Ramsay asked Sophie, ignoring me.

"For the internship? The one you agreed to?" Sophie spoke slowly, as though educating a three-year-old, and Ramsay's eyes shifted to mine.

"*Willow* is my intern?"

"I mean, I'm not yours, per se, it's not like you own me," I rushed out. No idea why I said that, because the idea of Ramsay owning *any* part of me didn't seem all that distasteful.

"No," Ramsay said. Turning, he left the room, and my mouth dropped open.

"Right, yes, he does have a habit of doing this. Don't worry, Willow. We'll figure this out." Sophie patted my arm, glaring at the empty doorway.

There was no way this was going to work. It was one thing for Ramsay to be here, on my new adventure, and another thing entirely to be working for him. I sighed, looking around at the expectant faces in the room.

"I'm sorry, but I don't think I can do this."

CHAPTER SIX

Ramsay

I didn't have time for this.

Or at least that was what I was telling myself. Somewhere along the way as a business owner, I'd learned that there were times when it was easier if I just cracked on with doing things myself. And this was one of those times. No way in hell was I allowing Willow to work in my shop.

I already had enough distractions as it was.

Checking my watch, I strode to the long table that hugged one wall of the workroom tucked behind my shop and flipped the slim laptop open. Settling onto the stool, I paged through my planner to look at the month ahead and answered the video call that popped on my screen.

"Good afternoon, sir. How are you today?"

I rolled my eyes at my cousin Sheila, who was also my virtual office manager, and a damn good one at that. Razor-sharp wit combined with an excellent eye for details made her the perfect addition to Ramsay Kilts. Even so, she'd been making noises about hiring more help recently, and I knew I'd have to give her the go-ahead to do so. It would have to be under her management though, as I certainly didn't have the time to train more staff.

Let alone a gorgeous American with the kind of body that was made for a man's hands.

"You only call me 'sir' when you want something. Out with it."

"It's Louise's wedding in May. In Portugal. I was hoping—"

"How long?"

"One week?"

"Approved."

"Grand, that's grand. Mark the dates down." Sheila nodded to my planner, and I dutifully flipped ahead to cross out the dates that she would be gone. "Next up, we've got the financials for the Edinburgh stores. First quarter is looking to shape up for your best yet, profit margins are up, particularly now that you've cut the bus ad campaign."

"I never should have approved that." My publicist had insisted that an ad campaign for our kilts would be huge on city buses, but it had barely moved the needle on sales.

"It's a data point. Worth trying out, but now you know it's not for us. I'd like to try a TikTok campaign though."

"TikTok?" I glared at her, as though she'd just suggested we sell cocaine in our custom sporrans.

"Bloody hell, Ramsay. Tell me you've heard of TikTok."

"Of course I've heard of TikTok. I just don't know why my kilts need to be on TikTok."

"Because people love looking at pretty videos of Scotland, even more so if there's a hot man in a kilt in them."

"Where are you finding these hot men in kilts?"

Sheila raised an eyebrow at me. I recoiled.

"Absolutely not."

"Och, come on! Who better to represent the brand than the owner?"

"No. Next item on the list?"

"No to TikTok or no to you being in the campaign?"

I sighed and tapped my pen, looking up as a knock sounded at the front door to the shop. Holding a finger up to Sheila's pouting image, I walked to the doorway and glanced out to see a group of women peering through the window. Ignoring them, I returned to the video call.

"No to me being in the campaign. But I'll have final say on the direction you take with TikTok, so don't start any campaigns until I give you the go-ahead."

"Aww, and here I was going to sneak the half-naked men coated in honey past you."

That caught my attention, and I glowered at her.

"Why in the world would you coat a man in honey?"

"It's less shiny than oil, but still gleams."

"Won't it just look like piss?"

"You think? Huh, I'll have to look into it."

"You can do that off the clock, Sheila. I'm not paying you to test out honey on naked men."

"More's the pity, I'm sure. Right, then. Carrying on. A spot has opened up at the airport."

I rolled my eyes.

"We've been over this. Move on."

"I think you need to hear me out because your brother

is trying to shoehorn his way in, but I managed to get the leasing agent to give us twenty-four hours before he opens it to other applicants."

My blood heated at the mention of Andrew. It was impossible not to. *Traitor.*

"Our kilts are custom-made. What do you suggest we do for an airport store?" I shouldn't be open to the idea, but the thought of my brother getting prominent placement with his fast-fashion, cheaply made crap, which he passed off as authentic Scottish merchandise, made me want to punch my fist through the computer screen. Not that any of this was Sheila's fault, it was just the closest thing to me. Instead, I drew multiple circles on the paper, stabbing little holes into the corner of the cover, while Sheila rushed through her pitch.

"I think you could choose one or two tartan favorites, our bestsellers maybe, and produce those in common sizes. Then we go all accessories. Bowties, braces, bags ... all of that can be made ahead of time without having to be a custom order. We have enough data to know what our customers like best, so we produce a lot of it. The revenue stream from this positioning would employ an entire new warehouse of employees at our production facilities."

She knew just where to fire her shots. It was vitally important to me that my employees lived and worked in Scotland, and each product was made with a careful eye to detail. Kilt-making was a time-honored tradition, and I made sure that each of our orders was crafted with that history in mind. But I also knew we were approaching a recession and that many employers were making cuts. If I was in the position to provide more jobs, I wanted to do so.

"What data do you have that supports purchases at that price? My brother's shite products would likely sell better."

"Maybe, maybe not. I'll send you the financials. I did a lot of research on high-end boutiques and their placement in airports around the world. Turns out, many people forget to buy gifts while traveling and are willing to splurge before they hop on a plane home. The data supports it."

"Send it over. I'll look at it today and get back to you by"—I checked my watch—"before end of day. I'm going to the pub for the match later."

"Look at you being social." Sheila gave me an approving nod.

"Hardly. I need to eat. And there's beer."

"Will any of your friends be there?"

"I dunno." I shrugged a shoulder. "Likely?"

"Aww, you have a man date to watch the rugby. See? You're growing. I knew moving to Loren Brae would be good for you."

"From my understanding, you're my cousin, not my mother, Sheila. I don't need you to hover over me."

"Not hovering. Just observing."

"I didn't see discussion of my personal life on today's agenda."

"Oh, speaking of!" Sheila continued unperturbed, tucking a pencil behind her ear. "Did your intern arrive?"

"I'm not talking about that."

"Wait, what happened?" Sheila's eyes sharpened. "I thought you'd agreed to this."

"Changed my mind."

"That's not like you. Usually, you're a man of your word."

My back went up. Sheila wasn't wrong. Once I'd given my word or agreed to do something, I rarely backpedaled. I didn't like people who were indecisive or changed tracks constantly. If I said I would do something, I did it. Which made me even more annoyed that Sophie had surprised me with Willow as an intern. If she'd just told me who was coming, I would have told her no.

You could have asked for the name of the intern.

"She's not a good fit."

"She?" Sheila perked up, dropping her chin onto her hands, and fluttered her eyelashes at me. "Tell me more."

"No."

"Oh, come on, Ramsay. Have a wee gossip with me. I'm bored."

"How can you be bored? You date a different guy every week and go out every night."

"Och, that's nothing interesting. Tell me about her."

She's perfect.

I couldn't believe that thought landed in my head, and once there, it burrowed in like a bear getting ready to hibernate for the winter. Horror filled me. Willow was *not* perfect. Sure, she was a stunning woman, but certainly not perfect. At least not perfect for me. Perfect for someone else. Away from me. Far, far, away from me.

"There's nothing to tell."

"Ramsay. Come on, give me something. I'm your manager, after all. I prepared an entire training program for this intern. You can't just call it off and not tell me why."

I grimaced. Why had I hired a family member again?

"She's Miles's sister."

"Oh. Well, that shouldn't be a problem, right?" Sheila

crinkled her nose as she thought about it, and then her eyes widened. "Ohhhhh. *Oh*. You fancy the lass, don't you?"

"No."

"Ramsay! You do, don't you?" Sheila's eyes lit and I growled, literally growled, as a smile widened on her face. "You've never had a problem hiring friends before."

"She's not suited."

"Why? Does she hate clothes? Criminal history? Passes wind a lot?"

At that, I rolled my eyes and reached for the top of the computer.

"It's not happening. Goodbye, Sheila."

"You've got a crussshhhhh," Sheila sang just as I slammed the computer closed and buried my face in my hands. *Great*. Now I'd never hear the end of this.

Fighting down the irritation that threatened to make me call Lachlan and tell him to rein in his woman, which I knew would go over about as well as a fart at a funeral, I picked up my phone and called Miles instead. I might as well deal with this sooner than later, and the last thing I needed was to have him chew me out because I'd canceled his sister's internship.

"Ramsay! I was just talking about you today. How's it going, man?" Miles's face filled the screen, and a knit cap pulled low over his head, snow blanketing the yard behind him.

I still remembered the first time I met Miles, attempting to skip rocks on the banks of Loch Mirren. Instantly hearing his American accent, I was intrigued and had decided to show him how a real Scot skipped a rock. Except my rock had only gone two hops and his three, and before

I'd known it, we'd entered an epic competition that had secured our friendship. Now we saw each other once a year on an annual trip somewhere, and though I didn't talk to him weekly, Miles was still an important part of my life.

"Hey, mate, how goes it?"

"Yeah, good enough, doncha know? Business is good, even in this weather."

"Cold?"

"Shit, man, another foot of snow forecasted for tomorrow."

"I don't know how you do it." I'd visited Minnesota twice, once in the summer and once in the winter, and I far preferred the summer. The winter wind had felt like someone was trying to carve into my face with an icy scalpel. My nose hairs had frozen instantly, my eyes had watered, and I'd, quite literally, gasped for breath when I'd stepped outside. All while the neighbor jogged by with a fuzzy hat on and had waved cheerfully like it was a balmy summer's day.

Don't get me wrong, growing up in Scotland had thickened my skin against cold weather. It wasn't *warm* in Loren Brae by many standards, but it wasn't Baltic. The days at least reached zero degrees Celsius. The lot of them in Minnesota were mental, I'd concluded. Nobody could survive, let alone thrive, in such conditions. Or I suppose with the right gear you could, but *why*? Why would you want to?

"Just used to it, man."

"I wanted to talk to you about something."

"What's up?" Miles's face instantly sobered. I wasn't one to call him much for advice or to talk matters of the heart, but we'd had enough important chats through the years to know when the other needed us.

"Your sister's here."

"I knew it! I asked her if she was going to see you and she denied it." Miles shook his head and glowered into the phone.

"That's not the worst of it. She's meant to be my new intern."

"Wait, you hired her as an intern and didn't tell me? What the hell, man?" Miles leaned back from the phone, affronted.

"I didn't know, mate. Sophie, who owns MacAlpine Castle, and is my best friend's girlfriend, badgered me into taking on an intern. Said she wanted to design a line of custom kilts for the castle shop. She didn't tell me who the intern was."

"Ah, okay. So, what's the problem? Did she screw up already?"

I tilted my head at that, the tone of his voice putting my back up the same way that Sheila's comment about keeping my word had. Why would Miles think she'd screwed up? Did she have a bad track record or something? I realized now how little I knew about Willow's life because, well, I never really asked Miles about it. We talked about work and girlfriends and planned the occasional guy's trip together.

"No, not at all. I barely saw her." Just pressed her luscious breasts against my chest while my hands gripped her thick thighs and my body begged to take her to a dark corner of the castle and sink into all her softness. Fucking hell, I was doomed. Even thinking about how her body had felt against mine earlier was causing an uncomfortable reaction.

"This is great, actually. Finally someone who can keep an eye out for her since she refuses to let me."

"You want me to look after her?" I kept my expression flat, hoping he couldn't read anything untoward in my eyes.

"Yes, please. Last dude she dated stole from her and slept with her only employee. The job before that? Tried to make her model lingerie for their ad campaigns instead of letting her design. The job before *that* one? Boss put his hands on her and tried to force her to sleep with him."

My blood boiled.

"His name?" My voice took on a sharp edge.

"I took care of it, bro. But thanks. She just needs a win. I'd hoped it would be here, in Minnesota, but she's allergic to me at this point."

"Maybe because you have the approach of a bulldozer?"

Miles laughed and looked away from the camera before turning back.

"Pot calling the kettle black and all that."

"Touché."

"Just look out for her, will ya? I feel better knowing she's there with you. And don't tell her I said that. Oh, and I wouldn't mind updates since she's pissed at me right now."

Great, now I'd been put in the position of protecting her *and* reporting back to her brother.

"Maybe it's best not to work with her. I don't want you coming after me if it doesn't work out. Doesn't sound like she's had a great track record at her jobs. Is she even a good designer?"

"Oh, hell yeah, she's great. Wait until you see her stuff. It's not her work ethic that's the issue, Ramsay. She's just so damn naïve. She'd give any dude off the street a roof for the night if he needed a place to sleep. How she didn't get mugged regularly in New York City I do not know. She's the most optimistic person I've ever met, and I think I'd be less worried if I saw she'd sharpened some edges. Unfortunately, the only person she seems to have claws with is me."

Not, quite. Och, I had a glimpse of those claws myself. At least now I understood why she'd been so antagonistic toward me when she first spotted me. What had she accused me of?

"I don't need you reporting back to my brother."

"We're hardest on those closest to us."

"Maybe. Either way, just keep an eye on her, yeah? I gotta run, my contractor's meeting me for a site walk-through."

"Aye, no problem, mate. Catch up soon."

I hung up and stared across the shop, my annoyance with Sophie growing even more. Why had I ever said yes to her proposal? This was all Lachlan's fault. Checking the time, I stood and grabbed my coat. He'd be at the pub tonight.

And I'd be happy to take my grievances out on him.

CHAPTER SEVEN

WILLOW

"Listen, it's not like you can hop back on a plane this second. Why don't you take a few days and learn more about the job and Loren Brae and then you can make your decision?"

Sophie's words echoed back to me as I finished getting ready for dinner.

Perhaps I had been a touch dramatic announcing my resignation before I'd even started my job, but between the ghost coo and Ramsay's sudden appearance in my life, I'd been more than rattled. Even so, my typical full-throttle approach to life would have meant that I shouldn't have been fazed by any of these hurdles.

It must be lack of sleep.

That was the only thing that I could chalk my behavior up to, since my gut was screaming at me to keep this job.

The minute we'd driven up the long road to MacAlpine Castle, something had clicked—like that definitive click that comes when you secure your airplane seatbelt—and I'd known I was home. *Home*. It was that same knowing, that deep-rooted understanding that I needed to be here in this moment, that had me standing in front of a mirror trying on outfits to wear to the local pub for dinner instead of looking up flights to go home.

I wondered if other people had the same internal voice that I did. This sense of knowing, the gentle nudges forward in life, was something I'd had as long as I could remember. Many a time it had saved me from disaster—like the time I'd stopped on a street corner and refused to step forward even though the walk sign had turned green. A car had run the red light, luckily not hurting anyone, but had I stepped out onto the street I would have been a goner. Numerous instances like that through my life had convinced me that when my gut told me to do something, I should listen.

Which is why, currently, I was more frazzled than was typical for me. My gut said "stay." My mind said "leave." I was at odds with myself and that was never a comfortable place to be. The reality was that Miles was getting in my head. My impatient, domineering, overprotective brother had been determined to chip away at my impulsive behavior through the years until finally, he'd managed to take a chink out of my freewheeling armor. I liked to believe that every life experience taught me something and led more toward where I needed to go. Miles wanted to control every situation so that the outcome was predetermined.

Was his way better or worse than mine? Considering

that thought for a moment, I pulled on wide-legged jeans, a fitted crewneck top with a vintage ice cream shop logo on the front, and my Adidas Sambas. I piled a few dainty necklaces together, added my hoops, and pulled back the top half of my hair with a cute bow. Bows were in this season. Grabbing my soft wool camel trench coat, I slipped it over my shoulders, added my black quilted crossbody purse with gold details, and turned in front of the mirror.

Cute, casual, chic.

The three Cs.

What Miles needed in life, I did not. My soul craved adventure and creation, and this job offered both. The needs of the castle shop would stretch my creative energy, all while allowing me a foundation of security to potentially build something of my own. While small-town Loren Brae, Scotland, wasn't exactly the hotbed of the fashion industry and the place I needed to be to grow a brand, maybe that was *just fine*. There were many roads to the lake, my father had always told me, and I reached for that wisdom now.

I loved new experiences.

I loved designing.

I loved being creative.

I loved meeting new people.

I loved building something of my own.

Loren Brae offered me all of these things, plus the opportunity to live in an actual freaking castle. And the reality was, I really, really, really wanted to build something of my own. I needed to do this for myself, and even *if* Miles had manufactured this job somehow, I still could prove myself. I didn't see how working for Ramsay was going to pan out, but surely Sophie would still be open to me designing for the castle shop. I'd ask her over dinner and maybe we could come to a resolution that suited both of us.

Since Ramsay clearly didn't want to work with me either.

Sniffing, I tucked my phone, lipstick, and wallet into my purse and left my apartment.

The rude bastard had simply walked out. Who even *did* that? He'd even been more dramatic than I had been, and that was saying something.

"Moo?"

It was just a whisper this time, like the softest of sighs, and I barely jumped. Schooling my breath, I turned to see Clyde in the hallway behind me, his head tilted, his eyes hopeful.

Could a ghost coo's eyes be hopeful? Was lack of sleep finally catching up to me?

Bracing myself, I lifted a hand that only trembled slightly.

"Hi, Clyde."

"Moo!" Clyde bellowed, dancing his little jig while I tried not to have a panic attack on the spot, and then winked from sight.

"You might want to work on decibel control," I called out, my hand at my chest, as I turned to continue downstairs. Really, how did someone *ever* get used to that? At least I didn't need that cup of coffee I'd been hoping for as my jet lag had been shattered at Clyde's shout.

"Are you okay?" Sophie stood in the foyer of the castle, and I paused to catch my breath and admire the grandiose room. Stone floors, high ceilings, and stately double wooden doors created an epic backdrop, and already I was itching to take a million photos here. Even though Sophie was dressed casually in a UCLA sweatshirt and jeans, she looked effortlessly cool against the worn wood door with black metal scrollwork. Oh yeah, I wouldn't have to look far for interesting and unique content for social media, that was for sure. "You look a little tense."

"Your resident ghost paid me a visit."

"Ah, yes. Clyde is a fan of the jump scare. Wait until you meet Lia. She'll tell you about the time he made her pee her pants."

"Seriously?"

"Oh, yeah. He's like a toddler on crack. There is nothing more exciting to Clyde than being able to scare someone. It's like he was given the rules of ghosting and took them to heart, but then immediately feels bad when he actually manages to scare someone, so he hangs around to make sure you're okay."

"He has feelings?" I hadn't imagined the emotion in his eyes.

"Oh, big time. But his mainline is cheerful."

"Fascinating. Is this something you're just … used to now? Or have you always been comfortable with ghosts?"

We left the front hall and stepped into the brisk winter night. Sophie nodded toward the twinkling lights of Loren Brae at the base of the hill on which MacAlpine Castle stood.

"Are you okay with walking?"

"I was just living in New York. We walked everywhere."

"Perfect. And yes, I'm used to Clyde now, but he still gets me from time to time. And no, I wasn't someone who was into ghosts before my uncle left me the castle. I was a marketing manager for my uncle's company in California. Huge fan of spreadsheets and things that add up and make sense. A highland ghost coo doesn't fit neatly in any of my life-understanding boxes."

"And yet, here you are. You inherited the castle?"

"I did."

"That's a pretty big deal. Also, sorry for your loss."

"Thanks for that. Yeah, now? I can't say I'd take it all back just to have Uncle Arthur with me again, because then I'd never have met Lachlan or started this new and amazing life, but I miss him. He was one of my favorite people, aside from his wife, Lottie, and the grief never fully goes away. It just sort of sneaks up on you in unexpected ways. Knowing him, though, he'd be happy as can be with how things have worked out for me. He was always up for an adventure."

"I understand grief. I lost my mom quite young, so the edges of my grief are dulled and mixed in with those blurred childhood memories you get. But watching those around me grieve probably added to that experience."

"I'm sorry." Sophie shot me a sympathetic look as we walked down the path, the gravel crunching beneath our shoes. "Do you have a big family?"

"No, just my brother and my dad. My mother was from here, actually. Well, close by. That's how we know Ramsay. We'd come to visit Gran in the summers and my brother, Miles, made friends. He was better at it than I was, always off fishing and playing sports, while I liked to stay home and cut up clothes to dress my dolls."

"And look where that landed you, though. A celebrated fashion designer."

"I don't know that I'd say celebrated. But I'm getting

there." I paused. Loren Brae revealed herself to me as we reached the base of the hill, and my heart sighed. Even though it was dark out, it was hard to ignore the charm of this village. It reminded me of a postcard, with twinkling lights reflected on the dark surface of the water, and old-timey lantern style streetlamps lighting up cobblestoned streets. Was everything here a picture? Already I wanted to pull my phone out and take a ton of photos for inspiration, but I didn't want to be rude to Sophie who pulled her coat more tightly around herself when an icy gust of wind rattled across the loch. Sophie turned to go up the main street of the village, but I paused, my gaze captured by the rippling waters of Loch Mirren.

When we'd arrived in Loren Brae, Sophie cheerfully chattering as she'd directed the car down a narrow lane that hugged the loch's shores, I'd barely had a chance to admire Loch Mirren. In the daylight, it had been stunning, icy greyish-blue water hugged by intimidating hills, but at night? She was breathtaking. It was really a sense of openness, like I was the only person standing on the edge of the world, with the wind whispering the secrets of the past at my ears. Something tugged in my soul, like my blood rising to meet its roots, and for a moment, the world seemed to shimmer and shift around me as a faint glimmer rippled across the surface of the loch. My breath caught.

"Beautiful, isn't it?" Sophie's voice was quiet at my side.

"Powerful," I said.

"Ah. Then you feel it already? Interesting."

At that I glanced at Sophie, a question on my lips.

"Sophie! Hi!"

Interrupted, we both turned as a slim woman with

messy curls and a puffy jacket waved at us from across the street.

"Agnes, hi! Are you going to the pub?" Sophie asked, nudging me toward her friend. We crossed the empty street, and I smiled politely at the woman.

"I am. I'm craving a bowl of soup on this brisk night. Hello." The woman smiled at me, nodding.

"This is Willow. She's here to help design a custom fashion line for the castle shop."

"Och, that's right. With Ramsay, eh? Welcome to Loren Brae, Willow. I'm Agnes, and I own Bonnie Books, just down the way." Agnes gestured to the village and shook my hand, her eyes bright and lively in the light from the streetlamp.

"I don't know about the 'with Ramsay' part, but I'm definitely here to design."

"Bloody hell. Is he giving you trouble already?" Agnes shook her head and turned down the main street and we followed, the icy wind driving us toward the warmth of the pub.

"He said no as soon as he saw her and walked out."

"He did not. Fecking eejit." Agnes shook her head.

"Oh, he did. But there's history there. My mom was from the area, so we'd visit in the summers. Ramsay is one of my brother's best friends, even though I haven't seen him in years. Guess he doesn't think I can hack it at his store."

"How would he even know if he doesn't try? God, he's such a grump," Sophie said, outraged on my behalf.

I wouldn't have described Ramsay as a grump in my teenage years. Reserved, I guess, but with a devilish smile, maybe, but not necessarily grumpy. He did spend most of his time with my brother, so perhaps I never saw that side of him.

"I wouldn't know. I haven't really talked to him in forever."

"He's a tetchy one, and that's the truth of it. Already it's becoming a bit of a thing around town," Agnes said, slowing her speed. "People have heard it's impossible to get an appointment at his shop, so it seems to be a game to see if they can get through the door."

"Like a VIP list at a club?" I asked, shaking my head. That was certainly no way to do business.

"Exactly that. There's no rhyme or reason to when he's open or accepting customers."

"I'm not sure he really needs the business, does he?" Sophie asked.

"Then why even open a shop? If he just wants to work in peace, wouldn't he have opened a workshop or whatever? Why have the storefront?" Agnes stopped in front of a pretty stone building. With paned windows that spilled warm light onto the sidewalk, a carved wooden sign reading *The Tipsy Thistle,* and an arched doorway at the entrance, I was instantly charmed. No neon signs and dismal sports bar exterior here. Instead, stone walls and carved wood framed the building, showcasing true historical design and aesthetic. Why the United States had succumbed to bland strip malls and basic design, I do not know. City planning gone awry, I guess.

"Maybe it just feeds Ramsay's ego to be in demand," I said.

Both women stiffened at my words, and I winced. Had

I gone too far? Ramsay was their friend, and I was new in town, so perhaps I'd put my foot in it.

"Ladies."

I closed my eyes at the word at my back, the voice a rough timbre that shivered across my skin, and I knew instantly that Ramsay had overheard what I'd said. Turning, I confirmed my suspicions when I found him glowering down at me.

Once again, standing this close, I couldn't help but feel overwhelmed by this man. His sheer size made me have to tilt my head to look up at him, and if possible, he made me feel like a fragile flower ready to shed her petals in the wind. Was this how thin woman felt around men all the time? Like delicate teacups that could break under their touch? If so, I was beginning to see the appeal. I'd never been one to aspire to have a man capable of manhandling me, but now that I was confronted with this rude, glaring, growly hunk of a man, my inner hussy wanted to roll over and flirt with him like a cat begging for more cream. His presence was potent, and my body instantly remembered how casually he'd carried me through the long halls of the castle as though he was rescuing a princess from a battle. Again, damsel in distress I was not, but damn it, Ramsay made me want to be one, just so I could press myself against his muscular body one more time.

"Ramsay. We were just talking about you," I said, not bothering to try and cover up my faux pas.

"As I heard. You think I have an ego?" Ramsay lifted his chin at me, his eyes shrouded in darkness from the newsboy cap he wore.

"Don't most men?"

"She has a point," Sophie interjected.

"Delicate, fragile, whiny little egos," Agnes muttered, and my lips quirked. I wondered who had annoyed her.

"Rough crowd," Ramsay rasped. "I'll be sure to keep my ego on the other side of the pub tonight."

"Oh, come on, Ramsay. We need to talk about this," Sophie protested.

Ramsay just shook his head and held the door open for us. Sophie sighed, and we clambered into the narrow front hallway.

"See?" Agnes hissed. "Fragile egos. Men need to be pampered at all times. It's why I don't want one."

"Me either," I agreed, though my inner hussy was still outside wrapped around Ramsay's muscular thighs.

"I, for one, will happily feed Lachlan's ego if it means I get as many orgasms as I do."

"Who needs a man when you have a vibrator? Have you seen the designs they have these days? Enough to make you sing."

Agnes nodded and high-fived me, while Ramsay made a sound caught between a laugh and a groan, and I winked at him.

"Nothing you need to worry yourself with, Ramsay. Women can take care of themselves."

"If you prefer rowing a boat yourself instead of a ride on a superyacht." Ramsay shrugged, and my mouth dropped open.

"A superyacht." Agnes snorted and patted Ramsay's arm while I tried to ignore the heat that warmed my body at his words. "That's an inflated opinion you have of yourself, darling."

"Never had any complaints." Ramsay flashed Agnes a grin so full of heat and oozing sexual promises that I felt the force of it from where I stood. Agnes blinked up at him, momentarily stunned, and I could not blame her. The man packed a powerful punch when he wanted to.

Which I was not going to pay attention to. No, sir. I was not.

The inner door to the pub opened, spilling enticing scents and laughter, and I rushed toward the lightness and warmth, because I quite literally had no answer for the lust that plagued me for my potential employer. Now I was stuck thinking about what a superyacht of sexual experiences with Ramsay would look like and that was *not* where my thoughts needed to be about my brother's best friend.

Superyacht. Indeed.

CHAPTER EIGHT

Willow

The Tipsy Thistle oozed charm and made me feel both welcomed and at home. Already, I itched to take endless photos of every nook and cranny of the building. The layering of textures here was something that interior designers would kill for, yet I suspected the design worked simply due to its authenticity. This was a place that had become what it was through decades of existing, not because it was carefully curated at the hands of a designer. It was a hodge-podge sort of space, like rooms had been added through the decades as an afterthought, and worn wood beams, stone walls, and a cheerful fire crackling in the wide fireplace dispelled some of the cold that seeped in from outside. A heavy wooden bar anchored the room, and one of the most handsome men I'd ever seen in my life gave me a slow smile designed to make a woman drop her panties at ten paces.

"Holy shit," I breathed.

"Och, admire him from afar but don't let him know it," Agnes advised me, "or we'll never hear the end of it. He's like a puppy—if you give him a treat he'll never leave you alone."

"Do I want him to leave me alone?" I wondered out loud.

"Yes," Ramsay growled at my ear and then stomped across the room to take a seat at the end of the bar.

"Do what you like." Agnes shrugged, but I caught a whiff of something there. She turned to walk to the bar and Sophie grabbed my arm. Meeting my eyes, she shook her head once, and then nodded at Agnes's back.

Ah. Message received.

I'd much rather make friends here than toy with the men, so I filed the hot bartender into the "Don't Touch" category and followed Sophie to sit next to Agnes at the bar.

"Och, there's a trio of bonnie lasses to warm my cold, dead heart on a blustery evening. I see you've brought a friend with you. To what do I owe this pleasure?" The bartender, with wicked eyes, a mouth made for sinful dreams, and muscular arms, leaned onto the bar in front of me and offered another unhurried smile. I'll admit, my inner hussy that had been momentarily considering wrapping herself around Ramsay now sashayed right over to the bar and fluttered her lashes at the bartender. It was hard not to be attracted to this man, who basically oozed sex appeal, and I realized he'd chosen the perfect profession if he enjoyed being ogled every night.

"Graham, this is Willow. She's come to work for MacAlpine Castle to design a customized line of clothing for the gift shop. She'll also be interning at Ramsay Kilts."

"Nope," Ramsay interjected from down the bar, and I turned to see him, arms crossed and staring at a sports game on a television screen.

"A few small details to be worked out," Sophie continued through gritted teeth. A look that I couldn't quite identify passed between Graham and Sophie, and then Graham turned the full power of his attention upon me.

"Well, now, sure and it's grand to have a bonnie lass such as yourself joining us in Loren Brae. It's been a particularly ... cold winter ... and you're like the sunshine peeking through storm clouds."

Oh man. This one knew what he was about. I blew out a shaky breath.

"Is it poetry you're spouting these days, Graham? For someone who never reads, that's certainly a new twist."

"What's life if you aren't growing, my sweet Agnes?" Graham shot her a honey-sweet smile before offering a hand. "I'm Graham, and I am the proprietor of this fine establishment."

"Which will go out of business soon if you forget to get your patrons drinks," Ramsay said. Graham's grin widened as he held my hand a moment longer.

"It's lovely to meet you, Willow. What are you drinking tonight?"

"Um, a gin and tonic would be great, thanks."

"We do a lovely pink gin and tonic with pomegranate seeds and a sprig of rosemary."

"Oh, yum. Sounds great. Thanks."

Graham slid me a leatherbound food menu and busied himself with drinks, working his way neatly down the bar and collecting orders from the other patrons who had gathered to watch the game.

"What's going on with Ramsay and not wanting you to work at his shop?" Agnes asked, her voice pitched lower than the game on the screen.

"He knows he needs to hire someone." Sophie leaned over, bending her head close. "His place is a nightmare when it comes to actually functioning. Maybe he just can't admit he needs help?"

"Or maybe my brother is making Ramsay report back to him."

"Your brother?" Agnes tilted her head at me.

"He's friends with Ramsay. We grew up coming to the area because my mum is from two villages over. Somehow Miles and Ramsay stayed close through the years. Now it feels like my brother managed to put this whole thing together and is just using it as a way to control me."

Whoops, I hadn't meant to say that last bit out loud. And I hadn't even had a drink yet. I'd have to be careful to watch my words with my new employer if jet lag was making me this loose with my tongue.

"Is that what you're worried about?" Sophie asked. "I can promise you that your brother had nothing to do with your job offer. I mean, I can't say whether he spoke to Ramsay or not, but on my end, I've never heard of Miles. I promise you we had our own reasons for hiring you."

A quick look between Agnes and Sophie had a question rising in my brain.

"Here you go, lass. Made with Common Gin, owned by that gentleman, Munroe himself, so if you hate it, be sure to say so loudly." Graham nodded to the man I'd seen with Lachlan in MacAlpine Castle's parking lot but hadn't met yet. He, too, was handsome in his own way, with gilded locks and broad shoulders, and I blinked as Lachlan entered the bar.

"Jesus." I turned to the women. "What is with the men here? They all could be models."

"Do you hear that, honey? You could be a model," Sophie said, wrapping an arm around Lachlan's waist as he leaned in for a kiss.

"You already made us model for your marketing campaign. What else am I modeling for now?"

"Did someone say model?" Graham brought his arm up and flexed his muscles, all while delivering a sultry, scowling look.

"You look constipated," Agnes said cheerfully. "A wee bit of fiber in your diet should sort you out."

"The only thing that needs sorting is—"

"A pint, please, Graham. BrewDog, ah, the Modern Mutiny please." Lachlan nodded toward the taps.

"The food looks good." I scanned the menu, trying to change the subject before Agnes and Graham got into it. "Oh, tough call. Steak pie or baked mac and cheese? I don't think I've ever had a steak pie before. Maybe when I was younger?"

"Seriously?" Agnes turned to me, distracted from scowling at Graham.

"Really. Meat pies aren't all that common in the States."

"Then you should give it a go. Unless you want to give the haggis a try?" Agnes winked at me.

"Nope. Tried it when I was thirteen. Not for me." I shuddered at the memory. Ramsay snorted, and I turned to him, though his eyes were still on the game.

"Something funny?"

"You spit it in the poor dug's face. Though he was pretty delighted about the situation."

My face heated. I'd forgotten that Ramsay had been there the first time I'd tried haggis. Honestly, it probably hadn't been as bad as I'd made it out to be, but everyone had revved me up so much for it to be this wild experience, so when I'd taken a bite, my first instinct had been to turn and spit it out. Which, I'll admit, was a pretty gross response. Particularly when it landed on the face of the poor dog who had been waiting for table scraps.

"It was a dog, Ramsay."

"That's what I said. A dug."

"No, a dog," I enunciated carefully, turning toward him.

"Och, lass. He was more than half the size of you. That was a dug if I've ever seen one."

"A dog," I insisted.

"A dug." Ramsay slid a glance my way, and the heat of his look made me want to rise to the challenge.

"Let me clear this up," Lachlan said, drawing my attention back from Ramsay. "Sir Buster is a wee dog. But the mastiff that Fergus our sheep farmer has? That's a dug. It's a fine distinction."

"Oh, so you *can* say dog. You're just saying dug when

it's bigger? Is this like where you call a thin woman beautiful, but a fat woman is just curvy?"

"I reckon I can't answer this correctly." Lachlan raised an eyebrow, glancing down at Sophie, as Graham passed him a pint. "I'm just going to watch the match, love." With a quick kiss he exited the conversation and joined Ramsay and Munroe at the end of the bar.

"I think I scared him away."

"To be fair, Lachlan is the least sizeist person I know." Sophie pointed a finger at her own large body. "He loves me exactly as I am and has never once made me feel insecure about my size."

"I don't doubt it. You can see the man is besotted with you. I was just trying to understand why the little dogs get to be called dog, but the big dogs are called dugs. It's like ... painting them in a poor light."

"Och, not at all, lass. Dug's a good word. A strong word. Trust me, Sir Buster wishes he was a dug." Graham held out his hand and made a fist, lowering his voice into a growl. "Now that's a *dug*."

"Hmm." I did appreciate his delivery.

"See the difference? A dug is a good thing, much fiercer than a wee dog. You ken?"

The men shouted, interrupting anything I was going to say, and we all turned to look at the screen.

"What is this? Rugby?" I asked.

"Yup." Agnes leaned over and picked up her cider. "Six Nations. Do you know rugby?"

"Not really. I mean, I've seen it on TV a few times, but don't know the rules."

"Go on, lads!" Ramsay shouted, banging his fist on the bar. It was the most animated I'd seen him yet.

"Push forward!" Lachlan shouted.

A bunch of men clenched in what looked like a group hug on the screen, inching slowly forward. Their shorts rode up thick tree-trunk like muscular legs, and there was a lot of grunting.

"Oh, my." I fanned my face and Agnes laughed.

"There's some perks to rugby, that's the truth of it."

"I see that. This is a game I could get into. Who are we rooting for?"

"The blue jerseys. With the tartan stripe down the side."

Something happened on the screen, a ball was tossed about, and everyone groaned.

"Och, get it out wide to Finn, you know better." Ramsay drained his pint and motioned to Graham for another. The men grappled once more on screen, and there were lots of beautiful shots of flexing muscles and sweaty skin. Oh yeah, I definitely could get into this game.

"I think I need to learn more about rugby."

"There's a local match next week. I'm happy to take you," Graham said.

"Back off," Ramsay ordered before I could even open my mouth. I whirled toward him and slapped my hand on the bar.

"Excuse me?"

"He knows better." Ramsay nodded at Graham, returning his eyes to the screen.

"Och, it's like that, is it, mate? Understood." Graham held his hands in the air.

"It's not." Ramsay shook his head.

"Like what? It's not like anything," I argued to Graham.

"I'm just looking out for her." Ramsay's tone put me on edge.

"Looking out for me?" My voice rose as anger snaked through me. The last thing I needed was another overprotective brother hovering over my every move. If I wanted to go to a rugby match with a hot bartender, then I could do so. Not that I'd really go, since I wanted Agnes to like me, but the point was about being controlled, not about being able to date. "I don't need you to look out for me."

Ramsay ignored me, his arms crossed, concentrating on the game.

"Excuse me? Hello? You don't get a say in my life, *sir*." Turning, I looked askance at Agnes and Sophie. "Can you believe him?"

"Unbelievable," Sophie agreed.

"Do you care if I say yes to this rugby match? Just to prove a point to Ramsay? I just got out of a bad breakup, so I promise I'm not looking to date anyone," I whispered.

"By all means, have at it." Agnes spread her hands out. "I hate men telling me what to do about as much as I hate loose men who date every woman that blows through town."

"Got it. No touching of Graham."

"I didn't say—"

"Graham?" I smiled sweetly at the bartender. "I'd love to go to the rugby match. Thanks for asking."

"No." Ramsay shook his head at Graham, completely ignoring me. My blood heated.

"Um, hmm." Graham looked between the two of us, a worried look on his face.

"Och, you've stepped in it now." Agnes hooted.

"Well? You did ask me on a date, didn't you? Are you not a man of your word?"

"Of course I am. The Scots pride themselves on honoring their word. I'd love to take you to the match, Willow."

"Did you hear that, Ramsay?" Sophie raised her voice, injecting a syrupy sweet note. "The Scots are known to be men of their words."

"Bloody hell." Ramsay rose and stormed toward the bathroom.

I looked around the bar.

"I missed something, didn't I?"

"Nothing that won't sort itself out in due time, lass. Now, was it steak pie you were thinking then?" Graham leaned in, tapping a finger on the menu in front of me. Confused about the undercurrents here, but needing food and a good night of sleep, I nodded and turned to Sophie.

"I think I'm going to need to crash after this. I'm dead on my feet. Plus, I'm not sure how much more I can take of Grumpy McJerkface tonight."

"Aww, you just reminded me of when Matthew and I called Lachlan Grumpy McHottie." Sophie sighed. "Matthew's my best friend. You'll meet him at some point if you stick around. He flies out when he can."

"I love Matthew," Agnes agreed.

Ramsay returned, ignoring us, and posted up at the bar again to watch the game. What was his deal anyway? There was no reason for him to step into this brotherly role. I didn't ask for it and I certainly didn't need it. I was tired of being treated like I was just a child. I was almost twenty-seven years old, had a fashion design degree, and had been in several relationships. It was all so ridiculous. What was Ramsay's deal? *Had he already tattled to Miles? Already been given the lowdown of my disastrous life?*

Thankfully, not long after, my delicious steak pie arrived, and I dug in with gusto. It was the perfect combination of soft pastry, thick sauce, and melt-in-your mouth steak. Perfect for a cold night, that was for sure. Conversation had been fun and easy between Agnes and Sophie, I could see us becoming fast friends, which was welcome given the last few months of my life. I'd needed this type of inclusion.

By eight o'clock, as much as I'd loved the atmosphere of the pub—*except for the belligerent, green-eyed Scot*—I was ready to leave. My annoyance with Ramsay had grown into full-blown anxiety. He'd roundly ignored me for the rest of the match, abstaining from joining in any more conversation that involved me. For being a family friend, he certainly wasn't acting like one. And now I supposedly had to work with this man?

"I don't see how I can work with Ramsay," I told Sophie on the walk home.

She sighed, nodding her head. "Yeah, he's being an absolute prick, isn't he?"

"Really is," I agreed, glumly. My fatigue clung to me like a heavy blanket as we plodded up the hill toward the castle, and all I wanted to do was go face first into a pillow and worry about everything tomorrow.

"Give it time. If it's any consolation, he really is known to be quite tetchy. It's not just you."

"Tetchy?"

"Um, crabby, grumpy, annoyed at everything. It's one of my favorite Scottish words."

"So, it's not just me who feels that way?" I heaved a sigh of relief when we got to the castle. The building looked lovely at night, with floodlights angled to light the four towers, and various windows lit from within. It would take some time to accept that I actually lived in a place as stately as this. It felt like I had an apartment in Grand Central Station or something.

"Get some rest. Everything's better after sleep. Keep an eye out for Clyde on the walk up."

"Thank you for taking me tonight. I had fun."

With that, I made my way carefully to my room, on high alert for any ghostly capers, but made it without any trouble. After a quick scrub of my face, I changed into some sweats and dove into bed, pulling the thick comforter over my head and dropping instantly into sleep.

I awoke with a start, hours later, and blinked into the darkness.

What had jolted me awake?

My brain felt fuzzy, as though my thoughts couldn't catch up with my reality, and when an otherworldly shriek sounded from outside, I did the first thing that came to mind.

I pulled the comforter back over my head.

Trembling, I took a few deep breaths, my brain finally waking up as another shriek rattled the window.

What the *hell* was that?

I couldn't wrap my head around any natural animal that would make such a sound, and steeling myself, I crept from beneath the comforter and pressed myself flat against the wall. Edging closer to the window, I tried to regulate my breathing as my heart hammered in my chest. Shaking, I paused at the edge of the window, scared that if I peeked out, I might become a target for the wrath of whatever that thing was.

In the end, curiosity won out.

Yeah, I know. I'd probably be the first to get picked off in a scary movie.

Dropping to my knees, I peered over the bottom of the window frame. Hopefully, since my room was dark, whatever was out there wouldn't be able to see me.

A sliver of moon hung low over the loch, shedding dim light across the dark surface of the water, trees swaying in the wind. Movement caught my attention, and my eyes widened to see Sophie, a sword in hand, walking the battlements with Lachlan at her side.

Whatever was out there, Sophie knew about, and if she needed a sword to keep it at bay, well, then it was something serious. But what? *And why a sword?*

Easing back from the window, I stood and dove back into bed, pulling the comforter over my head. Whatever was out there was not my problem for the moment. *I need sleep.* Next time I fly business class, I am definitely going to forego the ice cream treat and go for sleep instead. *They do say that sleep deprivation messes with your brain.*

. . .

"This is your adventure, Willow. Sleep now and ask questions tomorrow," I whispered to myself, hoping that would help calm my racing heart.

I needed answers, because if it wasn't Ramsay sending me home, that creature screaming in the night might just do the trick.

CHAPTER NINE

Willow

Surprisingly, I managed to fall back asleep, which was a testament to how fatigued I was. It wasn't just lack of sleep from the flight overseas, but the weeks leading up to my departure had been fraught with sleepless nights where I questioned my future. Like clockwork, I'd spring awake at three in the morning and question every life choice I'd ever made. Apparently, it had caught up with me, and even a screaming beast in the night couldn't sway me from the first solid sleep I'd had in ages.

Now to just find out what, exactly, had been screaming in the night and why Sophie prowled the castle walls with a sword in hand. No easy task, I'm sure, but since I couldn't conceivably think of a delicate way to bring up what I'd seen the night before, I figured I might as well do it in my usual manner.

Full wrecking-ball style.

I arrived for a late breakfast to find Hilda, Archie, and Sophie drinking their tea in the lounge by the fire, while the dogs sprawled on their beds. The two jumped up when I arrived, Sir Buster with a growl, and Lady Lola with a lolling grin, and I squatted to pet them.

"Good morning," Hilda smiled at me and rose, moving to a door. "Can I get you a tea or coffee then? Some eggs? Toast? Scone?"

"Coffee would be great. A scone as well, if it's not too much trouble."

"Nae bother, I'll just be a moment."

"How'd you sleep?" Sophie smiled at me, and I took a seat in a soft lounge chair with a side table next to it. This room was comforting in the way of rooms that are well used and well loved. A bit of a mix of design, with the tartan chairs pulled close by the fire, a few rugs thrown over the faded carpet, and high ceilings with stunning crown molding. A mix of paintings and photos lined the walls, creating a gallery wall effect that so many people tried to replicate in their homes, but few managed to do well. Here, I could tell it was the real thing, with each painting or piece of art hung at random points through the years to create an eclectic and charming atmosphere.

"Great until the screaming started."

"Oh dear." The coffee mug on Hilda's tray wobbled slightly as she came through the door and caught my words.

Sophie slid a look to Archie, and I followed her gaze, wondering if the older man would be straight with me. He had the look of it, a man who didn't seem to mince words, but still—you never knew what someone would be hiding.

Or protecting.

"That was the Kelpies," Archie said, holding a feather into the air and turning it this way and that, as though he had not a care in the world.

"I'm going to need more of an explanation than that," I said, nodding my thanks to Hilda as she placed the tray on the side table near my chair. "Starting with what the hell a Kelpie is."

"Mythological water horse. Except not a myth, because you heard it yourself."

I blinked at Archie and when no more was forthcoming, I turned to Sophie, a plea on my face.

"Right, so, I guess we'll just get into it then?" Sophie gave me one of those smiles that people used when they had to break bad news to you, and my shoulders tensed.

"This is going to be bad, isn't it?"

"Depends on what you're made of," Archie barked, and I looked at him in disbelief. Was he calling my character into question before I'd even had a cup of coffee?

"Och, Archie. Give the lass a chance to hear us out. It'll be your tetchy attitude sending this one running before the Kelpies ever will."

"Tetchy? Me?" Archie sniffed. "Being direct is hardly being tetchy. It's not my fault if kids these days can't handle direct communication."

"Kids these days …" Sophie snorted and shook her head, rose-gold hair tumbling over her shoulders. Today she wore jeans, hiking boots, and a cozy green cable-knit sweater. Dark circles smudged her eyes, a testament to the lost sleep she'd had the night before. "Yes, because the older generation is renowned for their ability to discuss their feelings."

"Feelings?" Archie's thick white brows shot up on his forehead. "What's there to discuss? You just crack on with it."

"There's that stiff upper lip we so love." Sophie made a fist.

"Och, who has the time to spend endless hours analyzing your inner workings when you could just be living your life?"

"Who has the time?" Sophie raised an eyebrow as Archie calmly pulled out a pair of scissors to snip at the feather for his fly. "I couldn't possibly imagine where you could find the time for therapy."

"Fishing *is* therapy, lass."

"Guys? The Kelpies?" I asked, my anxiety already at about a strong nine and inching toward a panicky ten.

"There's no easy way to say this, dear. We just ask that you hear us out." Hilda settled into the tartan chair next to Archie, for all the world looking like an attractive, genteel woman enjoying tea at her fancy country estate. Not like she was about to lean into a discussion about myths come to life. However, her calm tone and warm eyes soothed some of the panic that was currently threatening to send me running. "MacAlpine Castle has a rich history of being one of the esteemed places selected to protect one of the most sought-after historical artifacts in the world—the Clach na Firrin. Also known as The Stone of Truth. Some would refer to this as the Holy Grail, though different accounts through history will point to other artifacts that hold this title. The reason the stone is sought after is not just for its historical value, but also for the power it provides."

"Power?" A shiver rippled across my skin. I reached for

the cup of coffee, holding it between my hands to warm my palms.

"Aye, lass. Power. Magick. It's said that anyone who gets their hands on the Stone knows all the secrets of the world. This knowledge can be used for good, or for bad, and must be protected at all costs. The Stone has chosen to rest at Loch Mirren, and the Order of Caledonia was enacted to protect the Stone at all costs."

"The Order of Caledonia?"

"A round table of sorts," Sophie said, pulling my attention to hers. "But not your traditional round table of olden days. Honestly, it's quite progressive now that I think about it. So far all of the members have been women."

"And the Order is stronger for it," Archie said, causing me to raise an eyebrow. So talking about feelings was out, but supporting women was in? The man had layers.

"I agree on that. We're kind of just like this witchy round table of badasses, aren't we?" Sophie laughed and my shoulders tensed.

"Witches?" I said faintly.

"Depends how your power manifests," Sophie added.

"Your power?" My eyes darted around the room, but everyone was regarding me calmly.

"The Order of Caledonia came into being to protect the Stone. It is comprised of nine people, all of whom have different and unique powers. We're still trying to figure out how and why those powers play into the bigger picture, because we don't always know what the candidate's power will manifest until they accept their role and pass their challenges."

"Their challenges?" Was I just going to repeat everything they said?

"Yes, three challenges to determine your worth as a member of the Order of Caledonia. Once passed, you are part of the Order and sworn to protect the Stone from those who would steal it."

"Uh-huh. And the Kelpies?" We hadn't even gotten to the water beasts that scream in the night and I was ready to start packing my bags.

"The Kelpies are the last line of defense between the Stone and anyone who would try to steal it. When the Order of Caledonia is broken, or unfulfilled, the Stone is vulnerable. Basically, it creates fear and chaos using the Kelpies until the Order can restore the protections appropriately."

"Which is why Loren Brae is suffering," Sophie said softly.

"The Kelpies are driving everyone away." I mean, I couldn't blame people for running away when they heard a Kelpie scream. *That shit was terrifying.*

"Yes, and they almost killed someone a few months ago."

"They have killed in the past," Archie supplied, and a shiver danced across my skin once more.

"Great, just great. Killer water horses. Witches. Magickal powers. An angry truth Stone." I pressed my lips together. It was then that Sophie's words came back to me.

"I promise you we had our own reasons for hiring you."

So, this wasn't just about my design abilities? *I wish someone would just spell this out for me, as I am so confused.* "Where do I play into this?"

"Och, lass, haven't you figured it out? You're the next in line to join the Order of Caledonia." The way Archie looked at me made me think about how I'd hid in the back of science class, desperately hoping not to be called on because I didn't know the answer. My shoulders hunched.

"Good delivery, Archie. Shame her for not figuring it out in all of the five minutes she's had to try and process this information." Sophie glared at Archie. "You've lived with this knowledge your whole life. Give other people a chance to get up to speed, okay?"

"I've told you not to have him around when you talk to the new members," Hilda said, pursing her lips.

"Duly noted for the future." Sophie rolled her eyes while my thoughts scrambled to make sense of what was happening.

"Why me?"

"We don't always know. Agnes is queen of research, and she's trying to connect the dots on who the Order members are. So far, there's been some sort of blood connection between who is next in line."

"My mother?" I whispered, my hand at my heart. The memories of her were blurred in my mind, but I remembered her laugh, warm and all encompassing, and how she smelled like lemons.

"Perhaps. Or another member of that side of your family."

Gran? I hadn't had a chance to go see my grandparents yet, but I was hoping to borrow a car to go visit them soon once I found my rhythm here.

I didn't say anything for a moment, and the room descended into silence as I tried to process what they were telling me. None of them looked to be unstable, and I didn't get the sense that they were pulling a weird practical joke on me. I'd seen Clyde for myself, hadn't I? Unless Clyde was some super advanced animation they had rigged into the castle to dupe guests, but I just wasn't getting that vibe from them.

My gut told me this was real.

My head, though confused and scrambling to process this new information, confirmed the same.

This was the real deal. Kelpies, magick, and the Order of Caledonia. Which meant …

"So you never really wanted me to come here to be a designer, did you? That was just a ploy to get me to fly here so you could tell me this." My heart fell. For some reason, this hurt even more than thinking that Miles had manufactured this whole opportunity for me or that Ramsay wasn't interested in working with me. I'd been genuinely excited to design a custom line for the castle, in my mother's homeland, and now I realized how stupid I'd been to think they'd just landed on my website and had decided that I was the *only* designer who could help them with their plans.

Maybe Archie was right in his estimation of me. I *was* an idiot.

I'd been a happy little sailboat, my dreams the wind filling my sails, and now I bobbed in place, helpless to move forward. What had I been thinking? That a castle in Scotland needed a fashion designer? Of course they didn't. I'd just been blinded by the idea of actual job security for once and had ignored all the warning signs. Once again, my impulsivity had landed me in a sticky situation.

"Yes, and no," Sophie said, seeing the look on my face.

"We do need a designer, as it's part of the second phase of the marketing program I'm rolling out to encourage tourism to return to Loren Brae. The job offer is very real, and we wouldn't have offered it to you if you hadn't met the qualifications. Instead, we would have found another way to bring you to Loren Brae. Do we need you for the Order of Caledonia? Yes, we do. But do we also need a talented designer who can create beautiful, mouthwatering designs for tourists to drool over? Also, yes."

"Both of these things can exist at once," Archie barked, and I raised an eyebrow at him, somewhat mollified, though I remained skeptical of, well, *everything* they were telling me.

"We're just asking that you hear us out," Sophie said.

Sir Buster got up from his bed and padded over to me, his little body vibrating as he pawed at my leg. I looked down at him. *Suspicious*.

He pawed at my leg again.

"Is he magickal too?"

"Sir Buster? God no. He certainly thinks he is." Sophie laughed.

"Can I pick him up?"

"Seems he wants to be picked up, so yes, go for it." Hilda smiled, and I scooped up Sir Buster. He nestled into my lap, a warm, vibrating, little stress ball of a dog. Still, his presence soothed me.

"You realize this sounds crazy, right?" I said, looking around the room at the group that I had formerly taken for sane adults.

"Oh, absolutely. It took a whole sit-down with books and convincing before I was on board. But it also helped that my uncle Arthur sent me here. He knew what I was getting into, and he never, ever, would have set me up for something that he didn't have faith I could handle. That part made it easier."

"So just like that? Poof! You're off fighting Kelpies and using magick?" I looked at Sophie in disbelief.

"Pretty much. It's wild, but in some respects, it's also really freaking cool."

"What's your power?"

"I'm the Knight. I have a magickal sword and can use my voice to command the Kelpies back."

"Whoa." The memory of Sophie walking the battlements the night before flashed in my head.

"Lia's our resident Kitchen Witch. Shona's our Garden Witch. And you, well, we won't know what your powers are until you do the ritual. Unless you have an idea of what your powers may be. Shona's were already manifesting before she joined the Order."

You know.

A voice whispered deep in my soul and I paused, surprised by my thoughts. Could *that* actually be a power?

"Generally speaking, I feel like the word 'ritual' contains more negative connotations than positive," I pointed out, leaning forward as I stroked Sir Buster with one hand and reached for the scone with the other. I wasn't hungry, not really, but the few sips of coffee I'd had now churned in my stomach, and I needed something to cut through the acid. I chewed, Sir Buster straightening and sniffing the air hopefully in my lap, and watched Sophie carefully.

"It's not a blood ritual or anything. More a ceremony of sorts. I've learned that magick is all about intent. To welcome it in, you have to tell it that you accept it. If that makes sense? You accept that you want to be a member of the Order and that you welcome the magick in."

"And then what happens? I'll just be magickal?"

"More or less." Sophie shrugged.

"It can take time with some. With others, it manifests quickly."

"And then what?"

"What do you mean?" Sophie tilted her head at me.

"For like, the rest of my life?" I waved the scone in the air. "I just live here and protect the holy grail? That's it? That's my lot in life forever on? My future is now here?"

"That's a valid question." Sophie nibbled her lower lip and turned to Hilda and Archie. "For me it was an easier choice because I inherited the castle, but what about Willow? What if she wants to leave and expand her career past Loren Brae and whatever opportunities we can give her?"

"Our hope is that all members of the Order will stay until the final ritual that should subdue the Kelpies and secure the Stone. After that, so long as some members remain in Loren Brae to keep the wards strong, you should be free to leave."

"And if that doesn't happen? I have to stay?"

"No, but you would be sacrificing the needs of many for your own desires." Archie glared at me, and I had the ridiculous desire to stick my tongue out at him. First, he insinuated that I was dumb, and now he was suggesting that I was selfish.

"And what about now? If I get up right now and walk out that door? What happens to Loren Brae then? You can't tell me that every supposed member of this Order is going to just fall in line and join this magickal cult."

"Not a cult," Sophie insisted. "I've really tried to be clear on this. The only cult I'd join is one that worships cheese."

Archie sighed.

I grinned. I couldn't help myself. It was just random enough to make me smile and ease some of my tension. Plus, I could get on board with a little cheese worship.

"Have you considered leading with cheese? You might convince people more quickly to join," I asked.

"I have cheese." Hilda jumped up and left the room, and I laughed. I couldn't help it. My emotions were ping-ponging around inside of me. I closed my eyes, schooled my breathing, and then opened them to meet Sophie's.

"Is it scary?"

"The Kelpies? Yeah, they are. But we can beat them. Together. The power is cool, though. I mean, it's like you get to rescue yourself a little, you know? I've been thinking about having T-shirts made."

Archie snorted. "What would they say?"

"*I'll save myself, thanks.* Or ... *I'm no damsel in distress.* Or maybe, *Not your Damsel in Distress*?" Sophie tapped her lips as she thought about it.

In that moment, something clicked. The same click that I'd felt when we'd driven up to MacAlpine Castle yesterday. I wanted to stay and help Sophie design those damn T-shirts. I wanted to save Loren Brae, hell, save myself. And if that meant stepping into some honest-to-God magickal powers and battling a few Kelpies, well, why the hell not? It couldn't be harder than trying to eke out a living in New York City. I was made of tougher stuff than this.

"Not bad. I can work up a few designs for you."

Sophie jumped up and cheered, just as Hilda returned with a plate of cheese and crackers.

"I'm guessing we won't be needing the cheese after all?" Hilda asked.

"Oh no, we definitely need the cheese. Celebratory cheese for the win. Willow is staying!"

"For the foreseeable future." I slid a glance to Archie who gave me a gruff nod of approval. For some reason, that somewhat settled my anxiety.

"Now, about these T-shirts … what do you think about adding a sword design?"

CHAPTER TEN

Willow

How does one dress for a ritual where you join a magickal order tasked with protecting a magickal truth stone that knows all the secrets of the universe?

I mean, I'd packed a variety of outfits, but this situation hadn't quite made it onto my list of potential occasions. Sophie had warned me we'd be outside and tromping all over the estate to stand on some cardinal direction points or something, so my silver party dress was definitely out. In the end, I'd gone with black leather pants, a Ramones sweatshirt, hot pink Doc Martens, and my worn leather coat with studs up the arms. It felt a little punk rock, this stepping into power and taking on some water beasts, so I figured the Ramones would be on board with my outfit choice.

"Hey ho, let's go," I murmured to myself as I met Sophie, Hilda, Archie, and Lachlan outside. Icy wind whipped around the side of the castle, stopping me in my tracks, and I pulled my jacket closer around my body.

Sophie reached out and squeezed my hand when I neared them.

"It's painless. Promise."

An hour later, the ritual was complete, and Sophie had been right. The ritual itself, while steeped in words of old and exclaiming my willingness to protect the Stone of Truth at the four cardinal points on the property, had been fairly uncomplicated.

"I accept the responsibility of protecting the Clach na Firinn and promise to restore the Order to its fullness. In doing so, I show myself worthy of the magick of Clach na Firinn."

The smoke from the sage bundle that Hilda burned had coiled around me, carrying the secrets of my ancestors with it, and my blood had hummed in my veins.

"I accept the power bestowed upon me."

We'd all waited a moment after the final recitation, and I'd flexed my fingers, wondering if I was going to start shooting laser beams or something of that nature. When nothing extraordinary had happened, another blast of icy wind had sent us toward home.

"Time will tell," Archie assured me as we trudged back toward the castle, my feet almost frozen. I made a mental note to wear wool socks the next time I hiked around the property. We left the line of trees, three crows swooping low over our tracks, and Sophie chattered to them as they flew after her.

The sight of MacAlpine Castle made me catch my breath. If I was a different type of artist, I'd paint the castle, just as she stood, jutting proudly into the air with the wintry grey waters of Loch Mirren spread out below her. The whisper of those gone before us carried to me on the wind, and the urge to create something beautiful for this place rose. It didn't matter if this hadn't been my original plan for my future as a clothing designer. What mattered was that I was here now, standing on this land rich with history, and my story would be woven into its future.

Ramsay rounded the corner of the castle, wearing a thick grey sweater pulled over a muted tartan green kilt, and wool socks with workman's boots. He strode across the garden to meet us, as confident as any warrior of yore, and nerves made my stomach twist. I couldn't get a read on him, because he vacillated so quickly between terse and somewhat friendly, so I didn't know what to think. It was almost like he was considering being my friend and yet couldn't quite bring himself to do so. Maybe he just wasn't good at making friends?

"Did I miss something?" Ramsay asked after the group had greeted him, the soft burr of the highlands in his accent making my skin tingle.

"Just out for a bit of a wander to show Willow the lands," Hilda said, nodding briskly. "Tea, anyone?"

"Please," Lachlan said, starting toward the castle with Hilda and Archie while Sophie drew Ramsay and me aside.

"I called Ramsay to come by because I thought you two might want to look at some of the boxes of fabrics we have in storage. And maybe, from there, you might get some ideas for collaboration for the castle shop."

"I thought we weren't working together." I lifted my chin at Ramsay. His eyes narrowed slightly before he glanced out to the loch. The moment drew out in silence, before Ramsay shifted, and sighed.

"I gave Sophie my word."

"Oh, so honor is the only thing forcing you to work with me? Cool, cool." I rolled my eyes and looked at Sophie. She just shrugged, her lips pressed together in a thin line.

Another blast of icy wind shook us, this time bringing with it a smattering of rain that hit my face like little shards of glass. Ramsay said nothing, instead turning back toward the castle, as Sophie ushered us through a smaller side door that looked more like a service entrance, unlike the grand doors that led into the foyer.

"You can leave your coats here if you'd like." Sophie pointed to a bench just inside the door, and I squinted in the dim light.

"This feels like you're taking us to the dungeons."

"I could, at least if I'd remember the way correctly." Sophie tapped a finger against her lips, thinking about it. "I do still get a bit lost in here."

In contrast to the sweeping ceilings and ornate decoration of the grand foyer at the castle's entrance, this hallway had low ceilings, dull grey stone walls, and uneven flooring. Sconces lined the hall, lighting the passageway dimly, and I felt like I was in my Indiana Jones era. Maybe instead of a punk rock look, I should have channeled the explorer side and gone with a full khaki outfit and a knotted scarf around my neck. Ramsay stood back, allowing Sophie and me into the hallway first, and I was definitely aware of his nearness as we followed Sophie down the narrow hall. Glancing back, I noticed that Ramsay had to duck to avoid hitting his head on the ceiling and was once again reminded just how large this man was. I wondered ...

"Here we are," Sophie said, dragging my thoughts away from the naughtier direction than they needed to be going, and I snapped to attention as she turned an old iron knob in a worn wooden door with large bolts. The door creaked on its hinges as it swung open, and Sophie hit the lights.

"Oh wow," I breathed as I stepped inside the storeroom. It was like stumbling upon Aladdin's Cave, at least for someone like me who loved digging through thrift stores for cool finds. Here, the room opened, with higher ceilings showcasing exposed wood beams, and rows of shelves lining the walls. Old-timey steamer trunks were stacked in a corner, and hat boxes were piled on the shelves. Surprisingly, the room didn't smell too damp or moldy, nor was it all that dusty, so somebody must have taken care with the preservation of its contents.

"Anything in particular you'd like us to look for?" Ramsay asked as I trailed slowly along the shelves, my fingers already itching to open some of the boxes.

"Inspiration, I guess? I don't want to put thoughts in your head on what way the designs need to go for the shop, so I'll just invite you to dig around and see where your creative side takes you. If you need anything or have questions, just text me, and I'll pop back down."

"Nothing's off limits?" Ramsay asked and the way he said it made my blood heat.

"Nope, have at it." Sophie squeezed my arm on the way out and gave me a knowing look, which I interpreted to mean she wanted me to call her if any of my newfound magickal powers suddenly popped up.

Right. That should be interesting. What if I grew a third arm or something wild while we were digging in the boxes? I mean, I'd *just* done a magickal ritual. Was this really the right time to be stuck in a basement room with a grumpy Scotsman who'd already made it clear he didn't want to work with me?

"Keep an eye out for any, um, tools," Sophie said, holding that look.

She thought I might find my weapon down here.

Yes, apparently as part of the Order I was supposed to pick a "weapon" to defend myself, though the word *weapon* was defined loosely it seemed. More of a power item, I was told, so I assumed mine would likely be a needle or something of that nature. Not sure how much damage I could do with a needle, but at the very least I could annoy someone to death by pricking them a million times over.

If I had that kind of time, of course.

"Tools?" Ramsay asked after Sophie departed.

I shrugged one shoulder. "I think anything to decorate the shop with."

"I've seen the castle shop. It's well decorated as is."

"Okay," I said, determined to ignore his grumpiness. "*Don't* look for tools then."

Ramsay just grunted and moved to the other side of the room. I watched him go, his broad shoulders moving nicely under his sweater as he reached for a box on the shelf, and my eyes trailed down his backside to his muscular legs beneath his kilt.

Yup, the man was built.

I also wondered just why he was insisting on being so grumpy. I didn't remember a lot about Ramsay, but I could have sworn he'd been a touch friendlier in the past. Maybe life had changed for him since I'd last seen him. I couldn't just assume that I was the one making him grumpy, not when Agnes had mentioned that he tended to be stand-offish with others in town. Deciding to out-cheerful his grumpiness, I reached for a hatbox on the shelf next to me and opened it.

"Oh, this is cool. Look." I held up a man's fedora, with a neat tartan band. Turning it over, I noticed a smudge in the material on the brim. Putting it on my head, I reached up, and fingered the smudge. "He was left-handed."

"Why do you say that?" Ramsay turned and studied me.

"It's worn on the brim on this side." I took it off in a smooth motion and tilted it for Ramsay to see. "It would be natural to remove it with the left hand if you grabbed it there, right?"

"Humph." Ramsay nodded and turned back to his box, not saying anything else.

Right, man of few words.

We worked in relative silence for a while, well, aside from me exclaiming every time I opened a box. Most of the hatboxes indeed held hats, and I was beyond delighted to find a variety of fascinators. It wasn't a common fashion anymore in the States, and I dearly loved that the Brits still embraced the habit of wearing a fascinator at formal events. I mean, why the heck not? I was a big fan of any excuse to wear something snazzy on my head. I pulled out two of my favorites and set them aside. The first was one with peacock feathers, the lovely deep greens and blues surrounding a faux bird's nest, with three pearls in the nest to mimic the eggs. I mean, *come on*. How cool was that? The second had a bundle of silk flowers, hand painted by the looks of it, with a delicate lace bonnet and ribbons that wrapped around the chin. The lace was embroidered with tiny jet beads and shimmered in the light. I wasn't yet sure what inspiration I'd take from these pieces, but I kept them out because they'd caught my eye.

Humming to myself, I picked up what looked to be a small leather suitcase from the shelf. Different from the hatboxes, something rattled inside when I lifted it. Turning, I put the square suitcase down on a steamer trunk behind me and flipped the locks, popping it open.

"Oh, look." It was a sewing kit, full of ribbons, thread, needles, buttons, thimbles, and the crowning piece—a stunning pair of dressmaker shears. Crafted with a gold handle that showcased intricate scrollwork with Celtic knots and vines of flowers, the scissors were almost too pretty to use for work. Picking them up, I turned to brandish them at Ramsay but froze when the metal hit my palm.

Mine.

A wave of energy rippled across my palm, as though I'd brushed my fingers across a live wire, and I gaped down at the scissors. Were these my power item? My weapon? My magickal tool of choice? I mean, in fairness, stabbing someone with scissors this sharp would certainly do some damage, so it wasn't a horrible choice for protection. It would need to be a close-range battle of course, because I'd been horrible at sports growing up and I didn't see myself having the dexterity to impale someone with these from a distance.

"Och, what's that look about?"

I blinked at Ramsay, realizing that I was holding the scissors aloft like I was going to stab someone, having gotten lost in my thoughts of battles and destruction. Rightly so, he hung back, his eyes narrowed.

"Just testing their weight," I said, balancing the scissors on my open palm before putting them back in the suitcase. The instant they left my hand, I felt bereft.

Message received.

"These thimbles are grand, aren't they?" Ramsay forgot to be rude to me for a moment and held up a pewter thimble with dots and what looked to be the outline of a wolf etched in it. Grabbing another, he turned it in the light to reveal a curved Celtic pattern etched along the rim.

"They are. Oh, look. Each one is different."

Ramsay's arm brushed mine as he reached for another, and his nearness made my legs weak. Which, in itself, was unusual. I'm a sturdy woman, used to being on my feet for long hours as I worked, and wasn't prone to fits of dizziness or instability. And yet. Here I was feeling like my knees were about to start knocking together because Ramsay's arm lightly brushed mine. Was this how Victorian women felt when a man accidently saw their ankle? Was that what all the swooning was about? Moving slightly to the left to give myself some space, lest I, too, caught a case of the "swoons," I gestured to the suitcase.

"Should we take some of this stuff to your shop maybe? Or upstairs? I'm sure Sophie wants us to use some of it."

"I don't know that we'll need much of the bits and bobs when it comes to ribbons, but we can take the thimbles."

"And the shears."

Ramsay just shrugged and moved away, flipping the latches on a large steamer trunk.

"How did you even get into sewing? It doesn't seem like ..." I trailed off, not sure how to phrase my question without insulting him.

"Seem like what?" Ramsay's tone was as icy as the wind outside.

"Just ... you look like one of those rugby guys."

"So I can't be in the fashion industry then?"

"No, not at all. I just ..." Damn it, he was making me stumble over my words.

"My grandfather was a kiltmaker. My father didn't take it up, he was a bookish sort. I learned at my grandfather's knee."

"Right. A family tradition then."

Ramsay grunted, digging into the steamer trunk, and I pressed my lips together. Was every conversation with him going to be like pulling nails?

"No family tradition for me on my part," I supplied, determined to talk enough for the both of us as the siren's call of a huge trunk tucked in the corner was too much for me to ignore any longer. Crossing the room, I flipped the latches on the trunk and hefted the top open. "At least not that I'm told. My mother was creative, but more into painting and poetry. Nothing of a professional nature, either. Basically, I've always wanted to make clothes. Ever since I was a kid. I think fashion is such a great way to express yourself. It's like ... who do I want to be today? You can just choose your persona every morning and go with it. How cool is that? I've always wanted other people to feel empowered by their choices, and I think clothing helps you do that, you know?"

Silence met my words, and I rolled my eyes. Seriously, this man really needed to loosen up.

"How cool for you though, that your family has a history of kiltmaking. I mean, it has to make you proud, doesn't it? To continue the tradition?" I squealed as I pulled the wrapping back at the top of the steamer trunk and revealed several bolts of tartan fabric.

Gorgeous tartan wool.

Deep blues and rich muted browns, emerald greens.

"Ramsay, look. Imagine how much we could make with this! There's enough for kilts, or scarves ..." Turning, I held up a bolt of tartan wool in a warm umber tone.

Ramsay straightened, fury crossing his handsome face, before he turned and stormed from the room without a word.

"Excited, are you? *Great*! Really looking forward to working with you," I shouted after him.

Shaking my head, I put the fabric back and retrieved my scissors, my stomach twisting in knots. Despite my usually optimistic outlook—*despite Ramsay saying he's a man of his word*—trying to work with him would clearly be a disaster. We *should* have many things in common. This room *should* be something that binds us together. And yet ... he can't stand to be in my presence. *Why? Why was he being such a jerk about this?*

Was this because of Miles? Would he ever let me find my way?

CHAPTER ELEVEN

Ramsay

"*Imagine how much we could make with this!*"

Willow's words had sent me back to a happier time in my life.

Andrew and I had been in our grandfather's workshop after he'd passed away, going through boxes. Having found some unusual patterns for kilts, he'd brandished the sheets of paper in front of my face.

"Make those?"

"Yeah, mate. Why not? These would sell like crazy." Andrew's eyes had lit, the promise of fast money exciting him.

"These are custom patterns. It would take time. You'd have to build your clientele." At least that's what my grandfather had always told me. He'd built a careful and loyal clientele, having taken his time and care with each kilt, and it had provided him with steady work through his life.

"But we could make them faster. The two of us. Hire a few people. Just think, we'd make a killing."

Andrew had danced around the workshop, revved like he'd always get with a new idea, enthusiasm lighting him up. He'd always been this way, ever since he was a small child, chasing after the next big thing that excited him and then abandoning it the minute it no longer held interest. His childhood had been littered with half-completed projects, puzzles left unfinished, and failed school projects.

We'd been in our early twenties when our grandfather had died, and Andrew, having burned his way through several trade jobs, had seized the opportunity to design kilts. It was hard to ignore his enthusiasm, and even though I had my misgivings, I'd also been excited about continuing our family tradition.

Maybe this would be the idea that stuck, I'd thought, finally something that would save Andrew from an endless loop of failed projects.

We'd even gone so far as to ask our father for an investment in our company.

What a stupid, stupid kid I'd been.

Within months, Andrew had stolen the money my father had invested in us, taken our family's designs, and had outsourced the patterns overseas to create fast, cheap, and trendy kilts that would make my grandfather turn over in his grave. Synthetic fabrics, cheap fastenings, and pleather sporrans sold for bottom dollar in brightly lit tourist shops.

Andrew had never looked back.

Fifty thousand dollars. A huge chunk of our parents' retirement fund that they had generously agreed to lend us for startup. Gone. He'd stolen from our family, from his own brother, and had cut me out. Now he made money hand over fist on crappy fake products, in poorly run shops with high employee turnover and questionable business practices.

He hadn't come home to check in on our father after he'd had a stroke.

Andrew cared about Andrew. And I'd learned a hard lesson about trusting anyone with my future.

Did it make me a difficult business owner? Likely so. But Ramsay Kilts was run with honor and for that, I could be proud. Trusting others to share in my success? That was the biggest hurdle I'd ever faced. Because if my own brother could betray me, there was nothing stopping anyone else from doing so. I'd grown my company painstakingly slowly, only allowing others in after rigorous training and tests, and while it likely had stunted growth, now Ramsay Kilts was one of the top kiltmaking businesses in Scotland.

I'd paid my father back, even though he'd insisted that wasn't my responsibility to do so.

I'd considered it fair. Why should his retirement plans be thwarted because of one greedy, disloyal son? Being back in Loren Brae had unearthed many of those childhood memories for me, memories that I'd long buried, and they'd surface at inopportune times, reminding me that I'd never have the relationship with my brother that I'd once had. Or at least *thought* that I'd had.

Opening the shop here had been a point of pride for me. It paid homage to my grandfather and the little workshop he'd run for ages, and I didn't really need or want it to be busy. It was a space for me to design in peace, creating kilts in a time-honored tradition, and working off a penance owed by my brother.

I wouldn't let him dishonor our name.

Outside the castle, I gulped the cold air, knowing I'd been incredibly rude to Willow. She didn't deserve my behavior, particularly without giving her any explanation, but the slice of pain from my brother's betrayal had sent me scrambling outside lest I do something unheard of like discuss my feelings with her. Willow didn't need to be burdened with my problems.

It also didn't help that being stuck in a storage room with one of the most beautiful women I'd seen in real life was making my thoughts take a decidedly carnal direction.

My brother's betrayal was a sharp reminder that Miles had asked me to look after his sister. Miles was my friend—more of a brother to me now than my own—and lusting after his sister was its own betrayal.

No, that didn't sit well with me in the slightest.

Distance was needed, and frankly, I needed to just be honest with Sophie that I wouldn't be able to work with Willow in my shop. I didn't see any reason that Willow couldn't just go ahead and design for the castle on her own, and I could run my business as I saw fit. There was no reason for me to bring someone into my store, particularly when all I craved was silence. The last few years had been nothing but growth for my business, which had resulted in an endless slew of meetings. Had my father not had a stroke, I'd likely still have found myself driven back to Loren Brae, craving my roots and the quiet of small towns.

I'd just forgotten one thing.

Small towns were *anything* but quiet. Instead, everyone had promptly inserted themselves in my business, insisting they knew what was best for me, which was how I'd found myself sandwiched with Willow in a storage room where the scent of her perfume had gone straight to my groin and made me wonder what her skin tasted like. I gulped the cold air like it was a fresh pint, knowing that I needed to go back inside and explain myself to Willow.

"Needing a break? Overwhelmed by fabric choice?" Willow's voice at my back made my shoulders tense and yet, at the same time, I welcomed it. Welcomed her. I liked having her near, even when I wanted to push her away. She was both familiar and exotic, and decidedly her own woman. Her nearness tugged at those gentle memories of childhood, racing through the woods with her brother, picnics on the loch's shores with the whole family. Those youthful memories had taken on a warm fuzzy glow in my mind, but I remembered her laughing. Always laughing. And now I was the one to take that smile from her face.

"Aye, it's enough to make anyone faint," I said.

"Should I fetch the smelling salts?" Willow's voice had taken on a dramatic tone, as though she was soothing someone from Victorian times.

"It might be best to have some on hand. I can barely control myself around such grandeur."

"Same, same. See? I knew we'd get along, Ramsay."

At that, I turned to see Willow grinning at me, looking impossibly ethereal in the grey afternoon light, wind causing her hair to dance around her shoulders. A ripple of awareness worked through me.

"I don't like people in my space, Willow."

I don't trust people in my space, Willow.

I couldn't say what I really meant, because then I'd have to unpack years of family trauma, and that certainly wasn't going to happen, at least not here, in the misting rain outside MacAlpine Castle.

"That's unfortunate, as I've been hired to work in said space."

"Aye."

"Want to talk about it?" Willow asked, all sunshine and rainbows, and I glowered out at the loch. Looking at her made me think about things that would one hundred percent make Miles want to kill me. This wasn't normal, my reaction to her, and it annoyed me even further. It wasn't like I was a monk. I'd been with my fair share of women, even managed a few relationships that ended amicably. I wasn't some teenage lad unable to control his hormones in the presence of a woman. Yet one glance at Willow and my hands itched to touch, to sink into her softness, to wrap myself in her melodic voice.

This was not good.

Abort mission.

Instead, I glanced at her, helpless not to, and shook my head.

"Nope."

"Right, that's an American thing, isn't it? Talking about our feelings."

Feelings? She'd be terrified if she knew the particular feelings I was having about her right now. Namely centered on lifting her on top of one of those steamer trunks and unwrapping her slowly, discovering every inch of her delicious body, while she unraveled under my touch.

"Nowhere did Sophie mention that bringing on an intern required daily emotional discussions."

"Just business for you then, Ramsay?"

"Aye, just business, Willow. It's better that way."

"Is it normal for you to storm out of business meetings with zero explanation then?"

I winced at Willow's cheerful question, annoyed that she was pinning me so neatly into a corner. Despite myself, my lips quirked.

"Absolutely. Isn't it for you?"

"God, no. A woman isn't allowed to storm out of anything unless we want to be labeled *dramatic*."

I couldn't be certain, but it seemed Willow was poking fun at me.

"An unfair double standard, I'm certain."

"I'd say. For a man—it's a power move. A woman? We're too emotional. It's annoying, really."

"I wasn't pulling a power move on you, Willow. I just had a moment."

"Yet you're refusing to work with me and jeopardizing my new career here in Scotland. So how is that not a power move?"

I pressed my lips together, a trickle of shame working itself through me. I'd been so focused on my own shite, that I hadn't stopped to think about how my actions were potentially jeopardizing Willow's future. In my mind, Sophie would still work with Willow whether I was involved or not. I just hadn't bothered to clarify that point with Sophie. Now I realized that I was doing something that I, personally, hated. Meddling in someone's dreams.

Damn it all to hell and back.

I'd have to follow through on my word, allow Willow to work in my shop, and give her an opportunity to create something beautiful for the castle. It wasn't fair of me to stand in her way, and she'd come here under the promise of being able to apprentice with a kiltmaker steeped in Scotland's history. Taking that away from her simply because I thought she was pretty was decidedly unfair. My attraction to Willow was a *me* problem, not a *her* problem.

I'd just have to do better.

Resolving myself to a few nights of cold showers, I decided maybe it was just a newness thing. Once I'd spent more time with Willow, the "shiny new toy" appeal would wear off and she'd go back to being my friend's annoying wee sister. Not that I ever remembered her much being annoying.

Current circumstances notwithstanding, that is.

"I'll see you at ten tomorrow. Don't come before that. I like to have my coffee in peace."

With that, I left, knowing that I didn't have the patience to continue exploring the storeroom with Willow. I needed to recalibrate my idea of a quiet solitary workshop in Loren Brae to one with an employee and regular customers. Which meant I needed a training manual, systems in place, and a somehow magical ability to ignore Willow's obvious charms.

"Looking forward to it, *boss*."

Boss.

Damn it. Sophie was going to owe me big time.

CHAPTER TWELVE

Willow

Sir Buster had seemed determined to show me to my room, growling his way down the hallway, perhaps keeping Clyde from popping out of the wall to terrify me while I carried a box of treasures I'd found in the storeroom. After Ramsay had left, I'd spent another hour going through a few more boxes, finding it a touch easier to concentrate without him grumbling in the corner. The storeroom really was a treasure trove, with some dresses that I was dying for Sophie to put on display in the castle somewhere. Such finery was too fancy to be wrapped away in a box, never to be seen or admired. I was a strong believer that clothes were meant to be worn, or in this instance, displayed, and I catalogued the various outfits that I found and what trunks they were in to discuss with Sophie.

Now, settled onto my comfy bed and nestled in the thick duvet, I eyed Sir Buster at my feet.

"Are you allowed up on the bed?"

Sir Buster growled, turning three times before burrowing under a throw blanket at the foot of the bed. I took that to mean yes, but texted Sophie that he was with me just in case anyone would come looking for him. I'd never had a dog before, and while I dearly wanted to give the little guy a cuddle, I also could respect his need for space. Until he decided to snuggle with me, it wasn't worth losing a finger trying to give him a quick pet.

Instead of annoying Sir Buster in his nest of blankets, I opened the box I'd brought with me. Rain pelted the window, the wind rattling the panes, and I snuggled deeper, happy to be cozy and dry inside. At least it wasn't snow. I could handle most weather, as sometimes Minnesota had all seasons in a day, but the snow did begin to wear on your soul after a long winter. Rain seemed less of a bother, though I'm sure the locals felt differently if it stayed this damp and cold for months on end.

I pulled out the gold scissors that I had tucked away, wondering if I would feel the same response as I had in the storeroom, and shivered as the metal touched my skin. The scissors should feel cool against my palm, instead they heated under my touch, and a smile spread on my face.

Mine.

Yup, these were meant for me, even if there was no viable explanation for it, and it was just another piece that made me feel at home. That coming here had been the right decision, even if it was wildly different to the future I had envisioned for myself.

Thunder rolled, rumbling against the window, and I held the scissors as I gazed out at the loch, thinking about my ideal vision for my future. My own collection. The flash of runway shows, the pandemonium of backstage, the rush of seeing your own designs on fabulous models. It was what I'd thought I'd wanted, but at the end of the day, I really wanted to design clothes that people wanted to wear. Not everything that hit the runways translated to wearable fashion for women like myself. I'd rather sell something online that the plus-sized girlies loved, than be on fancy runways that excluded women that looked like me.

I mean, don't get me wrong—fashion shows *were* fun. Chaotic, exciting, and glamorous. But the fashion industry had a dark side, and what I did know was that it could take years before a designer could eke out even the most basic of living from their art. Surely there would be a way to blend my desire for a secure living wage with my dream to design beautiful clothes for people of all sizes.

Placing the scissors on my bedside table, I turned back to the box and picked up a brooch that I'd found. A penannular, I'd learned, after a quick Google search from my phone. It had a unique design, with a circle and a stick pin, and I played with it until I understood the mechanism for closure.

"Clever," I murmured, admiring the Celtic dragon design etched in the pewter circle. I wondered if I could modernize this design, making it a touch smaller for a scarf or to wear on a jacket, and pictured the brooches in a line up the side of a dress like Liz Hurley's famous safety pin Versace dress. Intrigued, I reached for my iPad and began to sketch, humming softly to myself as I drew ideas of interlocking circular pins.

"I wonder if we could play on chain mail." I often spoke to myself when I worked, needing to voice my thoughts, and Sir Buster's nose poked out of the blanket he'd buried himself under. "Oh, my bad. Sorry to disturb you, good sir."

Sir Buster huffed out a small sigh, as though he could hardly believe that he had to put up with me, and then disappeared back under the blanket. I sketched out a chain mail halter top, embracing the sheer trend hitting the runways at the moment, and wondered just how much work it would take to mass reproduce such a look. I liked the links a touch larger, so it had a bit of a steam punk edge to it, but I could also see how a tightly constructed chain mail would look cool, like metal mesh draped over the body. Either way, it could be worn on its own, or over a simple white T-shirt for effortless cool.

Perhaps we should be thinking about making jewelry?

I remembered a bracelet that a friend had worn in New York. It was a thick cuff, made of hundreds of little silver circles soldered together, very much in the style of chain mail. Yet the clasp had edged more to Tiffany & Co. in its design, and the style had ended up being something that would look equally as cool on a young mom to a chic career woman running a boardroom. Making a note to ask Sophie about accessories, I continued to sketch, my mind flowing with ideas. This was what I loved most, being in the flow, thriving on my ability to create beautiful things. Well, at least I thought they were beautiful. Fashion was subjective, but at the end of the day, anything that was created with love was beautiful in my opinion.

My mind drifted as I sketched, caught on the problem that was Ramsay.

"I'll see you at ten tomorrow. Don't come before that. I like to have my coffee in peace." If he was anything like Miles, he liked to be in control of his business—*and everyone else's*—and I knew how to work around that. After our discussion when he'd stormed off from the cellar, I knew I could break through that tough exterior. I just had to keep trying. I *could* be an asset to his shop. I might even make him smile. He'd laughed once, at the pub during the match, the sound low and rumbly, as though unused, and it had warmed my core.

I sighed.

It seems my girlhood crush had followed me into womanhood, and that was my problem to deal with, not Ramsay's. Maybe once I'd gotten settled into my new routine and was feeling confident with my path in life, I'd dip into the dating scene in Loren Brae. Not that I needed or wanted that anytime soon, of course. I was still licking my wounds from my last catastrophic attempt at a relationship.

"Love and learn," I hummed out loud, pausing as I realized what I had been drawing.

Instead of a sketch for a chain mail vest that I'd intended to draw, I'd sketched a scene of, well, *Ramsay* of all people. He stood, waist-deep in churning water, a kitten clutched in his arms, furious horses rising from the loch behind him with flames in their eyes. I gasped, as the vision came to life in my mind, as though I was there with him, fear rising inside me as the Kelpies rose.

"Run," Ramsay shouts, shoving the kitten in my arms, icy water splashing my skin.

"Not without you," I shout back.

A sharp bark startled me, and I blinked, the room coming back into focus, Sir Buster having left his blanket fort to come paw at my arm. Looking down at the trembling dog, my breath shuddered.

"Whoa," I said, reaching up a hand, daring to pet Sir Buster.

My mouth dropped open.

My hand was wet.

Patting my face, I realized my cheeks still stung from the spray of icy water I'd just had in the vision that had momentarily overtaken me.

What could that mean?

Taking a chance, because I needed the comfort more than I was worried about losing a finger, I drew the trembling dog into my arms and smiled when he huffed out a small sigh and cuddled in under my chin. We stayed like that, the warmth of his furry body like a little heating pad on my chest, his nearness calming my racing heart.

The vision had been so clear, as though I was actually there, wading into the ice-cold loch, worry for a small kitten and Ramsay driving my decisions. I'd been able to smell the damp winter air, read the fear in Ramsay's eyes, feel the sharp bite of freezing water nip at my skin. In any other instance, I'd be able to convince myself that I'd had a *very* lucid dream.

But I couldn't explain the water.

Considering, I leaned forward and licked a drop of water off the back of my palm. It tasted salty, and I felt like I remembered from somewhere that Loch Mirren was made of salt water. Or connected to the ocean in some way. Something like that. I'd played on her shores as a child, hadn't I? I closed my eyes, and smiled as I remembered screaming away from the icy water as the boys tried to splash me, blinking at the salty sting of water in my eyes. Yup, salt water it was.

This had to be connected to my supposed magick then. Was it ... was this something that allowed me to see the future? Or was I tapping into events or memories from the past? I wondered if Ramsay had a cat. Maybe he'd rescued a cat one time from the loch, and somehow, I was now able to tap into his memories.

How would that be helpful magick though?

I snuggled more deeply into the pillows, tightening my arms around Sir Buster when he grumbled at my movements, and stared blurrily at the window as my brain whirled with possibilities.

The future made more sense, though I couldn't quite see Ramsay racing anywhere to save a kitten, grump that he was.

I guess I would find out in the morning. Maybe he had a shop cat with a dramatic origin story. If anything, it would be a good way to connect with Ramsay, and maybe we could become friends. Given how close he was to my family, it just didn't make sense for us to be at such odds. *This is a good plan, Willow. Let's hope Ramsay lets you in.*

The bed shifted, and my eyebrows shot up my forehead.

"Clyde!" I hissed, my heart jumping into my throat.

The ghost coo had climbed onto the mattress and was

currently circling the end of the bed, much like Sir Buster had just done, before settling himself down onto the blankets. He tilted his head at me, almost as though he had a question in his eyes. I stared at him, frozen.

"Moo?" Clyde whispered, nudging my leg with his head, and I swear for a moment I could feel the press of his nose against my thigh.

"Um, I'm just fine, Clyde. If that's what you're asking."

Clyde bopped his head once and then settled his entire massive head across my legs, as though he was protecting me, while Sir Buster let out a rumbly little snore at my throat.

I gaped down at the chihuahua, and the massive ghost coo, both of whom had now decided I was their bed. Should I ... was this ... what exactly did one *do* in such a situation?

In the end, I did the only thing that I could think of.

I slipped into the most comfortable sleep I'd had in years.

CHAPTER THIRTEEN

Ramsay

I'd barely slept the night before.

Which certainly didn't help my annoyance this morning, as I poured my third cup of coffee. I stood at the back entrance of my shop, door open to the blustery morning, not caring that I'd have to light a fire to warm the place up when Willow arrived.

At the moment, I needed the caffeine and the cold to shock my system into tearing my mind away from thoughts that I most decidedly should not be having.

It hadn't helped that every time I did fall into sleep last night, a dream would slip through my mind, the softness of Willow's lips pressed against mine. I'd shake myself awake, even in dreamland knowing that she was off limits, and adrenaline would send my mind racing as I tried to force my thoughts away from this attraction that had a chokehold on me.

I couldn't remember the last time I'd been so instantly taken with someone, and the fact that it was Miles's little sister was like pouring salt into a wound. If Willow had been anyone else, I'd be rolling out the red carpet and wining and dining the bonnie lass until she'd give me a chance. But now, I had to keep Willow at a distance and the only way I knew how to do that was to be downright surly to her. Arsehole move, for sure, but it was the one that resonated the most with me. Being friendly with her danced too close to a relationship status that I wasn't ready for, so I'd need to enlist the time-honored tradition of Scottish banter coupled with my naturally grumpy exterior to keep a stern boundary between us.

Maybe I should set her up on a date.

The mere idea brought a scowl to my face, and I sipped at my black coffee, the liquid bitter against my tongue as I thought about Willow dating one of my mates. Miles would probably have my head if I went that route, so best to just steer clear of anything dating related when it came to Willow.

My laptop pinged, signaling an incoming Zoom call, and I turned from watching a crow swoop above a tree in the small courtyard behind my building and shut the door. The cold was finally starting to seep into my bones, and I flicked a glance to the empty hearth before picking up my laptop.

"Hiya, Sheila. How you getting on then?"

"Well enough, now that you've agreed to the airport

store. They've sent the contracts over for the lease. Tenancy will become available in three months."

"That's grand, I'm sure. I hope you've got a good plan for this."

I'd looked over the contracts Sheila had sent, largely because I'd promised her that I would, but also because she was right—if I didn't take the spot, then my brother would, and he only sold mass-produced fake crap. At the very least, I could send tourists home with authentic gifts, plus, based on Sheila's predictions, create a small factory's worth of jobs for locals. All in all, it was a sound business decision, even though I'd have to step away from what I largely loved to do —crafting custom kilts.

"I'm having display designs mocked up for your approval now. I've got a few of our more enterprising employees mocking up some design options that would be easy enough to produce in larger volume. Hopefully, we'll be able to get both the display designs and product suggestions to you within a matter of weeks."

"Scarves?" I asked, knowing it was one of the easier products to make quickly.

"Scarves, bowties, wool cottage socks, tartan bags, pens, whisky glasses—"

"Whisky glasses?" I interrupted.

"A partnership I'm teasing out. You'll see in the presentation. Wouldn't hurt for you to have a wee chat with Munroe either. I could see an easy collaboration there."

"Wouldn't he need to do something with duty free or VAT then?" I asked, checking the time and moving the laptop to the fireplace mantel in the main store before I bent and began to stack wood.

"He'll have merch. Even if he can't sell liquor, there's other options. Have a chat with him and see."

"He's still mad at me for beating him at pool."

"Do you have to beat everyone?" I could hear the annoyance in Sheila's voice even when I couldn't see her face, and I bit back a grin.

"Can't help that I'm a legend, lass."

"Oh, I'm sorry to interrupt—"

I brought my head up, narrowly missing banging my head on the mantel, to see Willow framed in the front doorway that I'd unlocked earlier that morning. I'd taken the bell off the door, the damn thing driving me crazy half the day, and now Willow's eyes darted between Sheila's smiling face on the screen and mine.

"I'll just leave you to your call then." Willow gave me a wink, implying that I was speaking to a date, and breezed past me into the back room. My head swung in the direction she'd just gone.

Nobody went into my workshop without my permission. My mouth gaped open, but nothing came out.

"Is that your new intern then?" Sheila beamed at me, correctly interpreting my expression. "Try not to chew her head off, Ramsay. She works there now too."

"But ..." I had never considered she'd invade my inner sanctum. Which was weird, of course. The shop was only so big, so naturally she'd have to come through my back workshop, even if she just needed to get something from the storeroom. This was how having employees worked.

"Go be a boss."

"I don't like being a boss," I hissed.

"So you've told me, repeatedly. And yet, you've built an

empire with very little turnover. Seems people like when you're a boss."

I narrowed my eyes at Sheila, and her grin widened.

"She's pretty. Loved her skirt."

"Don't start." On that, I closed the laptop quickly, because I, too, had loved Willow's skirt. At least the quick glimpse I'd gotten of it.

Sparkles.

Who wore a black sparkle mini skirt to work?

Willow did, apparently.

"All finished? Sorry I interrupted," Willow said, coming to stand in the doorway between the back room and the main shop looking like a damn sunflower that had popped up in the middle of a plowed field. She wore a loose button-down blue tartan shirt, cuffs rolled, and ends tied at the waist of her very short, very sparkly black mini skirt. Tights so dark they could be leggings lined her curvy legs, and low-heeled suede boots completed the look. She'd pulled her hair up in a messy ponytail, fastened with a silly bow, and I wanted to pull an end of the ribbon like a besotted schoolboy.

She was fresh, and bright, and just so … out of place here. Her very existence jarred something in me, and I forcibly had to work myself to close my mouth and swallow, before turning back to the fireplace to finish what I'd started.

I needed something to do with my hands lest I do something crazy like dive them into that mass of hair and drag Willow's lips to mine. I was an adult. An adult with a strong code of ethics and morals. I didn't date employees, I didn't use my position of power to intimidate or harass, and

I certainly didn't hit on my best friend's little sister. After a stern talk to myself, while Willow watched me in silence, I set a match to the tinder, and a cheerful flame lit the wood.

"Bit of a chill this morning. That should sort it out," I said. Straightening, I turned.

Sparkles flashed as a ray of sun shot through the window, illuminating the curve of Willow's bum, and I rolled my eyes to the ceiling, making a mental note to address dress code. Sparkles were definitely out.

"This place is fabulous, Ramsay. Oh just look." Willow all but cooed as she reached up to trail a finger along the raw edge of the rough-hewn shelves holding a few folded scarves. "This wood is fabulous. I mean, the ambience here is incredible. It hits all the right notes, doesn't it?"

"Does it?"

"One hundred percent it does. These gorgeous stone walls, the wood beams, and you haven't cluttered the space up too much. Just the chairs by the fire, a few kilts on display." Willow whirled around, a smile on her lips. "It really gives the customer a feel like they're getting a custom experience, doesn't it? They're coming here to see an artist at work, to have something tailored to their tastes, not just to grab something off a rung and try it on in the back. With the window showing the loch as the backdrop and all this stone and wood and careful lighting ... oh yeah, you've outdone yourself. I even like that you decided to leave the floors bare. It's nice, isn't it, to hear your soles on the hard-wood floor."

Willow demonstrated the sound by strutting across the floor, her hips swinging, and I swallowed a silent groan. What had I done to deserve this torture? I could have my pick of women if I so chose, couldn't I? Why did I have to suddenly be smitten with one woman who was decidedly unavailable to me? In so many ways.

My lack of sleep and earlier annoyance heightened, and I growled at her.

"It's not a runway."

"It could be though. Just enough room for a good strut and a fabulous turn." Willow stalked across the room, modeling a perfect runway walk, and flipped her hair as she pivoted at the door, and stomped back before striking a pose right in front of me.

She looked incredible.

"When you're done playing maybe we can get to work?"

"Oh, yes, boss." Willow saluted me, clicking her boots together for emphasis, a cheeky sparkle in her eyes. "What's the plan for today? Are we designing or am I interning?"

"Interning. I have two appointments, so I'll teach you that process, then we can go through intake, ordering, and customer service."

"Wow, a whole two appointments? Keeping yourself busy, aren't ya, Ramsay?" Willow winked at me.

"I find my tolerance for people ends after two appointments. Don't schedule more than that in a day for me. And I don't allow walk-ins."

"You don't …" Willow trailed off as I turned, tucking the laptop under my arm, and crossed to a large desk in the corner. I nodded to the chair in front, and took the leather armchair behind, taking a moment as I reopened the laptop, and hit Spotify. There, I selected my rock playlist of the day, and an edgy guitar riff from Greta Van Fleet came through the hidden speakers.

"Greta, nice." Willow nodded her approval. "Okay, wait, why don't you allow actual customers in the store? It looks like you have a few things that they could buy on site if they wanted."

"A scarf or two. It's a custom experience, Willow. Everything should be selected, made, and tailored directly for the client."

"And someone coming in off the street can't have that experience?" Willow stuck her nose in the air. "How rudely *Pretty Woman* of you."

"I don't know what you're saying to me."

"What? Oh come on. You have to have seen *Pretty Woman*. You know the scene where the fancy rich people won't serve Julia Roberts in their fancy rich store? She walked in off the street, and they looked down their noses at her?"

"I have no idea what you're talking about, and I certainly don't look down my nose at anyone." I looked down my nose at her, and Willow grinned.

"You sure about that, boss?"

"Stop calling me boss."

"Fine. Partner?"

"Ramsay will do."

"Ramsay it is then." Willow reached for her bag while I groaned internally. My name rolled across her tongue like a lover's murmur, and I berated myself for being an idiot. Boss was *much* more impersonal. Willow brandished a notepad and pen. "I'm ready to take notes. Why don't you run me through a typical day, and I'll try not to piss you off too much while you do so."

"Good luck with that."

"I don't doubt it. Seems most things annoy you." And yet, that fact didn't seem to bother Willow as she hummed along with the music thumping in the background.

"Then why do you want to work here?" Curiosity got the better of me.

"Why not? An opportunity to learn at the hands of a master kiltmaker—albeit a very surly one—is not something to pass up."

I pulled my mind away from the image of Willow under my hands and narrowed my eyes at her.

"Is it kiltmaking you're wanting to go into, hen?"

"Hen?" Willow looked at me, clearly delighted. "Did you just call me hen?"

"Aye?" Granted it wasn't super common to call a woman hen, but it wasn't all that unheard of around Scotland either. I'd learned from Graham and Lachlan to put it on a bit for the tourists, and it was true, they just ate up any stereotypical saying we had. I didn't much mind it, if I was honest. I liked keeping some stereotypes alive, if only because it partnered so nicely with keeping the history of our kilts alive.

"Should I cluck for you then?"

My eyes strayed to her pretty lips, and I imagined them pursed, making a clucking sound, and had to take a deep breath to settle myself. This was getting a bit ridiculous, and I had work to do, not sit here and ogle the intern all day.

"You can bark for all I care, so long as the work gets

done. First appointment is in a half hour. Typically, we like to offer tea or whisky, or champagne if that's their taste."

"Where's that?" Willow craned her neck to look around the shop and I stood, motioning her to follow. Her hand brushed mine as she stood, her skin warm against mine, and I bit my lip.

"I like to give my clients time to consider what they want. We don't push, we don't rush, this is meant to be an experience. I lock the door after they arrive so nobody else can interrupt. For some, this may be the only kilt they purchase in their lifetime. It's an important and monumental day, and here at Ramsay Kilts we treat it as such."

"Really? Some people only buy one in their life?"

"If they don't outgrow it. A well-made kilt should last. Most men will get their family's tartan as a gift when they turn eighteen."

"Surely you're not the same size you were at eighteen?" The way Willow surveyed my shoulders made me stand a little taller.

"Kilts have some flexibility to be let out as you mature."

"I wish more clothes were designed like that." An indiscernible look crossed Willow's face.

"It's the nature of people to change and grow. We design for that."

"Ah, a bit of life wisdom woven into the kilt." Willow held up her notebook. "So, what's next? Welcome the client, get them drinks, then what?"

"Typically, I leave them alone."

"What?" Willow laughed, a siren's song to my heart, and I raised an eyebrow at her.

"Aye. I give them time. No pressure. No rushing. Pull

the chairs up by the fire, cozy in with some fabric samples, take some time browsing. Only after about three-fourths of a cup of a tea do I wander back out and start answering their questions."

"Three-fourths of a cup of tea." Willow scribbled in her notebook, squinching her nose as she looked back up at me. "Does that translate to a specific amount of time for us non-Scots?"

"Figure it out."

"Got it. No rushing, no harassing, no pushing. A gentle welcoming appointment."

"Don't touch the music."

"No music changes."

"Don't come in my workroom."

"Don't—"

"And don't—"

"Wait, why can't I come in your workroom? I put my purse back there. Where am I supposed to go while the clients are ruminating on their fabric choice? Am I supposed to stand in the corner and turn my back to the room?"

"If you must."

"Ramsay." Willow rolled her eyes. "Don't be ridiculous. Also, is there a bathroom? An employee locker? Where are you brewing this tea?"

"There's a kitchen and bathroom in back." I gestured with my thumb.

"Which I access …"

"Through my workroom."

"Yet I can't go in there?" Willow put a hand on her hip, and I felt like I was being scolded.

"I don't like being interrupted while I work."

"But here we are, supposedly working together. I thought you were going to show me these famous kilts and how they're made. Plus, aren't we going to start tossing designs around for the castle shop?"

I raised an eyebrow at her. "I don't *toss* designs around."

"Brainstorm, discuss, collaborate, dream, spitball, whatever ..." Willow laughed up at me, not at all bothered by my gruff tone.

When she laughed, little lines feathered out from her eyes, and her face came alive. She was an animated person, talking with her hands, moving about the room as though she couldn't quite sit still, and the sparkles kept catching my eye.

She was sunshine to my storm clouds, and I wondered how the two could ever coexist.

"We can arrange time for that this week."

"Right, so what else, exactly, do you need me to do here?" Willow squinted around the shop as she ticked points off on her fingers. "Don't bother the customers, don't let new customers in, don't go in the workroom, don't change the music, don't design any kilts, and no runway walks."

Pinching my nose, I sighed. The woman had a point. Striding across the room, I flipped through my appointment book to the back where I'd started a list for Willow.

"Here's some tasks to get started. Managing the calendar, updating the website, answering emails, answering the phone. You'll meet Sheila at some point who manages my other branches, and I'm sure she'll have loads of things for you to do."

"Branch manager?" Willow pursed her lips as she studied me, amusement dancing in her eyes. "Are you a kilt mogul then, Ramsay? Hiding out down here in your quiet shop while your empire grows elsewhere?"

"Less people down here." I pointed at the clock on the wall. "Client should be here soon. Familiarize yourself with the space. I'll get the tea on."

"Yes, sir." Willow's grin widened when I glared at her. "What? You said no to 'boss,' but not to *sir*."

"I knew this was a mistake," I grumbled under my breath, turning and leaving her at the desk. "I don't like people in my shop."

"Great to be here, sir. Can't wait for our first day together. It's going to be so much fun. We'll be besties in no time," Willow called after me and I stopped in the doorway to my office. Turning my head, I glared over my shoulder.

"Besties?"

"You know … best friends. Making friendship bracelets for each other. Telling secrets." Willow fluttered her eyelashes at me. I shook my head, furious that I'd be stuck in her vicinity every day for the foreseeable future. How had Sophie managed to con me into this?

"Bloody hell."

It was going to be a long day.

CHAPTER FOURTEEN

Willow

Turns out, Ramsay really did need the help. Whether he was willing to admit it or not. His phone rang almost constantly, his inbox pinged with incoming emails, and people knocked on the front door often enough that Ramsay's curses carried through from the back room.

I realized quickly that becoming a natural barrier between Ramsay and people who interrupted him would likely bring his stress down tenfold. While I hadn't managed to follow his edict about not entering his workroom, mainly based on the logistics of working in the shop and needing to get to the storeroom or use the small kitchenette, it did allow me brief glimpses into how the man worked.

And it was with a singular focus that had to be admired.

I'd thought, of course, that Ramsay would be the one

crafting a kilt. But I didn't realize the breadth of his business, nor the sheer volume of acumen needed to manage so many moving parts at once. As predicted, I met with his manager, Sheila, who clued me into Ramsay's empire, and a quick search on Google showed me just how much Ramsay Kilts had accomplished. While Ramsay had recently tucked himself away in this little shop in Loren Brae, he truly had a veritable kiltmaking empire at his feet, which gave hundreds of Scottish people jobs and continued a time-honored tradition.

It was something he should be proud of, and I would tell him so, if he didn't glare at me every time I interrupted him.

I peeked in the back room, watching as Ramsay expertly measured and pinned, measured and pinned, methodically folding the kilt's fabric. His rhythm was smooth, his focus absolute, and I found myself entranced by the way his arm muscles bunched under his shirt as his large hands smoothed the fabric and neatly folded the next pleat. The tattoos winding up his thick forearms and disappearing under the fabric of his shirt made me want to move closer, to examine each design and ask him their meaning. He'd likely bite my head off, of course, so I stayed by the door instead, watching a master at work, even though my hands itched to join in.

I loved the process of creation. The feel of fabric under my fingers, testing the weight of a material, examining the stretch, the color, the sheen. All of it invigorated me, and I wanted to learn this too, even if making and designing kilts wasn't exactly what I wanted for my future. Any opportunity to learn a new skill was exciting, and for all I knew, it would spark an idea that would show up in a collection of mine down the road.

"I can hear you breathing."

"I'm pretty sure 'don't breathe' wasn't in the rules, but I can double-check my list if you'd like."

"Breathe elsewhere." Ramsay continued to fold, never breaking rhythm, and I sidled closer, ignoring his grunt of disapproval. I was used to dealing with difficult men, Miles being one of them, and if those two were best friends, well, Ramsay shouldn't be too difficult to handle.

I just had to outshine his grumpiness.

"I like this tartan," I said, directing his attention away from the fact that I was breathing in his space. "It's a pleasing pattern."

Ramsay grunted again.

"The colors balance well. Is it for a certain clan?"

After our first client of the day had left, a groom planning for his wedding, I'd spent some time paging through the fabric books that Ramsay had in stacks by the fire, reading about Scotland's history of clan tartans.

"Aye, it's a Douglas tartan. Shared with several other clans, in fact. One of our more common and popular tartans."

"Wow."

At that, Ramsay glanced up at me.

"What?"

"A whole, like, fifteen words. Careful, Ramsay, or you'll be accused of carrying on an actual conversation."

Ramsay just leveled me a look, which I'm sure would be considered withering by many who weren't used to rude and consistently angry older brothers, and I inched closer to the table.

"Can I touch it?"

"Bloody hell." Ramsay paused, his hands holding a pleat in place, a pin at the ready. He looked up at me under heavy lids, his expression mutinous.

I shouldn't find this hot.

Pasting a wide smile on my face, I shrugged.

"It sounds like you're particular about the type of fabric you use. Where the wool comes from. How it's woven. Dyed. I'm interested is all."

"In what part of my explicit instructions to leave me alone in my workroom could you interpret to mean 'come blether on in my ear while I'm trying to work'?"

"Jeez, that had to have been at least twenty words. You're doing great." I nodded encouragingly at him, and Ramsay's eyes narrowed. "Oh, I know that look. That's the look of a man who is dying to tell me all about how he sources his fabrics for his famous custom kilts. No problem, Ramsay, I've got all day. Go on ..." I waved my hand in the air, as though ushering him to continue talking.

"What do I have to do to make this stop?"

"Answer my questions. Show me your process. Talk to me like a real partner and not an annoying kid sister."

At that, Ramsay looked up, and something flashed behind his eyes, before it was gone. It was enough to make me want to squirm on the spot, whatever his thoughts were, and a delicious tendril of heat unfurled low in my stomach.

"It's not a kid sister I'm thinking of you as."

Say what now?

I was going to need clarification on that. Like, immediately. I opened my mouth to speak, but his warning look caused me to pause. The seconds ticked by—the moment hung suspended between us—as a log snapped in the fireplace and rain pattered on the roof.

"I pride myself on continuing the Scottish tradition of weaving our own fabrics." Ramsay methodically placed a pin and then paused, gesturing to the fabric. I gingerly reached out, running my fingers over the tartan, testing the weight of it against my palm.

"Worsted wool," I said.

"Aye, worsted wool with a twill structure. When woven in a particular sett, it creates the tartan pattern."

I nod vigorously as though I know what a "sett" is, and Ramsay catches my implication and sighs.

"Go on."

"So this isn't mass produced then? It's woven on an actual loom? Do they still make looms like they once did? Or are they all commercial now? What about the dyes? Where do they come from? And the wool? Is this all done by hand ... like in a hut down by the river? How long does something like this take to make? Is it expensive to produce? How do you determine your margins?" I rushed out, assuming he was not going to give me many opportunities to ask questions.

Ramsay looked to the ceiling, clearly attempting to muster the patience to deal with someone like me, and I beamed at him when he dropped his eyes to my face. Shaking his head slightly, he returned to measuring the kilt.

"I'll give you a wee lesson, lass, but then I need to finish pinning this kilt."

"Great, so …"

"Wheesht." Ramsay tucked a pin in the fabric and then straightened, disappearing from the room. "Cuppa tea?"

"Um, sure."

I wandered out of the workroom and added another log to the fire, before going to stand at the front window for what felt like the twentieth time that day. Dark clouds had moved in, rolling over each other in the sky, Loch Mirren a sheet of slate grey water. Shadows drew long across the shop floor, cut by the flickering light from the fire, and I shivered, my eyes caught on the loch. She held so many secrets, literal magick moving beneath her surface, and I still was processing everything I'd learned in such a short time.

I'd always been drawn to water, which wasn't wholly unheard of, being from the land of ten thousand lakes. I'd grown up spending long summers in the water, and my dad had always called me a fish because I never wanted to stop swimming. Our summers were so short in Minnesota that we made use of every moment we could. Because of that, I'd learned to really look at water, not just scan my eyes over it. I looked for currents, for changes in surface patterns, depths, that kind of thing. You couldn't live near water and not learn to assess the dangers of it. And to me, Loch Mirren was stunningly beautiful, but coldly dangerous. I would absolutely proceed with caution around her shores.

"Right then. Let's crack on with your lesson, since you'll no doubt be bothering about it if we don't."

"I can certainly Google it, if it's too much trouble." I smiled sweetly at his snort of derision.

"Google."

"It's a popular internet search engine. You have been on

the internet, I presume?" I crossed the room to where he'd put a tea tray on the table by the fire, and settled into one of the tartan chairs, a pile of books at his side.

"I try not to."

"Aww, you're like an Amish person or something then, aren't you? How cute is that? Living in your little bubble. Weird how this Spotify playlist manages to bring music to your speakers though."

"I'm instantly regretting agreeing to this lesson."

"No, no, I'm sorry. I promise to be on my best behavior. Please. Explain to me what sets Ramsay Kilts apart from the others. I should know this, anyway, if I'm going to be speaking to customers." I pulled out my notebook and settled back into the chair, pressing my lips together to indicate that I wasn't going to interrupt him again.

Ramsay regarded me for a moment, letting the silence draw out, as though testing my resolve not to speak. I'll admit, I almost broke the silence, but I really did want to learn about the kilts, and I sensed I could only annoy him so much before he'd chuck me out the front door and call it a day. He'd already stormed out on me once, and I'd only been in Loren Brae a matter of days. Firelight danced across his cheekbones, the teacup looked like a toy in his large hands, and he looked every inch a dominating Highlander sitting in his tartan chair by his fire. I crossed my legs at the response in my body, seeing him like this, because just for an instant, I wanted to straddle him where he sat. To feel his large hands gripping my thighs, reminding myself how it felt to be locked against his muscular body. With his sharp jawline, dark hair, and thick muscular arms, Ramsay could have stepped on the set of *Outlander* and been mistaken for an actor.

Ramsay lifted a brow, and I realized something in my expression must have changed. Picking up my pen, I poised it against the paper, forcing myself to look away from him.

Damn it, but my boss was a hottie with a capital H.

"Ramsay Kilts has one of the only mills that still produces tartans in a traditional manner. We do use a commercial loom at times, for bulk orders, but will still bring most of the process in house so our weavers can check the fabric every step of the way. A traditional kilt has a clean-cut edge at the knee." Ramsay held up a swatch of fabric draped over the side of his chair, showing me the edge of the tartan. "This can only be produced by a traditional shuttle loom, granted though we've been able to motorize them, so our weavers don't have to pedal."

"No way, that's awesome."

"We're not opposed to modernizing where it makes sense." A ghost of a smile crested Ramsay's lips. "A shuttle loom is called that because of the wooden shuttles, which create a back-and-forth motion that allows a clean natural selvedge. A traditional kilting selvedge doesn't need to be hemmed."

I forced myself to not think of other back-and-forth motions that I wouldn't mind trying out with my very sexy boss.

"Versus a commercial loom? The edge needs to be hemmed or tucked in?" I asked instead, making a note on my pad.

"A rapier loom will either leave threads loose for hemming or returned into the weave as a tuck-in selvedge."

"And ..." I paused when Ramsay lifted both eyebrows at me. "Sorry. Go on."

"We order our raw yarn from various local spinners, who transform raw fleece into the perfect fibers for our kilts. We ship the yarn directly to our dyers who carry almost one hundred different colors. That way we can match shades quickly and move forward with orders. That being said ... traditionally, tartans only came in black, white, red, green, and yellow as those were the colors of natural dyes. These days you have more options with synthetic dyes, obviously."

"And you'll use synthetic dyes?"

"I try to urge people to go natural with their color choices, but it's no longer a sticking point for me. So long as the yarn and the fabric are created with a careful eye to our history, I'm happy enough."

"A lot of the dyes are made nicely these days too."

"They are, and we do our best to find eco-minded ones. So, the yarn gets dyed, spooled onto bobbins, then onto cones, then onto pirns. Basically, smaller and smaller spools. The weaver will pull the yarns off the cones in sequence of the tartan's sett. Maybe it's sixteen green threads, then four yellow, then thirty green, then eight black and so on until the pattern is complete. Threads will always be in even number groupings."

"I may need a visual on this."

"I figured." Ramsay picked up a book and flipped it open, paging through until he found a photo of a shuttle loom. I was vaguely familiar with it, but now tried to place names to parts as he pointed out the shuttle, the pirns, and the cones.

"Once one sett is done, the weaver will start the sequence again, repeating the pattern, until the full width of the fabric is reached."

"Which is?"

"Twelve hundred threads for a heavyweight wool."

"Wow."

"Once the warp length is set, they move it to the loom, and we always keep a part of the last weave on the loom. We'll knot the new yarns to the old, pull it through the heddle"—Ramsay pointed to a gate of thin vertical wires—"and guide the new weave through."

"This is incredible," I said, beginning to understand the extent of effort that went into creating a tartan.

"The weaver sits at the front and will guide the new yarns through to tie on to the thread from its last weave. Then begins the actual weaving, and you'll see here the back-and-forth motion of the shuttle gives that nice clean selvedge."

Again with the back and forth.

"The weavers watch the loom, looking to catch any breakages, so as to fix any errors prior to completion. Once finished, it's off to greasy darning."

"Greasy?" I laughed at that.

"The fabric hasn't yet been cleaned and inspected. Our darners will examine the fabric both by sight and against the flat of their hands, looking for any breakages. From there, the fabric goes off to finishers. Unless you want a hard tartan, of course."

"A hard tartan?" I swallowed, my mind completely in the gutter. Ramsay's head dipped close to mine as he flipped through the pages of his book. He smelled like soap and leather, a clean masculine scent, and I wanted to run my hands through his hair.

"Aye, lass." Ramsay glanced up at me, his face close, and I could see the fire reflected in his eyes. "It's a term for what the fabric feels like before it's finished. A touch harsh, a bit uneven. True historians, the ones who like to do the reenactments, request it in that manner because they feel it's closer to how the fabric once felt in the olden days."

Ramsay handed me a square of fabric, a dark green tartan with red and yellow threads, and I ran my fingers over it.

"Okay, I see. It is rough, isn't it? A bit like burlap, maybe?"

"Aye. We'll clean it, removing any dust and grit it's picked up. Once we wash it, just in water, the fabric softens. We'll then press it and hang it on tenterhooks to dry."

"Isn't that a saying?"

"Aye, lass. That's where it comes from. To be on tenterhooks. Look." Ramsay flipped through his book until he found a picture of a stretch of tartan hung on a long row of narrow hooks. "After that, it's back once more to the darners for what we call a clean darning and then it's ready for me."

I could be ready for you.

Well now, where was my mind going? All I needed was a fire, a man with a sexy accent talking about my favorite thing, clothes, and I was ready to lift up my skirt and show him what I was about. While the thought had appeal, I mean, *a lot* of appeal, I also needed to stay focused on my job. This was my boss. My boss. Big bossman. Brother's best friend. Strict "No Touching" rule in effect.

Though it would piss Miles off, so that might be an added bonus.

"For you?" I cleared my throat and leaned back to take a sip of my tea, putting some distance between Ramsay and me before I did something stupid like asking him if he liked sequins on his bedroom floor.

"Aye. Then it's my time to shine. We hand stitch each kilt, measuring each pleat by hand, and deliver a final, custom-fit, tailored garment to their new owner."

"How much fabric is used to make a kilt?"

"Typically eight yards of fabric, but some are double length. In the olden days, the kilts were more than just something to wear. They'd also be used as protection against the rain or a blanket to bed down on in the wild."

"Ah, I get it now," I said, making a tsking noise with my lips. "Lazy men. You just rolled out of bed and wrapped your blanket around you, didn't you?"

Ramsay's mouth dropped open, amusement lighting his eyes for the first time since I'd seen him, though he pretended to glower.

"Och, I'd watch yourself, lass. That's my ancestors you're insulting. The kilt is a fine part of our history, worn for battles and trudging through bogs."

"Mm-hmm, sounds to me like you didn't want to leave home without your blankie."

"That's it, I knew this was coming." Ramsay shocked me by hauling me out of my chair and dragging me toward the front door. I laughed, seeing the smile he was trying to hide, and dug my heels in as he threw the front door to the shop open. Rain pelted the pavement out front.

"Noooo, Ramsay, stop. I take it back." I squealed as the first drops of rain hit my head.

"Bloody blasphemy," Ramsay growled, nudging me farther out into the rain. I twisted in his arms, pushing my butt against him, trying to leverage myself back inside the shop.

A motion on the surface of the water caught my eye.

"Wait. Ramsay. Oh my God. Look!" I straightened, no longer caring about the rain, and pointed at the water. "No, we have to help it."

"What is it, lass?" Ramsay's hands were at my shoulders, pulling me into his chest, instantly protecting me against whatever I'd seen.

"It's a kitten, I think. And it's drowning!"

A clap of thunder shook the skies, drowning out the soft mews for help I could now hear.

Ramsay took off at a run.

CHAPTER FIFTEEN

WILLOW

I sprinted after Ramsay, but *damn*, the man was fast. He was already waist deep in the water by the time I reached the shoreline, icy rain deluging us.

"Ramsay! Over there!" I shouted, pointing to where two little ears poked above the surface of waves that had kicked up with the storm. I wondered if the kitten had fallen from the embankment wall or from a boat or something. Either way, its desperate mewls for help were causing panic to rise in my throat. Another clap of thunder rattled the sky, and I hunched my shoulders against the rain that slapped my back.

I stumbled along the rocky shoreline, keeping my eyes on the kitten at all times, my arm pointed to where it was, determined not to lose sight of the little guy. It was one of the rules of boating we'd been taught—if anyone was ever struggling in the water, one person always kept eyes on them and directed the boat to help. Now, I did my best to be shore support as Ramsay pressed through the water.

"You're almost there!"

The kitten, hearing my cries, turned and spied Ramsay. Gratefully, the little guy seemed to understand help was on its way, and both Ramsay and the kitten closed the remaining distance quickly. Catching the kitten close to his chest, Ramsay hunched his shoulders, protecting it from the rain, and trudged toward where I stood, shivering and near tears on the shore.

Something shifted in the water behind Ramsay.

My heart skipped a beat.

"Ramsay."

It came out as a whisper, and I stood, frozen, as water horses began to take shape among the sheets of rain that pounded Loch Mirren. They were far out, merely silhouettes shifting among the water in the distance, but I knew.

I knew.

"Ramsay, *run*." This time it came out as a shout, as the shadows grew larger, the shapes taking more definition, lightning rippling along the mutinous storm clouds. A shriek split the air—the sound what nightmares were made of—and I stumbled as I ran toward the shore, needing to get Ramsay out of the water. Not that I had any idea of what to do about the Kelpies that careened across the stormy loch. I'd barely been in the Order of Caledonia for a day. I hadn't been given the rundown on what to do if a Kelpie attacked. Which, you know, might have been a helpful thing to know if attacks were happening on a regular basis.

Ramsay caught me as I slipped on the rocks, heaving me into his arms before I hit the ground, and I scrambled in his arms, hooking my arm around his shoulders as he carried me to safety. I peeked over his shoulder, my eyes widening as the Kelpies loomed closer, their heads tossed back and rage on their face.

"By the Order of Caledonia, I order you back!"

A shout at my back had me twisting in Ramsay's arms to see Sophie, sword raised, Lachlan at her side as the Kelpies raged to a stop at the shoreline, dissolving in a shatter of icy seawater.

It was shocking, really, how fast they disappeared. It reminded me of a water balloon exploding on a sidewalk. In one second, the Kelpies were a very real threat, and in the next, they matched the droplets of rain that smashed the surface of the loch.

"Holy hell," I breathed at Ramsay's neck, my heart hammering in my chest. Something squirmed at my chin, and I leaned back to see the kitten poke its head out from the neck of Ramsay's sweater.

"Meow."

Its meow was just a rasp in its throat, and it blinked greenish yellow eyes at me, its fur matted and spiky around its head.

"Okay, bud. We got you now. You're safe."

"You're both okay?"

Ramsay's voice was a rumble at my ear, and I looked up at him. Water dripped from his chin, his face set in stone.

"Seems so. We'll get him dried off. You're a hero, Ramsay."

Heat flashed in his eyes, a barely restrained storm, and

for one insane second, I thought he was going to kiss me. His lips hovered close, adrenaline racing through our systems, and my chest heaved as I shuddered in a breath.

Kiss me.

I wanted it. I realized that immediately. I wanted his lips on mine, to taste him, to feel what it would be like to have a man like him protecting me. I eased closer, the movement almost imperceptible, desperate for just a taste of him.

"Willow!" Sophie called and Ramsay turned, his lips brushing softly across my cheek with the movement.

My skin burned at his touch.

My eyelids fluttered closed, and I inhaled the salty sea air, trying to calm myself down.

It was just an impulse born of adrenaline. That was all. *You're not a damsel in distress, Willow. Just because a strong man swoops you up into his arms doesn't mean you need to kiss him.*

But the princess kissed the hero in the movies, didn't she?

"Are you guys okay? What happened?" Sophie asked as Ramsay stopped at her side, gently placing me back on the sidewalk before cupping the kitten that wiggled underneath his sweater.

"Let's get inside. We need to get this guy warm." Ramsay nodded to the kitten that now poked its head fully from his sweater, and if I hadn't been attracted to Ramsay before, it would be almost impossible not to be now. Both kitten and man were soaked, and there was just something about the juxtaposition between a big, strong dripping-wet man and the teeny-tiny kitten that he'd saved that made my heart melt.

"Awww," Sophie said. She clutched my arm after Ramsay walked away, and correctly interpreting my look, raised her eyebrows after him.

"Nope."

"Or, maybe, right? Why not?" Sophie hissed, dragging me with the arm that didn't carry the sword. Lachlan trudged in silence next to us, continuing to dart glances over his shoulder at the stormy loch until we clambered through the door of the shop.

"Towels. Flip the lock." Ramsay nodded to a pile of towels from where he sat on the floor by the fire. He'd already wrapped the kitten in a fluffy pink towel, its fur spiking around its head. It let out another small rasp.

"Oh, he's super cute. He was in the loch?" Sophie crouched and handed me a few towels. I did my best to dry off my sodden hair, before wrapping another around my shoulders and dropping to the floor next to Ramsay to peer at the kitten.

"Should I heat up some milk or something for it?" Lachlan asked, crouching.

"I don't think you can give kittens milk. It gives them a sore stomach," Ramsay said. "Maybe just a little fresh water? See if it takes it?"

"Should we get him checked at the vet?"

"Closed for the day now, I think. But if we think it's an emergency, we can call." Sophie eased back, reaching for a towel to wipe the rain from her face. We sat in silence, drying ourselves, and nobody seemed quite ready to speak about the Kelpies.

"It's pretty cold in the loch, though, isn't it? I'm

worried about the kitten's water exposure," I said, my eyes going back to the kitten.

"But not mine?" Ramsay arched a brow at me, and I smiled.

"You seemed pretty hot to me."

Yup, that's what I said. What I'd meant to say was he seemed fine, yet those were not the words that came out of my mouth.

"Mew."

"Oh buddy, your poor voice. May I?" I asked, needing to distract myself from the embarrassment that burned my cheeks. Ramsay handed the kitten over to me, his face inscrutable, and I shifted to cradle the kitten and turned my wet back to the fire.

The kitten tilted its head, and I held it to my face to meet its eyes. We'd never had pets growing up, so I didn't much know the protocol with a kitten, but I remembered desperately wanting one as a child. About two pounds, with dark stripes in matted grey fur, the kitten settled into my palms and surveyed me with the same interest that I gave him.

Mine.

Jeez, I really needed to stop claiming things around here. Pretty soon I'd be saying the same about Ramsay if I didn't stop myself. But the same feeling I'd had about the sewing scissors resonated with me about this cat.

The scissors.

I gasped, causing the kitten to stand in my palms, its back going up.

The vision.

I'd forgotten about it, but now as I stared at the kitten

who glared at me, I pulled my eyes up to a dripping-wet Ramsay.

I'd seen this happen.

Quite literally.

And had been coated with sea water after the vision. My mouth worked, but no sound came out, and Ramsay's expression shifted to concern.

"Willow?" Sophie touched my arm, startling me from staring dumbly at Ramsay, and I turned to her.

"I think I know what my magick is."

I blurted it, without thinking, and then winced. After the ritual, Archie and Hilda had discussed some of the matters regarding privacy around the Order and magick, and now I'd likely broken their trust. Granted, Ramsay had just been privy to the Kelpies, so it wasn't like he could ignore the existence of magick in the world, but he also didn't need to know that *I* was magick. Did he?

"Your magick? Did you call the Kelpies then?" Ramsay asked, looking taken aback.

"Excuse me? You think I'd put us in harm's way?" I asked, affronted.

"Och, lass, stand down. It's the only magick I saw, is all. Except …" Ramsay toweled his hair, lifting his chin toward Sophie. "That little trick you did with your sword. A bit magickal, no?"

"Aye," Lachlan said, surprising Sophie, and Ramsay looked up to him. "Both of the lasses have magick."

A look passed between the men, and then Ramsay just nodded.

That was it?

Nothing more? I mean, I'd had a thousand questions

yesterday and still felt like I'd barely scratched the surface, and the men could just accept it point-blank?

A knock sounded at the door, and Lachlan crossed the room, flipping the lock, and opening it to Agnes hovering under an umbrella, concern on her face.

"Sorry to interrupt, but I had to come."

Lachlan ushered her inside, closing the door against the rain again, and Agnes stomped her boots as Ramsay added another log to the fire. It was cozy in here, with friends huddled close by the fire, the rain hammering the window outside. It was almost easy enough to pretend that the last few horrifying minutes hadn't just happened. A soft rumbling drew my attention, and I realized that I was still holding the kitten aloft, but he'd settled back into my palms. His little body vibrated with purrs. Drawing him close, I wrapped him back in the towel again, and cradled him against my chest.

I could see the future.

That had to be it. It all made sense to me, these flashes of knowing that had occurred in my past, often saving me from danger. It was some sort of latent power that now had manifested with my indoctrination into the Order of Caledonia. Honestly, of all the powers, I expected something perhaps more physical, or something related to sewing, but not necessarily psychic abilities.

Was it psychic though? I mean, I'd drawn Ramsay holding the kitten in the water. But I'd also come away from the vision with sea water on my face. I didn't know any psychics that had that kind of power. Granted, I didn't know any actual psychics, so my knowledge was limited in that area anyway.

"I saw the Kelpies, and wanted to come check that everyone was okay."

Silence greeted Agnes as we all looked up at her. She tilted her head at us in question, concern furrowing her brow as she folded her umbrella and placed it by the door, before shaking her coat off and hanging it on a hook. "What's happened? What's wrong?"

"Willow's figured out what her magick is. And, apparently, also just informed Ramsay that we have magick. We're just processing ... I'm guessing?" Sophie twisted to look at me and I nodded faintly. "Also, they rescued this kitten from the loch."

"Aww, look at the wee lad. Sometimes they do slip off that sea wall, don't they?"

"Aye, we know it. Sir Buster did it himself, didn't he then?" Lachlan said and I gaped up at him.

"Sir Buster fell in the loch?"

"And Lachlan went after him. We almost lost him because of how long he'd been in there." A look passed between Lachlan and Sophie, full of so much love and tenderness that my heart twisted in my chest.

I wanted that. That inscrutable *something* with someone where a thousand words were said with barely a glance.

"Does this happen a lot? With animals by the water?"

"Here and there. Along that one side of the loch where there's the sea wall that protects the road, they've slipped a time or two." Agnes crouched by my side and ran a finger over the kitten's head and its rumbling increased. "He seems well enough though."

"Does he? I have no idea. I've never had a cat before.

I've always wanted one though." I looked down at the sleeping bundle, barely resisting the urge to rock it. The kitten was already sleeping, he didn't need me to rock him to sleep. "Can I ..."

I trailed off, not sure if it was too much of an ask and suspecting I wouldn't like the answer that I would get. Sophie had already done so much for me, and I'd hardly proven myself—not as an employee nor as a member of the Order—and to ask to bring an animal into her home was totally overstepping.

"Can you what?" Ramsay's voice was gruff.

"I really want to keep him. I've always wanted a cat, and I just feel like he's mine. I really do. But it's such a huge ask, and you've already got the dogs. Maybe I could keep him here? Or just in the apartment but not in the actual castle? Or bring him back and forth? I just feel like ... I don't know ... like he belongs to me." I stroked the kitten's soft fur, and it nuzzled closer, tucking its head beneath my chin, and I realized that I was dangerously close to tears. It was stupid, really, he was just a kitten. I'm sure I could find him a good home if I needed to.

Maybe I just needed something for me. Something to love me without reservation, or expectation of anything other than companionship. A silly thought, maybe, but I was in a different country, with new friends, a new job, and felt decidedly out of place as I tried to navigate these wild, new circumstances into which I'd been thrust. Last night, when Sir Buster and Clyde curled up on my bed, it had been decidedly soothing, and now, as I held this tiny kitten to my chest, I desperately wanted him to be mine.

The kitten, seeming to sense my distress, lifted its head and licked my chin, its tongue rough against my skin.

"What's his name?" Ramsay asked me.

"Calvin," I said automatically, and Sophie laughed.

"Like Calvin Klein?"

"No, like *A Wrinkle in Time*."

"Ah yes, a wee hero in his own right, eh?" Agnes scratched Calvin's ear, nodding her approval at me. "Great book."

"It was my favorite growing up. Love wins." I'd probably reread that book a hundred times. I could relate to the idea of a missing parent and feeling at odds with the world.

"Of course you can keep him," Sophie said, smiling at me. "We'll figure it out with the dogs."

"He can stay here too."

At that, I looked up at Ramsay, a smile on my face.

"Really?"

"Aye. But you'll need to get him a scratching post. If he rips any of my fabrics, he's in trouble."

"Oh shit, yeah, that would be bad." I tightened my grip around Calvin. "We'll train him. I promise. Thank you, guys. I just feel like he's mine. It's dumb, I guess."

"It's not dumb," Sophie and Agnes chimed in at the same time.

Ramsay stood and left the room, and shuffling noises came from the back room. In moments he was back, two chairs hooked under his arms, and he placed them by the fire, dragging over the other one from in front of the desk. Next, he draped towels on all the chairs, before stopping in the doorway between the rooms.

"I'm going to change, put on a pot of tea, and then we'll figure this out. Aye?"

"Aye," I said softly, nerves simmering in my stomach.

He wasn't talking about figuring out how to take care of a kitten. He was talking about the magick, and I realized I'd have to bare myself to everyone in this room when I still didn't know or understand what was happening to me. It was wildly disconcerting, not just picking up and starting over in a new place, but also discovering I was part of a mystical Order. I would say, one of the benefits of having worked on fashion shows, was that you needed to address things at lightning speed. Hopefully, that trait would help me now.

By the time Ramsay returned, we'd all moved from the floor to the chairs, towels wrapped around us, and my breath caught when he walked through the door, a tea tray in hand.

He wore sweatpants.

Grey sweatpants to be exact.

Hung low at his hips, with a navy-blue chunky sweater on top, and thick fuzzy cottage socks at his feet. He looked comfy, cozy, and impossibly sexy. It took everything in my power not to ogle him as he bent to put the tray on the table in the middle of the chairs. There was just something about a man in grey sweatpants that made my insides go loose and liquid. It made gruff Ramsay seem more approachable, a man to curl up with by the fire, and I distracted myself by readjusting Calvin in my arms.

Sophie winked at me, and I shook my head.

Nope.

She was not going to be a matchmaker. We weren't

going to do this. Ramsay barely tolerated my presence as it was. A love match? Not happening.

"All right, lasses. Have at it then. Magick?" Ramsay said, startling me from stroking Calvin with increasing adoration.

"Do you want the long version or the short?" Sophie asked.

"Short. The lass has been through enough today."

I blinked up at Ramsay, realizing he meant me, and gave him a soft smile. It wasn't like I'd been the one to throw myself in a freezing cold loch and been threatened by the Kelpies. Yet Ramsay was worried about me.

"Well, you know about the Kelpies." Sophie gave Lachlan a heavy look, and he nodded at her.

"He's safe," Lachlan murmured.

"So, the short version is that there is a magickal Order tasked with protecting the Stone of Truth buried on the island in Loch Mirren. Because the last of the old Order died, the Kelpies will now protect the stone until the Order is fully resurrected again."

"Right," Ramsay said. He steepled his fingers as he absorbed her words, the fire snapping in the background. "And the magick?"

"Each member of the Order will step into powers as they pass their challenges to become a fully standing member."

"Challenges?" Ramsay, the man of many words, asked.

"You can't just join the Order. You have to prove you're worthy of the magick, as well as being strong enough to protect the Stone."

"And Willow is a member?"

"Correct. She joined yesterday and, it appears, her magick has manifested already."

"It may have been there all along," I admitted, biting my lower lip as I thought about all the times that my gut had guided me in the right direction. That being said, I'd had a lot of times that I'd made poor decisions or things hadn't gone well for me. So was I really psychic then? Or had I simply ignored my instincts to my own detriment? A thought to chew over another day, I supposed. I looked up at the group. "I ... I don't know. I've had moments in life where my gut instinct made me do something. Like not take a bike tour in Costa Rica where they ended up getting stuck in a mudslide or not walking on a crosswalk when a car ran a red light. That kind of thing."

"That's a really strong instinct then. But you said you had an actual vision?" Sophie gave me an encouraging smile.

"I did. Last night. I was sketching out ideas for the shop and, well, yeah. So I guess I just drifted off? Hold on." I stood up, handing Calvin off to a delighted Agnes, and crossed the room to dig in my bag. A shiver went through me once I was away from the fire, and I realized I wanted to get home to change, curl up with Calvin, and just hit the pause button for a moment while my brain caught up with these changes. Hopefully, I could do that soon if we could just get through this conversation.

"Archie has kitten food. He feeds a few at the stables. He'll bring it to your apartment, along with a litter box, litter, and some food dishes. He says to keep him contained in smaller rooms for now, so he doesn't get too scared in a big place." Sophie held up her phone, and relief washed through me as I returned to the group, iPad in hand, and dragged a towel around my shoulders again.

"That's awesome, I hadn't even thought that far ahead."

"Calvin will be just fine. We'll get you tucked up in your new home shortly, bud." Sophie reached over to scratch Calvin's ear, and while I itched to bring him back to my arms, I needed to show the others what I'd drawn the night before.

"Oh, random question, but how did you know to be there? To help us?" I asked Sophie, sitting back down. "It was incredible to watch."

"I didn't. We were on our way to the shops. Lucky timing."

"You take your sword to the shops?" Ramsay asked, eyeing the sword by the fireplace.

"Doesn't everyone?" Sophie joked. "No, but I take it most places with me or leave it in the car. The Kelpies have been active lately. Doesn't hurt to have it around."

"No kidding. Glad you were there. So, I was sketching out some ideas …" I flipped my iPad on and scrolled through some sketches.

"Oh no way, those are cool. Is that chain mail?" Sophie leaned in and I paused, happy to hear a good response from her already.

"Yeah, I was kind of just playing with the idea of it. Maybe incorporating it in a modern way? Sort of a nod to the knight?"

"Even cooler. I'm the Knight."

"You are?" Ramsay raised an eyebrow at her.

"Sword, right?" Sophie indicated the sword, and Ramsay nodded and said nothing else.

A lot of nodding. Few words. It seemed like Ramsay absorbed wild news quite well.

"I'd like to see you in that top," Lachlan said to Sophie, and their eyes locked. I swear the temperature went up ten degrees in the room until Agnes swatted the air between us.

"No sexy talk right now, people. Focus."

"Right, so yeah, I was drawing and then I guess I kind of zoned out? But I kept drawing and then, well, yeah. It was this. And when I realized what I'd drawn I also noticed that I was wet."

"Wet?" Ramsay's voice shot heat straight through my core and I blinked at him, caught on whatever swam in the murky depths of his eyes. My cheeks heated.

"Like with sea water. It was salty. My face and hands were actually wet," I clarified quickly, realizing how that had sounded. I held up the iPad to show the image of Ramsay in the loch, clutching Calvin at his chest.

"Oh shit, Willow. That's a great drawing."

"You've taken some liberties with his looks, but it's not bad, I guess." Lachlan deadpanned and Ramsay punched his shoulder.

Admittedly, Ramsay looked very much the superhero in my drawing with bulging muscles and fearsome Kelpies hovering over his shoulder.

"You should send that to me. I'll print it and frame it for Lachlan," Ramsay said.

"Better to start a fire with, naw?" Lachlan and Ramsay descended into boy banter while Agnes tapped my leg and leaned in.

"This makes sense, you know."

"Does it? How?" I asked. Calvin awoke in Agnes's arms, stretching and looking around until he found me. Instantly he stood, and tried to clamber in my direction, and Agnes handed him off. Once he was in my arms again, Calvin settled in, purring contentedly in my lap.

Damn it, but I was already in love.

"It's the weaver. It's a common theme in many myths. The weaver foretold the future. It's like ... weaving threads of fate together, you ken?"

"Threads," I said, faintly. "That's my father's nickname for me."

Agnes's face lit with excitement. "Aye, that's perfect, isn't it? It's all over the place in history when it comes to the ability to foretell the future. The Fates. Like in Greek mythology. Or the Norns in Norse. And the Parcae in Roman. All spinners of fate and destiny. Oh, and in some Native American myths there's the spider woman. She spins fate and prophecies through her web. Yes, this all makes sense, given what you do."

"It does?"

"Sure, you're in fashion. You create, work with textiles, build something new."

"It fits." Ramsay joined the conversation again, and his easy acceptance of something that I was still coming to terms with pacified some of the nerves that twisted in my gut.

"It does."

Another clap of thunder sounded, and Calvin let out a tiny little "brrrrp" in my arms. Shifting, I hugged him closer.

"I don't mean to be like this, but do you guys mind if I go home? I think I just need to get out of these wet clothes and take a moment. This is all a lot, and I want to get him settled." I nodded down to Calvin.

"I'm glad you're already calling it home." Sophie hopped up and patted my shoulder. "Come on, Lachlan will grab the car. You don't have to walk in the rain."

"Is it okay for me to leave?" I asked Ramsay.

"It's far past closing time, lass. You're free to do as you wish."

"I'll see you in the morning then. Not before your coffee, of course."

"Bring Calvin."

His words warmed me all the way back to the castle. He may be rough around the edges, but there was a softness underneath that hard exterior of Ramsay's. The innate gentleness was what I remembered about him from when he was a teenager. Yes, he goofed around with my brother, but he hadn't been churlish. *Charming, kind, and sexy Ramsay was lethal to my heart.*

Now I just had to do my best not to annoy him, all while trying not to fall head over heels for him.

CHAPTER SIXTEEN

Willow

"Gimmee," Hilda demanded, arms outstretched, as soon as we entered the castle. I handed her Calvin, and he snuggled right in with a contented little "brraaap."

"Well now, isn't he just the sweetest? Archie's put a basket of things outside your door, Willow. I've got tea on if you're feeling peckish?"

"They call dinner 'tea' here," Sophie translated quickly, and I raised my chin in understanding.

"I'd like to change out of these damp clothes real quick."

"Please do. I'll just take this little man with me while you do."

"Will he be okay with the dogs? What about having to go to the bathroom?" I realized that I hadn't even put him down or outside and knew next to nothing about cats.

"Cats are surprisingly resilient, and quite smart. Once you get the box set up, put him in it and nature will take its course. The wee lad will get on just fine."

"Great, I'll go do that and be right down."

True to her words, there was a box brimming with goods at my apartment door, and I unpacked everything, setting up the litter box in the bathroom that connected to my bedroom. I figured I could keep Calvin in there while I was in the castle and bring him with me when I went to the shop. I'd have to make a note to ask Archie if he had any more supplies to take with me to the shop. Ramsay would have my head if Calvin peed on something.

I changed into fleece-lined leggings, Shearling lined Ugg boots, and a hot pink Barbie sweatshirt. Instantly feeling better now that I was no longer in my sodden clothes, I carefully hung my skirt in the bath to dry, and then I made my way downstairs to find Archie on the floor with Calvin, trailing a feather on a fishing line while Sir Buster trembled at Hilda's feet. Lady Lola licked a paw, entirely unbothered by the kitten's presence, lolling in the warmth from the fire.

"Oh, look at him go." I laughed as Calvin pounced on the feather, only to have it whisked from his paws. He gave chase, his little body springing everywhere, and happiness flashed through me. "This is great. I was worried he'd get pneumonia or hypothermia or something from falling in that cold water."

"He must not have been in there all that long. Lucky little lad." Hilda looked down at where Sir Buster whined and pawed at her feet. "Oh, for goodness' sake, Sir Buster. You'd think the kitten was a dinosaur the way you're acting."

"Is he scared?" I raised an eyebrow at the shaking dog.

"Appears so. They had a brief moment."

"No, what happened?" I gasped.

"Sir Buster barked at him. One bark, mind you. A warning, I'd say. Got a wee snipe right across the snout, didn't you?" Hilda kissed Sir Buster's nose, who looked decidedly rattled at the intruder. "We learned our lesson about kittens today, didn't we?"

"Aww, I'm sorry, buddy." I patted Sir Buster's head, and he curled his lips at me, but his growl was a touch less threatening than usual. "Got the wind taken out of your sails a bit, eh?"

"It'll happen. He's had it a time or two with a hedgehog as well. Go on, sit, sit. Food is ready."

Hilda nodded to the table, and I turned to see Sophie and Lachlan ladling soup into bowls, steam escaping from baskets of warm crusty bread. My stomach growled, and I realized that I hadn't eaten lunch.

"Are you okay with Calvin for a moment, Archie?"

"Och, nae bother, lass. The lad's enjoying himself."

At his name, Calvin turned to look at me, and a feeling of love flashed through me. He was happy to see me. I narrowed my eyes as I looked at the little kitten, his fur now dry, and wondered if I had ascribed that emotion to him, or if he had managed to transmit that idea into my head.

Okay, now that was getting to be a bit much. Shaking my head at my thoughts, I joined Sophie at the table.

"Potato leek soup. I like it with a dash of pepper myself."

"Thank you. This looks great." And it was. Simple food, made from locally sourced ingredients, I was told, and soon enough I was patting my stomach and refusing another bowl.

"Just wait until you meet Lia and Shona. They are a match made in heaven. Lia is the incredible chef at our restaurant here, and Shona is a local gardener who grew those leeks you just enjoyed in the soup."

"Oh, that's right. You have a pretty fancy restaurant on site, don't you?"

"It's world class, in my opinion, but Lia will tell you she likes to make comfort food with a touch of class," Sophie said, motioning with a piece of bread in her hand.

"I can't wait to meet them."

"I'm hoping for a girls' night this week."

Lachlan snorted. "Just a usual girls' night?"

"You know, talking magick, saving the world, that kind of thing." Sophie grinned at him.

"The usual." Lachlan mimed painting his nails, fluttering his lashes at Sophie. She leaned over to give him a lingering kiss.

"I love you so much," Sophie whispered, and he murmured something indecipherable against her lips. My cheeks heated, and at the same time, my heart sighed. It was hard not to want something like that even though I was meant to be on my independent "didn't need no man" journey at the moment.

"Enough fornicating at the dinner table," Archie barked from the floor, causing Calvin to spring into the air.

"This is hardly fornicating. Old age must be taking your sight."

"Yet I kicked your sorry arse at darts the other night, didn't I?" Archie said, and I laughed.

"That's an aim problem, not a sight problem," Lachlan protested.

"Your aim's never ... you know what? Never mind," Sophie trilled, and I laughed harder. For some reason, I felt at home with these people, even though I was still reeling over the fact that the Kelpies were really freaking scary and that I could see the future.

"Sophie tells me you think you found your magick?" Hilda neatly changed the subject, and I nodded, pushing away from the table.

"Should I take my plates into the kitchen?"

"Och, just leave them. Would you like a glass of wine?" Hilda asked, and I nodded my thanks as she held up a bottle of red. I moved to stand with my back to the fire, enjoying the heat, as I watched Archie trail the feather across the carpet for Calvin. The kitten licked its paws, apparently uninterested in playing anymore.

Until at the last moment, he sprang straight into the air and landed on the feather.

"Aha! You can't fool me," Archie said, whipping the feather away, and Calvin gave chase again.

"I thought he'd given up on it."

"Cats will do that. You'll find they're finnicky. Mercurial moods. Play hard to get one moment. Cuddly the next. They can be all over the place."

"Yes, dogs are *never* moody," Sophie said, side-eying Sir Buster.

"Here you go, dear." Hilda passed me a glass of wine, and I took a seat in one of the tartan lounge chairs and sipped it, a smile at my lips while Calvin pranced around.

"He really seems to be okay, doesn't he? Bounced right

back." Seeing him so bedraggled and tiny had been horrifying. Which, of course, reminded me of the Kelpies. "Um, so, yeah, the Kelpies were pretty freaking terrifying. Guys, I could've used a heads-up on how to stop them or whatever. Since I'm part of the Order and all. I felt pretty useless, standing there gawking on the sidelines while they almost creamed Ramsay and Calvin."

"It's my job, Willow." Sophie tugged at her hair that was woven in a braid over one shoulder. "I've got the power to command them back. We didn't know your magick, and it doesn't seem like what has manifested for you will actually help in the moment of an attack. Likely you'll be able to predict an attack. But in the moment? Not much you can do. I'd say, at the very least, try? Order them back. Let them know you're a part of the Order of Caledonia, that you're one of theirs, and try telling them to get back."

"Seriously, just scream for them to back off?"

"Pretty much what I do. Except I can feel it." Sophie brought a hand to her chest. "In here. I can feel the power to compel them back. It's, I don't know, like I've got this electrical current of energy that lights up inside me. And I push them back with it."

"That's ... wild. Why do you think they were there today? Why was Ramsay a threat?"

"I'm not sure, to be honest. It feels like they're becoming increasingly more active," Sophie said.

"The longer we take to fulfill the Order, the more often they'll appear," Hilda said.

"I thought that my being here was helping them calm down." Sophie stuck out a lower lip.

"It does, for a while. But keep in mind this stone has

weathered centuries. It likely looks at time very differently than we do."

"I guess. Wouldn't mind a solid night's sleep though." Sophie shrugged.

"Is it the future you see then?" Archie asked from the floor. "Sophie filled us in while you were upstairs."

"I ... I guess? I mean, it's never happened in quite the way it did last night, but I'm sure the more I think on it I'll be able to remember more times that it's happened. I just ... it's not like I could tell you what your future holds. I don't think at least."

"Want to try?" Sophie asked, and I jolted.

"Like how?"

"Like give me a reading?"

"I wouldn't even know where to start?"

"So, no pressure then." Sophie jumped up and grabbing her own glass of wine, settled at my feet. I looked down at her, confused on what to do. Reaching over I patted her on the head, and she snorted.

"Not sure that's how it goes."

"I literally have no idea what to do."

"Want a notebook? You said you were sketching. By the way, you have some serious skills. That drawing of Ramsay, whoo, boy." Sophie fanned herself.

"Is that right? I'll have to take a look." Hilda brought a small notepad and pen and I put my wineglass on the side table.

"I guess, just see if you can focus on me? If anything pops in your head? Or maybe I should ask a question?"

"Oh jeez, I don't know. Right." I picked up my wine and took a long sip, then put it down, jostling it a bit and sloshing the wine at the rim. "Ope, sorry. Jeez, I'm nervous."

"Don't be. You can't screw anything up. This is just for fun."

"Um, so I'll just do what I was doing I guess?" Silence fell in the room as I began to sketch on the paper, idly doodling, drawing Sophie's face, because that was what was in front of me. As a designer, sketching outfit ideas kind of went together with the design process, but as a creative, I'd taken many art classes growing up and considered myself a fairly proficient artist. Rarely did I take out my pencils and sketch for fun, but every once in a while, I'd pull out paints and have at it. In fact, designing prints was something new that I'd recently gotten into, and I could already tell that I would love to do that in some capacity for the store. Maybe a cute thistle scarf? I sketched one around Sophie's face when the room faded around me.

For a moment, I was carried away to a beautiful forest, standing beside a lovely river that burbled over smooth stones. Sunlight dappled the leaves, and I gasped as Lachlan crouched in front of Sophie, a ring in his hand.

Blinking back to the room I was currently in, I quickly scribbled out the drawing I had started, pressing my lips together because the last thing I needed to do was reveal a secret of that nature to Sophie.

"You saw something, didn't you?" Sophie demanded, starting to rise, and I shook my head.

"Nothing major. Just you standing on the wall with your sword." Like I'd seen her the night before.

"But no details? Nothing to indicate an immediate threat?"

"No, didn't seem that way. I'm sorry." I refused to look at Lachlan, though I wanted to squeal and do a little happy dance for Sophie. They were such a cute couple, and I could only imagine what a castle wedding would be like here.

"That's okay. It's your first real go at it. I'm sure Agnes can dig deeper in her books and maybe pull up some suggestions for how you can harness your power more."

An image of Calvin sleeping flashed into my head, and I turned to see him, his eyes drooping, staring at me.

"Oh, I think the little guy is tuckered out. I'd like to take him up and show him his litter box and food, get him used to the space. Is that okay?" Frankly, I needed some alone time just to get my head on straight after the day I'd had as well.

"Yes, go ahead. Do you need anything else? Do you want to take a bottle of wine up with you?" Hilda asked as I stood.

"No, I'm good. I'm going straight to bed. I have to admit, it's been a pretty exhausting day."

"You're back at the shop tomorrow? I didn't even get a chance to ask how you got on with Ramsay today," Sophie said, as she stood and stretched.

"He's … tricky," I finally landed on, and Lachlan barked out a laugh.

"That's one word for it. Good luck to you on that front." Lachlan saluted me with a glass of whisky.

"Oh, I just think he's a grumpy ol' bear. I bet he's all cuddly and warm beneath that tough exterior. I do like a grumpy man," Sophie said, going to wrap an arm around Lachlan's shoulders. He put an arm around her legs and leaned in, looking up at her.

"I am not like Ramsay," Lachlan protested.

"No, of course not, babe. You're a positive ray of sunshine," Sophie assured him, and I chuckled as I scooped up Calvin and Lachlan glowered.

"Goodnight, everyone. Thanks for your help today. A lot to think about."

"It doesn't all need to be resolved tonight, Willow. Take your time." This from Archie, as he stood, the feather still dangling in his hand. I appreciated the reminder, as my impulsive nature usually made me want to find an answer to a problem immediately. Calvin purred at my throat as I walked upstairs, a warm, little ball of comfort, and I placed him on the middle of my bed once we got into my apartment.

"Okay, let me just put my glass of wine down, then I want to show you your new digs." Putting the wine beside the bed, I picked the kitten back up from where he'd begun to knead the comforter and took him to the bathroom.

Placing him in the litter box, I stood there, hands on hips, while he regarded me solemnly.

"So, um, that's your toilet. You're meant to do your business there."

I sincerely doubted my ability to potty train this little cat. Surely just pointing at a box of sand wouldn't cause a cat to understand my meaning.

To my surprise, Calvin began to dig around in the sand and quickly, and neatly, might I add, took care of business. Color me impressed.

"Well done, good sir. I can't believe that worked so well. Okay, right. I bet you're going to want food and water. Here's your water dish." I picked him up out of the box and put him in front of a little tray with two dishes, one that I'd put water in. Calvin immediately lapped it up while I read the back of the food packaging that Archie had delivered.

"So there's wet food and dry food. But you seem kind of young, so I feel like you start babies on wet food. I'll go with that. Hold on." I backtracked to the little kitchenette in the apartment, dug out a spoon, and went back to the bathroom to dish out the right amount of wet food.

"There. What do you think?"

Calvin dove face-first into the food, which I took to mean he approved, and his little legs flew up in the back as he splayed out over the dish.

"Oh bud, hold on. Here, let me help." The sides of the dish were a touch too tall for him, so I ended up spoon-feeding him his meal. I made a note to get a small plate in the morning. Once we were done, I wiped his face gently with a damp towel where he'd landed in his food and then carried him to the middle of the bed.

"Mooooo!" Clyde jumped through the open door of the bedroom and skidded to a stop as Calvin arched his back and hissed. My hand shot to my heart, but it wasn't me that was scared this time.

If the coo could have screamed, I'm sure he would have.

The look on Clyde's face as he scrambled backward, his eyes wide with terror as little Calvin batted a paw in the air and hissed, had me convulsing in laughter. The ghost coo scrambled, tipping backwards in its haste, sliding across the floor, and winked out of sight right before he would have slammed into the wall.

Calvin stood, all eight inches of him, paw raised, waiting to see if the threat would return.

"I'm dying," I heaved, tears of laughter streaming down my face, as I went to stroke the fur that stood up at the back of Calvin's neck. "Well, done, my little hero. You protected me."

"Brrrrrpp." Calvin bumped his head against my fingers before settling into the comforter, kneading the material with his little paws.

"Oh man, I honestly don't know if I'll ever get used to this. What a day." Wiping tears from my eyes, I went to get ready for bed.

Who knew what the next morning would bring? At this rate, anything could happen.

CHAPTER SEVENTEEN

Willow

A gentle bump at my head woke me from a dead sleep, and I blinked up at the ceiling before the bump happened once more. Jolting, I focused on the small kitten that was currently headbutting me, and everything from the day before came flooding back.

"Jeez, I'm surprised I slept at all. Hey, bud." I scratched behind Calvin's ears and his eyes closed, a rumbling purr emitting from his little fuzzy body. He really *was* cute, even if he was waking me up before ... I craned my neck to look at my phone ... seven in the morning. "We're going to have to work on the concept of sleeping in."

Not that I slept in all that much, but since Ramsay didn't want me at the store until ten, rising before seven did seem a touch enthusiastic. Today it would give me some time to get to know Calvin better, maybe get a phone call in to my dad, and work on a few more designs. Picking up my phone, I scrolled to the world clock app, realized it was far too early to even contemplate calling my father who, albeit was an early riser, but not a *one in the morning* early riser.

My phone also showed a slew of text messages from Miles, increasing in frustration at my lack of response. I ignored them.

He didn't get a say in my life at the moment, and he probably already had all the intel he needed from Ramsay anyway. Would Ramsay tell him about the magickal happenings in Loren Brae? I doubted it, since the Kelpies hadn't been a surprise to Ramsay, and Miles surely would have brought something of that nature up to me, as protective as he was.

"I guess I'll have to get used to checking in with Dad later in the day. Ope!" I snagged Calvin before he tried to jump off the side of the bed. "That seems like a pretty big jump for you."

I guess I was getting up.

An image flashed in my mind of Calvin's food dish, and I paused in my attempt to extract my legs from the covers tangled around them.

"Are you doing that?" It felt weird, asking my kitten a direct question like that, but since nobody was around to judge me, I went with it.

Calvin licked a paw and didn't reply.

"Calvin?"

The cat looked up at me. Did he already know his name or was he just looking at me because I was the only one speaking in the room? How would I test that he was actually communicating with me?

Maybe Loren Brae was beginning to make me think that *anything* could be magickal.

"Can you show me what you want right now?"

The image of his food dish flashed in my head again.

Hmmm. Was I doing that because I knew he was probably hungry or was he doing that?

"Can you show me how you fell in the loch?"

An image of a car speeding, scaring him, and sending him careening off the wall into the water, surfaced in my brain.

"Really? A car ran you off the road? You poor thing."

I went to scratch his ears and Calvin bit my finger. Lightly, maybe even playfully, but I grabbed it back.

"*Sir*. Rude."

The food dish image popped back in my head.

"Okay, see ... I think you have to be doing this. Because I'm not thinking about your food as much as you're thinking about your food. I wonder what it means though?" Scooping Calvin up, I acquiesced to his demands, before showering and getting ready for the day.

My sequin skirt had dried from the day before, but now I paused as I considered my outfit choice for today. Yesterday I'd wanted to mix fun with a nod to Scotland in my tartan shirt, never considering that I'd be running through the rain to rescue a kitten. Since it was anyone's guess what challenges would arise for me today, maybe I needed to consider ease of movement and sturdy footwear.

Pulling out my pink Docs, I paired them with grey straight-legged jeans, a Nirvana T-shirt, with an oversized tweed blazer with rolled cuffs. Piling on a tumble of statement necklaces, I lined my eyes with a smokey liner, and pinned half my hair back. Based on Ramsay's preference of rock music, I figured he wouldn't be too fussed by me wearing a band T-shirt at his shop, but we'd never actually discussed work attire. I made a mental note to bring that up with him later today.

A crash sounded.

"Calvin!" I poked my head from the bathroom to see the small box of sewing accoutrements that I'd brought with me from the storeroom on the floor. Calvin, who was on his back on the carpet, didn't seem at all bothered by the mess he'd just made, and batted lazily at a ribbon.

"What the heck? Calvin, you naughty boy." I squatted and began gathering the items, placing the thimbles and buttons back in the box. Spying my scissors, I sighed. "You have to be careful. What if my scissors had landed on you?"

Granted, I guess *I* would have to be careful. I hadn't really thought about how to kitten proof a room, but now I looked around, wondering if there were other things that could pose a danger to the little man. The last thing I needed was to kill my kitten on day one of having him.

Something caught my eye, and I squinted down at the scissors in my palm. I'd been about to tuck them away in the box, meaning to take them to Sophie at some point to have a chat with her about the possibility of them being my power item—or whatever it was called—and the design caught my eye.

The pattern on the handle had changed.

Or something in the pattern had changed.

I'd always had a good eye for patterns, designs, and things of that nature. When I'd first picked up the scissors and had felt that pulse of energy against my palm, I'd taken time to study the design etched into the handle. Intricate Celtic knotwork and flowers had wrapped the handles, and while that design was still there, now, a singular tiny cat clambered on one of the vines.

"No way," I breathed, bringing the scissors closer. I held them up to the light, turning them upside down to see if there was a cat, or anything else, hidden among the vines.

Nope.

One little cat tucked among the vines that had most definitely not been there the day before. I was certain I would have noticed it. I looked between the cat and to where Calvin played with the ribbon.

"Did you do this?"

Calvin rolled over, twining the ribbon around his little body, and blinked his greenish eyes at me. I waited for some image or inkling to pop into my head, but nothing came. Rolling my eyes, I scooped Calvin up, tucked the scissors in my purse, and brought the ribbon along for him to play with. While Ramsay had been kind enough to tell me to bring Calvin with me to the shop, I wondered just how well that would actually work out.

"You can't knock his stuff over or he's going to kick you out of the shop." I pressed a kiss to the top of Calvin's head, and we went downstairs to find Sophie and Hilda having a coffee in the lounge area.

"There's my wee man. I've kept a bit of chicken out for him."

Sir Buster growled at my arrival, and Calvin perked up in my arms.

"Can I put him down or will there be blood?" I surveyed the growling chihuahua.

"Put him down. He's all bluster."

I put Calvin down, who immediately scampered across the room, sending Sir Buster running beneath the table from where he let out a near constant growl of warning.

"That's enough out of you," Hilda told Sir Buster before giving Calvin a small plate of chicken. The growling intensified. "Now, Buster. You can share your chicken."

"Coffee?" Sophie asked and I nodded.

"I need to go to the store at some point. I can't rely on you for all my meals."

"It's no bother for me," Hilda said, from where she was crouched by Calvin, "but I'm sure you'll want to have some food in your apartment as well."

"I can take you later," Sophie promised me.

Sophie looked comfortable in a baggy UCLA sweatshirt and leggings, and it was hard for me to remind myself that she was seriously wealthy, and the owner of this castle. Handing me a cup of coffee, she curled back up on a small sofa and tucked her feet under a blanket. The sky outside was just beginning to lighten, and I glanced at it in surprise.

"Does it stay dark this late in the morning?"

"Yup. And summer it will stay light longer."

"Really? That's kind of cool." I took the chair next to Sophie, and remembering Calvin's antics earlier, I dug in my purse one-handed and gave Sophie the scissors.

"What are these? Oh, cool. They're pretty, aren't they? Did you find them in the storeroom or are they yours?"

"Um, both. If that's okay with you?" I took a sip of my coffee and decided to just push forward with it, since, well I guess everything was on the table after the Kelpies had tried to murder us yesterday. "I found these in the storeroom, and for some reason I, like, instantly connected with them. I knew they were mine. Weird, maybe, but I could just feel it."

"Oh! These are your weapon. That's awesome."

"When you say weapon …" I looked helplessly at Sophie. "Am I meant to stab someone with them?"

I *really* didn't want blood on my Nirvana shirt. It was borderline vintage.

"Let's hope not. I think it's more symbolic than anything." Sophie wielded the scissors and Hilda chuckled, carrying Calvin with her to come sit next to Sophie.

"Let's have a look?"

Sophie snagged Calvin, tipping him over on her lap and scratching his belly, which he seemed to enjoy for a moment before he bit her finger and flipped over, stalking across the couch to jump from the arm to my lap.

"Ohhh, he's got a bit of an attitude, doesn't he? I like it," Sophie said.

"So, with the scissors, do you see the cat in the pattern?" I asked, stroking Calvin's back as he began to knead my knee with his tiny, sharp claws. I winced as one sunk deep and pulled his paw back.

"I do. Look." Hilda tilted the scissors to Sophie.

"Cute."

"It wasn't there yesterday morning."

"Ohhhhh." Sophie's face lit with excitement, and she slapped her hand on her thigh. "No way. You've passed a challenge already."

"Excuse me? I have?"

"I think so. I guess we'll only know if you pass another and see if a different design shows up."

"Aye, that's the way of it." Hilda nodded at me. "Between using your power to predict Calvin's wee spot of danger, to rescuing him, you completed a challenge."

"But did I? I mean, I didn't rescue Calvin. Ramsay did." I took another sip of coffee, mulling it over. "Maybe I was on alert for it. Subconsciously. As I did find myself going to the window a lot yesterday, in between work, and staring out at the loch. But also, that could just be because it's beautiful. Or because you told me about Kelpies and now that I know it's magickal, I'll probably stare at the water a lot."

"Speaking of Ramsay ..." Sophie leaned in, brushing over the monumental discussion about me passing magickal challenges and moving one step closer to banishing murderous Kelpies. "He's hot."

"Nope." I wagged a finger in the air. "Don't even go there."

"Oh, come on ..."

"Aren't you my boss? And you're advocating that I hook up with the man who is technically my other boss? Wouldn't HR have, like, a million things to say about this?"

Sophie glanced to where Sir Buster had crept to Hilda's feet now that Calvin was tucked safely on my lap.

"HR, do you have a problem with Willow dating her hot boss who looks like he should be chopping trees down for a living instead of sewing kilts?"

Sir Buster pawed at Hilda's legs, giving her a smile.

"See? He's got no problem with it."

"Sir Buster is your human resources department?" I asked, amused.

"Sure, why not? But, in all seriousness, was I reading

that wrong? I swear, for a moment yesterday I thought you two might kiss."

So did I.

The feeling of his lips across my cheek had done more for me than many a moment with my last boyfriend, so I'm not sure what that said about my last relationship.

"I don't think I'm really in the space to think about him like that. He's my brother's good friend. He's my boss. I just got out of a bad relationship not too long ago. I've moved to a new country. Learned I have magick, apparently, and you know, the whole Kelpies thing. One might say it's not the best time for love."

"Ohhhh, she said love." Sophie elbowed Hilda gleefully, and the older woman gave me a gentle smile.

"There's never a perfect time to find love, dear. You either make space in your life for it or you don't."

"I don't have space for it." I gave Sophie an emphatic look. "I don't."

"If you say so." Sophie held up her hands, backing off. "We haven't known each other long enough for me to harass you into dating your hottie boss, but we'll get there eventually."

Despite myself, I laughed. I really *liked* Sophie.

In fact, I'd liked everyone I'd met so far in Loren Brae. The town itself was charming, the castle stunning, and the countryside breathtaking. Be it magick or just the natural allure of a well-connected small town, I was beginning to fall in love with the direction my life was taking me. New beginnings could be challenging, I knew that from experience, but this time felt different.

There was a rightness to this move that was already

making me want to settle in and make a name for myself. Maybe, just maybe, I was finally stepping into my own. I couldn't wait to start collaborating on designs for the castle, I already loved working at the shop, and I'd even acquired a kitten.

All in all, I felt like I was ready to take on the world.

Kelpies and all.

CHAPTER EIGHTEEN

RAMSAY

Like I needed something else to make Willow more attractive.

But the fact that she had magick? Yeah, that was damn sexy. I'd always loved the fact that Scotland was renowned for its magick and myths, even more so when I'd discovered the Kelpies were real. Granted, they were terrifying, and we all should rightly be cautious of them, but a part of me was still the little boy who had fought dragons with his brother on the hill.

Life was just more exciting with a hint of danger in it.

I was just finishing up my project when Willow breezed through the door, Calvin in her arms, and a tightness in my chest released at seeing her. Maybe a part of me had been a bit worried that she'd turned tail and run after yesterday's encounter with the Kelpies. She'd said she needed time to process when she'd left the shop yesterday, and it had made me wonder if she'd be strong enough to hack it here.

I'd resisted texting her to check in, only just, but also because she hadn't technically given me her phone number. I'd taken it from the intern information that Sophie had given me.

I had acted completely on instinct the day before, racing into the loch to find the wee kitten for Willow. My thoughts flashed to her face, the terror she'd felt, both when she saw Calvin in the water and then the Kelpies. *But she'd been fearless.* Despite being soaked to the bone from the rain and the loch, she'd felt so perfect in my arms. *Right.* And the expression of awe in her eyes when she'd looked up at me, the kitty in her arms ... I hadn't been able to get her beautiful face out of my mind all night. *And that was a problem.*

"What is that?" Willow skidded to a halt, and I took the moment to appreciate her curves in motion, before glancing down at my project.

"This? It's a cat tree. Or I guess, a jungle." I surveyed my work, tilting my head. Yes, it was definitely more of a jungle than a singular tree. Knowing that a kitten would likely shred the first thing it got its wee paws on, I'd hammered a few scraps of wood together when I'd stopped to visit my parents the night before. My father's workshop had provided a plethora of loose ends to work with, and before I'd known it, the simple cat tree had turned into a playground that had barely fit into my truck. My father had enjoyed helping, and because it had been the first thing he'd really been interested in since his stroke, we'd spent a fun few hours adding burlap, engineering a cat bridge, and adding various ropes and tassels to keep the kitten entertained. Maybe it was overkill …

"No way," Willow breathed, and I looked up to see admiration in her eyes. "This is incredible. I hadn't even thought about something like this. I literally know next to nothing about cats. I brought a ribbon along as a toy. But seeing this … yeah, okay, I'm dumb. *Of course,* he needs something like this. Is that burlap? He already almost shredded my jeans this morning. His claws are sharp."

"Aye, burlap. And some nice strong rope. See how it's wrapped here? Then he can really dig in." I pointed to where I'd wrapped rope around one of the poles.

"I'm just in awe. This is, like, professional work, Ramsay. Thank you for doing this for him."

I shrugged off her praise, though her words warmed me to the core. I'd just done this so the wee cat wouldn't rip up my wool. It had nothing to do with seeing the smile that bloomed on her face, making her look like a damn ray of sunshine after a rainy day.

"Let's see if he takes to it?" I nodded to Calvin, sitting back on my heels, and Willow crouched by my side, her thigh brushing mine as she put Calvin in front of the playground.

"See? It's for you to play on, buddy."

Willow's thigh was warm against mine and I tried not to notice that her perfume smelled faintly like toasted marshmallows—was that even a thing?—and willed myself to ignore my body's response to her nearness. I was used to working alone in my shop each day, and lately, when I did socialize, it was with my mates. Having someone as overtly feminine as she was, her body rounded and curved like a seventeenth century master had painted his vision of a goddess, was making it difficult for me to concentrate. I wanted to touch her, to listen to her gasp as I figured out what aroused her, to see that same admiration in her eyes that she'd just given me for building a damn cat tree.

Och, this is not good.

I prided myself on being a good boss. Many of my employees were women. Weaving, particularly darning, tended to be a female-dominated industry. I'd always been aware when an employee was trying to flirt with me and had kept it professional at all times. It was important to me that my employees knew they were respected and that they worked in a safe environment. Sheila knew this as well, in fact she had drilled it into her managerial staff so much so that we had very little turnover, and in the few instances where a line had been crossed in a work situation, the employees had felt comfortable reporting it to management. We'd swiftly dealt with any such occurrences, and now, as I tried desperately not to think about kissing Willow's perky mouth, I berated myself for not following my own code of ethics. Even if it was just my thoughts that wanted to get down and dirty with Willow. *Not to mention she's Miles's sister. Completely. Off. Limits.*

Calvin launched himself at the cat tree, clinging to one of the poles, clambering quickly up the side and racing across the wee bridgeway I'd built. He pounced on a knot of rope I'd frayed at the end, batting at the fringe, and almost fell off the side of the bridge in his attempt to tear it apart.

"Ope, bud, careful." Willow laughed, the sound sending a shiver down my back, and I stood, needing to distance myself from her.

"Now, Calvin." The cat looked at me, seeming to already know its name, and I nodded, impressed. "This is for you to play on. Not my fabrics, understood?" The cat regarded me for a moment, and then went back to batting at the fringe. Even though I hoped to keep him distracted with the scratching post, I'd still cleaned up the workroom, putting most of the bolts of fabric away in the closet. Less temptation was better.

I glanced at Willow where she lectured Calvin about the importance of being a good shop cat.

Less temptation was *definitely* better.

"Meeting in ten minutes." I indicated the chairs by the fire and went to make a pot of tea. Sophie had dropped the bomb on me that MacAlpine Castle had decided to host a cèilidh in a month as a Spring Fling of sorts. They'd asked if I could have some extra kilts available. Apparently, both Willow and Sophie were having a hard time understanding the bespoke nature of my work, and Sophie had steamrolled me into stocking any ready-to-wear kilts that we had on hand, as well as a few accessories for those wanting to liven up their wardrobes for the dance.

"Sashes," I grumbled, returning to the fire with tea and biscuits for Willow. I'd noticed she'd been partial to the Tunnock's tea cakes I'd supplied yesterday and had made sure to add two to the plate. Not that I cared what she ate, I was just being a good boss, was all.

"Sashes?" Willow perked up, notebook in hand, and crossed her legs. She'd already sat in a chair by the fire, and I'd positioned the cat tree in perfect view of where we sat so we could keep an eye on Calvin.

"For the cèilidh."

Willow nodded vigorously, her eyes wide. "I have no idea what you're saying to me."

My lips quirked as I sat, my calendar in hand, and I stretched out my legs. "A cèilidh is a traditional Scottish dance. Sophie has informed me the castle has decided to throw one in a month. To get rid of winter blues and welcome spring she said."

"A dance?" Willow heaved in a breath, her eyes going wider.

"Aye, you've heard of them?"

"I have." Her face dropped, something flitting behind her eyes that I didn't like, a vulnerability that made me want to protect her, and I looked away, trying to stay focused on work.

Don't ask her about dancing, Ramsay. Don't.

"Everyone in the town, and likely surrounding villages, will attend. It's grand fun, if that's your thing."

Again, that flash of sadness in her eyes, and I bit back a sigh.

Damn it.

I didn't care whether Willow liked dances or not. I cared about making sure we had enough stock in the shop for said dance. That was it.

"Sophie would like us to have some accessories, kilts even, on hand for anyone looking to perk up—her words— their wardrobe. Completely ignoring the fact that we largely custom-make everything."

"And yet you'll do it, won't you?" Willow's lips curled in a hint of a smile.

"It's not my preferred way of working, you ken? But she's a force of nature that one. Sashes she says. Sashes for the women. Not as difficult to make and can be fixed with a pretty brooch around any dress you wear."

"Oh, I was looking at some examples of a penannular brooch the other day. There are some really beautiful ones made by a shop not too far from here. Hold on." Willow dipped into her bag and pulled up her iPad, flipping through the screen until she found what she was looking for. "Here. See? The thistles are nice, as are the ones with the dragon's head. Maybe we could stock them? Sell them on commission for the artist?"

"Not a bad idea. Would provide some more options for people."

"Great, I'll reach out to them today. I also had some ideas …" Willow trailed off and looked up, wincing. "Sorry, I'm just so excited to start our designs. But I know we need to work on other stuff before we get to our collaboration."

She looked so crestfallen. *But I want to see her smiling again.*

"Let's make a list of what we can feasibly stock in time for the cèilidh, and then we'll take a look at your ideas for the castle."

"Oh great. Tell me more about the … dance."

"Kay-lee," I said, pronouncing it for her slowly and she followed suit. "A cèilidh usually has a series of well-known dances, and there's a caller who'll instruct the moves."

"Like line dancing?" Willow asked.

"Somewhat, yes. It's fun. Everyone tries it … all ages. You don't need experience to give it a go." Again, Willow shuttered her eyes.

"Don't like dances?" I finally asked, despite my promise to myself to keep the topic just to business.

"I wouldn't know. I've never been asked to one." Willow scribbled something on her notebook, avoiding my eyes.

"Do you need to be asked to one to go?" I asked, genuinely curious. Anyone could attend a cèilidh, and most people went with groups of friends or their families.

"Most of the ones in high school you did. Prom, that kind of thing, all needed a date."

"Why wouldn't anyone ask you?" I asked, genuinely surprised. Willow was a knock-out, both in personality and looks, and I couldn't imagine a man not being proud to have her on his arm. Or a boy, I supposed, if we were talking about high school. I cast my mind back to my impression of her as a kid. I remembered her dying her hair some weird colors, and she'd definitely worn some outlandish clothes. Had she been pretty then? I honestly couldn't remember because I'd been older and had had my eyes on the lasses in the class above me.

They were more developed.

Sad to say, but hormones were a powerful thing. And, yeah, I'd been pie-eyed over a lass two years older than me who'd barely known my name. Nothing had ever come of it, much to my teenaged broken heart, but I couldn't remember paying much attention to Willow one way or the other. But surely boys in her class had.

Willow huffed out a laugh and gestured with her hand to her body.

"And?"

"Oh, come on, Ramsay. Don't make me say it."

"Say what?" I asked, surprised to see anger flash across

Willow's face. She was so perpetually cheerful that it was rare to see that bite of frustration.

"Seriously?" Willow scoffed. When I just looked at her, dumbfounded, she rolled her eyes. "I'm fat, Ramsay. Curvy. Plus-sized. Whatever you want to call it. But to highschoolers, it was just fat with a capital F. I embrace that word now, because I've learned to love my body, but it sucked growing up. Kids can be pretty cruel."

"You're not …" I stopped myself and held up a hand when Willow looked ready to bite my head off.

"There's nothing wrong with being bigger, Ramsay."

"I'm not saying—" I pinched the bridge of my nose, feeling like I was navigating a minefield. "Och, I hear what you're saying, aye? I stopped myself. I didn't mean. Yes, you're right, the word fat is often used as though it is a bad thing. Which is stupid, really, because we welcome it in food, don't we? Add more fat in and everything tastes better, doesn't it? I guess what I meant to say is that I think you're mind-blowingly beautiful, and any man, or boy, who couldn't see that needs to get their eyes checked. It's their loss, isn't it then?"

Willow's mouth had rounded to a perfect O shape at my rant, and I wasn't sure how to take it, so I rushed to reassure her that I wasn't trying to insult her body and that I accepted her just as she was.

"Seriously, Willow. You're a damn goddess. You would be at *any* size, because you have the personality of a fecking angel, but add in those killer curves and that damn mouth, and och, it's enough to bring any man to his knees. Or woman, if that's, um, your thing."

I'd never asked her if she preferred women, had I? I

hadn't asked her much about herself at all, I realized, instead just doing my best to scramble away from her so my heart didn't do something stupid like jump off a ledge and fall head over heels for this woman. She'd been sunshine in a bottle as a child, and now, literally lit my shop with the smile that beamed from her face.

I could use this type of light in my life.

Where the hell had that thought come from? And how?

I seriously hadn't had time during the last decade to date all that seriously. I'd taken a lass or several out to the occasional meal, but it had only really been a precursor to a night of sex. At least I was always honest and up-front with my expectations. A few short relationships had sprung up here and there. But anything long-term had been completely off the radar.

So why was I thinking about wanting light in my life?

Standing up, I bent to help Calvin unhook one of his wee claws from a particularly gnarly piece of rope, grateful for the distraction, yet helpless to stop the sudden flow of words from my mouth.

"And that's braw if that's your thing. It's none of my business, you ken? Either way, I'm sorry you missed out on dances growing up. You won't have to miss out on this one, and I'm happy to go with you if you're nervous about attending."

Shite, had I just asked her to the cèilidh?

"Are you asking me to the dance?" Her tone was incredulous, and I couldn't bring myself to look in her direction. She was giving me an out, and I could clarify that I'd meant just as friends, or that we could go as a group, but since she'd clearly been hurt by stupid teenage boys not asking her to stupid dances in the past, I'd just add to it by backpedaling now. I certainly didn't want to contribute to more hurt for her.

Bloody hell, I'd neatly boxed myself in, hadn't I?

"I'd be honored if you'd accompany me to the cèilidh, Willow."

"Jeez, well, yes, thank you very much, Ramsay. I'd love to go."

A quick glance showed me she was glowing, literally glowing, and I had to restore some sort of balance here or I was about to break my code of ethics and bury my face in her lap.

"I need to show Calvin where his litter box is. Then I'll take a look at your designs before the first appointment of the day."

As I left the room, her voice floated after me.

"Oh, and while I find women to be beautiful, Ramsay, I prefer men."

My blood heated, and I glared down at where Calvin bit my finger, testing his strength on me.

I guess we both were testing our strength now.

CHAPTER NINETEEN

WILLOW

I was going to my first dance.

I couldn't believe it. I mean, I could, because I was an adult and had gone to clubs and stuff in New York, but not while on a date.

Sixteen-year-old me was still freaking out, even though it had been over a week since Ramsay had asked me to go with him and thus far, he hadn't retracted his invitation.

Time was already starting to fly by. Ramsay and I had neatly fallen into a rhythm where we spent an hour or so each day collaborating on ideas for the castle where time allowed, and the rest was trying to manage his admittedly impressive business. He still barely talked to me, grunting his answers most days, but that didn't mean he was cold to me.

Not in the slightest.

He always had my favorite "biscuits" on hand. He'd smacked my hand—*gently*—when I'd called them cookies one morning. He noticed when I was cold, and would add a log to the fire, or if the music annoyed me, he'd switch the playlist. One day, I'd been struggling with a headache and two paracetamols had shown up with a glass of water by my desk. He badgered me into taking breaks, tried to force me into letting Calvin stay with him each night, and more often than not, gave me a ride home from work if the weather was bad. And still, getting him to open up was as easy as chipping away at marble.

I was beginning to learn a few things though. His dad had recently had a stroke, which was what had brought him back to Loren Brae. He and his brother didn't speak anymore, which made me sad for him, but I didn't remember his brother at all from our time in Scotland. He was older than Ramsay, and while I wasn't sure where his brother had been when we'd been over to visit, I knew I'd never met him. It had always been just Ramsay and Miles, wreaking havoc around town. Ramsay made it clear he didn't much care for small talk, even more so when it danced too close to anything personal. That didn't stop me from talking to him though. I talked to him all day long, taking his grunts as encouragement, and told him random tidbits about my life as we worked together. I liked to chat, and since Ramsay hadn't yet specifically told me to shut up, I figured he was accepting it. For now.

On one memorable occasion, Ramsay had startled me rearranging the closet, and I'd almost fallen off the small ladder I'd climbed up to reach the highest shelf. Which had landed me in the impossible situation of Ramsay's face pressed firmly to my butt, his hands grazing my breasts, as he caught me before I broke every bone in my body.

Neither of us spoke about that moment.

I *may* have dreamt about it though.

In turn, I badgered him into trying new music, made sure he ate regularly, and encouraged him to be more sociable by inviting customers into the shop even when he skewered me with looks that would have made most grown men cry. I updated his website, researched ideas for our collaboration, and in general, fell in love with small-town life. Who knew that I'd love it so much more than the hustle and bustle of New York City?

When I'd finally called Dad, he'd been cautiously happy for me. At least he knew Ramsay. That had helped him accept where I'd landed. Naturally, there had been no talk of Kelpies, kittens who could somehow insert thoughts, or magick sewing scissors.

In all honesty, I felt as if I was where I was meant to be.

Now, we sat at the table after a walk-in client had just left, gushing about the cèilidh, ecstatic after having ordered a pink sash for her pink dress. Even I couldn't believe it when Ramsay had calmly shown her a few swatches and promised it would be finished in time for the dance. And now my teenaged self was back to having an inner meltdown about the dance, because I didn't even know what to wear, let alone how to dance.

But adult me was calmly sitting with Ramsay, showing him my sketches, trying to push down his monologue about my body the other day that surfaced every time he leaned his head close to me.

I think you're mind-blowingly beautiful, and any man,

or boy, who couldn't see that needs to get their eyes checked. You're a damn goddess. You would be at any size, because you have the personality of a fecking angel, but add in those killer curves and that damn mouth, and och, it's enough to bring any man to his knees.

No one, and I mean *no one*, had ever made me feel so beautiful like I had that day. Somehow, though, I'd pretended that his words hadn't made my insides go liquid. It had taken everything in my power *not* to climb into his lap and kiss him until we both were senseless.

Because that would be wrong.

He was just being nice because he was my brother's friend, I told myself, and helping me acclimate to a new town. He'd told me himself that groups of people attended these dances together and that nobody needed an invitation, hadn't he? I really needed to not read into this. Particularly when he'd come back from showing Calvin the litterbox and had barely said two words to me afterward. In fact, his little rant about my body had probably been the most consecutive words the man had ever spoken to me yet. I'd just tuck that away to examine another time, because let me tell you, a man saying those things about me, in that delicious Scottish accent? Oh yeah, I had been secretly feasting off that compliment for days.

"Tartan fanny packs." Ramsay eyed me in horror, and I rushed to explain.

"See? Look, I know they were popular in the eighties and all that, but they're making a comeback. For real."

Ramsay pointed carefully to a sketch of a bag that I had on my iPad.

"You want us to make a *fanny* pack?" Something indecipherable hovered in his expression.

"Um, yes?"

"How much can you fit in it?"

"Well, a good amount, I suppose. Depending on the size. We can try different types and see."

Ramsay's face remained passive, yet I sensed I was missing something.

"And will you let other people use it, lass?"

"Um, I guess? It depends on if the owner wants to share it?" What an odd question.

"Is it free or do you pay for it?"

"*Of course* you pay for it." I squinted at Ramsay in confusion.

"How, um, big is it?"

"Ugh, Ramsay, I don't know, big enough."

"Can more than one person use it at a time?"

"What? I have no idea. I'm sure more than one person can put something in it if needed." Had he lost his mind?

"Is it for men or women? Or both?"

"Both, if they like it."

"That tracks." Ramsay sniffed, wiping his hand across his face, and I caught something in his eyes. "Do you post photos online of it or is that private?"

"Why would it ... Ramsay! What is going *on*?" I threw up my hands in exasperation. "If you don't like the fanny pack, just say so."

"Oh no, darling, I dearly love a good fanny, that I do."

At that, Ramsay smirked. "Maybe not for the beach though. Tough when you get sand in them."

"Fine, forget the fanny pack. Clearly you think this is dumb." I made to get up and stopped when Ramsay threw his head back and laughed, the sound rolling over me in one delightful thunderous wave. It was the first time I'd been the one to make him laugh, freely like this, and the sound stopped me in my tracks. I swear my toes curled in my boots. I gaped at him as he wiped his eyes.

"Och, lass. I'm sorry to be the one to tell you this, but fanny means something different over here."

"Excuse me?"

"Fanny is ..." Ramsay nodded toward my pants, and I looked down at myself.

"Is what?"

"Your, um ..."

Calvin meowed and Ramsay threw back his head and laughed once more. He got up from the table, howling, and walked into the back room while I furiously googled the Scottish meaning for fanny on my iPad.

Oh.

Ohhhhh.

"Damn it, Ramsay! How was I supposed to know it meant vagina? What the heck do you call them here?"

"I mean, colloquially, we have many terms ... fanny, fud, vulvarine, honey pot, bearded clam if you're crude—"

"The bags, Ramsay, the bags," I said quickly, my eyes rounding in horror.

"Oh those? We call them bum bags."

"Fanny means bum in the States," I said, enunciating

clearly in case he still didn't get it. "I would not, nor would I ever, suggest we make a—"

"Kitty bag?" Ramsay winked at Calvin and laughed again when I cringed.

"I might hate you. I think that I do. I can't believe ..." I winced thinking about his questions. "How many people can use it, he asks. Like it's a damn toy to be passed around."

"It's a fair question, lass."

"Do people pay for it?" I mocked him in a high voice, and he threw his head back and laughed once more.

"Also a fair question."

"I can't. I can't be with you." I glanced at the time because I had to look away as my cheeks were burning. "Our first appointment is almost here. Go away."

"It's my shop."

I glared at him long enough that he retreated into the back room while I tidied the shop, staunchly ignoring him when I went to wash the teacups, and then positioned myself back at the desk to welcome our first client.

Pulling out my iPad, I drew a big X through my fanny pack design. Nope, no way in hell were we making those. I would never live this down.

By the time we'd worked our way through the appointments, as well as successfully fended off random passersby who I cheerfully welcomed into the store, staunchly ignoring Ramsay's "no walk-ins" rule in between appointments just to annoy him, I'd largely lived down my embarrassment from earlier. Just as I was getting ready to close up, a pretty woman with dusky skin and a shock of red curls popped through the door.

"Am I allowed in? I'm told Ramsay bites." A whisper of Boston tinged her words and I immediately warmed to my fellow American.

"He's more bark than anything. Hi, I'm Willow."

"I'm Lia, the chef up at the castle."

"Lia! Finally, we meet. I've been meaning to stop at the restaurant, but I heard you were gone." I rushed over and gave her a hug, my Midwest niceness propelling me to do so, and she laughed, accepting it. I mean, we were in the same Order, right? It was fine to hug her. I happened to be a touchy-feely person in general, and I couldn't help but notice that Ramsay stiffened every time I laid my hand on his arm. He never shook it off though. And I didn't stop.

The man had serious muscles.

"Munroe stole me away for a mini vacation. We're planning a wedding, and it has been a bit hectic. But since this is our slow season, I was able to take some time from the restaurant."

"Well, I'm glad you stopped in. I've heard nothing but great things about Grasshopper."

"Good to hear it." Lia glanced around the shop, interest in her warm brown eyes. "This place is nice. I know Munroe has several kilts, but maybe we should get something special for the wedding."

"I'm happy to spend Munroe's money any day," Ramsay said from the doorway to the back room, Calvin cradled in his arms. "Good to see you, Lia."

"Awww, who is this guy?" Lia walked over to Ramsay, patting his shoulder in greeting before scratching behind Calvin's ear. Even in a week the kitten had grown, and he'd become more adventurous for it. We were constantly lecturing him about things, but strangely enough, Calvin seemed to understand exactly what was off limits for him and what wasn't.

He also continued to communicate with me in images.

Sometimes it was when he was hungry.

Other times it was if he didn't like a customer.

Lately, it had been a lot about Ramsay. I couldn't quite piece together what he was trying to tell me.

Or maybe I was just ignoring it.

Either way, Calvin had grown just as attached to Ramsay, and I had to admit, watching the tiny kitten follow the massive muscular man all over the shop made my heart twist. I mean, it would for anyone, no? One time, I walked into the back room to see Ramsay on the floor on his back, a screwdriver in hand, adjusting something under his worktable. At his side, Calvin lay on his back, mirroring Ramsay, surveying his work. I'd been tempted to offer both hard hats, but instead had pulled out my phone and snapped a photo without them knowing.

Not that I'd ever tell Ramsay I'd taken his photo.

And I'd only looked at it a time or two since. Maybe twice.

Okay, like ten times.

Either way, it was just a cute photo. That was all.

"I'm popping by because I was on the way to the market and Sophie had mentioned you wanted to stock up."

"Oh, I do. That would be great." I glanced between Calvin and Ramsay. "Can you watch Calvin? I can come back for him after."

"He can stay with me tonight."

"Absolutely not. I wouldn't want to put you out."

"Nae bother, hen."

"Nope. We're coming back for him."

We had this argument at the end of every day at the shop, and so far, Calvin had come home with me every night. I loved how he snuggled into my side, comforting me if I was restless.

My familiar, Agnes had suggested when she'd met him.

I'd never heard of such a thing, but now I loved the idea that Calvin might be magickal as well. I mean, why the hell not? It seemed anything went in the magickal world these days. I'd even heard about Shona's gnomes, though I'd yet to meet her. That was next on my list. Because, are you freaking kidding me? Of course I wanted to meet a real live gnome.

"Shall I let you guys box this one out while I wait in the car?" Lia winked at me.

"Nope. He's mine. I'm coming back for him."

"I saved him. He's mine." Ramsay glared at me.

"Maybe I *will* fight you," I said. "I do love a good throat punch."

"Oh, me too," Lia gushed. "My Boston side can't help but love the occasional throwdown."

Ramsay blinked between the two of us, muttered something about "bloodthirsty women" and disappeared with Calvin into his back room.

"Thanks for taking me, I appreciate it. At some point I'll probably have to look at more serious transportation," I said, grabbing my purse and stepping out front with Lia behind me. The last of the afternoon light was just fading, and while it was starting to warm up just a smidge, the blustery wind that rocketed down the side of the hills wasn't quite ready to give up on winter yet. I hurried to her car.

"How's it been living in Loren Brae? I mean, Boston is a pretty big city to leave behind. Do you miss it?" I asked Lia as she drove to the outskirts of Loren Brae where there was a larger supermarket along with a pharmacy and small post office.

"I do, at times. But not enough to make me want to go back. I miss baseball." Lia laughed when I pumped my fist in the air. Then I gasped.

"Oh no. Sox fan?"

"Duh."

"Twins fan."

"Well, I guess this friendship is over already." Lia pretended like she was going to pull the car over and kick me out, and I laughed.

"Hey, it's not as bad as being a Yankees fan."

"Truth, I'll give you that. Okay, I'm going to run into the chemist then I'll meet you in the market?"

"Great, thanks. I don't think I need too much. I just feel bad that Hilda is making like every meal."

"She loves it. I promise you she does. There is nothing that lights that woman up more than having people to cook for. But I get it. Some nights you probably just want to be on your own too."

"Yeah, it's still an adjustment coming here. Plus, you know, the Order stuff. I need some me time too."

"I know. Come by for breakfast tomorrow. It's the only time of the day that I'm really alone. We can talk more about the Order, and I'll make you something yummy."

"You don't have to cook for me," I protested, and Lia

laughed again as we got out of the car, waving my words away with a hand.

"Cooking is my love language. It's fine. Okay, see you in a bit."

I wandered into the store, pleased that I would have a moment to shop for a few things and gathered a few bags of sweet and salty popcorn in my arms, along with a new addiction—salt and vinegar chips. Or crisps, as they were called here. Chips were French fries, apparently. Humming to myself, I turned the corner of an aisle and ran smack dab into someone, my snacks going flying to the floor.

"Oh, shite. That's my bad." A handsome man winked a smile at me, grabbing my arms to stop me from tumbling forward. I looked up at him, gasping in surprise as he laughed down at me. Seriously, what was with the men here? They were all so damn good-looking.

"I'm so sorry. I truly wasn't looking where I was going. Daydreaming, I guess."

"American, are you? Here on holiday?" The man bent, gathering my snacks before I could get them, and held up the bag of crisps, shaking his head at me.

"No, I live here now." It was funny to say it, I realized, but it also felt really good.

Loren Brae was home now.

And I was actually doing something with my life that I was excited about. Warmth filled me, and I beamed up at the man, not for the reasons he likely thought, but nevertheless, I was in a good mood.

"In that case, I'd better show you the secrets if you're planning to make your home here. Come on then." The man motioned me back down the crisps aisle and pointed to a different brand than I'd picked up. "It's Mackie's you're wanting. The best."

"Oh, I didn't know." I switched bags and smiled at him. He vaguely reminded me of Ramsay, now that I looked more closely at him, but they had different hair color, and this man was shorter and stockier than Ramsay. Much more charming though, since he'd already spoken more words to me than Ramsay did most days.

"Trust me on this one. You'll never look back."

"I'm so glad I ran into you then. Any other grocery store secrets I should be aware of?"

The man crossed his arms and thought about it for a moment.

"What are you shopping for?"

"Largely a few snacks for my apartment. Late night nibbles. Light dinners."

"Ah yes, snacks for the flat. So far, you're doing grand with your choices. You'll need shortbread, naturally. Have you tried Irn Bru yet?"

I looked at him, confused, and he threw his head back and laughed.

"Tell me you know what I'm talking about."

"Nope, no clue."

"Och, lass, you're in for a real treat. I wish I could be there when you tried it." The man led me toward an aisle with soda. "My name's Andrew, by the way. Yours?"

Something niggled at the back of my brain, but I couldn't figure it out.

"Willow."

"That's a nice name for a bonnie lass. If it's not too forward of me, maybe I could take you for a proper drink this week? If my Irn Bru recommendation doesn't turn you off us Scots forever, that is. I've got loads of insider tips I could share about Loren Brae."

A date?

Was I getting picked up in a grocery store of all places? I'd heard of such things but had never been privy to it before. Flustered, I smiled shyly at him.

"Um, maybe? If this Irn Bru doesn't kill me that is."

Andrew laughed, and the sound made me warm to him even more.

"Tell you what, lass. I'll give you my number. Text me later after you've had the Irn Bru. If you survive, I'll treat you to a proper drink."

"Okay, you're on." I cupped my snacks in one arm while I added Andrew's number to my phone. Then he handed me a neon orange can that I eyed suspiciously.

"Is this an orange pop?"

"I don't know what pop is." Andrew shrugged a shoulder.

Ope, my Minnesota was showing.

"I meant soda."

"Mmm. Irn Bru is its own experience. Trust me on this."

"Okay, random person I just met in a grocery store. We'll see."

"I'm off then. Hope to hear from you soon, Willow." With that Andrew waved and left the store without buying anything, and I squinted after him. Why did he feel so familiar to me? Shrugging, I took my items to the checkout, still eyeing the neon can suspiciously.

"Is Irn Bru any good?" I asked the cashier.

"Oh, it goes down a treat."

Well, I guess that was that. I'd be trying something new, *and* I had a date. Maybe it would take my mind off my burgeoning crush on Ramsay. The more I thought about it, the more I realized that a date was exactly what I needed.

Nothing serious, of course. I didn't actually want or need a relationship right now. But the novelty of being picked up in a grocery store was just too much for me to pass up. Plus, maybe it would provide a tiny distraction from thinking impure thoughts about my boss.

CHAPTER TWENTY

Ramsay

"Dad? Mum?" I called, pushing inside the back door of my childhood home.

I'd grown up near Loren Brae, in a comfortable two-story, three-bedroom cottage on a large plot of land that allowed plenty of space for growing boys to work off pent-up energy from long days confined at our school desks. Andrew and I used to race across the garden, clambering up any trees we could find, certain we were knights protecting our castle.

A simpler time, and one I didn't like to think about now that Andrew had grown to be the man he was.

It had been over a week since I'd last checked in on my parents, and I wanted to update them on how things were going with Willow in the shop, as well as see if they'd heard about the cèilidh at MacAlpine Castle. When I'd found myself mooning around the store once Willow had collected Calvin after her trip to the shops, I realized that maybe I needed to socialize more than I had been lately. I was beginning to lean into hermit life with gusto. Prior to Loren Brae, while I hadn't been exactly a social butterfly, there'd been a weekly dart and pool league I'd try to stop in for and, when I was in Edinburgh, I loved going to see comedy shows at Monkey Barrel Comedy Club. More or less though, it was an unattached life, with nobody to answer to and an empty flat to come home to.

Muffled voices sounded from the sunroom, and I wandered past framed photos of my childhood—me in my school uniform, the family on a day trip at Edinburgh Castle, my parents at my graduation—and followed the scent of peanut butter through the house. Mum must have baked her famous crispy peanut butter cookies.

"Ramsay!" Mum beamed at me. A woman just shy of sixty, she had a trim figure, dark hair that curled to her shoulders, and was partial to matching knit sets and colorful silk scarves. Today she wore a plum cardigan with a floral and striped knotted scarf and stood when I entered the room.

I skidded to a stop.

"What are you doing here?" I demanded, my fingers curling into my palms, forming fists.

Andrew sat next to my father on the loveseat, a crossword puzzle between them.

It had been six years since I'd last seen Andrew, and he looked healthy enough, aside from a bit of weight he'd put on and the dark circles that hung under his eyes. He took after our mother's side of the family, with lighter coloring and a shorter build. I hated that I wanted to hug him just as much as I wanted to shove a fist in his face. We'd once been close, and it was hard to see through the hurt that clouded the good memories. I didn't *want* to see through the hurt. I no longer trusted Andrew, and the pain of his betrayal only served as a reminder to keep my guard up with him at all times.

"Can't a son visit his father when he's ailing?" Andrew held up his hands, as though he hadn't stolen and lied to our entire family.

"He had a stroke months ago, Andrew. Which you knew about because I called you and left a message. As did Mum. You're just showing up now?"

"Unfortunately, I was on a work trip in China. I'm just now home."

"You were months in China? I find that hard to believe."

"Truly, I was. Working on factory arrangements."

"And taking jobs away from our people."

Andrew's lip curled, and his eyes heated.

"Boys, that's enough. Andrew is our son, and he's always welcome here," Mum jumped in, trying to ease the tension that hung in the room.

"Even after he stole your money? Lied to us?"

"Bloody hell, Ramsay. You're always blethering on about this. I've apologized, haven't I then?" Andrew sighed.

"Saying sorry doesn't mean you've pulled your head out of your arse. Your actions don't show you're sorry. You're never around, you've done nothing to help, and I haven't seen a damn pound of the money that you stole, have I?" My blood heated as I stepped closer to him, wanting him out of this house. "I'm the one who paid Mum and Dad back."

"So? It's not like you need the money."

"That's not the point."

"Ramsay." My father's voice was soft, and I tore my eyes from my brother's face, where his expression bordered on a smirk.

"What? I'm not wrong, am I?"

"Let's just have our tea as a family," Mum urged, and I turned, catching the pleading look in her eyes.

My father hadn't been able to handle big emotions since his stroke, preferring calm environments with low stress. He didn't drive anymore, much to his frustration, but day by day he was growing stronger, and his faculties were returning to him. As much as I wanted to drag my brother from the house and toss him in the yard, locking the door behind me, I needed to respect my parents' wishes.

"I'm watching you." I pointed a finger in Andrew's face, and he rolled his eyes.

"Enough with this shite. There's bigger stuff in life to worry about, isn't there?" Andrew stood, his head only coming just above my shoulder, and I resisted the urge to shoulder check him.

But just barely.

"There now, that's lovely. My two boys home for tea. Come on then, I've baked your favorite cookies, Ramsay."

"You always were her favorite," Andrew mumbled at my side.

"Likely because I'm not a thieving bastard."

Andrew sighed and Mum, sensing danger, hooked an arm through mine and pulled me toward the kitchen. I glanced over my shoulder, catching my brother handing my father a folder, and my eyes narrowed.

"What does he want?"

"Nothing, Ramsay. He's just here for a wee visit."

"I doubt it. He wants something. What did he ask for?"

My mother sighed and opened the fridge, pouring herself a glass of white wine. Holding up the bottle she raised an eyebrow at me.

"Can't. Drove over."

"Och, right." Mum shook her head, waving a hand in the air, clearly distracted. "Don't be so hard on him, Ramsay. He never had what you had."

"Good character?"

"Your smarts. Your drive. Your heart." Mum smiled gently at me, and I went to her, pulling her in for a hug. She'd always been my biggest champion, and it had infuriated me when she'd cried over what Andrew had done with their savings.

"He wasn't always bad. Something changed."

"He's blinded by money, Mum. It's all that matters to him."

"He needs to find his way is all."

"At the expense of others?" I opened the fridge and pulled out a bottle of sparkling water. Pouring a glass, I lounged at the table as Mum went to the stove. "Need any help?"

"No, thanks. Just reheating a curry I made earlier this week."

"I don't trust that he's here. Is he staying with you?"

Mum shot me a guilty look over her shoulder.

"Oh, come on."

"He's my son, Ramsay. I've always said you'd both have a place in our home."

"How long is he here for?" Worry kicked up. Andrew could do a lot of damage in a short time, and I didn't like that he'd be here unsupervised. He was up to something, I could feel it in my bones.

"I don't like it."

"You don't have to like it. But you'll respect my wishes." Mum, for as sweet as she was, had a backbone. I watched her as she stirred the curry. It hadn't been easy for her, these past few months, managing my father's recovery. A once active and vibrant man, it had been a change for him to slow down and allow himself to heal. His frustration often boiled over on those closest to him, and I knew my mum took the brunt of it. That was love, though, wasn't it? Being there for your person at their best and their worst?

I want that.

Love wasn't something that had been particularly high on my agenda, so the thought startled me. Even more so when it was Willow's face that came to mind when I thought about my future. While I could admit that I'd had many a sleepless night over my gorgeous intern, love was an entirely different thing.

Lust had me wondering what her kiss would taste like.

Love had me thinking about cooking dinner together, laughing over clothing designs, taking long walks by the loch on mild summer nights.

"Understood." I narrowed my eyes at Andrew when he walked into the kitchen, his hand clamped on my dad's shoulder, the two laughing.

Catching my eye, the clarty bastard winked at me.

Och, I didn't trust him. Which meant I'd have to be extra vigilant over the next few days.

Starting with seeing what was in that folder that Andrew had passed to my father.

"I'll just use the loo before dinner." I didn't know how I was going to get through dinner, as I could barely stand to be in the same room as Andrew. Standing, I left the kitchen and detoured to the sunroom, scooping the folder off the table from where it was largely concealed under stacks of crossword books. Flipping it open, I scanned the contents, my anger reaching a boiling point.

He was asking my parents for more money.

Because, of course, he was.

This for an investment in a start-up company, that I'm sure once I did some research, would likely be a front for something nefarious. I could barely breathe through my anger, and it took everything in my power not to stalk back into the kitchen, drag my brother out into the yard, and beat him into a bloody pulp.

But the thing was? People like him would never learn. He'd keep coming back for more. If it wasn't this investment, it would be something else. What I needed to do is figure out a way to protect my parents from his slimy hands. Sliding the envelope into my coat, I returned to the kitchen and gave my brother a smile that was close to feral.

"What?" Andrew eyed me.

"How's business, Andrew? Booming? Taking advantage of people who don't know the difference between good products and fake crap?" I took my seat.

"Ramsay." My mother's tone was sharp.

"Sorry, sorry. I'll be good." Lifting my chin at Andrew, I

gave him the same look I'd give an opponent on the rugby field. His shoulders hunched.

Dinner was excruciating, but Andrew regaled my parents with tales from China, and I barely spoke, biding my time. Once dinner was over, I declined dessert and rose, having come to my decision. My mother's cheeks were flushed, clearly happy to have both her sons home, and I wasn't going to ruin that for her.

"I have to go. Andrew. A word?"

"Ramsay," Mum warned.

"Just a word. Promise." I gave her a hug, kissed the top of my dad's head and squeezed his shoulder, and Andrew followed me out into the yard. Once the door was closed, I turned on him.

"How much?" I asked, without preamble.

"How much what?" Andrew pretended to not know what I was talking about, shaking his head and raising his eyebrows. I pulled out the folder and tossed it at his feet, the wind taking a few sheets across the yard.

"Damn it, Ramsay."

"What's the investment really for?"

"It's a proper invest—"

I hauled him up by his throat, slamming his back into the stone wall of the garage, and he gasped, grappling at my hands.

"What's it for? I won't ask again." My voice was low, and I could hear my mum singing inside.

"Let me ..." Andrew gasped. I dropped him, and he gasped for breath. "For feck's sake."

I didn't respond, waiting while he caught his breath, my fists ready if he launched himself at me.

"I owe people money," Andrew finally admitted, his hands on his knees.

"Why? I thought your business was super successful."

"In theory. I have some debts."

"Gambling?"

Andrew didn't have to say it. My brother was the ultimate risktaker, always chasing a dopamine hit, and gambling was one way he fulfilled that need.

"Some." Andrew shrugged, straightening and crossing his arms over his chest. "But these guys ... they're bad news."

"I don't care."

"Bloody hell, you've gone cold."

"I stopped caring about you when you broke Mum's heart."

Andrew had the decency to wince, his eyes not meeting mine.

"How much to keep you from ever asking them for money again?"

"I don't know." Andrew shrugged, his gaze dancing around the yard, refusing to land on mine.

"If you don't answer now, I'll up it to–how much for you to never *ever* contact them again?"

"What? Come on, Ramsay." Andrew's eyes met mine in shock.

"This is the last time I'll ask. How much for you to never ask them for money again? Not for a loan. Not for a gift. Not for a donation. Never *ever* anything to do with money or investments or anything shady. When you come here, it's as a son visiting his parents only. You won't so much as accept a Christmas gift from them." My hand came up, pressing him back into the wall again. "How much?"

"One hundred and fifty. Two hundred if you've got it." Andrew's voice dripped with shame. I closed my eyes, furious that he'd gotten himself, and now me, into this situation.

Again.

"You'll sign something. Agreeing to our terms. If you break them, you sign your businesses over to me."

"That's ..."

I pressed my thumb to his Adam's apple, pushing hard enough that Andrew coughed.

"I'm not asking you to pay me back. Your payment is to leave them the hell alone. They're good people, Andrew. How they raised a piece of shite like you, I don't know."

Yeah, it was mean. But I didn't care. I protected those I loved at all costs. Even if it was against another so-called member of the family.

"Understood."

"I'll get the paperwork drawn up."

With that, I left him standing there, his head down.

As far as I was concerned, he was no brother of mine.

I was done pretending I cared emotionally.

The stupid shite had gone too fecking far. "One hundred and fifty. Two hundred if you've got it." Of course, I've got the fucking money, but I hate that I have to give it to the clarty bastard.

And even still, my heart twisted at the memories of what he'd once meant to me. I wasn't sure I'd ever get over the person he'd turned into, but I guess that was my own problem to deal with. For now, I just needed to get out of here and contact my solicitor.

I wished I had Willow to go home to. I could use her sunshine right now. Even if I couldn't reciprocate, it was hard to not be around her and absorb her constant cheerfulness. I knew she'd had some issues with her brother, but they were still in contact, even though she was keeping him at arm's length at the moment. I wondered if she would agree with what I'd done here tonight. To my surprise, I wanted to ask her opinion, her viewpoint mattering to me.

Maybe I'd bring myself to talk to her about it tomorrow. She had a good head on her shoulders, and she might be able to ease the sadness currently banded around my heart. I didn't really need anyone to validate my decisions, but something propelled me to want to speak to her about this. Maybe it wasn't such a bad thing to lean on a friend once in a while.

CHAPTER TWENTY-ONE

WILLOW

"Come on, Calvin. We're going to find the restaurant. Somehow." Calvin struggled in my arms, so I put him down on the hallway floor and he scampered forward. I'd already learned that I wouldn't lose him, he never strayed far from me or Ramsay anyway, and I took a turn down another passageway in the castle.

It was positively pouring this morning. It was the kind of rain that made me want to burrow deeper into the comforters and hold on to the tendrils of the sexy dream I was having.

I'd been sitting on the worktable in the shop, my short sparkly skirt on, and Ramsay had been towering over me.

His hands gripping my thighs, spreading my legs, until he scooted me forward so I brushed against his hardness.

One flick of a button, and my breasts had been exposed to

his mouth, and I'd bowed back as he'd suckled, his mouth hot against my skin.

No. Stop thinking about that.

He's your boss. He's not interested in you like that.

I'd promised Lia that I'd come by for breakfast, and grateful that I didn't have to step outside in the sleeting rain to do so, I now took myself on an adventure through the castle, hoping that at some point I'd land at the restaurant's door.

"Moo?"

It came out almost as a whimper, and I hurried to catch up to where Calvin had the ghost coo cornered.

"Clyde. He's just a kitten."

Calvin arched his back and pawed the air, and Clyde whimpered once more, hunching his shoulders and stomping the ground with a hoof. He shook his head, his large horns looking threatening, shaggy coat sticking out around his head.

He looked at me, pleading.

If a ghost coo could plead, that was.

Somewhere along the way, I'd stopped being so scared of Clyde, likely because he had demonstrable feelings about my little kitten. I took a moment to marvel at the ghost, the dim rays of light from the wall sconces filtering through his transparent image and wondered just how many other ghosts wandered the castle halls. Sophie hadn't indicated there were any others that called the castle home, but if Clyde could wander about this massive place, so could anyone else, I supposed.

An image flashed in my head, of Calvin laughing, and I narrowed my eyes down at the little kitten. We were getting better at communicating through mental imagery, which was wild in itself, and now I realized that he was just having fun scaring Clyde.

Because he could.

Not because he was scared.

"You stinky little devil." I scooped up Calvin, and he blinked at me, the picture of innocence.

"Clyde, he's just playing with you. Don't let him scare you."

Clyde tilted his head, and I held Calvin out to him.

"Truly. He's just playing."

The ghost coo tentatively leaned forward until his nose reached the kitten's. The two booped noses, making my heart melt, and then Clyde raced down the hallway, bellowing his joy.

"Jeez." I almost jumped out of my skin at his bellow. "The acoustics in this place are ridiculous."

MacAlpine Castle was built as a square, yet some of the passageways inside the castle twisted and turned in odd ways. I wonder if that had been planned as protection from an attack so there wasn't an easy in or out. I'd possibly read somewhere about having different-sized steps to trip up intruders running up the stairs. I took my time, not caring too much if I got lost, just enjoying exploring one of the oldest buildings I'd ever been in. I found myself in a drawing room of sorts, with a glass case that housed three different wedding gowns from days of yore.

"Oh," I whispered, breakfast forgotten, as I made my way to the display. Three different styles, reflecting three different eras, and my eyes drank in the details. One dress had a deep V at the waist, likely worn with a corset, and a large, pleated silk skirt. Lace flounced at the shoulders, and tiny seed pearls had been embroidered at the neckline. How many hours ... days—*months?*—would it have taken to hand sew all those pearls? How were they all such similar sizes and shapes? Where did they find them all back when this dress was made?

What would *my* wedding dress look like?

Where did that thought come from?

Likely because I was still working on a design to wear for the upcoming dance. I'd consulted Sophie, who had been absolutely useless when it came to attire for a cèilidh, but Hilda had stepped in and offered some suggestions. From my understanding, anything could go, but because I was who I was, I wanted to make something special. I was so used to modifying or creating my own clothes for myself, that I reasoned it wouldn't take much to create something pretty for the dance.

Ramsay loved my body.

I think you're mind-blowingly beautiful, and any man, or boy, who couldn't see that needs to get their eyes checked. You're a damn goddess. You would be at any size, because you have the personality of a fecking angel, but add in those killer curves and that damn mouth, and och, it's enough to bring any man to his knees.

A shiver ran across my skin, and I turned away from the wedding dresses, pressing a kiss to Calvin's head, and left the drawing room, my mind on Ramsay. I'd probably replayed his little monologue in my head far more than I'd needed to, and he'd never once mentioned my looks in any capacity since then. In fact, the more I tried to get close to him, the further he pulled back. I could read signals, and I wasn't the type of woman to throw myself at a man who wasn't interested in me, so I'd fallen back into a routine of trying to make him less grumpy. So far, I hadn't largely succeeded, but I had sensed a subtle softening in him. I'd call that a win and be happy I had a date to redirect my attention to. Not that I thought Andrew was going to be a sweeping romance or anything like that, but since the only man I currently spent all my time with barely grunted answers at me most days, a decent conversation with someone else would be a nice distraction at the very least.

And sometimes we just did things for a bit of an ego boost, didn't we?

The reality was, I wanted Ramsay to find me desirable. It was stupid. I knew it was reckless to have these feelings for someone I worked with, let alone for Miles's best friend. I'd already been burned by crossing lines in a professional relationship before. Adding the brother component to it? Yeah, those feelings were just plain stupid. Yet the more I spent time with Ramsay, the more I genuinely enjoyed his company, respected him as a boss, and really liked him. Not that I'd tell Miles that.

My brother had been hounding me for information about my new job, to the point where I'd threatened to block him if he didn't let up. I'd finally brought the matter up to my father.

"Threads, he's just worried about you."

"Can't he worry about something else? I'm fine. Thriving, in fact."

"I'm glad to hear it. Be patient with Miles. He's never been the adventurer that you have. What you do? It's outside his comfort zone. And when he doesn't understand some-

thing, he just assumes it's the wrong way. But it's not, I promise you. Your way is equally as good as his way. You're both just different."

That had stopped me in my tracks. I'd never really considered it from that angle before, that my brother worried about me not because he didn't trust my ability to handle new experiences, necessarily, but because he wouldn't take those same risks. My father was absolutely right. Miles was a down-home Minnesota boy who thrived in the predictable routine of darts league at the corner bar, opening day tailgating, and early summer mornings on his boat. While I enjoyed aspects of that life, I didn't thrive there. But here? Where life was unpredictable, and the days were filled with new things and experiences? Growing knowledge and seeing an expert at his craft? I was glowing.

I wasn't sure if it was this newfound magick, or if it was that I so enjoyed bantering designs back and forth with Ramsay, all while getting to know Loren Brae better, but I could feel my roots starting to curl into the earth here. Maybe Miles and I both enjoyed small-town life, just in different countries. It could be a connecting point, at the very least, and I made a note to try a different approach with him the next time I decided to answer one of his text messages.

"Oh, here we are."

"Brrrp." Calvin did one of his half-meow's half-purrs and I ducked my head into a doorway.

"Lia? You here?"

"Yup, come on through," Lia called, and I entered directly into a kitchen that was far more impressive than I was expecting it to be. I mean, I guess I hadn't really much thought about kitchens being extraordinary or not, but this one really was. Likely because it was in a badass historical castle and all, but the room was this incredible blend of both historical and modern that made my mouth drop open.

"Wow," I said, and then motioned with Calvin in my arms. "Also, can I bring a cat in here?"

"Likely not if the health inspector came through, but I've got some assistance to keep this place magickly clean." Lia beamed at me from where she whisked something in a bowl at the counter. Her hair was tied back under a bandana, and she wore a navy apron. A green grasshopper pendant sparkled from a chain around her neck.

"I've heard ..." I glanced around. "Sophie mentioned a brownie?"

"Broonie in Scotland." Lia came forward and scratched Calvin's ear, the cat bumping his head against her hand. "You can put him down. Though I'm not sure if Brice likes cats or not."

"Is that the broonie's name?"

A soft chattering had me glancing to the corner, but I didn't see anything out of sorts. A shiver went down the back of my neck. I mean, listen, I was doing pretty well with accepting magick, but I had no idea what to expect with a little kitchen elf. All I kept picturing was the scary trolls from an old eighties movie I'd seen back in the day that kidnapped children and ate them.

"That it is. He's around somewhere. He'll make himself known if he feels comfortable. Coffee?"

"Please." I put Calvin on the floor, and he did a long stretch before wandering after Lia while I turned to take in the room. A massive spice cabinet caught my attention, the wood worn with age, each tiny drawer labeled with the name of the spices. A double arched wood door was closed against the rain, chunky stone walls reflected the age of the castle, and music played softly in the background. It was a cozy spot, and I sat at a table with kitchen stools tucked beneath and put my bag against the wall. "Mind if I sketch while you cook? I just had this idea in a dream that I want to get down."

"Not at all. Tell me more about it."

"I kind of want to play with tartan vests for women but in the style of motorcycle jackets, you know? A little edgier, a little bit punk. Maybe mixed with some dark lace. I just think there'd be such a fun way to add tartan on different looks without always having to be just a kilt or just a jacket. Trimmings, accessories, hints of tartan, you know? I also really like mixing prints, and if Ramsay would be open to it, I bet we could do something really cool with tartan and flowers."

"Like how?" Lia came over, bringing the bowl with her, and whisked while she looked over my shoulder. I swiped through some images to find where I'd designed a black and white tartan silk scarf with huge hot pink peonies plastered across it. "Oh that's fun. Good travel scarf. Could wear it with anything, dress up or down."

"That was my thought. By making it silk, we'd give it an elegance."

"Smart. People are always looking for gifts from their travels and I think something more unique like that is a good talking point. Sophie will love it, I'm sure, even if Ramsay doesn't."

"We'll see. I haven't asked him yet."

"How's that all going?" Lia pulled out a cast iron skillet and put it on the stove. "I heard he can be a bitch to work for."

"He has his moments." My lips quirked. "I'm sure you've had to work with your share of personalities in the service industry."

"Oh, for sure. I kneed my last boss in the nuts and quit on the spot. Trust me, I know difficult."

I threw my head back and laughed, immediately feeling a kinship with Lia.

"And now you're in Loren Brae. And getting married, I hear."

"My own restaurant. Love of my life. Magick. I mean, hard to believe for a poor girl like me from the streets of Boston." Lia tossed a few drops of water on the skillet, testing the temperature. "It all seemed to fall in place in a way I could never have expected."

"That's kind of how I'm feeling," I said, beginning to sketch. "Minus the love part, of course."

"Ramsay's wicked hot."

"He is."

I let the silence draw out until Lia cursed.

"Throw a girl a bone, would ya?"

"He's hot. He's also my boss and good friends with my brother."

Lia whistled, long and low, and shook her head, pouring batter into the skillet.

"That's spicy, isn't it?"

"Just a bit. But, in other news, I do have a date tonight," I said, wanting to direct her away from asking questions about Ramsay. Largely because I had no answers for her. Ramsay *was* hot. And that was that.

"Oh, with Ramsay?" Lia's face lit with excitement, and I shook my head.

"Simmer down. No, with a man I met at the grocery store yesterday. He's cute enough, friendly, and asked me out for a drink. Can I be honest with you? I've never been picked up like that before. Not, like, out in the wild."

Lia snorted, her eyes on the skillet. "I find that hard to believe, a pretty girl such as yourself."

"For real. Not once. Maybe it happens to women like you, but a lot of men are put off by my size."

"Then they don't deserve you." Lia flipped the pancakes, not missing a beat, and I smiled in her direction. I didn't need her validation, but it was nice to hear the compliment, nonetheless. I'd become such an advocate for body acceptance in the fashion industry that I'd *had* to become my own personal cheerleader along the way. While occasionally the insecurities of growing up as a big girl surfaced, for the most part I'd learned to love how I looked. Sometimes it could be a battle, since society badgered us constantly with messages that thin equals healthy, but I just took that as a challenge to prove to people otherwise. I was big, I was strong, and I was usually the most fashionable person in any group I was in.

And yet still, I'd never been picked up in a grocery store before.

There was a first for everything, and I was going to enjoy this little moment as another win for all the plus-sized women out there who thought that they didn't deserve a fun meet-cute like in a romance novel.

A strange sound drew my attention.

It was a cross between a purr and a roar and I jumped up, realizing I'd lost sight of Calvin.

"Calvin?"

Lia went to a door that led to a hallway and turned, a look of delight on her eyes, and waved me over. Crossing the room, I leaned through the doorway, my eyes widening at the sight that greeted me.

A small man, or, um, elf, I guess, with wrinkled skin, faded overalls, and big brown eyes was currently having a mutual lovefest with Calvin. He cradled the kitten in his arms, and Calvin licked his face, cleaning him like he'd found his baby. A soft purring of sorts was coming from the broonie's mouth, and he looked delirious with joy.

"Holy shit," I breathed.

"So this is Brice. Brice, meet Willow. Calvin belongs to her."

Brice looked up at me, and squeezed Calvin harder, a mutinous look coming over his face.

"Who I will bring to visit you whenever you want," I said quickly, realizing that Brice wanted to keep Calvin. "We live here too, so you two can play whenever."

At that, the broonie brightened, chattering softly in Calvin's ear, and Calvin flashed an image of happiness in my mind. *Friend*.

"I think they're besties," I said, happy to see Calvin not striking terror into the heart of at least *one* of the magickal beings in this place. "Also, I'm kind of freaking out right now."

"It's crazy, isn't it?" Lia darted back to the stove, and I left Calvin and Brice to play in the pantry, not wanting to be rude and stare at the little elf guy for too long in case I offended him.

But seriously. A house elf?

"Wild. Man, just wild."

"I'll admit, once you get used to him, he's pretty useful. He likes to clean up, often anticipates my needs ahead of time, and will have ingredients for spells ready quickly."

"Spells. Right. About that, how does that all work?"

"Turns out I come from a line of kitchen witches." Lia plated food for us, bringing it over to the table, and topping off our coffee cups as she spoke. "There's this amazing book of magickal spells for like teas and food and ointments that my gran helped contribute to. It's become my guide as I learn how to use my powers."

"Was it … like, I don't know, how do you feel about all this?" I felt that I could speak with Lia in a way that maybe I couldn't with Sophie, since Sophie technically employed me and financed my future.

"At first? Yeah, it was a lot to take in. Particularly having Brice around. But once I found the book and realized that this power was connected to me through my bloodline, I don't know, I guess it brought me comfort. I've always been close with my family, so it just felt like another piece of them shared with me." Lia's eyes warmed, and she wrapped both hands around her cup of coffee, looking out the window at the rain that continued to come down in relentless sheets.

My stomach twisted. My family was small, but tightknit when my brother wasn't acting like a controlling butthole, yet there'd always been a piece missing. At times, it seemed like my mother's absence was stronger than her presence had ever been. I'd been a pretty resilient little girl, always able to gauge when someone needed cheering up, determined to be the sunshine on someone's rainy day. Maybe I could be the one to fill the hole my mom had left in her death—*my young self had reasoned*—and I'd been determined to never show that I was missing out on having a mother growing up. Now, as Lia's face filled with love while speaking about her family, and her grandmother, a part of me wished that I could find that connection here too.

Even if I could just be one branch of my mother's tree. Which reminded me—I needed to go see Gran. Maybe I could get Sophie to take me at some point.

"My mother was Scottish. We have some roots here. I haven't had time to explore, but I'm hoping, hearing your story, that maybe I'll find a similar connection."

"Was?" Lia's face took on that familiar expression of sympathy that I'd seen hundreds of times over the years.

"Yes, she passed when I was young."

"I'm sorry to hear that. I'll help you look for any connection, if I can. In fact, if you give me her name, I'll look for it through my book. It's really cool, here, let me show you."

I let out a shaky breath and sat back from the table, anticipation traveling through me. What if my mother had been blessed with magick as well? It would be a link between us, one that maybe I hadn't known I'd needed, and the thought made nerves twist low in my stomach.

"Welig," I said faintly. "Her name was Welig. It means Willow."

"Aw, that's sweet," Lia said, returning to the table with a beautiful leather-bound book with a pretty Celtic design on the front. She glanced at the clock on the wall. "I won't have time to look just now, but isn't this fabulous?"

I opened the book and was surprised when a zip of energy buzzed through me. The pages were old, with handwritten recipes and spells, illustrations, and notations edging the margins of the recipes. It was a book made with love, I could feel that much, and my eyes caught on a recipe for patience.

"I could use this. I'm always wanting things now, now, now." I laughed, tapping the recipe.

"Let me make it up for you before you go. It's just a quick tea I can brew. You can finish your design that you wanted to get down on paper."

I pulled out my iPad, and Lia and I fell into easy silence as Lia took the book to her prep table to brew the tea and I tried to bring to life the design I'd seen in my dreams.

And suddenly I was no longer in the kitchen anymore.

CHAPTER TWENTY-TWO

Willow

My mouth fell open as I looked around the room, which now resembled a doctor's office. A compact, curvy woman, with thick curling hair, dusky skin, and warm brown eyes gaped at a man in a lab coat, an expression of horror on her face.

"Cancer?" the woman whispered, bringing a trembling hand to her mouth.

"I'm so sorry to give you this news. Yes, ovarian cancer."

"How, um, how long? How far is it?" The woman ran a finger over a cross on a chain at her neck.

"It's stage four." The doctor cleared his throat.

"Out of—"

"Four stages."

"Oh." Tears filled the woman's eyes.

"I wish you would have come to me with your symptoms sooner." The doctor reached out and squeezed the woman's arm. "But we're going to fight this."

The kitchen snapped back into focus, with Lia's hand on my shoulder, concern on her face.

"Whoa, are you okay? It looked like you were in a trance."

"I ..." I gulped, seeing the same brown eyes in Lia's face as the woman in my vision. This must be about her mother. Oh hell, what was I going to say? I swallowed, trying to collect my thoughts, and something cool and metal slid from my fingers to the floor.

"Meow," Calvin said, flashing an image into my head of me helping Lia, hugging her. I looked to the floor to see what had fallen from my hand and found Calvin batting a necklace around.

"Oh, my locket." Lia bent, picking up a heart-shaped locket that had inexplicably just been resting in my hand, and secured it back around her neck. "My mother gave this to me."

My heart hammered, and my thoughts scrambled as I tried to make sense of my vision. Was this something that I should share with Lia? What if her mother already knew and wasn't telling her? What if this was something that was too personal for me to say?

Calvin sunk his claws into my ankle.

"Ow," I gasped, glaring down at him.

"Willow ... is that my mom?" Lia leaned forward, narrowing her eyes at the picture I'd drawn of her mom, worry on her face, clutching her necklace in her hand.

Shit.

"Um, jeez, Lia, I don't know how to say this."

WILD SCOTTISH BEAUTY

"Just say it. What's going on here? She's upset." Lia tapped the screen.

"So, you know how I've figured out that I might be able to see the future?" We'd talked about my magick in the car the night before, and Lia had seemed pretty stoked about my powers.

"You just had a vision, didn't you? That's where you disappeared to, wasn't it?" Worry furrowed Lia's brow. "About my mother? Just tell me. Give it to me straight."

"I had a vision of her in a doctor's office. He told her she had stage four ovarian cancer and said if only she'd come in sooner."

"No." Lia's fists clenched, and she paced the room, shaking her head. "No, no, no."

"I'm sorry. It might not be true. I'm new to this."

"You're sure that's what you heard?" A sheen of tears coated Lia's eyes when she looked over her shoulder at me.

"Positive."

"Okay." Lia blew out a breath, nodding her head. "Right. Okay. We've got this. We'll handle it. You said this was from the future ... so, we could jump on this now, right?"

"Um, I think so? I'm sorry, I wish I knew more. I just got that flash." I wished I could *do* more, but that was all I had to offer.

"No, Willow, you've done *more* than enough! I have to call my father. The thing with my mom is that she never goes to the doctor. She's always so busy taking care of everyone else that she brushes off her own issues. He's the only one who will be able to bully her into going. We might have caught this in time, with your help."

I stood up and gave Lia a quick hug, worry curling through my stomach. "Let me know how it goes, please?"

"Am I interrupting?"

We pulled apart to find Ramsay leaning into the kitchen from the interior door.

"No, it's fine, come in," Lia said, pulling her phone from her pocket. "We were just finishing up."

"What are you doing here?" I asked instantly noticing how happy I was to see him. I slid the image away, closing the app, and tucking the iPad into my bag. Calvin scampered across the kitchen floor, and Ramsay bent to scoop the cat up into his arms. I couldn't help but admire how handsome he looked, his large arms cradling the tiny kitten, and it made me go soft and gooey inside.

"Thought I'd come pick you up since it's heaving out there today."

"That's nice of you, thanks." I wasn't about to turn down the offer of a ride. I'd been walking most mornings, enjoying the brisk morning air, the time giving me a chance to soak in the stunning countryside.

"Everything good here?" Ramsay looked between the two of us, clearly sensing the tension in the air.

"Of course. Lia, I'll see you later?"

"Yup, thanks, Willow. I mean it."

"No problem." I squeezed her shoulder, her phone was already at her ear, and started to leave.

"Oh, have fun on your date later," Lia called after us, then started speaking softly into the phone.

"Will do."

"Date?" Ramsay skidded to a stop in the hallway, and I almost bumped into his back.

"Yes, a *date*. You know, where two people go for coffee or a glass of wine and size each other up to see if they want to jump each other later."

"I'm aware of the concept."

I didn't say anything else as we left the castle, my mind on Lia and her mother, and Ramsay also stayed silent. Tucking Calvin inside his coat, he held the door for me and gestured to where he'd pulled his truck as close to the castle door as he could. The rain hammered the earth, and I could barely make out the loch in the distance, let alone the end of the parking lot.

"Make it quick." With that Ramsay dashed into the rain, flinging the passenger side door open, before sprinting around the side of the truck. I tucked my bag beneath my coat, and followed suit, and gasped as icy rain splashed against my cheeks. Diving into the car, I slammed the door after me, my chest heaving, as I wiped my face.

"Maybe we should have waited."

A grunt was my only answer.

Calvin crawled out of Ramsay's coat, picking his way across the seats to my lap, and I curled him to me. His little body shivered in the cold, and Ramsay turned the key, heat pouring from the vents.

"It rains a lot here."

Ramsay didn't even bother with a grunt this time, instead flicking his lights on and shifting into gear, before steering the truck carefully across the parking lot.

Giving up on any conversation, because based on the way his expression looked like it could be chiseled from marble, Ramsay was in a mood, I leaned back into my seat. Staring out the window, I watched as the raindrops exploded against the glass and wondered if my vision had come in time to help Lia's mother.

Would my life always be like this from now on? When I'd first learned that I'd be able to see the future, I'd thought it would be a cool tool to have at my disposal. But something like this? Yeah, it carried a lot of weight. I realized that I'd need to be careful in how I used my so-called powers in the future, because who was to say how my visions could forever impact someone's life? Now I was beginning to understand that line in Spiderman about great power bringing much responsibility. Since I wouldn't have any control over the visions coming to me, I would have to decide what I shared with people. Like, what if I saw that someone's husband was cheating and she hadn't asked me about it? Did I just share that information? It could ruin someone's life. Gnawing my lower lip, I stroked Calvin's fur, his soothing purr rumbling under my hands, and let the heat wash over me. By the time we'd pulled up in front of the shop, Ramsay angling the truck as close as possible, the windows had started to steam.

"I'll unlock the door."

With that, Ramsay disappeared into the rain, unlocking the door before he ducked inside.

And that was it. No waving for me to come in, nothing. I looked down at Calvin.

The cat blinked up at me, telegraphing me an image of Ramsay with a grumpy look on his face, and I giggled.

"He is a grump, isn't he?"

"Brrrp."

"Well, let's see what we can do to change that."

"Brrrraaaap." Calvin stood and bumped his head against my chin, rubbing his face against mine.

"You're seriously cute, you know that?" Gathering the cat in my arms, I raced inside, ducking my head against the rain. Once in, I slammed the door behind me with a laugh. Ramsay was crouched by the fireplace, building a fire, and I took a moment to admire his butt.

I mean, I wasn't dead, okay? The man was seriously built. Thick muscular legs led to a perfect bubble butt, and his broad back showcased his strength. I mean, he'd carried me easily around, and I was no lightweight. Remembering the number of times he'd already lifted me easily in his arms sent a shiver down my back, and I took my bag to the desk, before hanging up my coat and depositing Calvin on his cat jungle gym.

At the strike of a match, I sprawled in the chair next to where Ramsay crouched at the fire and dangled my head near his.

"I've always loved a fire. It's cozy, isn't it?"

Ramsay grunted.

"How was your night? Did you get a good night's sleep?" Maybe I was crossing a line asking about his sleep, but we'd moved over the line into friendship category when he'd invited me to the dance. Or at least that's what I'd thought.

"No."

"Ah, that explains the mood."

Ramsay didn't move, just turned his head to skewer me with a look.

I grinned.

"Is tetchy the word I'm looking for here?"

"Bloody hell." Ramsay rose and disappeared into the back room, switching on lights as he did so. I got up and followed him, determined to pester him back into his slightly less grumpy self. There was an edge about him today that made him unreadable, and I wanted to set us back on an even keel.

"No? What about crabbit? I learned that one recently too."

Ramsay glowered as he flipped the switch by his sewing machine, mumbling something under his breath.

"What was that? I didn't catch it."

Ramsay ignored me, continuing his routine of flipping all his lights on, and I moved to the doorway that led to the kitchen, knowing he was going to make tea. He always brewed a pot for us in the morning. When he stepped close, assuming I would move, he pulled up short when I didn't.

"Move."

"Why don't you tell me what's going on? I promise you'll feel better."

"Move, Willow."

"Nope." I grinned up at him, crossing my arms over my chest.

"I'm not in the mood for this."

"Aw, come on, Ramsay. Give it up. Tell me what's wrong."

"Move. Or I'll make you move."

I just raised an eyebrow at him, and when he reached out, grabbing me beneath my elbows and lifted me, I couldn't help it.

I giggled.

"Oh, you think this is funny?" Ramsay's face was close

to mine, his expression furious, and I desperately wanted to lean forward and sink my teeth into his bottom lip. Ramsay stepped backward, moving me out of the way, while my heart pounded and my gaze remained transfixed on his mouth.

This is not a good side of you, Willow.

But I couldn't help that every time he casually picked me up, and moved me around at his will, a baser side of my self went all fluttery and faint like a damsel in the days of yore. It shouldn't be so hot, the sheer strength and grumpiness of this man, and yet here I was. Lusting after Ramsay once again.

He dropped me unceremoniously to my feet, and then brushed past me, leaving me with my eyebrows raised. I virtually skipped after him, bouncing into the narrow kitchen as he put the kettle on. "Oh, for feck's sake."

"I'm just gonna bug you until you tell me." I was pulling out every annoying little sister trick, and I went over to him, poking him several times in the back until he turned to glare at me.

"Has anyone told you how annoying you are?"

"It's part of my charm."

Ramsay inhaled, closing his eyes for a moment.

"Och, you're not going to leave this alone, are you?"

"Nope." I mean I would have, if he'd really wanted me to, but since I sensed he was weakening, I pressed my advantage.

"Fine. I had a fight with my brother."

"Ah, yes, I'm familiar with those. Sucks, huh?"

"You could say that." Ramsay gritted his teeth and pulled out a canister covered in cheerful daisies. Opening it, he pulled some teabags out and dropped them in a pot, and the electric kettle clicked off. "He was at my parents'. Harassing my dad. I wasn't nice about it."

"I don't blame you." I knew he'd had some falling out with his brother years ago, something to do with stolen money, and I wished I could remember more about his family from the times we'd visited when I was a child. Honestly, those recollections just blurred together as childhood memories often did, and I truly couldn't remember his family at all. I just remembered Ramsay and Miles, thick as thieves, and lovely summer days by the loch. "I probably wouldn't have been nice about it either."

"You don't have to excuse my behavior."

"I'm not excusing it. I'm just saying that I might have done the same."

Ramsay nudged me back as he bent to open the undercounter fridge for milk. I gave him the space, moving to sit at a tiny banquet table tucked under a paned window that looked out over a small stand of trees whose branches currently clung to their trunks like my hair plastered against my face after a shower. Calvin appeared at the door and padded across the floor. He hesitated briefly before jumping up on the counter and bumping his head against Ramsay's arm. Ramsay scratched his ears idly, waiting for the kettle to click off.

"He used to be my best friend."

At that I almost went to him, but the way he held himself, rigid against the counter, his eyes trained on the kettle, I suspected he'd reject any advance from me.

"Family's complicated. It's hard to lose someone you care about."

Ramsay's eyes closed briefly.

"Here I am moaning about my brother being a fecking eejit when you've lost a mother."

"It's okay. I barely remember her." I shrugged, not wanting the focus on me when he was the one hurting. "One loss doesn't diminish another, Ramsay. Do you know I looked up the meaning of a willow tree the other day?"

"The meaning?" Ramsay raised an eyebrow at me as he brought the pot of tea over to the table, settling across from me. The table was so small that our knees touched, but I didn't try to move away and neither did he.

"Yeah, like the spiritual meaning, you know? How people look for signs in things. My mother's name was Willow as well. I don't know, I just looked it up. Know what I found out?"

"That the lads used to whip the lassies with pussy willow branches?"

"Wait, what?" Pausing I gave him an incredulous look. "Why would they do that?"

"Anything to torment the lasses, I suppose."

"Ugh, boys are the worst. You and Miles used to take me into the woods and pretend to lose me."

"Did we? God, I'd forgotten that." A ghost of a smile crossed Ramsay's face as he leaned back, his hand at his chin.

"It sucked. I was convinced a troll was going to eat me."

"And yet, here you are. Stronger than ever." Ramsay's stormy eyes met mine. "Tell me about the willow tree."

"Ah, yes. The willow tree. One of the meanings I found was that it's symbolic of a human's ability to withstand hardship and loss."

Ramsay's eyes held mine, and something shifted in his look, a gentling, I guess. He brushed one finger across the back of my hand resting on the table.

"Apt."

"I thought so."

"Thanks for being a friend, Willow. I guess I did need to talk about it."

I blinked at Ramsay a moment, realizing he was done with the conversation. In what world would his three sentences about a fight with his brother, which barely explained anything or scratched the surface of the conflict, count as talking about it? Then, movement outside the window caught my eye.

"Ramsay," I breathed, gripping his hand. "*Look*."

Calvin leapt up on the windowsill, freezing at the sight that greeted the three of us.

A unicorn had appeared beside the trees.

Just ... like, it was there. Just there. Out of nowhere.

It stood, unbothered by the rain, tossing its luxurious mane in the air. It reminded me of a meme I'd seen going around recently.

Unbothered. Moisturized. Happy. Thriving.

This unicorn was all those things.

It glowed lightly in the rain, its pearlescent horn jutting proudly into the air, its eyes seeming to hold all the knowledge of the world. I don't know why it appeared then, when we spoke of family and loss and love, but for a moment I thought of my mother—her warmth, her laughter—and saw the same in the depths of this magickal being's eyes. The unicorn stepped forward, plodding lightly toward the window, sparkling.

Ramsay hooked his fingers through mine, and I held my breath, waiting.

The unicorn bowed its head to us once, as though it was giving us some sort of all-knowing blessing, and then turned and raced into the rain. Jubilation bubbled up inside me, and I wanted to jump up and run after it, to call it to come back, just so I could bask in its presence for longer.

Never had I seen anything so incredible, and I'd seen some pretty incredible things since landing in Loren Brae. Slowly, I turned my eyes from the window and met Ramsay's look.

"Tell me you just saw that."

"Och, aye."

For once, I was at a loss for words, and we just stared at each other until Ramsay realized he was still gripping my hand. He pulled his hand back, and I felt the loss of his warmth immediately.

"That was ... I don't know. I feel like I want to strip my clothes off and go dance in the rain and scream and cry with joy and make music and babies and like start fires and end wars and I don't know ..." I babbled, flailing my hands in the air. Unable to sit, I jumped up and did a little dance in the kitchen, needing to work through the excitement that coursed through my body.

Ramsay leaned back, arms crossed over his chest, and arched an eyebrow at me.

"Oh, don't give me that look." I waved a finger at him. "I'm not letting you yuck my yum. That was freaking incredible, and you know it."

"Aye, it was, lass. I've never heard of this before. Did you know the unicorn is the national animal of Scotland?"

"It is?" I stopped bouncing for a moment and gawked at him.

"Aye."

"Oh my God. So they are real. I mean, of course they are. We didn't just have a double hallucination. Ramsay, we have to put a unicorn in our designs somewhere."

Ramsay's eyebrows lifted.

"Unicorn kilts?"

"Yes!" I pointed a finger at him. "Yes, yes, yes. Unicorn kilts." I bounced around the kitchen and through to the front room, Calvin scampering with me.

When Ramsay's laughter followed me, I felt a tightness inside me loosen. At the very least, I'd accomplished my mission and restored Ramsay to a better headspace. He was still a grump, but he was my grump.

At that thought, I paused, my eyes wide.

My grumpy *friend*, I mentally amended.

He'd said it himself, hadn't he?

Thanks for being my friend.

Which was fine. It was *fine*.

A friendship was probably the least complicated place to be with Ramsay.

Especially because I just saw a freaking unicorn.

CHAPTER TWENTY-THREE

Ramsay

The imagery was almost too much for me.

Between seeing an actual unicorn in the flesh—something I had never ever believed existed in real life—and Willow talking about stripping naked and running around in the rain, I'd had to excuse myself for a moment.

Upstairs, I sat on the corner of the bed and tried my hardest not to think about Willow.

Willow naked in the rain.

Water running down those delicious curves.

Her bum bitable and glistening with rain.

It didn't help that I'd chosen my bed to sit on, because now all I could think about was bending her over the mattress and pressing myself into her softness.

I groaned, running one hand through my hair, and stood to pace.

A real, live unicorn had just visited us.

And all I could think about was Willow.

Willow on a date with another man.

A man who wasn't me.

Which was fine. Dating was a totally normal thing that single people did, and I should have expected that an attractive woman such as Willow would eventually be asked out on a date. Particularly when she was a new face in a small town. The dating pool was limited here, wasn't it? And I should be the last person to begrudge Willow a chance at having some happiness with some stupid fecking eejit who probably had no idea how to treat her well.

Maybe I should tell Miles. Get him on her case. Yeah, that might be a good idea.

Even as I thought it, I dropped back on the bed and ran my hands over my face. Willow would destroy me if I told Miles she was going on a date. It was her business to share or not share, not mine. She'd already made it abundantly clear just how much she hated his interference in her life.

And instead, I had to go downstairs and pretend like it wasn't driving me absolutely mental knowing that she was going on a date with another man tonight.

Another man? Shouldn't I mean *any* man?

Why did my brain seem to insist that I should be the one going on a date with Willow? No matter how many times I lectured myself that I had no reason to think of Willow other than as a kind and caring co-worker and friend, for some reason, I wanted more with her. I liked sitting in the kitchen, talking to her over a cuppa while the rain fell outside. She'd poked me into talking to her, and my instincts to share about the night before had been right. I'd felt better once we'd spoken, and I didn't want to lose that newfound closeness I'd found with her.

I wanted to be the one taking her to dinner.

I wanted to be the one wrapping my arms around her at the end of the night.

I wanted to be the one making her laugh so hard that she snorted and slapped a hand over her mouth.

And yet here I was, refusing to say the things that I wanted to say.

They say pride made for a cold bedfellow, but I was beginning to think loyalty did as well.

Cursing Miles for having such an incredible human as a sister, I returned to work.

CHAPTER TWENTY-FOUR

Willow

So, you admit it, lass? Irn Bru is good.

> I don't know if I'd say "good."

Those are fighting words in Scotland.

> Uh-oh, am I going to get kicked out?

We might make an exception for a bonnie lass such as yourself.

Later that afternoon, I smiled at my phone and looked up to catch Ramsay glowering at me from across the room. Neither of us had spoken much since the morning—Ramsay clearly having exhausted his word limit for the day

—and I'd been busy with finalizing a few concepts I felt we were ready to take to Sophie in between appointments.

"What?"

"You're on your phone a lot today."

"Oh? Is that not allowed? I didn't see any rules about that in your extensive training manual." I pretended to look around for the nonexistent employee manual.

"Is that your date?" Ramsay asked, crossing to the fire to add another log. Calvin jumped on my worktable and rolled on his back to bat at a piece of ribbon I'd given him. I reached over, tickling his belly, and Calvin sunk his teeth into my hand.

"Damn it," I hissed, pulling my hand back, and glaring at Calvin. The cat just blinked his eyes lazily at me and flashed me an image of himself sleeping alone by the fire. "Well, if you're tired, then go to sleep. You don't have to bite me."

Surprising me, Ramsay crossed the room and took my hand in his, examining the bite. My skin heated at his touch, my hands looking positively dainty in his, and I wondered how he was able to make his stitches so straight with such large hands. My eyes dropped to our joined hands as his thumb brushed across the bite.

"Just a surface wound. No blood." I cleared my throat. My phone buzzed again beneath our joined hands. Ramsay's fingers tightened on mine.

"Do you really think you should be going out on dates?"

"What's that supposed to mean?" Was he going to turn into my brother and start monitoring my every movement? If so, Ramsay better think twice about pulling such a move.

I was my own woman who could make my own choices. I didn't need another Miles looking over my shoulder and dictating my every decision. Annoyance flashed through me, and I took a deep breath, forcing my emotions from bubbling over. I already knew that Ramsay was in a mood today, and he likely didn't realize just how much he was overstepping his boundaries at the moment. I just needed to keep my cool so as not to pick a fight with him because his questions were intrusive.

"When did you even have time to meet someone?"

"What ... why do you even care?" I asked, glaring up at him. He still held my hand in his, and I could feel my heart thump slowly, as he shifted closer, his head lowering.

"You told me you weren't dating anyone right now."

"When did I say that?" *Had I said that?* I might have. I chattered at Ramsay constantly during our time in the shop, so maybe I did say that in passing. It was hard to think straight with my hand caught in his, and he shifted, leaning his hip against the table.

"You said you weren't looking for a boyfriend right now. That you'd had a bad breakup and wanted to focus on figuring out your new life." Wow, a positive monologue from the man of few words. I guess he did listen to me on occasion.

"Um." I swallowed. Was his head dipping closer to mine? My eyelashes fluttered against my cheeks for a moment, and I took an unsteady breath. Ramsay's thumb continued to caress my palm, heat trailing across my skin at his touch. "Yeah, that sounds like something I'd say."

My phone buzzed again, and Ramsay's hand tightened on mine.

"He's eager."

"Is there a reason he shouldn't be?" I asked, affronted. I tried to pull my hand from Ramsay's but he held it tight, keeping me at the table.

"No." Ramsay's response was simple and direct. "I'd be too."

My thoughts scattered at that, and I lost the power for words as he brought my hand to his lips, kissing the spot where Calvin had bitten me. I sucked in a breath, desire pulling long and low in my stomach, and I pressed my thighs together. Ramsay's music playlist had run out, so the only sounds—aside from my heartbeat thundering in my ears—was the rain pattering against the window and the crackle of flames in the fireplace. Seconds passed.

And then he licked my palm.

A shiver drifted across my body and my breath hitched. A low sound rumbled in Ramsay's throat, and then he blew a breath across my hand. Lust ravaged my core. It was hands down the simplest and yet most sensual thing someone had done to me. I didn't know what that said about my sexual experience, but the combination of his hot breath across the dampness of my sensitive palm made my insides go liquid. I dragged my eyes from our joined hands, forcing myself to look up to where his mouth now hovered inches from mine.

My phone buzzed again.

A corner of Ramsay's mouth quirked, forever cementing this moment in my head, and then he closed the gap between our mouths, capturing my lips with his own. And while I'd imagined kissing Ramsay on more than one occasion, nothing could have prepared me for this kiss.

It wasn't sweet.

It wasn't gentle.

Ramsay took.

He feasted on my mouth, angling my head and slipping his tongue inside when I gasped, wet heat making my insides melt. His kiss felt as though he was branding me, making me his own, and I could feel it all the way to my toes. My body lit up, and when he took the kiss deeper, clasping my chin with his hand, controlling my movements, I almost melted on the spot. His tongue was hot against mine, my brain short-circuiting as his kiss eradicated the word "sweet" for Ramsay from my vocabulary forever. When he stepped back, ending it as soon as it had begun, I gasped up at him, my lips burning from his touch.

I didn't want him to stop.

I wanted to see beneath his rigid exterior, to see what he looked like unraveled and spent, vulnerable as he was with no one else. My body shook with need for him.

"Think of me on your *date*."

With that, Ramsay scooped up Calvin, muttering something about how he'd watch him tonight, and disappeared up the stairs that led to his rooms over the shop. I raised my eyes to the ceiling, hearing his heavy footfalls above me, and held a hand to my chest to try and steady my breathing.

That jerk.

He'd done that on purpose, hadn't he? What was with the men in my life who refused to let me just go out and live the way I wanted to? Ramsay knew, *he knew*, that I'd never be able to sit across the table from a date tonight without thinking of his kiss stealing my very soul. Gingerly, I picked up my phone to cancel, but then saw the text messages that Andrew was already at the pub.

Damn it. I wasn't a rude person, and canceling last minute would be rude. I could go, have a single drink, and then leave. There was no reason that I couldn't have a friendly drink and then later I could try to sort out my complicated thoughts about what Ramsay had just done. Because I swear, if I hadn't had a date at that moment? I'd be barreling up those stairs and demanding an explanation from him.

Grabbing my bag, and an umbrella from the stand at the front, I flounced out of the shop, refusing to look back to see if Ramsay watched me from the window above. What I needed was a few minutes in the cool air to tame my tumultuous emotions, and then I would have a pleasant conversation with Andrew and enjoy a drink. It didn't have to mean anything more than that.

Light beamed from the windows of The Tipsy Thistle, a cozy, safe haven on a cold, rainy night. I beelined for it, the pub an oasis for the storm of emotions that raged inside me, and then ducked inside, dropping the umbrella in the bin just inside the door. Music and laughter drifted to me through the hallway as I hung up my coat and pulled a small mirror out of my purse to apply some lip gloss and to make sure that I didn't look like I'd just been making out with another man.

Because who went on a date directly from the arms of another man? Annoyed with Ramsay for making me feel like I was doing something shady, I ducked inside the pub and smiled when Graham winked at me from the bar. I scanned the room, not recognizing anyone else, until my eyes landed on Andrew far across the room from the bar, sitting at a small table tucked by the fire. Waving to Graham, I crossed the room as Andrew stood to greet me.

He looked handsome enough, I supposed, but now I was comparing him to my towering boss and his impossibly magnetic presence, and while I definitely saw some similarities between the two, hugging Andrew was like hugging a brother.

Not a single blip of excitement on my sexy-time radar.

Nothing.

Andrew was like a tepid cup of tea whereas Ramsay was an icy margarita on a humid summer's day.

"Sorry for being late," I said.

"Nae bother, hen. Just glad you came." Andrew grinned at me. "Can I get you a drink? Irn Bru, right?"

"White wine, please," I said, tilting my head and smiling at him. Andrew crossed to the bar to order my drink, and I took a moment to settle myself at the table, staring into the flames that danced in the fireplace as I tried to recalibrate my emotions.

"Think of me on your date."

Was that really why he'd kissed me?

Had I misread him all along? Was his invitation to the cèilidh an actual date? Maybe he'd been looking forward to the dance as our first date for a while now and I'd managed to hurt his feelings by accepting a date with another man. Confused, I mulled over my thoughts.

"Tough day?" Andrew asked, returning to the table with a fresh pint for himself and my wine.

"Thank you," I said, accepting the wine with a smile. Taking a sip, when I actually wanted to gulp the whole glass, I tapped the rim against his pint. "Sorry, I should have cheersed you first."

"Slàinte." Andrew saluted and took a drink. "So, tell me, how are you settling into Loren Brae then?"

"I think okay? I mean, it's a wild change from where I'd been."

"And that was?" Andrew leaned in, interested, and I swallowed a sigh. He seemed like a perfectly nice man, and yet my brain couldn't seem to focus on him, or this date. I was back in the shop with Ramsay, that moment hung suspended between us, and I had to force myself to stay in this conversation.

"Ah, I was in New York City, actually."

"Och, that's a huge change, isn't it? A lot quieter here. Boring."

At that, I raised my chin at him, the comment surprising me.

"You don't like Loren Brae? I thought you said it was a great town."

"Don't get me wrong, it is. Just a bit small." Andrew sniffed and looked around the room, shrugging. There was something about his mannerisms that seemed familiar to me, but I was still so distracted from Ramsay's kiss that my brain couldn't make the connection.

"I'm learning that maybe small is a good thing." I looked over to see Agnes had entered the bar and that she and Graham were having a heated discussion about something. She slapped her hand on the surface of the bar.

And then they both looked directly at me.

What the hell? Were they arguing about me?

Andrew followed my gaze.

"Oh, those two. Same old thing, you know? Nothing ever changes here."

"How long have you lived in Loren Brae?" I took another sip of my wine, forcing myself to focus on the date.

"Grew up outside here, lass. But I don't come here often anymore."

"Oh, so you're just passing through?"

Why had he asked me for a drink then? That seemed weird. Unless he was looking for a quick hookup. Did I look like the type? Maybe I had? I'm not sure what about me with my arms full of crisps at the grocery store, had signaled a quick hookup.

"That's the plan." Andrew tipped back his pint and I arched an eyebrow at him.

"So ... what was this exactly?" I waved my hand between us at the table.

"A pint with a bonnie lass." Andrew tilted his head at my expression. "Do you Americans plan your marriage on the first date then? Or do you keep it casual for a bit and get to know each other?"

What he said made sense, but there was just something in his tone that put my back up. I leaned back, tapping a finger against my wine glass.

"Fair point. Tell me, Andrew, where do you spend your time then if not in Loren Brae?"

"I like to travel as much as I can. In fact, I just got back from a trip to Hong Kong."

This was a topic I could warm to at least. I'd always loved to travel as well, even though I'd had to do so on a limited budget. Either way, I loved exploring new places and discovering new experiences, seeing how fashion changed with different cultures, and so I leaned in to ask him about his travels, enjoying learning about someplace I hadn't visited before.

"Not sure if you have trouble walking a lot or not, but if you don't, the Great Wall is well worth it."

"Why would I have trouble walking?" I raised an eyebrow at Andrew, confused at his words.

"Um, I just know, a lot of Americans prefer to drive."

I held his look for a moment, wondering if that's what he'd really meant to say or if he was making a backhanded comment about my weight. It wouldn't be the first time that I'd been on a date and someone had made a joke about hoping they could afford the bill or stupid shit like that. So I wasn't sure if he was insulting me, or my country, but I did know that I didn't like it.

"We don't have great public transportation. You're lucky you have a train system that is so easy to navigate." Look at me being all grace and kindness here.

Silence fell in the pub, and that was my only warning before Andrew was hauled out of his seat.

"Bloody hell, Ramsay."

I squeaked as Ramsay grabbed Andrew by the back of his neck, crushing him with brute strength until Andrew began to crumple.

"Enjoying your date with my brother, Willow?"

CHAPTER TWENTY-FIVE

Ramsay

What had I been thinking? Kissing Willow like that? I stood at the window and watched her leave, the taste of her still on my lips, while she left to be with another man.

A date.

It had been bothering me all day. In fact, probably more than the fact that I was emptying my savings account to pay off my brother, which said a lot. But I couldn't get the fact that Willow was going on an actual date, with someone who wasn't me, that very evening.

I was the one who was supposed to be going on a date with her.

No, I corrected myself. I was the one who was supposed to be watching out for her. Not kissing her senseless and then sending her out on a date with another man. What a bloody eejit I was. For weeks I'd been telling Miles I'd look out for her when all I'd wanted was to get closer to her.

And now I'd kissed her, and I would never not know the taste of her on my lips again. I'd never be able to erase the memory of the soft sigh she made when she sank into the kiss, or the breathy moan she made deep in her throat when I'd deepened the kiss. I'd taken her kiss like I owned her, and I was going to have to apologize, to her—to Miles probably—and yet a part of me knew I'd do it all over again.

Sunshiny Willow, who never stopped talking, to the point that the shop seemed dull and dark when she wasn't around. Flowers had appeared on the shop's windowsills. New music had entered my playlists. Customers were arriving at the shop, not so scared to enter now, and business was booming.

She'd gotten under my skin, weaving herself into the threads of my soul, and somehow, I could no longer fathom life without her. *How had that happened?* A month ago, I'd been content with my bachelor status, and since her arrival, I'd thought about dating and love and marriage. *What the actual fuck?*

"I should go there, shouldn't I? Profess my ... whatever this was to her?" *Was it love? Isn't it too early to be believing this is love?* And that kiss. Bloody hell, that kiss had been one of the hottest of my life.

And she was out on a date with another man.

Was it really necessary to keep reminding myself of that?

Yes, because you hate the idea. What if she kissed him? What if his kiss replaced mine? What if he were the one that would receive Willow's smiles and joy and sunshine ... because I'd been too fecking slow to act on my "feelings"?

And if that didn't tell me that I felt a lot for Willow, what would?

Do I love Willow?

What would Miles say to that?

I looked down at where Calvin sat in the window, waiting for Willow to return. I understood how he felt.

My phone buzzed in my pocket, and I pulled it out to see a text message from Graham.

> Did you know that Willow is on a date with your brother?

MY HEART SKIPPED A BEAT.

Ice flooded my veins.

Graham knew my history with Andrew, so his text was as much a warning as it was a question.

> On my way.

> Please don't break anything. I like my pub.

I DIDN'T RESPOND to that, rage clouding my vision as I stomped downstairs, tamped out the fire, and locked the door after myself. I didn't take an umbrella, I didn't grab my jacket, anger fueling me as I stomped through the rain to the pub, furious that my brother, once again, was trying to take something that was mine.

Granted, Willow wasn't mine, but she was all that was good and pure in this world, and I didn't need someone like Andrew dulling her shine with his slimy ways. As I neared the pub, a thought occurred to me.

Had Willow known she was going on a date with my brother? I'd said his name when I'd spoken about him. Hadn't I? She must have met him when she'd been here as a child. Was this all a game to her? I shook my head as I shoved the door of the pub open.

There was no way we would have had that moment today, when I opened up about my brother, and then Willow would have gone out on a date with him. If I were a betting man, I'd lay money that, for some unknown reason, she had no idea who she was on a date with.

I caught Graham's eyes as I stormed inside, and he lifted his chin to the corner. The pub fell silent as I turned, my vision narrowing to where Willow laughed at something my brother said. Stalking across the room, I wrenched him out of his seat by his neck, fury making me want to slam his head into the table. The only thing that stopped me was the look on Willow's face and the feel of Graham's presence at my back.

"Enjoying your date with my brother, Willow?"

"Your brother?" Willow gasped, her hands flying to her mouth, confirming my suspicions. She had no clue who she was on a date with. "*This* is your brother?"

Andrew wrenched himself from my grasp, straightening and rubbing the back of his neck, the expression on his face mutinous.

"What are you doing with her?" I asked, pitching my voice low, as Andrew raged back.

"Just on a date, brother."

"You're meant to be leaving town."

"I'm getting around to it." Andrew gave me a meaningful look, insinuating that he was going to stay around to mess up my life until he got the money he needed.

"Why did you ask her out?"

I realized my mistake in asking that question the instant that Andrew's expression changed. A corner of his mouth quirked up, and he lifted his eyebrows, a calculating look in his eyes.

"Oh God." Willow rose, interrupting his response. "You knew who I was, didn't you? It wasn't happenstance that you bumped into me and asked me out, was it? You were looking to mess with Ramsay. I'm just a pawn to you."

"A girl like you would have let me have a taste though." Andrew laughed, confirming Willow's fears, and I wanted to murder him on the spot for the defeat that I saw on her face. Her shoulders slumped and tears shimmered. "It was just by chance that I saw you in the shop, and I knew you were working for him. The plan kind of came together on the fly."

Two things happened at once.

Tears fell from Willow's eyes, and she grabbed her handbag, while I drove a fist into my brother's stomach, toppling him at the waist. Willow turned and ran from the pub, and I raised my fists again, determined to take my brother apart, piece by piece, until he could no longer hurt someone else that I cared about.

"I've got him, lad. Go after her." Graham shouldered

me aside, and my chest rose with the exertion it was taking not to lay into Andrew. Graham grabbed my chin, forcing my eyes to his. "Go. After. Willow."

"Don't be nice," I hissed.

A very dangerous smile flashed across Graham's face, and he pushed his sleeves up his arms.

"It won't be my fault if he bangs his head a time or two while I assist him off the premises."

Satisfied that Graham would finish the job, I crossed the pub. Agnes was by the door, worry on her face.

"You're going after her? Should I come?"

"No."

Agnes took one look at my face, and a smile bloomed. She patted me on the arm as I passed her.

"Good on you, lad."

I ran outside as Willow turned the corner at the end of the street. Hell if I was going to let her disappear into the night, feeling like she wasn't worth a man treating her well. The rain pounded down, water running in rivulets down the street, and I caught up to her as she turned on the street to the shop. She must be going to get Calvin, but she didn't know yet that I wasn't letting her out of my sight. No, tonight was going to be about showing Willow just what she was worth.

"Willow."

Willow wheeled around, her face drenched in sadness, and she held up a hand to stop me from stepping closer.

"I'm fine, Ramsay. Just go."

She was clearly not fine. Her body shook as she gulped for air, trying to stem the flow of tears as she dashed the back of her palms against her face, even though it was useless given the deluge of rain.

"Willow." I stepped forward, putting my hands on her shoulders and nudged her backward until her back hit the door of my shop. I wanted to get her inside, away from the rain, to protect her from anything that would hurt her in this life. "Look at me."

"I said I'm fine, Ramsay. I'm sorry, okay? I wouldn't deliberately do that to you. I didn't know it was your brother."

"I know, darling."

"You do?" Willow's hands gripped my arms, and she lifted her eyes to me, her face ravaged. "I wouldn't have hurt you like that."

"I knew when Graham texted me that you were there with him that you didn't know who he was, Willow. I came to stop him from hurting you."

"God, I'm so freaking dumb." At that, the tears started all over again. "Of course he wouldn't pick me up at the store. Women like me—"

"Women like you what?" I was dangerously close to dropping to my knees and burying my face between her legs to show her just what I wanted to do with a woman "like her."

"No, that's *wrong*. That's an intrusive thought." Willow lectured herself, literally smacking the side of her head lightly. "It's my fault. I put expectations on this date. I'd been caught up in the novelty of having a fun meet-cute, you know?"

"I have no idea what a meet-cute is." But she was talking to me, so that was something.

"Just the idea of someone seeing you across a room and asking you out." Willow flailed a hand in the air. "It's in all the romcom movies and stuff. I wanted that for me. Even if just once."

"You wanted a stranger to invade your space in public and demand you have a drink with him?" I raised an eyebrow at her, and reached for the key in my pocket, all while trying to shelter her from the worst of the rain.

Willow gulped out a sound torn between a laugh and a sob.

"No. Yes. I don't know. Not *demand*. And yes, getting hit on in public can be super awful and crude and make women feel unsafe. Yet in a weird way we've been taught to feel like it can also be flattering or bloom into a relationship. That's how people met before dating apps and all that. But it's just ... it's just nice to feel wanted, sometimes, you know? But I'm good, Ramsay. I'm *fine*." Willow schooled her expression, clearly seeing something on my face. "You don't have to fix this for me. This is just a me thing, not a you thing, okay?"

"Are you sure about that, Willow?" I brought my face close enough to feel her breath tickle my lips. "Because I'm pretty sure it's an *us* thing."

"Us?" Willow's voice caught.

"Aye, lass." Brushing my thumb across her lower lip that still trembled from her tears, I opened the door and angled Willow to step backward, and out of the rain. The shop was still warm from the fire, a few lamps that I'd left on casting their light around the room.

The click of the door closing behind us sounded amplified, an audible marker of the line we were crossing, the boundaries I'd set for myself with Willow being burned to the ground.

Because I'd always followed the rules. I was the fair one. The reliable one. A good son, a good brother, a good boss, and a good friend. And for some reason, even with my less-than-stellar personality, people were drawn to me and trusted me. I'd been suppressing my feelings for Willow from day one, because that was what a good person did. They respected boundaries. They did the right thing.

But just this once, as Willow's lower lip trembled, and tears still shimmered in her eyes, I wanted to be very, very bad. I wanted to kiss her until she knew that every man who'd hurt her in the past had been too stupid to understand the gift they had in their hands. I wanted to wipe any last trace of uncertainty from her mind that she was anything less than a goddess. And I didn't care, not in this moment, if Miles would be mad at me or if it was crossing lines between a boss and employee. The only thing I cared about was wiping that dejected look from Willow's face forever. And showing her what she means to me.

Crowding her, I backed her into the desk at the corner of the room, and she gasped, grabbing the edge and catching herself from falling backward. Leaning over, I caged her in place with my arms, bringing my mouth close to her ear.

"You and me, Willow. Tell me you've thought about it like I have." I pressed my face to her hair, inhaling that toasted marshmallow scent of hers, and I swear my knees almost went weak.

"I ... um—"

"You've been driving me crazy since the moment you turned around in the car park at MacAlpine Castle."

"I have?"

I shifted my head and nibbled lightly at the pale, delicate lobe of her ear, her breath hot at my neck.

"Aye. Driving me to distraction at work. I can't look at you and not want to touch."

"Really?" Willow drew the word out as though she didn't believe me, and I sunk my teeth into her lobe, biting just hard enough for her breath to catch.

"I told you what I thought about your body, didn't I?"

"Oh, um, yeah, I guess you did."

"Do you think I'm a liar?" I shifted slightly, finding the pulse at her neck with my lips, and holding my mouth to it while her skin heated.

"No, I don't." Willow swallowed, the sound audible against my face, and I smiled into her neck.

"Now let me tell you what I think about you as a woman."

"Ramsay, you don't have to ..." Willow tried to shift out of my arms, but I held her in place, kissing my way up her neck, across her chin, until I pulled back just enough to meet her eyes.

A thousand emotions swam in their depths, and I was drowning, drowning in the sea of her glory, gasping for her to throw me a lifeline.

"Once I got over the shock of how beautiful you'd become, I quickly learned that beauty transcended your looks. You're sunshine in a designer dress, Willow. You care, deeply, about those around you, and always look to make their day a little better. You don't hesitate to help, and jump without looking, not caring how you land. You're wickedly funny, surprisingly so, and I've laughed more in a few weeks than I have in ages since you've arrived. You're loud, completely disobedient, disruptive, and yet I find myself looking for you, wondering when I'll see you next. And when you're gone? The shop feels empty without you."

Willow's eyes filled again, and I cursed myself for fumbling this.

"Do not let my piece of shite brother, or anyone, for that matter, ever let you feel like you're less than enough."

"Damn it, Ramsay." Willow shuddered in a deep breath, a tear tipping over the edge of her lashes and streaming down her cheek. "For a man who never talks, you certainly have a way with words."

"I save them up for when they matter."

"And this? *This* matters?" Willow's words were a whisper, a plea, which I answered with my lips on hers.

"Aye, it does."

Willow's hand came to my face, her fingers tracing my jawline, and I bent my forehead to hers.

"Say you want me as much as I want you." I needed to hear it, my control tenuous at best, and when she nodded, her teeth sinking into her lower lip, I pressed a touch harder with my forehead. "The words, lass."

"I ... I want you, Ramsay. So, so much."

"As you wish, darling." There would be time to be gentle another time. I'd spent weeks on edge, fighting my urge to touch her, and now it was like I'd been given the winning lottery numbers. Scooping her into my arms, I carried her through the shop, Calvin meowing as I went past where he sat on his cat tree.

"You're staying down here, you wee beastie." The last thing I needed was a claw sinking into a delicate spot at an inopportune moment, and I didn't trust the kitten enough not to pounce. I dashed up the stairs as Willow gasped against my neck, laughing as I careened into my bedroom and kicked the door closed behind me. The room was dark, and I found my way to the bed by memory and dropped her onto the mattress. "Don't move."

Stepping back, I flipped a small bedside lamp on, the light soft against the wood beams that ran the length of the ceiling. I loved this room, which was the perfect space just for me, and I'd kept the decorations to a minimum to let the rustic beauty shine. The bedroom ranged across the entire top floor, with high ceilings, stone walls, and antique wood doors on the closet. I had sourced a thick rug in earthy tones to toss over the wood floors and had somehow managed to wrangle a king-sized bed up the stairs. Which I was exceedingly grateful for now as I prowled forward to where Willow sat, a myriad of emotions running across her lovely face.

"That's better. I want to be able to see every inch of your body, to watch you come undone under my touch, to learn what makes you moan."

"Oh." Willow's lips rounded to a perfect *O* as I dropped to my knees in front of her. "Don't the Scots use the word moaning to mean complaining?"

I buried my face in her lap, laughing against her thigh, as my hands worked to pull the tights down that she wore underneath that ridiculous sparkly skirt that I had a love-hate relationship with. I loved it because it curved around her bum so nicely, and I hated it because the shimmer drew my eye constantly.

This was also new for me. This laughing during sex. I'd always prided myself on being a focused lover, determined that the woman would find her pleasure first, and I was very good at staying focused on the task at hand. But now, as Willow's words made me laugh into the supple skin at her leg, something inside me loosened. Maybe there could be both. An ease and an intensity in lovemaking.

With the right person that is.

Desperate for a taste of her, I put my hand on Willow's stomach and pushed back. She fell with a gasp of laughter, and then howled when I bit the inside of her thigh as I worked her boots off her feet. Once done, I barely hesitated before ripping the tights from her legs.

"Ramsay!" Willow shrieked, struggling to sit up, but I just pushed her down again. "Do you know how hard it is to find good tights?"

"Fuck the tights. I'll buy you a dozen pairs. I've been dreaming of doing this since the first time you wore this stupid skirt to my shop."

"Eeep," Willow squeaked, her head falling back to the bed as I licked my way up her inner thigh, loving how her legs felt under my hands. Easing them wider, I pushed her skirt up and ran a finger over her black lace thong.

"How much do you care about these?" I asked, tracing my finger up and down the lace that covered her seam, loving how she jerked beneath my touch. "Because they're in my way."

"They're my favorite," Willow admitted on a groan, and I smiled, leaning over to kiss her through the lace, blowing a hot breath across her skin as she jerked. Hooking my thumbs under the material, I rolled the lace down her legs and tossed it behind me, growling as I returned my mouth to her. With the lace no longer impeding me, I sank into her softness, licking her straight through. Willow's body jerked under my face, and I reached under her, sinking my fingers into that juicy bum that I'd been dying to touch for weeks, and pulled her harder against my face, needing to tip her over the edge as much as I needed my next breath.

Desire raged through me, my body taut with the need to be buried deep inside of her, and when she shattered around my face, her hands digging into my hair and pulling tight as she cried out, spasming as I licked her, I smiled.

One day I'd take my time with this. Savor her like an expensive dessert at the finest restaurant. Linger over her pretty petals, teasing her until she begged for more. But today, I had no patience.

Bringing my head up, I gripped her thighs as Willow propped herself up on her elbows.

"Take off your top. I want to see you."

"Um."

"Undress for me, Willow. I want to watch."

Her eyes widened as I cupped myself, the need too great, and stroked myself through my pants as Willow pulled her jumper over her head, revealing a see-through black mesh bra that almost had me coming into my own hand. Her breasts hung heavy and voluptuous against her round stomach, and the black bra contrasted with the sparkles of the skirt and glorious expanse of smooth, gorgeous skin almost had my eyes rolling back in my head.

"Bloody hell, you're magnificent."

Willow's cheeks pinkened as I stared at her, frozen at her beauty, as I stroked myself. *Fecking hell, she's glorious. Absolutely glorious.* Realizing how dangerously close I was to losing my cool, I reached for her. "I promise to go slowly next time, lass, but if I don't feel you clenching around my cock in about three seconds, I'm going to lose my mind."

"Why do I find this so hot?" Willow wondered as I dropped my head to her breast, the mesh barely acting as a covering for her pert nipple, and sucked.

"Because you like being told what to do?" I bit the inside of her breast, chuckling as she swatted my back, and then hauled her farther up the bed so I could cover her with my body.

"I do not!" Willow's protest was lost as I kissed her, open-mouthed, needing the slick slide of her tongue against mine as I unbuckled my belt with one hand.

"Pull my jumper off." I leaned back, and Willow ripped my jumper and the shirt below it off, running her hands down my naked chest as soon as she got access to my skin.

"There's a good lass." I bent to take her mouth again and swallowed her laugh.

"Damn it, Ramsay, I shouldn't like this."

"But you do, don't you, darling?" I ran my hand up her stomach, tracing small circles at her side, before cupping a breast with my palm and running a thumb over her hard nipple.

"I don't like when other people take control of ... ohhhh," Willow moaned against my mouth as I slipped a finger inside her, caressing her wet heat, testing her readiness for me.

"Your body seems to say otherwise, Willow."

"She's a lying whore," Willow promised me, and once again, I found myself laughing as I pulled back and divested myself of my trousers.

"I like her," I said as I ran a condom over my length and then angled myself over the bed. "I'm going to need you to scoot back on the bed there, darling."

"Ohhhh ... kay," Willow said, inching her way backward, her cheeks flushed. I crawled after her, rolling to my back at her side, and she blinked down at me.

"Whatcha doing down there?"

"Admiring the view," I said, brushing my thumb across her nipple and sending a shiver across her body. Willow was incredibly responsive, and I was enjoying watching her react to my touches. Trailing my hands down the satiny skin at her side, I tapped her thigh.

"Willow? I'm going to need for you to open up."

"Like this?" Willow spread her knees a bit, and her hips jerked when I brushed a finger over her.

"Yes, just like that. Good. Now, I'm going to need you to put a knee on either side of my head so I can settle in for a good long while, otherwise I'm going to throw you down and take you so fast you won't know how to pronounce your own name anymore."

Willow gulped.

"Admittedly, that doesn't sound awful."

I grinned, still lying on my back, and tapped my shoulders.

"Come on darling. Have a seat."

"Oh my God," Willow breathed, interest sparking in her eyes. "Seriously?"

"Haven't you done this before?"

"I mean, the basic mechanics of it, yes, since you so nicely brought me to orgasm that way just a few moments ago. But not, like, in this particular position." Willow worried her lower lip, curiosity in her eyes.

'Trust me, you'll love it."

"But—"

"What are you worried about?"

"Um." Willow leaned over and stage-whispered, "What if you die?"

I laughed, tugging on one of her curls to bring her lips to mine.

"Willow?"

"Yes, Ramsay?" Willow's voice rasped against my mouth.

"First of all, that's a fine way to go if I'm meant to go that way. And secondly, have I not, on more than one occasion, very easily lifted you when needed?"

"Um, yes, you have at that."

"I'll tap your thigh if I'm in distress," I promised, grinning as her eyes widened, "but I don't think it's going to be me needing assistance soon."

"I mean if you're that cocky." Willow climbed over, her gorgeous thighs cocooning my head, and I reached up, gripping her juicy bum with my hands and pulling her close until she landed perfectly on my face.

And then I feasted.

It didn't take long for Willow to stop supporting herself, holding her body off me out of fear of hurting me, and lean into the experience. Her thighs trembled against my face as I licked, spreading my tongue across her, opening her up to find her most sensitive spot like it was a present to be unwrapped. There, I took my time sucking and nibbling, varying my strokes and pressure, until Willow's hips began to jerk in my hands, and soon she was riding my face. I held her there, enjoying the noises she made as she bucked against me, taking her pleasure at my mouth.

Bloody hell, but she tasted sweet.

"Oh, Ramsay!" she cried. Her release was like honey. *Bliss.* Fecking hell, this woman was incredible.

She rolled off me the instant she was finished, surprise on her pretty face.

"Miss me?" I asked, sitting up.

"Oh, was it you who was down there?" Willow pretended nonchalance, and I laughed, leaning over to kiss her while I easily rearranged her body on the bed, kneeling between her legs.

"Just your friendly neighborhood kiltmaker," I said.

"*Very* friendly by the looks of it."

"It's why I'm so grumpy with people. Otherwise, all this friendliness will just pour out of me." Willow snorted as I brushed my hard length against her. Her eyes widened as I teased her, running myself between her slick folds, before bringing my face to her neck and biting.

"Bitey too, are you?" Willow gasped, rolling her hips against mine, trying to take me inside of her.

"It must be this perfume you wear. It smells like toasted marshmallow. Makes me want to take you apart, bite by bite."

"You never talk. Like never. And once you do, this is the stuff that comes out?" Willow said and I laughed softly against her neck.

"That's why I don't talk a lot. Danger of all these dirty thoughts slipping out."

"I had no idea," Willow said. "I would have forced you to talk sooner."

"Is that right? There's something you should know about me though, Willow."

I lifted my head so my eyes met her, as I positioned myself at her entrance.

"What's that?" Willow gasped.

"You can't force me to do anything. I take what I want." I thrust inside her in one long stroke, and Willow's eyes fluttered closed for a second, a soft keening sound leaving her lips. "And I've wanted you. Just like this. For weeks now."

"Well, jeez, why didn't you just say so?" Willow gasped against my lips and then we were both lost as she rolled her hips sharply to meet my thrusts, her hot wetness enveloping me so completely that when she clenched around me, I let go, falling over the brink into a pleasure so deep that spots danced behind my eyes. Helpless not to, I plunged into her again, needing to feel her clench around me as much as I needed my next breath. Over and over, I drove into her soft, wet heat, and my body tensed, pleasure careening through me. Unable to stop, I thrust a few more times, as Willow shattered around me, and then I dropped to the mattress, still buried inside of her.

Turning my head, I found her looking at me, her cheeks flushed, her eyes happy, a smile loose around her lips. This. This was how I wanted her to look. Not that pinched expression of sadness and resignation. Now she looked satiated, happy, and relaxed. I vowed to keep that expression on her face.

"I promise I can last longer when I'm not pent-up from weeks of wanting you."

At that, her eyes lit. She lifted her wrist, pretending to check an imaginary watch.

"I was going to say ..."

I tackled her, pressing kisses against her throat, while she howled with laughter.

And then I wondered what I had to do to keep this—*keep her*—like this forever. *Mine.*

CHAPTER TWENTY-SIX

WILLOW

Neither of us had brought up my brother yet.

I wasn't quite sure what to say. Maybe Ramsay didn't know either. There was a part of me that felt like I was doing something wrong, like I was sneaking around behind Miles's back, but at the same time, we were both consenting adults.

It had been seven days since Ramsay had carried me upstairs and had his way with me, and yes, that is exactly how I liked to think of it. *Had his way with me*.

Because, I'm telling you, I never thought I was one for the whole Alpha male, order-me-around, take-charge type, but holy hell—in the bedroom? *Yes, please, and thank you.* I will take it any and all days of the week apparently. My cheeks flushed as I thought about how just that morning he'd ordered me to my knees, and I'd taken him in my mouth, touching myself while I'd pleasured him.

And all this was before my morning coffee.

I'd moved a few things over from the castle, nothing much, but just enough that could get me by, because I'd been spending most nights at Ramsay's place. Calvin didn't seem to mind, as a secondary cat jungle gym made by Ramsay's father had appeared, and I couldn't believe what an easy rhythm Ramsay and I had fallen into.

This morning I sat at the sewing machine, ready to put the finishing touches on my outfit for the upcoming cèilidh when my phone buzzed with an incoming text message. Picking it up, I dangled a knotted ribbon in front of Calvin absentmindedly while I scrolled.

> Mom got a favor called in and got her tests done. Stage one. Good news though. There are virtually no signs at this stage, so the outlook is great. All because of your vision. Dinner's on me. Bring Ramsay. I hear you two are shacking up.

I blinked back the rush of tears that threatened.

My gift had done some good.

I could make a difference here.

Calvin sunk a claw into my calf, and I yelped, looking down at him, and he blinked at me, a vision of my scissors flashing into my head.

"Ope, you think this was a challenge?" I squinted down at him. "You know, you don't have to be so rude about getting my attention."

Calvin butted his head against my leg, purring, and I pursed my lips.

"Yeah, like that. A much better route than the claws."

Digging in my sewing kit, I pulled out my scissors and turned the handle over in my hand.

I gasped.

Sure enough, nestled among the vines was a heart with a thistle in the middle of it, much like the locket that Lia had worn. I held the scissors to my chest, closing my eyes to settle myself, and that's how Ramsay found me.

"Don't do it. I quite like having you around."

Grinning, I opened my eyes to see him smiling at me from the other side of the table.

"I passed another challenge."

"Did you? That's grand, isn't it? When were you off accomplishing side quests?"

"Ah, well, it's a private matter. Do you mind if I let her tell you as it's not my story to share?"

"Who is she?"

"Lia."

"That's fair. I suppose you'd have to be careful with what you know, now that you can get a behind-the-curtain view to people's lives. But she and Munroe are okay?"

"They are. And, yes, it feels kind of like I need to have a confidentiality clause." I reached out and squeezed Ramsay's hand, grateful for his understanding, and pulled him closer. "Look at my scissors."

I showed him where the new design had shown up in the handle, and appreciated how he took the time to carefully listen and appreciate the gift that I'd been given.

Ramsay didn't try to steamroll me or tell me what was best for me to do, nor was he a pushover.

He'd truly been proud of me for being a part of the Order of Caledonia and was fascinated by how deeply the magickal roots ran in Loren Brae. As was I. He'd asked me more about my mom and my gran and brought up the question of whether one of them had maybe had magick as well.

Despite my lack of knowledge, instead of feeling threatened or trying to tell me what to do with my gift, he asked intelligent questions and listened when I answered. I was beginning to think we would make a really good team.

"Also, I have a fun project for us."

"Does it involve your mesh bra that I love?" Ramsay leaned against the table.

"It could," I said, my brain immediately leaving the work train and hopping on the sex train.

He laughed and gestured for me to go on.

That was something I'd noticed. Ramsay laughed more now. He wasn't as uptight, and he'd let me start making changes to the shop, allowing more clients in. I was starting to feel like I was finally finding my footing here. Our first round of designs were almost finished to show Sophie, but I wanted to add in one more extra touch.

"Let's go sit by the fire."

It had become my favorite part of the day, cozying in by the fire, tossing design ideas back and forth, and I looked forward to this time with him. Ramsay had warned me the fire wouldn't be lit in the summer, but maybe I'd be able to convince him to light a candle to at least set the cozy mood that I so craved.

"Okay, sooooo, I know we're almost done with the designs, at least for presentation purposes, but since we haven't actually settled on our top tartan patterns, I thought I'd introduce an idea."

"Unicorns?" Ramsay raised an eyebrow at me, and I laughed. He leaned back in the chair, stretching his legs out in front of him, and steepled his fingers as he watched me with an intensity that had my thoughts scattering. Bringing it back, I tapped the screen of my iPad and brought up a website.

"Did you know that you can design and trademark your very own tartan pattern?" I asked, looking at him with excitement.

His lips twitched.

"Right. Duh. Of course you know that. You're a kiltmaker. And Scottish. This is your job. So, yeah, well, I thought ... could we make one for MacAlpine Castle? Together."

"Hmmm." Ramsay brought his fingers under his chin, his eyes distant as he considered it. "The castle has a family tartan."

"Right, it does. But it's connected to the family name, right? Not to the MacAlpine name?"

"Correct."

"Look at this website. You can bring up all the tartan patterns, riff on them, or start from scratch with your own. You can even submit the pattern for commercial use after. Want to give it a go? Just for fun? See if we land on anything good?"

"Of course we'd land on something good. Everything you design is brilliant."

My heart stilled at his words.

"You really mean that?"

"Aye. You're extremely talented."

I blinked at him, and my heart trembled in my chest before it tumbled off the cliff into love. God, I loved this grumpy, impossibly handsome, steadfast man. I knew it was too soon to tell him that, so I just looked down at the iPad, heat flooding my cheeks.

"Thank you," I said softly, not realizing how much I'd needed to hear those words. My father had always supported me, but in sort of a bewildered way, and my brother had demanded I leave this career on more than one occasion. To have a man I cared about, particularly someone who was successful in the industry, compliment me in such a manner made my heart swell.

"You should be proud of yourself, Willow. And I do think these designs are going to be popular with the tourists, though I'm not sure how I feel about the bum bags."

"Fanny packs," I grumbled.

"Bum bags. Or the pet bowties."

"Those are going to sell like hotcakes," I promised him.

"Nobody is going to buy a tartan bowtie for their dog."

"Everyone is going to buy a tartan bowtie for their dog. Are you kidding me? Haven't you seen how cute Sir Buster looks in his kilt?"

Ramsay rolled his eyes.

"Laugh all you will, but I'm going to win that bet." We'd put money down on whether the tartan dog and cat collars would be one of the bestsellers, that is if Sophie agreed to stock them, and I was certain I'd win.

Ramsay grunted, but his eyes twinkled.

"All right, lass. Show me your program."

Two hours later we'd hammered out a pattern we both liked, in red, grey, black, and white with the tiniest thread of blue running through. Sitting back in my chair, I smiled, pleased with the result.

"I dig it."

"It's nice. Even though I had to pull you back from pink."

"What's wrong with pink?"

"It's not exactly a traditional kilt color."

"I suppose." I poked his chest. "Look at us. Agreeing on things. Designing together. Working together. And here you wanted nothing to do with me when I first arrived."

"I still have my moments. If you change my music one more time …" Ramsay held a fist in the air and I laughed. "Right, then. I've got a meeting with Sheila to go over some store plans."

"I'll finish up here."

"Dinner later?"

"Mmm, can we do takeout? I need to finish my outfit for the cèilidh." The dance was tomorrow night, and all of Loren Brae was in a tizzy about it. It had been a long, cold winter, and with the Kelpies continuing to keep the tourism industry at an all-time low, the dance was a bright spot for everyone.

For me, as well.

I was part of this community now too.

People weren't so scared to come in the shop anymore, I was beginning to learn the names of the locals, and I'd even been invited to join a book club at Agnes's bookstore. I didn't read much, but when I was told audiobooks counted, I agreed to join. The first book was a vampire romance, and I idly wondered how Ramsay would feel about having some romance played at the shop. I grinned, imagining his glowering as I asked, and modified one of the dog collars to have a tartan floral rosette instead of a bow. Picking up my scissors, I cut a swatch of fabric to see if I could fashion a rosette.

Flames licked up the walls and I gasped, dropping the scissors.

I looked around, but where it had been daytime, it was now night, and the room had changed enough for me to know I was smack dab in a vision.

A horrible one at that.

Heat singed my skin, and I jumped up, turning in a circle, panic clenching my gut as fire ravaged the shop.

A man's voice cried for help. I turned to go, to see where it came from, and ran into something hard.

"Willow." The voice was sharp, a command, and I came to with a start, realizing Ramsay was shaking me.

"Oh my God, oh no," I cried, gripping his arms, panic still holding me in its clutches.

"Shhh, calm down. Tell me what happened." Ramsay ran his hands up and down my arms, soothing me, and I swallowed, trying to find the words.

"I ... I had another vision. I think. Oh my God, Ramsay. It's the shop. The shop was on fire."

At that Ramsay stiffened, his face going hard, his eyes darting around the room.

"Walk me through it."

"It was ... it was so fast. It was night. That's how I knew

I was in a vision and that the fireplace hadn't suddenly erupted." I wiped a hand across my brow where sweat had sprung, and Ramsay grabbed my hand.

"Look."

A dark wash of soot coated the backs of my hands and I grimaced, long threads of worry unraveling inside me.

"I didn't see much else. There were flames everywhere. I heard a man's voice call for help, and I was running ... that way I guess? I needed to find him."

"Did you see anything else that might indicate a time? A date on your iPad? Was there a fire in the fireplace? Snow outside?" Ramsay ticked off the points, his face deadly serious.

"No, nothing that I can recall." I shook my head, furious that I didn't have more information to give him.

"Here, sit. Let me get you a glass of water." He nudged me back into the chair, pressed a kiss against the top of my hair.

"Incredible. Your hair even smells like smoke."

"I'm scared," I whispered, tracing a finger against the soot on my skin.

"One sec." Ramsay hurried away and then returned, depositing Calvin in my lap, and handing me a cup of water. Then he crouched at my feet. Calvin, sensing my distress, butted his head against my chin, and I stroked his soft fur. "Listen, I know this place looks cozy and rustic, but I've got all the modern things here. I have Nest alarms set up, ring cameras, all the bells and whistles. If you burn a piece of toast, the alarm will go off."

"Okay." I blew out a breath and then took a very long,

slow inhale. "I mean, we can't know that all of my visions come true, right?"

"We don't. But even if it's true, we can't just live on edge, you ken? We have to leave the shop. And I've done all the precautions I can to protect the space. There's nothing that can be done unless you can think about anything else that might help. Do you think you can drop back into the vision?"

"I have no idea. I can try."

"What do you need from me?"

"I don't know. Maybe, just, go back into the other room again? I'll try to replicate what I was doing?"

"Good luck. I'll be right here."

I waited until he'd walked into the other room, and then picked up my iPad. Led Zeppelin played in the background as I continued to sketch. But even when I tried to put myself back into the vision, nothing happened. I emptied my brain, forcing myself to just focus on the sketch, but still no dice. Frustrated, I put the iPad down, cupped Calvin in my arms, and stood. Striding across the room to the window, I looked out across Loch Mirren. The sky was moody today, as it was most days, and I found myself transfixed on the island far out in the water. The wind was high enough today that tinges of white capped the waves, and the grey clouds moved at a fast clip across the sky. The sun filtered through the clouds, an occasional ray spearing the loch, and I stroked Calvin's coat as I tried to push down the worry.

Intellectually, I understood that Ramsay was right. There wasn't much I could do about protecting the shop, and I hadn't been able to give him any helpful details.

Heavy footfalls sounded, and I sighed as Ramsay's arms came around my waist, pulling my back to his chest.

"Anything?"

"Nope."

"Would it make you feel better if we moved some of our important stuff out? To your place? Just in case?"

"I think so, yeah. Just to be on the safe side? Maybe we stay at my place?"

"I'm fine with that, if it makes you feel better."

"I don't know what's better. To be on site if a fire starts or to be away?"

"Again. Alarms. They'll alert me quickly. I'd be more comfortable keeping you at the castle."

"Keeping me," I snorted, turning to look up at him, "like a maiden in the tower."

"Do you need rescuing, darling?" Ramsay leaned down, stealing my answer with his lips.

I didn't need rescuing, no, but somehow, I felt like Ramsay had managed to do so anyway. I'd been lost, and landing here, with him, had given me a foundation that I hadn't known I'd needed. That being said, this was still so new, and I had a habit of jumping into things headfirst without looking for a safe landing. I needed to remind myself to take this day by day or soon I'd be designing my wedding dress before the man even told me he loved me.

We needed to speak to Miles. That would be a good first step.

"I have to hop on that call." Ramsay backed up, brushing a thumb across my lip, and smiled softly. "Don't worry, Willow. I'll take care of you."

That's what part of me was afraid of. I was supposed to

take care of myself, wasn't I? To prove I could do this on my own? Torn between wanting to prove to everyone that I could be a successful designer in my own right and loving this budding professional collaboration I had going with Ramsay, I watched him walk away, worry still hovering in my heart.

CHAPTER TWENTY-SEVEN

Willow

The preparations for the cèilidh that night were in full swing at MacAlpine Castle. True to his word, Ramsay had packed his truck full of anything we were worried about for a fire, including special-order fabrics, any personal mementos he cared for, as well as business papers and legal documents. Lachlan had ribbed him about moving up in the world when he'd seen all the boxes but had quickly helped move his stuff up to my apartment where we'd stored it in the spare bedroom. I'd appreciated that even though it was a deep inconvenience to move everything from the shop, Ramsay hadn't complained once.

Again, he'd listened and trusted my insight. *And again, I wanted to tell him that I truly loved him.*

We'd agreed that we'd just bring the bolts of fabric for the day's work with us down to the shop and transport it back at night. It would be devastating to lose some of those custom fabrics, especially with how long they took to make. If it took a few moments longer to bring each roll of fabric with us each day, so be it.

I just wondered how long we could operate that way. There'd been no timeline on when this supposed fire would start, and I'd been anxious all day thinking about it.

Calvin had been invited for a playdate with Archie in the library so I could finish my outfit and help with the dance preparation. I carried him downstairs, eyes peeled for a sudden Clyde appearance, and pushed open the door to the library, pleased that I'd successfully navigated the winding castle hallways to find it.

Pushing the door open, my mouth dropped open at the chaos I found.

"What the—"

"Och, lass, come in, come in. We're having a bit of a game." Archie motioned me over to where he crouched in front of a lounge chair, lecturing Sir Buster. But it wasn't the dogs that I gaped at.

Two gnome statues, a man and a woman, two hedgehogs, and Brice were all lined up in a row on the carpet.

Let me rephrase that.

Two gnomes.

Real, live, moving gnomes.

Apparently, once they'd decided I was cool, or whatever, they'd snapped out of their statue mode and immediately started arguing with each other.

"You're not going to the dance without me."

"Maybe I'll meet one of the castle gnomes." The female

gnome fluffed her hair, giving the male gnome, who wore a kilt and had tattoos on his arm, a wink.

"You can meet them all you want. You're coming home with me, lass."

"Um," I said, waving awkwardly at them. "Hi."

Calvin clawed at me to put him down and Brice let out that strange cooing sound again, racing across the room to hug Calvin, best friends reunited. The hedgehogs edged backward, cowering behind the gnomes, as my cat drew nearer.

"Calvin." Calvin turned and looked at me. "Be nice to the hedgehogs and, well, everyone here. Okay? This isn't a hunting ground for you."

Sir Buster peeked out from where he now cowered beneath Archie's legs while Lady Lola lay sprawled on the carpet, watching the others with lazy interest. Calvin bumped his head against Brice, curling around the broonie's body, and then winked at me. I couldn't decide if it was deliberate or not, but I figured if Archie could manage a playdate with all these magickal beings, then he could handle my cat.

"Are you ... Shona's gnomes?" I hadn't met Shona yet, but I hoped to tonight.

"Gnorman and Gnora, both with silent Gs." Gnorman nodded to me, and it took me a moment to work out what he meant about the silent G.

"Nice to meet you. I'm Willow."

"We know that." Gnora sashayed forward, her skirt swishing around her knees. "I hear you design clothes. I'm in the market for some new dresses. Something to drive this one crazy."

"Och, you drive me crazy just by existing," Gnorman grumbled.

"Isn't he sweet? What do you think, Willow? Could you design for someone my size?"

"I design for all sizes," I said automatically, and smiled when she beamed up at me.

"In that case, I'll get Shona to bring me by one day. I like a really deep cleavage. Maybe some lace?"

"What about a pencil skirt? That drives men up the wall," I offered and Gnorman put a hand to his forehead and pretended to faint.

"That'll do the trick. I'll come see you soon."

"I look forward to it." And I did. I'd always said I would design for all shapes and bodies, and I thought it would be a fun challenge to design for Gnora.

"You go on and help with the preparations. We're taking turns on daycare duty." Archie nodded at me.

One of the hedgies ran forward and bumped his head against my toe, and I crouched, tilting my head as he smiled up at me.

"Hey, bud."

"That's Eugene. He's a sweetheart."

"Och, lass. Not as sweet as I am," Gnorman protested, scowling at the grinning hedgie.

"Who said I like 'em sweet?" Gnora winked at me as Gnorman fumed, caught.

"Then I'm tough as nails."

"Well, which is it then?" Gnora shot a flirtatious look over her shoulder.

"Are you going to race or not?" Archie interjected, and they all lined up in a row again.

As much as I wanted to watch the little magickals in a race, I had promised I'd stop by to see Lia, and to help with any prep work that was needed. Plus, I had to finalize my outfit. I hoped to knock Ramsay's socks off when he saw me tonight. With a wave goodbye, I took myself down to the kitchen, a smile on my lips.

I mean, seriously, how cool was that?

I was living a literal fairy tale and had the handsome prince to boot.

Humming, I walked into chaos in the kitchen, as people raced about, arms full of this and that. I paused in the doorway, not wanting to interrupt, as Lia issued orders from where she chopped vegetables at her prep table. A pretty blond woman stood by her side, unloading a basket of herbs.

"Willow! Come in, come in. Willow, this is Shona."

"Finally." Shona's blue eyes crinkled at the corners as she smiled at me. "I've been meaning to stop by the shop."

"I think I just met your gnomes."

"Cheeky bastards, aren't they?"

"They are." I laughed, amazed that I was even having a conversation about live gnomes at the moment. "And Brice and Calvin were having a lovefest."

"Oh good. I told him to clear out while everyone was here. He has a tendency to get over involved in the party planning and can freak a few people out." Lia's knife flew as she spoke.

"I can imagine," I said dryly, looking up as Hilda poked her head in.

"Shona? Should we do flowers?"

"Put me to work. I just need like an hour to finish my outfit before the dance."

Before I followed Shona into the other room, I leaned close to Lia.

"How's your mom?" I whispered.

"Wicked good, thanks to you. She's got next level care." Lia's eyes warmed as she smiled at me. "I'll always be indebted to you."

"No, it's nothing. Really." I wanted to tell her about the vision I'd had about the fire, but figured she, quite literally, had enough on her plate. It could wait.

By the time I'd helped with the flowers, put out games for the kids, and packaged cute party favors, I was running out of time to finish my outfit. I couldn't wait for Ramsay to see me in it. Ducking out, I stopped by the library to find it empty. Archie must have taken them somewhere, but since I trusted him with Calvin, I figured he was probably stuffing the cat full of chicken and other various treats. Feeling excited for my first real Scottish dance, I opened my apartment door to find Ramsay with his back to me, his voice raised as he spoke to someone on the phone.

"I understand if you don't like it. But I'm not going to stop dating your sister."

My shoulders tensed. He was on the phone with Miles.

I'd meant to bring it up to Ramsay again, but we'd been so busy with other things. I hung back, nervous, as Miles let out a string of curses.

"You call yourself a friend? A brother to me? And you go and sleep with my sister?"

"It's not like that." Ramsay glowered at the phone.

"Some friend you are. I considered you a brother. You told me you'd look out for her. And instead you're hooking—"

"Watch yourself." The warning in Ramsay's voice sent a shiver down my back.

"*You* watch yourself. If I was there, I swear to God, I'd lay you out. Screw you, man. You're no friend."

Miles's face disappeared from the screen, and Ramsay's shoulders slumped.

"Ramsay."

Ramsay turned, his face set in stone.

"He'll calm down. He's just … that's how he gets. You know Miles doesn't handle anything out of his control well. He sucks. Like, legit sucks. It's going to be okay once he calms down."

"He's not wrong."

I tensed at his words, stepping farther into the room, clenching my hands at my chest.

"What do you mean? Are you … ending things?"

I felt like I was being dumped the night of prom. My stomach twisted, and tears threatened.

"What? Och, no. *No*. But he's also not wrong. I crossed a line." Ramsay lifted his eyes to meet mine, and I stepped forward until we were inches apart. Still I didn't touch him. I lifted my face to his.

"Did you though? It's not like you took advantage of me. If this is what we both want, who is he to stand in our way?"

Was it what we both wanted? I loved this man. But I can't tell him I love him, not if he's unsure about what he feels for me.

Damn you, Miles. Ramsay's expression was virtually unreadable as he looked down at me. For once, I wished Clyde would spring into the room to break the tension, but no such reprieve presented itself.

"I should have told him ... before. Asked his permission."

"Excuse me?" I reared back, annoyed. "Permission for what, exactly? I'm my own woman and can make my own decisions. I certainly don't need my brother's permission for *anything* that I do in my life."

"I still should have spoken to him." Ramsay's expression remained stony.

"You know what? You're starting to piss me off. And I don't like that, because I've got a pretty dress, and this is my first Scottish dance. Yes, I get it sucks that Miles is mad about this ... whatever this is. But he'll come around. Or he won't. But either way, get it very clear in your head, Ramsay, that I'm the only one who gives out permission on what to do with my body, my future, and my life. Not Miles. Not anyone. So you can take your antiquated patriarchal notion of asking permission and shove it up your ass." I poked my finger into his chest for good measure and turned to flounce into the bedroom, where I could cry in peace. I'd *really* been looking forward to this dance.

I made it two steps before Ramsay grabbed me around my waist and buried his face in the back of my neck.

"I'm sorry. It's been weighing on me, not telling him. You're right. I don't need his permission to date you. I'm upset because I crossed a line with him is all."

And line crossing with brothers is a very sore spot with Ramsay.

My breath was shaky as I turned in his arms. I needed to give this man some grace, because he, too, had his own issues he was working out.

"You're still taking me to the cèilidh?" I'd been working on my pronunciation.

"I'd be honored to have you on my arm this night, my fair maiden," Ramsay joked, playing up that we were now sleeping in a castle. I closed my eyes, and pressed my forehead to his chest, and he wrapped his arms around me. We stood like that for a moment, our world recalibrating around each other, so many words left unsaid and yet nothing else needing to be said at all.

"I need to finish getting ready." My words were muffled against his shirt.

"Just a moment, darling." Ramsay reached a hand under my chin, lifting my face until his lips found mine. I sunk into the kiss. "There. That's better then."

"He won't stay mad long. Give him time."

"He's always had a short fuse." Ramsay shook his head, and I arched a brow at him.

"This from the man who exploded when I turned off Foo Fighters the other day?"

"Och, you can't turn off music mid-song. At the very least wait until the end."

The tension eased in my shoulders, and I tapped a finger against his nose before pulling myself from his arms.

"You need to get ready in the other bedroom. I want my Cinderella moment."

"You look amazing in anything you put on."

"Keep that up, sir, and you may just get lucky after the dance."

Ramsay flashed a wolfish grin that had desire tugging at my core.

"I plan to."

I hightailed it to my bedroom before I did something silly, like skip the dance so I could jump Ramsay, and closed the door behind me. Unzipping the garment bag that I'd laid across the bed, I pulled out my outfit and grinned at it. I'd taken inspiration from images I'd scoured online of traditional Scottish attire for women, and then I'd done my own spin on it to modernize it.

If I had to say, it was like Madonna meets Outlander.

Naturally, I'd gone with a pink tartan that I'd sourced. I'd sewn a wide high-waisted circle skirt that had plenty of flounce and movement when you twirled. I'd ended the skirt at the knees, and then had designed a black tulle petticoat for beneath the skirt to give it added pouf. For the top, I'd cut and sewn a bustier with a sweetheart neckline in black silk. I'd lined the edges with a slim strip of the pink tartan fabric and added pretty jet beads down the front. It was fun and fresh, as Sophie had told me that while people would be dressed up, it wasn't as formal as a wedding, so I designed something that would make me feel pretty and would have a lot of movement on the spins.

A few more stitches on the bustier and I'd be all set. Humming to myself, I finished off the outfit, rolled my hair into hot rollers, then took a lightning-fast shower. After, I did my makeup, smokey eyes and soft lips, and then unfurled my hair from the rollers and brushed it softly for big bouncy waves. Piling a few sparkles around my neck, I slipped on my dress, and realized my error.

Shit. I was going to need Ramsay to zip me up.

Annoyed, I went to the door.

"Ramsay."

"Aye?"

"I need you to zip me up but it's going to ruin my Cinderella moment."

"I'll keep my eyes closed."

"How will you zip me then?"

"By touch."

"I really don't see how that will work, but okay, let's try it. I'm coming out now."

Stepping out into the living room, I almost swallowed my tongue at the sight of Ramsay in formal kilt dress. Slick black boots, chunky socks, and a proper fitted vest and jacket outlined his broad shoulders perfectly. Did I really want to go to the dance? Maybe Ramsay had the right of it and we should just stay here.

He held his hands in front of him like a mummy, his eyes squeezed closed.

"Okay, I'm backing up into your hands," I said, turning around right before him and then backing up, holding the dress at my chest. His hands brushed my shoulders and then he grabbed my arms.

"Hmm, let's see if I can figure this out."

One hand reached around and cupped a breast, and my eyes widened.

"Zipper is at the back, Ramsay."

"Oh, right. Right. Just checking." His hands came around my waist and then landed on my butt, squeezing enthusiastically.

"A bit higher."

"Really, just *so* sorry, darling. I'm sure I'll get this sorted."

I suppressed a giggle. I liked this teasing side of Ramsay and hoped I'd be able to bring it out in him more.

Finally, his fingers found the zipper, and he tugged it closed, his breath warm at my shoulders as he did. Once secure, I danced away before he could distract me, and slammed the door to the bedroom so I could put my shoes on and take a moment to catch my breath. I nearly melted every time he called me darling. The way the *R* rolled off his tongue ... it was so freaking sexy.

He just looked *so* handsome in his kilt. And he was my date to the dance tonight. Well, to anywhere, I guessed, though we hadn't actually had a conversation yet about what we were doing or the actual status of our relationship. I mean, it was too soon, wasn't it? Best to just let these things take their time.

Sliding on black sparkle high-heeled Mary Jane's, I straightened and went to the mirror, and clapped my hands in front of my chest. Twirling, I kicked my foot out, loving the flounce of the skirt, and how the sweetheart neckline accentuated my curves. My skin was flushed, my eyes sparkling with excitement, and I took a second to appreciate this experience.

Everything was happening for me.

I was finally coming into my own.

I had a new direction in my career that I loved. Designing with Ramsay was turning out to be challenging and exciting, and I enjoyed it immensely. I loved Loren Brae and the people that I was forging new friendships with here.

My magick was coming into fruition and offered a new avenue of power for me to explore, which I think with time, would give me an added layer of confidence.

And then there was Ramsay.

A man right out of a fairy tale really.

And he was taking me to the dance.

Letting out a breath, I grabbed a small clutch I'd made from the same black silk as the bustier with the pink tartan edging, and cracked the door.

"Ready?"

"Aye, lassie."

I chuckled. He knew I loved it when he called me "lassie."

"Okay, ta-da," I said, stepping out of the bedroom with my arms wide, nerves fluttering in my stomach.

"Och, lass." Ramsay's eyes heated, and the look that crossed his face was almost feral. "You look incredible."

"You like it? You made fun of pink tartan the other day."

"On you? It's fantastic." Ramsay circled his finger and I twirled obediently. "Och, it's going to be impossible to keep from pulling you into a dark corner tonight and having my way with you."

"Sir," I said, pretending offense. "Is that how you talk to a lady?"

"That's how I talk to my lady," Ramsay said, his hands at my waist, his mouth hot at my ear. "Who I happen to know for a fact would enjoy me having my way with her in a dark corner."

"I mean, I suppose I wouldn't object." My skin heated as he trailed a finger across the silk at the scooped neckline.

"This silk feels nice," Ramsay said, brushing his palms across my chest, and I had to clench my thighs together.

"Keep that up, and we'll never make it to the dance."

"I'd be okay with that, but I need to show you off in this dress." Ramsay pulled back, and I laughed as he adjusted his sporran over where it was clear how much he wanted me.

I loved that. Loved knowing I could have that effect on this handsome and powerful man.

"Shall we then? Show me what this cèilidh stuff is all about."

"I hope you're ready to dance."

"I'll do my best," I promised as we wound our way through the castle. Excitement made me a bit giddy—it was hard not to feel like Cinderella going to the ball with her dashing prince.

"I hope you can dance in those heels," Ramsay said, as we stepped inside the bustling restaurant that had been transformed into a dance hall for the night. Tables had been pulled to the room's perimeter, and strands of twinkle lights and colorful streamers ran from one side of the room to the next. Candles were tucked at intervals along the rugged stone walls, and a small bandstand had been set up in the corner where the singer had just started to speak into the microphone.

"Welcome, everyone! We're Scottish Storm, and I hope you're ready to dance tonight. We're kicking off the party with a traditional Gay Gordon's. Partner up!"

"Oh God, just right in, huh?" I said as Ramsay dragged me into the circle. He came to stand at my side and placed his arm straight across my shoulder.

"Yup. It starts with three steps forward, swivel, then four steps backward."

"Wait, how many steps?"

"Three forward, turn, four backward." Ramsay's eyes twinkled. "He'll call it out, just listen for the instructions."

A fiddle struck up, playing a jaunty tune, before the band swung into a rousing song and the singer shouted into the microphone.

"And we're off. Three steps forward. Turn. Four steps back."

Ramsay's arm at my shoulders propelled me forward and I giggled as I missed the turn and bumped into a couple who was already moving backward. Everyone laughed, and the pace picked up as the singer called off the steps.

"Gents, turn your ladies."

Ramsay surprised me with a quick twirl.

"And once around the room."

Ramsay grabbed me and ushered me in the circle, everyone following suit. It took about three more tries before I didn't end up bumping into other couples, but soon I had it down and tossed my hair over my shoulder, my cheeks flushing as I laughed and stomped my way through the dance. It reminded me very much of country line dancing, and it was surprisingly fun. By the time the song ended, my skin had heated, and I was thoroughly enjoying myself.

"This is fun," I gasped to Ramsay when he pulled me aside.

"It is. Can I get you a drink or do you want to jump right into the next dance?"

"What's the next dance? Is it different steps?"

"Aye, lass. They'll keep changing it up, and then cycle back through the dances later on."

"Oh, I'd better learn them then."

"Gentlemen, line up on one side. Ladies on the other. This is called Strip the Willow," the singer called, and we followed instructions. I had to laugh at the name of the song when Ramsay winked at me.

"This dress is fabulous," Sophie said from my side. She looked amazing in a silky wrap dress in soft pink, and Lachlan had barely taken his eyes from her.

"Look at them," Lia said, leaning in from the other side. She wore a fitted simple black dress that showed every curve. Agnes appeared in a delicate sheath dress the color of the sky at dawn. Shona joined us, in a pretty floral flowy dress, and we all examined the men across from us.

Lachlan, Munroe, Owen, Graham, and Ramsay stood across from us, all different, and yet equally as magnificent. I hadn't met Owen yet, but I'd seen him dancing with Shona already, so I figured that was him. The men looked at us, each with equally hungry looks in their eyes, and we gave a collective sigh.

"It should be illegal to be that hot," Sophie said.

"Seriously," I breathed. The combined punch of these men standing together, all kilted up and knowing exactly what they were about, was enough to make any woman swoon. If swooning was still in style, that is.

"Starting from the top, couple number one ... gentleman, swing your lady."

"And we're off," Sophie exclaimed, grabbing my hand. Ramsay winked at me from across the room, and I tossed my hair and winked back, feeling wanted in a way that I never had before. No matter what came next, I'd always have this memory, dancing in a centuries-old castle with a handsome man who only had eyes for me.

As life choices went, I was pretty pleased with where I'd landed.

CHAPTER TWENTY-EIGHT

Willow

"I'm going to sneak away for a whisky and cigar with the lads. Alright by you?" Ramsay asked during the band's break. We were all glistening with sweat, and none of us gave a damn. I was officially a convert. I loved cèilidhs.

"Go, enjoy. I'll go help Lia in the kitchen."

Ramsay brushed his lips over mine, and I smiled into his kiss, happy that he had no problem showing affection in public. Whether we were official or not, he wasn't hiding anything from the people of Loren Brae. Humming, I made my way through the crowd to find Sophie and Agnes helping Lia in the kitchen.

"What did you think?" Agnes asked, offering me a small crust of bread with chutney on top.

"Too much fun. I'm going to sweat right through this dress, but I don't even care."

"That's a cèilidh for you." Agnes grinned.

A vision flashed in my mind, and I froze, gripping Agnes's arm.

"Willow? What's wrong?"

It wasn't a psychic vision. It was Calvin. He was trying to get my attention.

"The shop," I gasped. "It's burning. We have to go."

"What?" Sophie exclaimed. "It's on fire?"

"Now, now, now," I shouted, and Lia ran to where keys hung on a hook by the door.

"Brice," Lia shouted. "Go find the men and tell them there's trouble. Let's go, I'll drive."

"I'll call the fire house." Agnes, Sophie, Lia, and I raced out the door and piled into a truck parked near the back door.

"Go, go, go," I shouted, and Lia floored it, racing toward Ramsay's shop.

"How do you know?" Agnes asked.

"Calvin. He can communicate with me. Somehow, he's gotten out, and he's down at the shop."

"Is he in the fire?" Sophie gasped.

"No." Panic gripped me. "But I think someone else is."

"Willow, no," Agnes said.

"I saw it in a vision. Someone gets stuck inside. We have to help."

"But how?" Sophie demanded as we turned the corner up the lane to see flames dancing in the front window of Ramsay's shop. My heart twisted. I was out before Lia had fully stopped the truck. The front door stood open, and I hesitated at the stoop.

"Willow, don't go in! The fire brigade will be here soon."

"I have to. Someone's in there," I insisted.

Smoke billowed from the front door, and I paused, my heart hammering my chest.

"Screw it," I said, and reaching down, I ripped off a swatch of my skirt and tied it around my face. We'd left a fire extinguisher just inside the front and back doors, and I reached for that now as I ducked inside to their shouts of protest.

Acrid smoke burned my eyes, and flames licked up the walls. Crouching, I found the fire extinguisher and pulled the pin, blasting the wall as I stepped forward.

"Help!"

It was faint, but I caught it.

"Hello? Where are you?" I screamed, unleashing another stream of foam at the fire.

"Back here," the voice shouted, and I turned toward the back room, trying to find my way in the smoke and darkness, coughing into the fabric at my mouth. I inched closer, trying to stay low and beneath the smoke, but it burned my eyes. My chest heaved, and I struggled for breath.

It wasn't the fire, I'd been told more than once, it was the smoke that would get you.

I tried to push forward, but the smoke kept billowing from the back room, and I blasted it as much as I could. Dots began to swim in front of my eyes, and I stumbled, dropping to my knees.

"How far back are you?" I screamed. I'd have to crawl.

"God damn it, Willow." Ramsay's shout behind me had

me turning, as he scooped me up from the floor and carried me through the flames and smoke back outside.

"No, Ramsay, someone's in there." My body shook with a wracking cough, and I burrowed into his arms, tears running down my face.

"You idiot," Ramsay seethed. "You could have been killed."

"Someone's in there," I insisted, pulling the strip of cloth down as cool air washed over me.

"And that's not for you to take care of," Ramsay shouted at me. I don't think I'd ever seen him so angry before. He put me down, and Sophie wrapped her arms around me. To my utter shock, Ramsay turned and stormed back inside.

"Ramsay, no!" I shouted. I'd made some headway with the fire extinguisher, but not enough to truly brunt the force of the fire. But he was gone, disappearing into the smoke and flames, taking my heart with him.

Seconds felt like eternity as the fire brigade wailed in the background, and my entire body shook as I counted the time. Waiting. Waiting. Waiting.

Forty-one.

Forty-two.

Forty-three.

"It's too long, it's been too long." I gripped Sophie's arm, tears almost blinding me.

"Shhh, the fire brigade is here. It'll be okay."

The firemen shouted at us to step back, unfurling their hoses, when movement appeared at the door.

"There are two people in there!" I shouted.

Two firemen heard me and changed course, heading

toward the front door, when movement showed through the smoke.

My heart caught.

Ramsay stumbled out, a body thrown over his shoulder, and collapsed to his knees outside. Immediately the firefighters converged on him, lifting the body from his shoulders and I broke away from Sophie, racing to his side.

"Ramsay." I crouched, as he doubled over, his body wracked with coughing, and held him as I looked around for the paramedic. "He needs help."

"It's fine," Ramsay gasped, between coughs.

"Smoke inhalation is no joke."

And then a flurry of activity descended around us as paramedics nudged me aside to help Ramsay, the firemen started their hose, and general pandemonium ensued. I was pushed back to the edge of the crowd, and I had to wait, helpless, as the shop burned.

Everything except the sign, it seemed.

Ramsay Kilts.

Would he rebuild?

What did this mean for us?

"It was his brother," Sophie said, joining me, and I gasped, turning to see a sympathetic look in her eyes.

"Andrew did this?"

"That was who he pulled from the fire. Whether he did it or not, I don't know."

"Is he ..."

"No, he's not dead. Barely breathing, but not dead."

A bump at my leg caught my attention, and I looked down to see Calvin twining himself among my legs.

"Oh, buddy. You did good." I scooped him up into my

arms, and he purred against my neck, nuzzling in. "I'm so glad you weren't hurt."

I had to count my blessings. Calvin was safe, I was safe, and Ramsay would hopefully be fine based on the cursing I'd heard him let loose on the paramedics. His brother had been taken away to the hospital. There wasn't much else to do but watch the firefighters work.

And so I stood there and watched our dreams burn.

CHAPTER TWENTY-NINE

Willow

Ramsay didn't come home that night.

I'd hoped he would, but he had gone to the hospital for a checkup and to see his brother. He'd been short with me when he'd left, instructing me to go home, and it was hard for me to read what he wanted or needed from me in this moment. Deciding not to push it, I'd agreed to take Calvin home and said I'd hoped to see him later.

But morning had come and there was no text message from him.

Worry filled me.

Needing to know what had happened, I tried calling, but it went straight to voicemail which meant either his phone had died or was off. It wasn't surprising, Ramsay wasn't much for texting or being on his phone, but I couldn't help but wonder what had happened with his brother and if he was feeling okay.

"The brother lived. I hear he's being charged with arson." Archie snapped his newspaper closed and held out his hands for Calvin when I arrived in the lounge. Dangling a feather from his basket of flies next to him, he smiled as Calvin rolled on his back and swatted at the toy. "He's a good cat."

"He is. He must have gotten away from you yesterday because he's the one who told me the place was on fire."

"Is that right?" Hilda asked, swinging into the room with a tray of scones and toast. "How are you able to communicate with him?"

"I'm not entirely sure. I just figured out that he can kind of flash images into my brain of what he wants. Like he's really interested in what's on your tray there."

"Nothing for you, wee lad." Hilda clucked her tongue at Calvin.

"And Ramsay? Has anyone heard from him?"

"I heard he didn't have to stay in the hospital or anything. He was there because of his brother, and then went home to his parents' house."

"Of course." I sat at the table and buttered a scone, eating it idly even though I wasn't very hungry. "That makes sense."

It did make sense. He'd want to be with his parents after an event like that, particularly where both sons ended up in the hospital. I just wished ... well, it didn't matter what I wished. Ramsay had been clear about me not following him to the hospital, so I had respected his decision.

"What will you do today, with the shop like it is?" Hilda leaned against the table, concern in her pretty eyes. She must be picking up on the undercurrent of what wasn't being said.

"I'm going to go down and see the shop. See if Ramsay needs any help clearing it out, and then I don't know. I guess work on designs from here."

"Library's yours to use if you need it then."

"Thanks, I appreciate it. Mind watching Calvin while I go to the shop this morning?"

"Of course not. The wee lad's not a bother at all."

Sir Buster let out a little growl from beneath the table, and Hilda snorted.

"They'll figure it out soon enough," Hilda said, squeezing my arm. "As will you. Even the darkest of mornings have light."

I held on to that thought as I made my way into Loren Brae after breakfast, the air crisp and fresh this morning, sunlight drifting softly across the calm shores of Loch Mirren. On any other day, my heart would be full, and I'd be admiring how pretty the buildings looked lining the water.

Water that held unimaginable magic and depths.

I'd passed my third challenge.

After breakfast, I'd checked my sewing scissors to find the tiniest of flames etched among the vines next to the heart and the cat. Three challenges met. Which meant I was now officially a member of the Order of Caledonia, and I hadn't told anyone. Not yet. I felt ... adrift this morning, without the shop to work in, my future hanging in the balance while I waited to hear from Ramsay.

Was he hurting?

I couldn't imagine how awful it must have felt to have one's own brother destroy something you had worked so hard for. Granted, we'd been smart about the vision I'd had, taking most of the important items from the shop and storing them safely at the castle, but it was really the symbolism of the act that mattered most, no? What bigger betrayal than having your own brother take a match to your dreams? I wanted to hug Ramsay and tell him that I was there for him, in whatever capacity he'd allow me to be.

Which currently, was nothing.

But I could change that. I just needed to find the man and squeeze him.

Turning the corner to the store, I skidded to a stop. A few men were climbing in a truck to leave, and Ramsay stood alone in front of what had once been his beautiful store. While I know the store only represented a small piece of Ramsay's palatial business, it had been a great spot to work.

I nodded at the men in the truck as they passed, and silently came to stand next to where Ramsay stared at the remains of the shop.

"Hey," I said softly, bumping his shoulder with mine. "How are you feeling?"

"How do you think I'm feeling?" Ramsay rasped, and he didn't look at me. Worry kicked up.

"I imagine pretty shitty," I said. "For a lot of valid reasons. But first I want to know if you had any major smoke inhalation issues or what the doctor said."

"All clear." Ramsay shook his head, dismissing my question.

"Your brother?"

"Broken ankle, smoke inhalation, and facing time in prison."

I pressed my lips together at that, my heart rate picking up as I studied the mess in front of us. Something had changed in Ramsay, and I didn't know how to reach him.

"Oh, Calvin's cat tree." I moved to step into the mess to see if we could fix the half-burned tree, but Ramsay snagged my arm and pulled me back.

"Can't touch anything. The site is part of an investigation. The inspector has been out, but he's coming back again this morning to take more photos."

"Oh, sure. Makes sense." Drawing in a breath, I turned and wrapped my arms around Ramsay. His body stiffened under my touch. "I'm just so glad you're okay."

"That *I'm* ...?" Ramsay pulled himself out of my arms and took a step back. "Okay? You think that I'm okay?"

The anger in his tone set me back a step, and I blinked up at him, torn on how to react. I wasn't sure that I knew this Ramsay. Carefully controlled rage hovered behind his face, and his fists were clenched at his sides.

"No, I don't think any of this is okay, Ramsay. But I'm glad you're not hurt, physically at least," I said, my hands in the air. "But the rest of this? Ramsay, we can fix this. We can build the shop again. We saved your fabrics. We can do this."

"We?"

The way he said it, as though I was a speck of dirt on his perfectly woven fabric, had my breath catching in my throat.

"Yes, *we*. I'm here to help."

"I don't need your help, Willow. You still don't get it, do you?" Ramsay swept his hand out in front of the store. "This is not a 'we' problem. This is a *me* problem. Stop trying to make this shop your own. It's not. This is my shop, and you don't belong here."

My heart fell at his words, and I turned to look at the smoldering remains of the store that I'd pinned my hopes on.

Had I done it again? Trusted my future with someone who didn't feel the same way about what we were building? I'd been so certain that Loren Brae was my spot and that designing for the castle would be my future—well, at least a step in the right direction, and I'd genuinely enjoyed working with Ramsay. We'd formed a connection, as designers, and we'd just finished all of our designs and had been ready to present them to Sophie. What had changed?

"But ... what about our designs, Ramsay? We've worked so hard on them. I thought we were really creating a beautiful collection."

"I was just humoring you because Sophie had asked me to. I've told you from the beginning that I work best alone."

I blinked at him, tears filling my eyes. I wish I could be one of those people who didn't show my emotions, that I could hide the pain from my face, but I just wasn't built that way. Instead, I stood in front of Ramsay, my heart bleeding.

"So the shop is gone and that means we're done too?" I whispered.

"You almost died." Ramsay whirled on me. "I was supposed to protect you, and I didn't. So yes, we're done. Go back home, Willow, where Miles can keep an eye on you, and I don't have to look out for you every second of my day."

The tears spilled over, and I took a step back, hating the expression I saw on Ramsay's face. *Scorn. Anger. Resolute.*

He's done.

He's completely done with me.

Once again, I'll be alone. How freaking wonderful. And that was when the anger began to boil within me.

"It's not your job to protect me. And it's not Miles's job either. I can take care of myself."

"Well do it elsewhere, Willow. I don't need someone else in here trying to take over my business."

"I'm not trying to take over your business. We were working together," I shouted, pointing at him. "Don't pretend like we weren't."

"You're just an intern, Willow. Go home."

With that, my heart cracked in two, and I turned, refusing to give this man another ounce of myself. Whatever had transpired between his brother and Ramsay since the fire had closed him up, made him cold. I didn't have the energy to be his sunshine anymore.

No, maybe he was right. It might just be time for me to go home. *If only I hadn't been so sure that Loren Brae was my home.*

CHAPTER THIRTY

Ramsay

In that moment, I hated myself.

But I needed Willow to walk away.

I'd failed spectacularly. *And I almost lost her forever.* Seeing her disappearing into that burning building had done something to my heart that I wasn't sure I'd ever recover from.

She'd almost *died* because of me and my messed-up family dynamics.

That brilliant burst of sparkles and light could have been snuffed out because Andrew had taken his vengeance too far this time.

Willow needed to go home where she was safe, because clearly, I couldn't keep her safe here.

I was angry.

Angry that Andrew had betrayed me again.

Angry that Willow had almost gotten hurt.

Angry at myself, for betraying Miles by sleeping with his sister.

It was more than just sleeping together, my brain whispered to me. Which, I fecking knew, because it took everything in my power not to chase Willow down and beg her to forgive me for being an absolute jerk just now. Because I had been. On purpose. I needed Willow to put the distance there. I couldn't do it myself. I'd fall head over heels for her and somehow try to figure out how to spend the rest of my days keeping her safe.

She'd infiltrated my business. My bedroom. My mind. Like someone shooting off a confetti cannon in my heart. There were colorful pieces of her everywhere I looked, even now in the smoldering ruins of my shop, the vase of flowers she'd put on my desk half-melted.

And so I let the best thing that had ever happened to me walk away because I was just so damn angry that I couldn't see straight. Turning, I stomped down the street and straight through the doors of The Tipsy Thistle, even though it was early for the lunch rush. Graham looked up in surprise from where he held a clipboard behind the bar.

"Hey, mate. Sorry to hear about the shop. That's a rough go of it."

"Whisky."

"Yes, sir."

And so it began.

. . .

A WEEK LATER, Graham told me I was no longer welcome at his pub.

Turns out, I'm not a good drunk when I'm miserable. Who knew?

Still, I decided to test how "really" kicked out I was by returning to The Tipsy Thistle after I downed a bottle of wine by the ruins of my old shop.

It had been a hell of a week.

The absence of Willow in my life was becoming unbearable.

Which was ridiculous. I'd been fine before she'd come along. I should have been fine after.

And yet I wasn't.

Not even a wee bit.

Not even at all.

The reasons that had made sense to me the day after the fire had begun to blur under my need to see her, to hear her laughter, to dive into the softness that was Willow. Instead, I was driving my parents crazy by coming home late, sleeping on the couch until noon, and overall being such a crabbit beastie that even my own mum had suggested that I return to my place in Edinburgh.

My own mother.

Could you believe it?

Willow's laugh stopped me in my tracks, just inside the door, and I drank in the sight of her like a prisoner seeing the outside world for the first time in years.

"Nope, mate. You're out," Graham snapped, rounding the bar and coming toward me.

Willow turned from where she sat between Agnes and

Sophie, her eyes wounded as she looked at me. I'd been the one to put that look on her face.

"Just let me talk to her," I said, pushing past Graham.

"You've been drinking."

"Just some wine. I thought she'd gone home." Graham checked me with his shoulder, stopping me in my tracks. I met his eyes.

"Watch yourself, mate." My tone was deadly serious.

"It's not me that needs to watch himself. You're not welcome here until you get your shite together." Graham shoved my shoulder, and I rocked back on my heels, my fists clenching at my sides.

"I shouldn't find this hot, right?" Agnes asked.

"Willow," I pleaded over Graham's shoulder. When she looked away, my heart cracked, and I shoved past.

"Bloody hell, Ramsay." Graham shook his head before cocking his hand back and clocking me in the gut and the wind went out of me. I doubled over, clenching my stomach, as Graham gripped the back of my neck and propelled me from the pub. "You're a lousy drunk when you're miserable, mate."

"I need to talk to Willow," I gasped, trying to catch my breath as the cold air slapped my face.

"Then you'll do so sober. But not in my pub and not like this."

With that, Graham left me slumped against the outside wall of his pub, sadness and anger brewing in my gut as I gasped for air.

"Ramsay."

I turned to see Sophie standing in the doorway.

"Is she okay?" I asked, hating that I had screwed things up so badly.

"That'll depend on you. You really hurt her. What the hell were you thinking?" Sophie hissed.

"I'm an idiot."

"Clearly. The grump thing was cute and all until it wasn't. You really messed up."

"I thought she'd left."

"God, no. Willow's made of stronger stuff than that. I convinced her to stay, no thanks to you. She'll still work for the castle."

"She's not leaving?" Relief filled me. I straightened, rubbing my hand over the tender spot in my gut.

"She might. It's hard to say. The whole town has been talking about you picking fights with people left and right, breaking a table. You even insulted Fergus and his gingerbread house skills."

I winced.

"Not my finest moment."

"What the hell are you doing, Ramsay? Why are you being like this?"

"Because I'm an eejit?"

"Clearly. But you'll need to dig a bit deeper if you're going to convince Willow to talk to you. Acknowledging you're an eejit barely scratches the surface."

"What do I do?" I asked and Sophie crossed her arms over her chest, an annoyed look on her face.

"Oh, so now I'm supposed to solve all your problems?"

"Bloody hell, Sophie. Do you want me to make it up to Willow or not?"

"Fine, but you'd better dedicate your wedding vows to me or whatever comes out of this."

"I am not dedicating a wedding vow to a woman other than my future wife."

"I suppose that wouldn't make sense, would it?" Sophie scrunched up her nose as she thought about it, and I almost lost my cool.

"Sophie," I warned.

"Fine. But before I help you, I need to know one thing. Do you love her?" *With all my fecking heart.*

"Aye. With everything in me. She's it for me, lass."

Sophie sighed, as if relieved at my confession. "Well, in that case, I know she hasn't had a chance to visit her gran since she's been here. And I know she'd like that. Maybe you could go talk to her and do something sentimental to win her back."

"Like what?"

"I don't know, Ramsay. Figure it out. You want to win the woman back, think about what you did to hurt her. Her last boyfriend stole all her money and her business from her. You kicked her out of your business after she did all this work for you. She's not feeling really confident at the moment. Fix it."

With that, Sophie turned.

"Wait. Her gran's address?"

"I'll text you it. Now go sober up and figure your shit out. As much as we enjoy watching Graham flex his muscles, we can't have him doing it every night, or Agnes might finally have to admit she's attracted to the man."

"God forbid." I rolled my eyes and moved away from the wall, purpose filling me.

"Good luck, Ramsay. Remember, we all screw up sometimes. Make it right."

"I plan to."

With that, I walked into the night, thinking over Sophie's words. She was right, I'd hit Willow's insecurities dead on, and now I needed to fix it.

I'd stupidly told her to go home, but *this* was Willow's home. Loren Brae.

With me.

CHAPTER THIRTY-ONE

WILLOW

It had been two weeks since Graham had punched Ramsay at the pub, causing Agnes to grow all flustered, and me to grow more miserable. I'd hated seeing Ramsay hurt.

Even though he'd ripped my heart out.

I loved the stupid man.

I couldn't believe it myself, to be honest, that I'd fallen for this grumpy, taciturn man, who was surprisingly thoughtful and interesting when I'd managed to break down his walls.

Or so I'd thought.

I still didn't understand why he'd pushed me away the day after the fire. Sure, I would have been angry too. If Miles had lit a match to my business, I'd be furious. But I was different than Ramsay. I would have turned to him, leaned on him for support, and built it back up together. Instead, he'd shut me out and made me feel unwanted, untalented, and unnecessary to his future.

"I was just humoring you because Sophie had asked me to. I've told you from the beginning that I work best alone."

My ex's betrayal had nothing on those words.

Sophie kept telling me not to give up on him. She said he was just an idiot man unable to process his emotions correctly in the moment. The question was—did I need to put up with that from someone I wanted a future relationship with? If Ramsay couldn't grow or change and learn to be an actual partner, there was no point in considering a future with him anyway. I just had to heal my broken heart and learn how to exist in a small town where I'd likely run into him at the pub once in a while. In time, maybe it would sting less.

He'd looked awful.

I'd hated that for him.

Usually so robust and confident, instead Ramsay's eyes had an almost feral look to them when he'd spotted me at the pub, his hair messy, his face gaunt. He'd been punishing himself and Loren Brae with his anger for the better part of a week, and more than one person had been pleased with Graham's punch.

But not me.

It had taken everything in my power to not run out and hug Ramsay when he'd gotten hurt, to fix him, to fix us. It's what I normally would have done. But I'd held strong, thanks to Agnes lecturing me about protecting my boundaries, and I'd forced myself to turn back to the bar and order another drink when Graham returned.

Now, I tried to push those thoughts away as I arrived at my grandparents' cottage on the outer end of Loch Mirren, about a half hour drive from Loren Brae. I'd finally been able to make time to see them and had borrowed Sophie's car to visit. I won't lie, it was harrowing driving on the other side of the road, but I was proud of myself for managing to arrive incident-free at their doorstep.

Instantly, I was greeted with memories of my youth when I stopped in front of their cottage. Set across the street from the loch, the house was a cute two-story stone cottage backed up to rolling, green hills with an abundant garden full of flowers and vegetables. My gran loved pottering in the garden, and my grandpa had indulged her whims through the years, building small greenhouses for year-round herbs and veggies, and creating trails through the land. I remembered running through the flowers as a child, feeling like I was lost in the Secret Garden, one of my favorite childhood books.

"Willow! Just look at yourself. All grown up." My gran and grandpa crowded the front door and tears pricked my eyes. It had been years since I'd seen them in person, only over Zoom calls, and this felt like coming home. We stood in the doorway in an awkward three-person hug, and the scents of cinnamon and apples drifted from the house.

"Come in, come in. I just have some apple fritters from a recipe I was fussing around with coming out of the oven." My gran, a round woman with wild curls and a stack of necklaces at her neck, motioned me back to the kitchen. I inhaled the scents of her cooking, stopping at a hallway of photos, and smiled at a photo of my mother holding me as a baby.

She'd been so happy.

It was one thing I'd always noted in every photo I had of her, plus the memories that I held close to my heart. Her laugh. Always smiling, always laughing. It was something that I'd tried to emulate my whole life, and whether it was because of her, or because of who I was at my core, I'd always tried to be everyone's sunshine.

It just hadn't been enough for Ramsay.

Shrugging off thoughts of him, I let my grandparents fuss over me, putting together a little tea tray of sweets and mini sandwiches.

"This is a proper tea, I'm so lucky," I gushed, appreciating the Scottish tradition of a three-tiered tea tray with miniature food. I mean, I don't know what other people think, but I love tiny food presented well. It was just so cute.

"This is the first proper day of sunshine we've had in a while. I thought we could take our tea down by the edge of the garden. Near the rose bushes?" my gran asked. "Would you mind carrying the tray out?"

"Of course." I picked up the tray of mini sandwiches, and hummed as I left the back door, and wandered down the stone path that ran between opulent rose bushes, and several lilac trees that would likely be in bloom in a few weeks. It was quiet out here, the soft tinkling of running water in a bird bath, the light breeze rustling a few branches. The garden was still dormant, ready for spring, and I tilted my face to the sun.

It was time for rebirth.

Rounding the bushes, I skidded to a stop and almost dropped the tea tray.

"Ramsay," I gasped.

"Here, let me." Ramsay strode forward, gently removing the tray from my fingers, and put it on the table.

I stood, frozen, my world tilting.

Ramsay looked, well, he looked incredible.

This part of the garden was almost fully enclosed from the rest of the backyard by clusters of rose bushes and one beautiful willow tree. In front of the tree sat a lovely wrought iron bench, and a matching bistro style table with two chairs. There, a basket piled with fabric had been placed, and Ramsay stood next to the table, his muscular arms crossed over his chest.

I drank in the sight of him, and tears filled my eyes when I realized what I was seeing.

He'd made *our* tartan.

The one we'd designed together that night, when we'd laughed and argued, picking out colors and patterns until we got it exactly right.

He wore a proper kilt in our pattern, along with matching vest and suitcoat, along with a sporran, boots, and thick wool socks.

I'd been right. The tartan we'd created together was perfect.

Helpless not to, I met his eyes and saw nothing but pain and sadness there.

"You made it," I said, my voice watery.

"I had to. I stopped all production on any other tartan until I could get this made."

"It's good."

"It's perfect," Ramsay said, stepping slightly forward and grabbing something from the table. "Just like you."

I swallowed, hope blooming, but not wanting to be led astray once more.

Ramsay fastened something around his waist and tears spilled over.

It was a fanny pack.

A unicorn one at that.

"Why are you here, Ramsay?"

"Because I screwed up. Royally. And I needed to get my head on straight so I could apologize properly."

"It's fine," I said automatically, shrugging it off as was my habit.

"No, it's not fine. Not in the slightest." Ramsay stepped forward. "Can I show you something, darling?"

"Sure." I stepped forward as he motioned me toward the willow tree. He kept a careful distance, not touching me, and I ducked my head as he pushed some branches aside.

My heart twisted.

There on the trunk of the tree, in a scratchy childlike script, was my mother's name.

Welig.

"Your gran told me this is where your mother had carved her name. I wanted to bring you here, in front of this carving, to say I'm so, so sorry. And I want to promise you, and her, that I will never take you for granted or push you aside like I did after the fire."

Tears spilled over, and my chest tightened as I reached out and ran my fingers over the carving. A tingle of energy raced through my palms at the touch, and I closed my hand around it, as though I could keep that magick with me forever. And maybe I could. Her blood was as much of mine and I of hers, and we were forever connected, our roots entangled in this earth.

I shuddered in a breath and turned to look up at Ramsay, his expression pained at my tears.

"You really hurt me, Ramsay. You made me feel like ... nothing. Like less than nothing."

"I know it. And all I can say is that I'm a fecking eejit. Truly. I was just so angry and the only thing I could land on was that I needed to do everything alone."

"But why? Why do you have to do everything alone, Ramsay? You run a veritable kilt empire. You have employees. You don't do it all on your own." I crossed my arms over my chest, lest I dive for him and wrap my arms around his waist and bury my face in his chest and howl like I wanted to.

"I know, I *know*. Guess what I've learned recently? Emotions aren't logical." A ghost of a smile crossed Ramsay's lips. "I was gutted when Andrew betrayed me. Absolutely gutted. I'd looked up to my brother my whole life. When he stole from me, from my parents, and took off—it just changed me. Because if my own brother could do that to me? Well, anyone could. Och, it hardened me. I was determined to succeed, but I needed to do as much of it myself, you ken? It took me a long time to take on help, and even then, it was tough. Poor Sheila's been through it with me, I'll tell you that much."

"I don't doubt it," I murmured.

"Miles has been a good friend to me," Ramsay continued, his face set in hard lines as he worked through what he needed to say. Again, this man didn't talk a lot, but when he did, it just all poured out of him. "A really good friend. In some ways, he replaced the relationship that I had with Andrew, and his friendship is important to me. When you arrived and he asked me to look out for you, I took that responsibility seriously."

"I'm not *yours*, or his, responsibility." I rolled my eyes. "Do you have some misguided notion that women just flounder about in the world needing male protection?"

"It's not like that, Willow. We know you're capable of taking care of yourself, but when your people love you, they want to look after you."

My breath caught.

He'd just said that he loved me. I wasn't even sure if he realized what he'd said.

"And so I hated that I looked at you as more than just my friend's sister," Ramsay barreled on, clearly needing to work through his speech while I was basically unraveling inside. "Every time you laughed, every time I caught the scent of your hair, every time you bent over in front of me, I hated myself for wanting to dive into you. It was like I'd been living in black and white, and you were this explosion of color in my life. All of a sudden, I was feeling feelings that I didn't want to, I was thinking things I wasn't supposed to be thinking, and I found myself looking forward to every moment that I got to spend with you."

"Ramsay," I whispered.

"You're like this tartan, you ken?" Ramsay held up a piece of the fabric. "You weaved yourself into my life, Willow, and when I thought it was something that I didn't want or wouldn't like, it turns out that I'm stronger with you there. Together, we were creating something incredible, and I'm so very sorry that I hurt that, hurt you, and made you think you were anything less than incredible. Not only are you the sunshine to my rain, but you're so very talented, and I loved working by your side. I hate that I might have made you second-guess yourself, in any capacity, because of my cruel words."

"Ramsay." I gulped, stepping forward.

Ramsay held up a hand and took a deep breath, still on a roll.

"When I saw you disappear into the burning building, I almost lost my mind. I was furious with you. Furious. Bloody hell, what were you thinking? You could have died, Willow. Died because of my brother. It would have been one more thing he tried to take from me. Do you know how angry I was? How scared I was?"

"It wasn't easy watching you go into the burning building either," I reminded him gently, feeling like I was approaching a big bristling bear. I laid a hand on his arm. "How do you think that made me feel?"

"I didn't think about it. I wasn't thinking. At all. And the next day, I let anger take over, and I just couldn't think straight, so I hurt the most important person in the world to me. And for that, I'd like to spend the rest of my days making it up to you."

"Oh, Ramsay." Tears just flowed down my face.

"I love you, Willow. And I'm so sorry that I hurt you. Will you give me another chance to prove to you that I'm not a complete eejit?"

"Of course, I will. I would have ten minutes ago if you'd let me get a word in." I laughed, wiping the tears from my eyes. "I love you too, you big grump. You hurt me, but I can understand now why you reacted the way you did.

Emotions were high. But I just need you to know that you can rely on me, Ramsay. You don't have to do it alone anymore, if you don't want to."

"I don't. I really don't. I can't imagine building my shop back and not having you by my side."

"I love you." I looked up at him and then his lips were on mine, relief and joy flooding me. I wanted to stay here, forever locked in this moment with him, but a throat cleared behind us.

"I have one more surprise," Ramsay said as he pulled back, holding my face in his hands. "And I hope this doesn't make you angry."

"Oh, no."

Turning, I found Miles and my father standing a few feet away, both with those expressions men wear when they're disgruntled about overseeing too much emotion, but were happy, nonetheless.

"Dad!" I shrieked, launching myself at my father.

"Threads, I've missed you." Dad hugged me close, and my tears just continued to fall.

"Oh sure, I get nothing?" Miles complained and I turned, giving him a hug.

"I'm not sure you deserve anything, you jerk," I said, even though I pulled him tighter against me. Stepping back, I wiped my tears as my grandparents came forward and joined them. "What are you guys doing here?"

"Ramsay flew us out," Miles said. "Said he'd screwed up and wanted to grovel in front of an audience."

"Good job, by the way." My dad nodded his approval.

"Epic job." I laughed, dashing tears with the back of my palm.

"There's just one more thing to do," Ramsay said, reaching into his pocket and pulling out a small box. My heart clenched. "Willow, this is for you."

Oh my God, was he proposing? I wasn't ready for that, but I wanted to be with him. My thoughts tumbled over each other, and my hand shook as I eased the box open.

Inside sat a simple brass key on a bed of velvet.

"What is this?" I asked, looking up at him.

"I'd like for you to be my partner. This is the key to the new door at the shop, and I'm asking if you'll join me, as an equal partner, in my business. I think we can weave a beautiful future together."

He knew. Ramsay knew I wasn't ready for marriage, that I needed to have confidence in securing a future and a career for myself first. He'd known how upset I'd been with the way things had turned out with my last relationship, and how important it was for me to find my foundation in my design career. Just like I understood how difficult it was for him to trust someone as a partner again. For both of us, this was a huge, and deeply meaningful, step.

"I'd love nothing more," I said, beaming up at him. "So long as we can mass produce those unicorn fanny packs."

"Don't say fanny in front of your gran." Ramsay's eyes widened, a horrified look on his face as he glanced at my grandparents.

"And why ever not, Ramsay? I've got a fanny, don't I?"

Ramsay's face flushed bright pink, and I threw my head back and laughed, while my brother looked between us.

"What's a fanny?"

"Och, lad, if you don't know by now, well, it sounds like your dating life needs to improve." Ramsay clasped a hand on my brother's shoulder, while I hugged the key to my heart.

"Shut it," Miles growled.

"And, for the record, I just want to say—your sister never needed looking after. Not only is she incredibly talented, but she's strong, fearless, and has a great head on her shoulders. You should be proud of her."

I blinked tears away as Miles turned to me.

"He's right, Threads. I guess, hell, I don't know…" Miles combed a hand through his hair. "Losing Mom made me want to keep everyone close. Like that was the only way I knew how to keep them safe."

Now the tears did spill over, and I walked over to my brother, giving him a hug.

"I get that. You just didn't have to be such a butthole about it," I said, poking him in the side.

"Noted," Miles said, wincing.

"I'm proud of you too, Threads. Your mother would have been as well," my dad said, nodding toward the tree. "This was her favorite tree. It's nice we can be here, all together again."

"Can you feel her?" I asked, walking back to put my hand out to touch the bark.

"I don't need to," my dad said, holding his hand to his heart. "She's always here with me."

"I know," I whispered, tracing her name with my finger. "That's love, isn't it? Something intangible woven into the fabric of our souls."

EPILOGUE

Willow

"The builder's coming out today," Ramsay said, as he brought me a to-go cup of coffee in front of the castle. "We'll see what's what and hopefully get things sorted enough to start rebuilding the shop."

"I hope it won't take long," I said, accepting the coffee and tucking Calvin under my arm as we made our way to Ramsay's truck.

Calvin pretty much came most places with us these days, aside from the pub, and surprisingly most people didn't seem to mind when we brought him along. Agnes particularly encouraged him joining her at the bookstore, and I often dropped him there for hours at a time. Agnes told me that cats and bookstores went hand in hand, and we'd even moved a small cat tree in there for him to lounge by the window on the mornings where he felt like schmoozing with Agnes. I figured once we'd rebuilt the kilt shop, he'd make his way back over to us, but since Calvin very much knew his own mind, I let him tell me what he wanted to do each day.

He was our little hero, after all.

I was beginning to suspect that he was becoming Loren Brae's cat, and he'd end up having a daily rotation of spots that he would grace with his presence.

Today he'd informed me he wanted to go to the bookstore, so I was planning to drop him there after the meeting with the builder. We'd more or less cleaned everything salvageable from the shop and had tarped the floors and exposed masonry against the elements. Surprisingly, two of the larger machines would be working with the replacement of a few parts.

A woman stood in front of the shop when we drove up, standing next to a pickup truck. Short, with a thick red braid down her back, and a canvas coat zipped against the weather, she had a messenger bag slung over her shoulder. She looked like a student, with a smattering of freckles across her face, and bright blue eyes and upturned lips.

"If you're looking for the kilt shop, we're obviously closed." Ramsay exited the car while I put Calvin in the back seat and followed suit.

"Och, I'm not in the market for a kilt at the moment." The woman smiled, her voice surprisingly rich and melodious, and I realized I'd misjudged her age. She had to be closer to my age and gave me a brisk nod before turning back to Ramsay. "Clarke Construction."

"*You're* the builder?" Ramsay wasn't able to hide the

surprise in his voice, and I rolled my eyes as I brushed past him and held out my hand.

"I'm Willow, part-owner of the shop, and this is Ramsay. Excuse his sexism."

"Och, not a problem at all. I'm used to it. I'm Orla Clarke." Orla beamed up at me as we shook hands, and I felt an odd tremor of energy zip up my arm when our palms touched. Her eyes jumped to mine, speculative.

She'd felt that.

Did Miss Orla Clarke carry magick? I narrowed my eyes in thought as Ramsay stepped forward, apologizing.

"My esteemed business partner is correct, lass. That was rude of me, and I shouldn't have expected a man to be meeting us. I apologize on behalf of my gender." Ramsay shook her hand as well, and Orla laughed.

"Trust me when I say I am very much used to it. Can't say it's been easy making my way in the construction business as a woman, but I've got a solid crew that I trust with my life. We'll get you sorted out soon enough and at a fair price."

"Your company comes highly recommended," Ramsay said, putting his hands on his hips as he turned to look over the shop's ruin. Orla mirrored the move, and I grinned, already liking this pint-sized powerhouse.

"I would hope so. We take great pride in our work. Why don't you walk me through what you're thinking, and I'll work up an estimate for you?"

"So here was the line for the front room." Ramsay stepped through the doorway that still stood, and began to walk around. As a stone building, much of the framework was intact, but we'd need to see about the structural integrity of the stones and if masonry work would be needed to ensure their stability. *All part of the process.* Ramsay had promised me it would be fine, and I trusted that we'd build back something beautiful together. "And then we had a back workroom, a kitchenette, and a downstairs loo. Upstairs was one single room with a bathroom attached. I was thinking that I'd like to extend farther out into the garden here."

"You would?" I came up next to them as Orla measured and made notes, running her hand across the stone and jotting her impressions into her notebook.

"Yes, don't you think? Look, there's quite a bit of room back here. Since we don't use it for parking, we could extend farther back, almost to those trees. That way you could have your own workroom, and we could have an actual walk-in closet upstairs."

"Did you say walk-in closet?" I hissed, grabbing his arm and pretending to faint.

"Och, lass, I've seen your clothes. I know what I'm getting in for."

"Are you asking me to move in with you?" I met his eyes, my heart hammering in my chest. We were taking all these big steps, and currently Ramsay was technically living with me in the castle, but we hadn't had a talk about if that would be official or not.

Orla made a humming note low in her throat and stepped discreetly away. I liked her. She clearly had good instincts when it came to reading people.

"Or if you prefer to live at the castle, that's fine with me as well. But if I could have my way of it, yes, I'd like you to live here with me." Ramsay squinted down at me. "Unless you'd prefer to have your space. Which I understand as well. It's what you want, darling."

"Well, then, yes, I'd like that. But we might need to extend the kitchen a bit then too, don't you think?"

"Orla, what do you think?" Ramsay turned, and Orla picked her way back over to us and held out her pad.

"On a rough sketch, I'd say you could extend the kitchen here, add a breakfast alcove here, and then build out the second workroom in an L shape here." Orla sketched quickly on the pad, showing us her thoughts. "If you carry that upstairs, the workroom space could become the walk-in closet, and the kitchen space could be a luxury bath."

"I like the sound of that," I said, nodding over the drawing.

"And here, you'll still keep some green space and have the trees, so you could fit a darling wee table outside under the trees if you prefer to take your tea outside when the weather's nice." Orla jerked her head back and looked around the space, her eyes narrowing.

I felt a low hum in my gut.

"What's wrong?" I asked.

"Oh, sorry, nothing. Thought I heard something," Orla lied neatly to me and, for some reason, I decided to press the point.

"Tell me what really just happened."

Orla's blue eyes snapped to mine, and she measured me for a moment. Raising an eyebrow, I crossed my arms over my chest.

"I got the sense something happened that you just lied about. If we're going to work together, I'd like to know I can trust you."

"I have impeccable business standards," Orla said, pressing her lips together as she studied me.

"I don't doubt it. But something just happened there." I was being rude at this point, but something compelled me to push.

Orla sighed and looked up in the air for a moment, before seeming to collect herself.

"Have you had any paranormal activity here?" Orla surprised me by asking and Ramsay scoffed, leaning in.

"You think the shop is haunted?" Ramsay asked.

"I mean it's not that far-fetched, is it?" I gave Ramsay major side-eye. He must have remembered our resident ghost coo because he eased back a bit.

"So you've sensed some activity then?"

"I personally haven't in this particular space," I clarified. "But I have seen ghosts in Loren Brae if that's what you're suggesting."

"You can see them too?" Orla burst out and then closed her eyes, realizing what she'd revealed.

"Yes, we both have. I think Loren Brae has a lot of unusual activity. It's not so uncommon, particularly if you're someone who's sensitive to that. Which it seems you are, am I right?" I asked, gently, not wanting to scare her off, but my mind was whirling.

Agnes had told me about how she'd been working to uncover the next potential members in the Order of Caledonia. Traditionally, the Order was made of people who held various roles that would help run or protect a village. We had the Knight, the kitchen witch, the garden witch, and the weaver. We'd run through some of the other possible scenarios, and a builder or carpenter had been one of them. A house witch, we'd thought. Now, as I stared at Orla, I realized that I might have inadvertently stumbled on our next member.

"Yes, I might have a bit of a proclivity for the paranormal. But I promise it doesn't affect my work. I can help clear some of the energy of a space is all."

"A useful talent in your line of work, I'm sure," Ramsay said smoothly, while I calculated how weird it would be to pounce on Orla and parade her to Agnes.

"Do you live in Loren Brae?" I asked.

"Grew up the next village over," Orla said, relaxing as we shifted the conversation. "Been here or around these parts most of my life."

"Well, well, well, isn't that interesting?" I beamed at Ramsay who was looking at me like I'd lost my mind, and Calvin began to wail from the car. "I'm just going to take Calvin over to Bonnie Books while you two finish up. Orla, lovely to meet you. I look forward to working with you."

"Same to you. We'll shine the shop up in no time," Orla promised.

"Don't you want to see her estimate first, lass?" Ramsay asked, raising an eyebrow at me.

"Nah, I've seen your books. You can afford it."

Ramsay chuckled as I walked back to the car and scooped Calvin up, my heart hammering as I walked toward Bonnie Books.

Maybe, just maybe, we'd be able to banish these dangerous Kelpies sooner than everyone hoped.

Are you ready to experience Willow and Ramsay's first fashion show? Word on the street is that Agnes and Graham are walking in it... download this enticing bonus scene to get a peek at Willow's hot new fashion line. Join the catwalk here - triciaomalley.com/free

Fall in love with Calvin? He has his own line of merchandise! Shop here - triciaomalley.myshopify.com

WILD SCOTTISH FORTUNE

The tension is ramping up in Loren Brae. Will the newest member of the Order of Caledonia be ready to join? Be sure to order today.

ORLA

"Surely you just need to jam it in there."

"When does jamming something in ever help the problem?"

"Depends, is your date in a huff with you or not?"

I rolled my eyes at the two men currently bent over a lock on a stall door in an old outbuilding outside MacAlpine Castle. Munroe Curaigh of Common Gin was opening a new branch of his famous distillery here, and I'd bid for the project knowing that it would give my crew enough steady work for months if we'd got it.

And we'd landed it.

We were already two months into the project, and I'd been able to hire in more help, as well as take on a few other local projects like the rebuilding of Ramsay Kilts which had recently suffered from a tragedy.

Such a shame, that fire. I'd heard his brother had started it and everything.

I was excited to work on the kilt shop, largely because the space wasn't very large, which meant Ramsay and Willow wanted more attention to detail and I always enjoyed the challenge of crafting out useful small storage or interesting details in unique spaces. The distillery, on the other hand, was a much larger project where form needed to meet function. Yet the building itself held history, which Munroe hoped to preserve, and we were working with a team to blend the old with the new in a seamless design that should offer a light and airy workspace for his crew.

"I'd suggest a gentle touch," I interrupted the two men, coming to the intricate latch at the stall door. "As most women prefer that over getting jammed." Both men straightened as I slid my hand softly over the locking mechanism, and turned it lightly, unhinging it so the door opened smoothly.

"Ah," Munroe cleared his throat sheepishly.

"Your technique is noted," the other man said, a twinkle in his grey-green eyes.

"Your future dates can thank me," I said, and Munroe winced.

"Apologies for our crudeness."

"I'm well used to it lads," I said, continuing through to the tack room that we were converting into a front office.

"Orla, this is Finlay Thompson. Our Chief Operations Officer. He's just arrived to town to have a look over everything and will be moving here once things are up and running."

I glanced over at Finlay, my eyes taking in his crisp grey trousers with a muted tartan print, well-shined shoes, and gold watch peeking out from beneath his collared shirt.

Posh bastard.

"Are you here to clean then?" Finlay asked, smiling at me, and Munroe cursed under his breath.

"Aye, that's me. The cleaner. What would you recommend needs cleaning in here, sir?" I tipped my head at him, pretending to give a wee curtsy, and his eyes narrowed.

"Well, I imagine everything, no? Och, it's quite dusty in here. Will need a good brush down," Finlay surveyed the room which was smack dab in the middle of a literal construction site, covered in saw dust, and had the gall to suggest it needed a good dusting. Clearly the man didn't know his head from his arse, and I opened my mouth to suggest a replacement when Munroe intervened.

I knew Finlay's type.

Hell, I'd dated his type.

They walked into everywhere they went, assuming they knew what was what, and acted like a cock of walk. He had the air of confidence about him, a man used to getting his way, and I didn't doubt that most things in life worked out exactly the way he wanted.

It didn't hurt that he looked like he'd just stepped out of a glossy magazine.

The man was seriously good looking.

But in the way of a man that might roll back his cuffs and go a few rounds, if the need called for it.

I shouldn't find it appealing, but it was probably my

incredibly long dry spell that made me find him attractive. It certainly wasn't the nonsense he was spewing from his mouth.

"Finlay. This is Orla Clarke. Owner of Clarke Construction and our head builder and project manager. Basically your partner for the next six months as we finish the build out."

"You're Clarke Construction?" Finlay didn't even bother to conceal his surprise.

It was a reaction I was used to. I was a female in a male-dominated industry. I'd been on more job sites than I could count at this point, and still most people mistook me for a delivery girl dropping off food to the site or something of that nature. Maybe I could have chosen an easier industry to break into, but my first love was construction work, and I'd fought hard to end up where I was.

Which meant I'd developed a fairly thick skin through the years.

"Aye," I said, accepting his hand when he held it out. "At your service."

"My apologies," Finlay said, holding my hand a moment longer than necessary, his lips curving up in what must be a practiced sultry smile. "I shouldn't have made assumptions."

"Everything good here, boss?"

All three of us turned at the word 'boss' but it was my head joiner, Derrick, who was extremely protective of me as if I was his own daughter. He'd likely overheard the conversation since sound carried easily on an open job site.

"Aye, all good, Derrick. Thanks for checking in."

"When you're ready, I'd like to review the install on the

cabinets by the storage room. I think we can integrate sliding shelves depending on the weight of the contents."

"I'll be right through." I gave Derrick a quick nod and then turned back to the two men, hands on my hips.

"Are there any more doors you need me to open for you, gentlemen?" I gave Finlay a tight smile and he winked at me, appreciating my thinly veiled insult.

"No, Orla, go on ahead. We'll catch up with you shortly," Munroe squeezed my shoulder in thanks. I liked him. He was a fair man who was besotted with his fiancé, and his employees loved him. Low turnover at a business always spoke highly of a good boss to me, and I'd found my dealings with him to be smooth and easygoing.

Finlay, though, I'd be withholding judgment on.

"Nice to meet you, Orla. I look forward to working with you."

I withheld comment, giving him a curt nod and a wide berth as I left the room.

The Finlay's of the world and I did not mix well, but I knew well enough how to get on with them when it came to work. For now, I'd bite my tongue and crack on with my job, knowing I'd have one more challenge to deal with now that Finlay was on the project.

I glanced back to see him watching me as I walked away, a considering look in his eye.

Och, the man was going to be a problem. I could sense it already.

Be the first to enjoy this delightful addition to the Enchanted Highlands series. Order Wild Scottish Fortune today!

AUTHOR'S NOTE

I'd like to dedicate this Author's Note to my sweet soul puppy, Blue. Unfortunately, I lost him at the tail end of writing this book, and it was quite a struggle to finish. I've never *not* had a dog by my side while writing. As many of you who have followed me since The Stolen Dog know, my writing career started because my dog, Briggs, was stolen from me and, on the path to recovering him, I also rescued sweet Blue.

One day, while I was searching for Briggs, someone

texted me a picture that they'd found of my dog. Except it wasn't Briggs. This dog, tiny, beaten up, malnourished, chained to a fence with a chain far too thick for a dog's neck, looked miserable and sad. And I knew in that instant I had to rescue him.

When I bought him off the street from this man, Blue's eyes never left my face. Not once. I took him to the vet, to the pet store for food, and then back home. And still, his eyes stayed on my face. When I put him in the crate next to my bed that night, knowing that Briggs was still gone, but already falling in love with this puppy, I cried myself to sleep. The next day, I had to take him to a doggy day care for the day while I went out putting up fliers to find Briggs. A pet psychic contacted me, promising to channel Briggs. Later that day he called back and told me that Briggs was in a new home. He was madly in love with the woman. He refused to come home. He was *so* in love with her. He had a new blue collar, was playing with puppies, and got vaccinated that day.

I was shocked. When I went to pick Blue up from the day care, he ran out and fell at my feet. *He was wearing a new blue collar*. My friend told me that she'd never seen anything like it. After I'd left, he'd jumped a wall, ran into an office, and put his paws on the window to watch me go. "I've never seen a dog so in love with his owner before."

The psychic had channeled the wrong dog.

The next day Briggs was returned to me, and I had two dogs to call my own.

The thing about Blue was, besides his incredible smile, and his ability to make every day better—is that nobody will ever love me like he did. I know that may sound weird to say, but I think most pet owners will understand. Blue was happiest if he was by my side. Always. I learned quickly that he would follow me everywhere—even to his own detriment—like launching himself off a pier when I dove into the water and immediately sinking to the bottom of the lake. Blue was simply at his happiest by my side, and what greater compliment is there in life than that? Blue was my rock through some very tough times in my life, and he never begrudged me a bad mood or a sad day. He just loved me. And I think that's the greatest gift that a dog can ever give—just pure, unconditional love. It's a gift that I'll treasure forever.

Safe home will you go, my sweet soul puppy Blue. Never will there be another like you. Love you always.

ALSO BY TRICIA O'MALLEY

THE ISLE OF DESTINY SERIES

Stone Song

Sword Song

Spear Song

Sphere Song

A completed series in Kindle Unlimited.

Available in audio, e-book & paperback!

"Love this series. I will read this multiple times. Keeps you on the edge of your seat. It has action, excitement and romance all in one series."

- Amazon Review

THE ENCHANTED HIGHLANDS

Wild Scottish Knight

Wild Scottish Love

A Kilt for Christmas

Wild Scottish Rose

Wild Scottish Beauty

Wild Scottish Fortune

"I love everything Tricia O'Malley has ever written and Wild Scottish Knight is no exception. The new setting for this magical journey is Scotland, the home of her new husband and soulmate. Tricia's love for her husband's country shows in every word she writes. I have always wanted to visit Scotland but have never had the time and money. Having read Wild Scottish Knight I feel I have begun to to experience Scotland in a way few see it."

-Amazon Review

Available in audio, e-book, hardback, paperback and Kindle Unlimited.

THE WILDSONG SERIES

Song of the Fae

Melody of Flame

Chorus of Ashes

Lyric of Wind

"The magic of Fae is so believable. I read these books in one sitting and can't wait for the next one. These are books you will reread many times."

- Amazon Review

A completed series in Kindle Unlimited.

Available in audio, e-book & paperback!

THE SIREN ISLAND SERIES

Good Girl

Up to No Good

A Good Chance

Good Moon Rising

Too Good to Be True

A Good Soul

In Good Time

A completed series in Kindle Unlimited.

Available in audio, e-book & paperback!

"Love her books and was excited for a totally new and different one! Once again, she did NOT disappoint! Magical in multiple ways and on multiple levels. Her writing style, while similar to that of Nora Roberts, kicks it up a notch!! I want to visit that island, stay in the B&B and meet the gals who run it! The characters are THAT real!!!" - Amazon Review

THE ALTHEA ROSE SERIES

One Tequila

Tequila for Two

Tequila Will Kill Ya (Novella)

Three Tequilas

Tequila Shots & Valentine Knots (Novella)

Tequila Four

A Fifth of Tequila

A Sixer of Tequila

Seven Deadly Tequilas

Eight Ways to Tequila

Tequila for Christmas (Novella)

"Not my usual genre but couldn't resist the Florida Keys setting. I was hooked from the first page. A fun read with just the right amount of crazy! Will definitely follow this series."- Amazon Review

A completed series in Kindle Unlimited.

Available in audio, e-book & paperback!

THE MYSTIC COVE SERIES

Wild Irish Heart

Wild Irish Eyes

Wild Irish Soul

Wild Irish Rebel

Wild Irish Roots: Margaret & Sean

Wild Irish Witch

Wild Irish Grace

Wild Irish Dreamer

Wild Irish Christmas (Novella)

Wild Irish Sage

Wild Irish Renegade

Wild Irish Moon

"I have read thousands of books and a fair percentage have been romances. Until I read Wild Irish Heart, I never had a book actually make me believe in love."- Amazon Review

A completed series in Kindle Unlimited.
Available in audio, e-book & paperback!

STAND ALONE NOVELS

Ms. Bitch

"Ms. Bitch is sunshine in a book! An uplifting story of fighting your way through heartbreak and making your own version of happily-ever-after."

~Ann Charles, USA Today Bestselling Author

Starting Over Scottish

Grumpy. Meet Sunshine.

She's American. He's Scottish. She's looking for a fresh start. He's returning to rediscover his roots.

One Way Ticket

A funny and captivating beach read where booking a one-way ticket to paradise means starting over, letting go, and taking a chance on love...one more time

10 out of 10 - The BookLife Prize

ACKNOWLEDGMENTS

Thank you to everyone who helped me finish this book. To my lovely editor, Marion, who so gracefully handled my delays due to Dengue fever and losing Blue, as well as to Dave and Trish for having final eyes on the manuscript, you all are the best!

To my beta readers, who are so lovely to help find any last minute issues with the story or helpfully raise questions that I hadn't yet considered, I so appreciate your help.

Finally, to my love, Alan, thank you for helping me through this book. I know we were both grieving at the end of this manuscript, and you did a great job of supporting me over the finish line. Love you always!

CONTACT ME

I hope my books have added a little magick into your life. If you have a moment to add some to my day, you can help by telling your friends and leaving a review. Word-of-mouth is the most powerful way to share my stories. Thank you.

Love books? What about fun giveaways? Nope? Okay, can I entice you with underwater photos and cute dogs? Let's stay friends! Sign up for my newsletter and contact me at my website.

www.triciaomalley.com

Or find me on Facebook and Instagram.
@triciaomalleyauthor

Printed in Great Britain
by Amazon